ONCE UPON A
WINTER'S
NIGHT

By Dennis L. McKiernan

Once Upon A Winter's Night

Caverns of Socrates

The Mithgar Series

The Dragonstone

Voyage of the Fox Rider

HÈL'S CRUCIBLE:
Book 1: *Into the Forge*
Book 2: *Into the Fire*

Dragondoom

THE IRON TOWER:
Book 1: *The Dark Tide*
Book 2: *Shadows of Doom*
Book 3: *The Darkest Day*

THE SILVER CALL:
Book 1: *Trek to Kraggen-cor*
Book 2: *The Brega Path*

Tales of Mithgar (a story collection)

The Vulgmaster (the graphic novel)

The Eye of the Hunter

Silver Wolf, Black Falcon

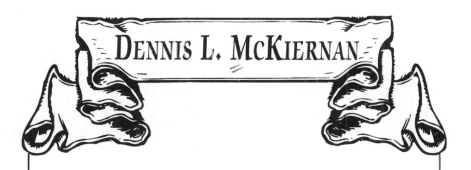

DENNIS L. MCKIERNAN

ONCE UPON A WINTER'S NIGHT

A ROC BOOK

ROC
Published by New American Library, a division of
Penguin Putnam Inc., 375 Hudson Street, New York, New York 10014, U.S.A.
Penguin Books Ltd, 27 Wrights Lane, London W8 5TZ, England
Penguin Books Australia Ltd, Ringwood, Victoria, Australia
Penguin Books Canada Ltd, 10 Alcorn Avenue, Toronto, Ontario, Canada M4V 3B2
Penguin Books (N.Z.) Ltd, 182–190 Wairau Road, Auckland 10, New Zealand

Penguin Books Ltd, Registered Offices: Harmondsworth, Middlesex, England

First published by Roc, an imprint of New American Library,
a division of Penguin Putnam Inc.

First Printing, July 2001
10 9 8 7 6 5 4 3 2 1

REGISTERED TRADEMARK—MARCA REGISTRADA

LIBRARY OF CONGRESS CATALOGING-IN-PUBLICATION DATA

McKiernan, Dennis L., 1932–
Once upon a winter's night / by Dennis L. McKiernan.
p. cm.
ISBN 0-451-45840-0 (alk. paper)
I. Title.

PS3563.C376 U65 2001
813'.54—dc21

Printed in the United States of America
Set in Trump Mediaeval
Designed by Leonard Telesca

PUBLISHER'S NOTE
This is a work of fiction. Names, characters, places, and incidents either
are the products of the author's imagination or are used fictitiously, and
any resemblance to actual persons, living or dead, business establishments,
events, or locales, is entirely coincidental.

To all lovers,
As well as to lovers of fairy tales

And to the many folks who grace
The Encyclopedia Mithgar,
The Halls of Mithgar,
and
The One-Eyed Crow

Acknowledgments

My dear Martha Lee, my heart, I appreciate and am grateful for your enduring support, careful reading, patience, and love.

Additionally, thank you, Tanque Wordies Writers' Group, for your encouragement throughout the writing of *Once Upon a Winter's Night*.

Lastly, thanks goes to Christine J. McDowell for her help with the French language. I would add, though, that in all the various words and phrases of the several languages the reader will find herein—Arabic, Irish, Japanese, Latin, and Norwegian, as well as French—any errors in usage are entirely mine. Of course, the errors in English are mine as well.

Contents

Foreword

I don't remember when I heard my first fairy tale or even what it was. It could have been *Hansel and Gretel,* for I did act the part of Hansel in a school play when I was but six.

Nor do I recall when I actually read my first fairy tale, though I *do* remember checking out fairy-tale books from the library when I was nine or so. I read through the full spectrum of the Andrew-Lang-edited fairy-tale books, and I do mean "spectrum," for the books were called *The Crimson Fairy Book, The Red Fairy Book, The Pink Fairy Book,* and on through *Orange, Yellow, Olive, Green, Lilac, Blue, Violet, Grey,* and *Brown*: i.e., the spectrum.

I loved those books, for, just as a *Captain Future Quarterly* had launched me into science fiction, these launched me into fantasy.

But, you know, it is my contention that many of the old fairy stories were severely shortened as the number of bards dwindled, and the people who were left to remember and pass on the tales simply didn't have the oratory skills to tell stories of epic scope. Too, we also know they were altered to help promote different religions from those in the societies where told, hence they were shortened merely to get the point across.

And so, it is my thesis that back when bards and poets and minstrels and the like sat in castles or in hovels or mansions or by campfires, or entertained patrons as they travelled along the way, surely the original stories were much longer, with many more wondrous encounters than the later, altered versions would have them be. After all, in the case of a bardic storyteller, she or he would hold audiences enthralled for long whiles with accounts of love and seduction and copious sex and bloody fights and knights and witches and dragons and ogres and giants and other fantastic beings all littering the landscape of the tale as the hero or heroine struggled on.

Don't get me wrong, I am not putting down the altered versions of the fairy tales; after all, I loved them. What I am saying instead is I've always felt that many wonders were lost by the shortening and altering of each folk and fairy tale to fit a different song from that which the old bards and my Celtic ancestors would sing.

For this reason, I decided to tell a fairy tale (in the traditional manner and style) as I would like for it to have been told had I either been one of those bards or one of those in the audience. Consequently, in telling the story herein, just as I think did happen in the past, I too have amended the tale, adding back those things—sex and fights and other such trappings—which might or might not have been in the original telling once upon a time long, long ago in a castle far, far away.

The tale I chose is one of my favorites, one you can find in *The Blue Fairy Book*, one that is said to have come from the Norse. But, you know, I always thought that this particular story should have come from the vales of France—it is a romance, after all, and who better than the French to have started it? Hence, sprinkled here and there throughout my telling, you'll find French words to give it that flavor. You'll also find other languages scattered therein, but the seasoning of French is strong.

By the bye, in my version of *The Blue Fairy Book* this story is but eleven pages long. I thought that much too short, and, as is apparent, I did lengthen it a bit.

Dennis L. McKiernan
Tucson, Arizona, 2000

It seems one cannot see the full flow of time
lest one starts at the beginning.

ONCE UPON A
WINTER'S
NIGHT

1

Knock

They lived in a one-room, stone cottage on the edge of Faery, there where the world ends and the mystical realm begins, there where golden sunshine abruptly becomes twilight all silver and grey, there where night on one side instead of the other is darkness, sometimes absolute, sometimes illumined with a glorious scatter of bright stars and silvery moonlight, sometimes illumined by small, dancing luminosities atwinkle among hoary trees, there where low, swampy lands and crofters' fields and shadowed forests on this side change on that side into misty fens and untilled meadows and deep, dark, mysterious woods.

There at the edge of Faery . . .

There at the edge of the world . . .

There where they lived in days long past, when the mystical yet touched the real.

They were a large family—father, mother, six daughters, and a son—scratching out a mean living from a meager plot of land on this side of the marge where the world ended and Faery began. Yet the meek father and bitter mother and their six daughters—ranging in age from twenty to sixteen and in manner from whining to cheerful and sweet—and their uncomplaining young son of nine managed to eke out a bare existence from the scant land and to make do with what they had. Although they had enough to eat, beyond that they did not live well, working the poor soil, laboring hard, father and mother and daughters. As to the son, he was quite sickly, yet even he did what he could, though he did tire most easily and seemed always out of breath. It was but a scrape of land, standing remote at the edge of the world, and passed down through generations from poor fathers to equally poor sons. Neighbors they had none, the nearest croft miles away, the town even farther. None of the daughters was married, and no dowry did any have, and no suitors came to call, living in poverty and isolation as the daughters did. And so they were yet maidens all, though in face and form quite fair, especially the youngest with her golden hair, who often sang in a voice that would put the larks to shame as she worked in the field near the woods, there on the edge of Faery.

But then . . .

. . . Once upon a winter's night . . .

"Oh, Papa, listen to the wind howl," said Camille, raising her head from the hand-carved game of échecs over which she and Giles pondered, some of the shaped pieces arrayed on the squares of the board, other pieces sitting to one side, captured and no longer in play.

"Howl indeed, and I am freezing," grumbled dark-haired Lisette, eldest of the six sisters, hitching the blanket tighter 'round her shoulders, then huddling closer to the meager fire and reaching out with her cold hands.

The chimney moaned as would a lost wraith, and the bound thatch across the sparse beams above rattled and thumped and shook like a rat in a terrier's jaws, and dust drifted down to swirl about in the darts of air whistling in through chinks in between stones in the walls.

"Move back, Lisette," snapped Joie and Gai nearly together, the twins in their shared blanket crowding inward, Gai adding, "you are taking all the heat for yourself." Colette and Felise chimed in, agreeing, at the same time crowding inward as well.

"Now, now, mes filles," began the father, "do not bicker. Instead—" but his words were cut short.

"Complain they should, Henri," snapped the mother, Aigrette, her downturned mouth disapproving, her glaring blue eyes full of ire as she pulled at the blanket she shared with him. "I told you time and again this summer to mortar the gaps, but you didn't, and now the wind blows as fiercely within this hovel as it does without."

As the tempest rattled the plank door, through the firelight the father looked about the mean dwelling, with its hard-packed clay floor and rough, field-rock walls and its aging and thinning reed roof. This single room was all they had, a fireplace in one corner, now crowded 'round by the family on three mismatched chairs and a wobbly, three-legged stool and a small, splintery bench. Near the fireplace stood an inadequate worktable for the preparation of meals, such as they were, with a wretched few pots and pans and utensils hanging from the beams above. Several rude shelves on the wall at hand held a small number of wooden bowls and dishes and spoons. A water bucket sat on a shelf as well, a hollowed-out gourd for a dipper hanging down from the bail. To one side of the fireplace stood a tripod holding a lidded iron kettle dangling empty. Swaying in the shadows above, strings of beans and roots and turnips and onions and leeks and other such fare depended from the joists. Ranged along the walls stood a cot for the boy and three beds, two of which were stacked—upper and lower, shared by three girls each—and in the center of the room stood the table on which they ate, one short leg propped on a flat stone to keep the whole of it from rocking. Pegs here and there jammed into wall cracks held what few garments they owned, and by the door a meager coat for braving the cold hung over a single pair of large boots. In one corner a coarse burlap curtain draped from a rough hemp cord, behind which sat a wooden chamber pot, in truth nought but a bucket, though it did have a lid.

The father sighed and stroked his care-lined face, for they would spend much of the remainder of the winter jammed together in this insufficient, single room—bickering, fighting, glowering at one another in sullen ire, or sunk in moody silences—for in the cold season the out-of-doors was brutal, and the meager clothes they wore would not protect them from the bone-deep, bitter chill. Even indoors as they were, they kept warm only by huddling within well-worn blankets, and these they had to share.

As the wind shrieked 'round the house and battered as if for admittance, in the dim shadows beyond the clustered fireside arc of family Camille said, "Giles, I shall win in four moves."

"What?" exclaimed the lad, staring at the board, perplexity in his hazel eyes. "You will? Four moves?"

Reaching out from the blanket they shared, Camille slid a miter-topped piece diagonally along three unoccupied squares and into the occupied fourth. "Hierophant takes spearman. Check. Now, Frère, what is the only move you have?"

Giles studied the board and finally said, "King takes hierophant," and he smiled his crookedy smile.

"Yes," replied Camille. "Then my warrior takes this spearman. Check."

After a moment, Giles said, "This spearman takes your warrior."

Camille nodded. "Now, with that spearman moved, tower takes tower. Check."

"Oh, I see," said Giles. "Then I have no choice but to move my king here, but then you reveal the mate by—" Of a sudden, Giles broke into racking coughs.

Camille wrapped the blanket tighter around Giles's narrow shoulders, yet he gasped and wheezed, unable to gain his breath. "Here," said Camille, helping the boy to stand, "let me get you closer to the fire."

As Camille shepherded Giles toward the hearth, "You just want to steal our warmth," declared Lisette. "Well, I for one do not intend to move." An immediate squabbling broke out among the girls, the mother joining in.

Sighing and without saying a word, the father stood and yielded up his place, leaving the blanket he had shared wrapped about his wife.

But before Camille and Giles reached the vacated space, there came a hard pounding on the door, the cross-braced planks rattling under the blows, the barricading bar jumping in its wooden brackets.

Startled, the girls looked at one another and then at the father, who had jerked about to stare at the entry.

"Who could that be?" whispered Lisette. "Thieves? Brigands come to rob us? Kidnappers come to grab up one of us for ransom?"

"Ha!" snorted the mother. "And just what would they get, these thieves and robbers, these kidnappers? Rocks? Dirt? Straw?"

Again the pounding came.

"Papa," said Camille to her father, even as she huddled closer to Giles, "perhaps you had better see who it is; they may need shelter from the storm."

Looking about for a weapon, finding none, the father stepped to the door and pivoted the bar up and aside on its axle. Glancing back at Camille and receiving a nod, he placed a shoulder against the rattling planks to brace against the wind and lifted the clattering latch and eased the door on its leather-strap hinges open a crack, putting his eye to the narrow space as a snow-bearing sheet of wind swirled in. *"Ai!"* he wailed and slammed the door to and crashed the bar down into its brackets.

"What is it, Papa?" cried the children at the fire as they leapt to their feet and clustered, all clutching one another for support, the mother standing and shrinking back against the trembling knot of girls.

"A Bear! A white Bear!" wailed the father, backing away from the barred planks. "A great white Bear of the North!"

As the father retreated and the girls and the mother pressed even tighter together, and Camille held on to wheezing Giles, once more came the massive knock, the planks and bar shuddering under the blow, there at the cottage where the mortal world ended and the realm of Faery began.

2
Offer

Silence fell, but for the storm, and but for Giles's racking cough. Moments passed, none daring to say aught, none daring to move, except to stare wide-eyed at one another. Finally, Lisette whispered, "Perhaps it's gone." Yet no sooner had the words passed her lips, when again came the thunderous pounding, and all the girls but Camille screamed, she to wince and clutch Giles tighter, the lad yet gasping and wheezing with his cheek pressed against her breast.

"Papa," asked Camille, "how large is the Bear?"

"Huge," quavered the father, backing away from the entry.

"Large enough to smash down the door?"

"Oh, yes, Camille. Quite easily."

"Yet he does not," observed Camille. "Here, Papa, take Giles." She gave over the lad and blanket to her sire.

"What are you going to do?" cried the mother.

"I'm going to see what it wants," replied Camille, stepping toward the door.

"Oh, oh," cried Joie, clutching her twin, "now we shall all be killed." At this the girls began to weep, and huddled even closer together.

But Camille rotated the bar about its end axle and cautiously opened the door.

With the blizzard shrieking all 'round, the frigid squall howling inward and threatening to blow out the meager fire, a huge white Bear stood on the doorstone, its paw lifted as if to strike the planks again, the wind rippling its fur.

In the fluttering light cast by the struggling blaze, Camille, her loose golden hair aswirl, called out above the blast, "What is it you want, O Bear?"

The Bear raised its head up and turned it aside and stood very still, revealing a leather canister affixed to a strap about its neck, the cylinder a foot or so long and some three fingers in diameter.

Leaving the door to swing wildly in the wind, Camille knelt and with trembling fingers unfastened the tube, her heart beating frantically, for she was fearful of the Bear's great claws and teeth, though if the creature decided to attack there was little she could do to defend herself or her family within. The moment the canister was free, the Bear backed away a step or two, Camille suppressing a gasp of startlement at the great white beast's sudden move. But the Bear stopped and once again became still. Camille then stood and, shivering with cold or dread or both, stepped back into the cottage and grabbed the door and latched it shut. Inside, she heaved a great sigh of relief and slumped against the wind-battered planks, the storm howling to be let in again.

"What is it?" cried the father, he and Giles now huddled with the others, spinning snowflakes yet swirling through the air within and drifting down to the clay floor.

"It is a message tube," said Camille, pushing away from the door and moving to the table. She held the leather canister up for all to see, her hand yet trembling with residual fright. "Now and again by courier, Fra Galanni would receive one similar to this"—she glanced back at the rattling door—"but never one borne by a Bear."

Camille twisted off the cap and shook out a scroll from inside and set the canister down on the board.

"What does it say?" asked Aigrette, the mother moving opposite.

"It is sealed, Maman," replied Camille, showing her mother the fix of green wax holding the scroll closed, wax impressed with an ornate signet depicting a wide-branching tree—an oak, perhaps.

"Well, open it, for surely it was meant for us, else the Bear would not have brought it here."

Camille nodded and broke the seal and unrolled the parchment. The message it bore was written in a very fine hand.

"Read it to us," urged Lisette, now stepping to Camille's side.

"Oh, do," cried Colette, she and Felise rushing forward as

well, the others crowding 'round the table after, including the father and Giles, the lad's coughing finally come to a stop.

They all craned their necks to look at the writing, which none could read but Camille, for, unlike them, she had been taught by Fra Galanni to read and write. Her mother had bound Camille over to the elderly monk as a servant girl at the age of eight, and she had attended him for nearly four years, until he had died of the ague.

Tilting the letter toward the firelight, the better to see the script, Camille quickly scanned down the scroll and sharply drew in a breath. She looked up at her father.

"Come, come, daughter, what does it say?" he asked.

Camille looked again at the letter and, her voice slightly quavering, read, "To the parents of the girl who sings in the field . . ."

To the parents of the girl who sings in the field: Greetings.

Fear not the Bear, for he would do you no more harm than would I. Think of him as my ambassador, and offer him your hospitality ere reading on.

Camille looked up from the page. "Papa, let the Bear in."

"Bu-but, what if—"

"The Prince of the Summerwood has so ordered," said Camille, gesturing at the letter.

"Prince?" gasped Aigrette, her eyes flying wide, a gleam of expectation within. "Henri," she barked, "do as Camille says."

Sucking in air through gritted teeth, Henri loosed his hold on Giles and stepped to the door and lifted the latch and opened it wide, the wild wind and snow howling about to set the strings of beans and turnips and other such to madly sway, the pots and pans to clang, and the fire and wrapped 'round blankets to whip and flutter in the blow. "Enter, Monsieur Bear," Henri called, his voice trembling, and then quickly stepped wide of the way. The great Bear ambled inward, the girls scrambling together and in a body retreating, Camille and Giles standing firm on the side of the table nearest the Bear, the mother cringing but remaining opposite.

Taking up most of the free space, with a *"Whuff!"* the Bear sat down and grunted as if in satisfaction.

Shutting out the storm, the father closed and latched the door, though momentarily he peered out into the fury beyond, as if perhaps seeking more bears or mayhap thinking of bolting.

With pale eyes, the Bear looked at Camille and the opened scroll and cocked his head.

"He wants you to go on," Aigrette whispered across the board.

Camille nodded and peered at the scroll again and started at the beginning once more:

To the parents of the girl who sings in the field:
Greetings.
Fear not the Bear, for he would do you no more harm than would I. Think of him as my ambassador, and offer him your hospitality ere reading on.
That done . . . I am smitten by your golden-haired daughter, and I seek your permission to marry her—

"Not fair!" cried Lisette, outrage honing her words as she glared with dark blue eyes at Camille. "I am the eldest, and I should be first to marry. And to a prince at that."

"And I next!" called out Colette indignantly, her own blue eyes ablaze. "And a prince for me as well."

The Bear swung his great head toward the pair and a growl rumbled deep in his chest, and with small yips the two fell silent.

"A prince," hissed Aigrette to Henri, her eyes narrowing in calculation. "A prince wishes to marry our daughter. Go on, go on, Camille; pay your sisters no heed. Go on, read the rest."

Taking a deep breath, Camille continued:

. . . I seek your permission to marry her. If you accept, she will be the mistress of a grand estate, and my holdings in Faery are—

"In Faery?" blurted Giles, and then began coughing again.

Embracing the rail-thin lad, the father repeated, "In Faery? But therein dwell monsters most dire, and—"

"Quiet, both of you," snapped Aigrette. "Our daughter is to marry a prince. Read on, Camille. Pay no heed to your father and brother."

. . . my holdings in Faery are considerable. Too, if you accept, I will settle upon you a sizeable bride-price of gold as well as an annual stipend, enough for you and your remaining children to live in modest luxury.

I await your answer. If it is yes, my ambassador will bear her to me.

Until your decision, I remain,

Lord Alain
Prince of the Summerwood

Now the Bear sat back on its haunches and glanced from fretting father to avid mother and back again.

"Oh, but isn't this wonderful," said Aigrette, rubbing her hands together and beaming, her usually downturned mouth smiling for the first time in months. "Our own Camille is to be married to a rich—"

"But, Maman," protested Camille, "I don't wish to be wedded to someone I have never met."

"Hush, child," replied the mother. "You knew someday we would arrange a marriage for you."

Lisette shoved forward. "But you should first arrange a marriage for me," she angrily snapped, "for I am the eldest, while Camille is the youngest of all."

A clamor arose from the other girls, each crying out that they were certainly older than Camille, and the twins began arguing with each other as to which of the two had been born first, Gai crying, "Me!" and Joie crying, "No, me!"

"Be quiet, all of you," shouted Aigrette.

When a disgruntled silence fell, Aigrette said, "Don't you see, the prince asks no dowry, but instead will pay us a bride-price and an annual stipend for the hand of Camille. By accepting this proposal, not only will we have wealth to escape this dismal life your father has visited upon us, we will also have dowries for each of you, wealth to attract suitors."

With sharp intakes of breath, the girls looked at one another, realization illuminating the face of each. And then, clamoring, they turned to Camille, and she in turn looked at her father, tears in her eyes, but he could not meet her regard. In that moment Camille wished that Fra Galanni were there to comfort and advise her. Again she looked at her father and whispered, "Papa."

Henri turned to the Bear and said, "We will sleep on it."

"*What?*" demanded the mother in shock. "Sleep on it? Henri, the one who made the offer is a *prince!*"

Henri flinched, but then took a deep breath and gritted his teeth. "I said, we will sleep on it."

The great white Bear grunted, and lay down and closed his ashen eyes.

Henri took to his bed; Aigrette, sissing angrily, followed him. The girls, too, retired—Camille and the twins sharing the lower bunk, Lisette, Felise, and Colette sharing the upper—and Giles took to his cot by the fire.

In spite of the blizzard, the cottage was cozier that night, made so by the presence of the Bear, his huge bulk shedding warmth into the room. Yet at the same time the chamber was distressingly chill, for Aigrette seethed in frigid ire. Camille lay a long time awake in the angry whispers coming from her parents' bed—Aigrette raging at Henri, her furious hissings muted by the storm rampaging without and the great sleeping breaths of the Bear within.

The next morning dawned to quiet, for the blizzard had blown itself out sometime in the night. At breakfast, at the mother's urging, once again Camille read the letter to them all, and over their gruel they argued, and only Camille and Giles were opposed to the proposal: Camille would not wed someone she had never seen, and Giles would not lose the one sister he had come to love, who made him laugh and played riddle games and taught him échecs and who sang so sweetly. Henri did not speak, his ears weary from Aigrette's late-night harangue. The mother and sisters, though, clamored for Camille to quickly accept the fact that it was a prince whom she would wed.

The Bear sat silent, though he did share a bowl of the porridge with Camille, who had no appetite at all.

Finally, Henri said, "We must write a response unto the prince."

"Papa," said Camille, sighing, "we have no parchment, no pen, no ink."

"And even if we did have such," hissed Lisette, "how would we know what she had written on any note we would send?"

At this the Bear growled, and Lisette snapped her mouth shut.

"He seems to know what we are saying," said Aigrette, nodding toward the Bear. "Simply tell him that we accept and send him on his way to bring back the promised gold."

Tears in her eyes, Camille silently gazed at her father. Henri once again could not meet her mute stare. He turned to the Bear. "Come back in a sevenday, for then we will have our answer."

Angrily, Aigrette glared at him.

Grunting, the Bear moved to the door, and, before anyone else could stir, Aigrette sprang to her feet and opened the wooden-planked panel and led the Bear outside. 'Round the corner of the cottage she went with him, and there she said, "Come prepared to pay the bride-price and bear Camille away, for I shall see to it that she goes with you."

The Bear growled low—whether in ire or agreement, Aigrette could not say—and then ambled away from the stone hovel and toward the twilight border of mysterious and dreaded Faery, for therein strange and terrible creatures did dwell, or so it was said. Hugging herself against the cold, Aigrette didn't blink an eye as the Bear rambled across a pristine white field of new-fallen snow, leaving heavy tracks behind, to pass into the silvery twilight and vanish; but inside the cottage, with an eye pressed to a chink in the back wall, Camille watched as well, her heart beating swiftly in fright.

3
Decision

"But, Maman, he may be old beyond years and ugly," cried Camille.

Pushing out a hand in a swift motion of disallowance, Aigrette said, "Camille, if he's old, then you will inherit his fortune and estates more quickly"—she gestured at the letter on the table—"and he is a prince with a great mansion and considerable lands." She glanced at Henri. "And as for ugly, it matters not. After all, look at what I got."

For his part, Henri merely sighed.

"Papa is not ugly," rebutted Camille, reaching out to touch her father's sleeve.

"But Mère is right," said Lisette. "And if the prince had made the same offer to me, as he should have, I would have accepted without hesitation. Camille, he is a *prince!*"

"It is not yours to choose," said Giles, receiving a glare from Lisette in return.

"Your frère is right," declared Aigrette. "It is not yours to choose, nor, I add, is it Camille's to choose. It is mine to say whom she will marry, or no."

"What about Papa?" exclaimed Camille, turning to her sire. "Has he no voice in this whatsoever?"

Henri sighed and peered at the floor.

"Would you not marry a *prince?*" asked Joie.

"Aye, a *prince,*" echoed Gai.

"But he lives in Faery among monsters dire and creatures fell," said Camille, "a place Humans are not welcome."

"*Pah!*" snorted Aigrette. "As far as not being welcome, the prince invited you, and so you are welcome to travel within that realm, to travel to his principality of Summerwood, for he wishes you there as his wife."

"But what of the peril?" asked Giles. "The monsters and other dire creatures of Faery? Ogres and Trolls, Bogles, Dragons, and Goblins like the Redcaps, who dye their hats in the blood of Humans, or so Papa says."

Although the other girls blenched, Lisette glanced at her brother, and then at Henri. "*Bah*! As for things of peril, Camille will have the Bear for protection, and a finer guardian none could want."

Camille touched Giles' hand in thanks, then looked at her mother. "Then answer me this, Maman: what if this Lord Prince is not right in the mind, a simpleton or other such."

"He would have to be a loon to have chosen you," gibed Felise, her blue eyes dancing, her sprinkle of freckles wrinkling 'round her nose as she grinned.

"This is no laughing matter, Felise," said Camille, though she grinned at the light-brown-haired girl in return.

"If he is simpleminded," said Aigrette, "then you will command his wealth all the easier."

Camille sighed. "Then what if he has the deadly plague or some other spreading ill?"

"All the better," said Lisette, glancing at her mother, "for as Mère says, it means you will inherit sooner than late."

Camille glanced about the table "What if the prince himself is a monster dire, a terrible thing to behold, perhaps even a murderer of women?"

Even as the sisters' eyes widened in alarm at this newly imagined possibility, Aigrette again pushed out a hand of negation. "Then you can merely run away, Camille, but only after we get the gold."

"Is that all you are interested in, Maman? The bride-price, the gold?"

Aigrette gestured at the room. "Would you have us live in destitution, when wealth is within our grasp?"

"Oh, Camille," said Colette, turning to her sisters for support, "would you deny us dowries to attract suitors?"

"Aye, dowries," chimed in Gai, glancing at Joie, who added, "Would you have us be old maids?"

"Do none of you think of aught but yourselves?" asked Giles in anger. "Camille is the only—" But the boy began gasping for air, leaving the rest of his words unsaid.

Camille embraced the lad as he wheezed, and Aigrette's eyes narrowed in cunning. "With the gold we can afford a healer for Giles, Camille. Would you deny him such relief?"

Tears welled in Camille's eyes, and she did not answer her dam.

"Yes, a doctor for Giles," said Lisette, following her mother's lead. "We could afford the medicine needed to make him well."

"D-don't pay h-heed," panted Giles, but he could say no more.

"With the gold, we could have a bigger and better house," declared Aigrette. "One of warmth and light. One where Giles could escape the draft and damp and dust of this hovel."

"And warm clothes," added Felise. "Something to keep Giles cozy."

Catching his breath at last, Giles said, "Oh, Camille, I don't need doctors that badly. You shouldn't go off to an unknown fate, no matter the count of coin."

Camille smiled at the entirely too-thin nine-year-old, but she knew in spite of his bravado that he was truly ill.

And thus did the arguments and harangues go for the full sevenday: the mother harping that she deserved a better life, the one her failure of a husband had promised her when they first were wed, ". . . but look at what he gave me instead"; the father looking everywhere but at Camille, though often tears ran down his cheeks, for he knew that his achievements as a provider had never amounted to much, and whatever spirit he might have once had as a young man had been nagged into abject submission; the sisters' eyes lighting up at the thought of rich dowries and the suitors to come; and all the women arguing that with the gold they could afford a doctor for Giles, even though Giles denied that a doctor or medicine or other such was needed, that he was healthy enough.

. . . And so, all told, did a sevenday pass.

And late in the evening of the seventh day, just as the sun was setting, the great white Bear came padding across the snow and to the stone cottage plank door, where he gave the panel a heavy knock. Rushing to the entryway, Aigrette flung it wide. "Come in, Monsieur Bear, Ambassador of the Prince." Aigrette moved aside. The Bear swung its head this way and that as if seeking, and then he stepped inward, making straight for Camille. 'Round his girth was a harness on which were affixed bundles, several on each side. The Bear presented a flank to the girl and looked over his shoulder at her. "*Whuff,*" he breathed, and nuzzled the pack-roll at hand.

Camille loosened the thongs holding the bundle fast and set the whole of it on the table.

"Untie it, untie it," demanded Gai, jittering from one foot to another.

"Yes, do," added her twin, fidgeting at Gai's side.

Inside was clothing, all of it sized to fit Camille. First revealed was a splendid dark green, all-weather cloak, made of a woolen cloth. Then came soft leather trousers and a leather vest and boots and cotton socks, all of these dark brown. Next revealed was a jerkin, made of pale green silk, and green silk full-length hosiery. Lastly came undergarments, made of green silk as well. Father and mother and sisters and even Giles *ooh*ed and *ahh*ed over the richness of the attire.

Camille sighed. "Travelling clothes." Then she turned to the Bear. "But, O Bear, I have not said I would go."

The sisters gasped, and Felise whined, "Oh, Camille, but you must, else we will be without dowries."

"Nonsense," snapped Aigrette, stepping to Camille's side, but addressing the Bear. "She will go."

"I have neither said yea nor nay, Maman," replied Camille, glancing at her father, but Henri merely hung his head.

Now Joie and Gai broke into tears, and Lisette ground her teeth in fury. Felise plopped down in a chair and moaned, while Colette cried out, "Stupid! Stupid! Stupid!"

Of a sudden the Bear gave a great roar, shocking them all into silence, all but Giles, that is, for he began wheezing and gasping, desperately struggling for breath. And then his eyes rolled up in his head and he collapsed to the floor, falling slack as if slain. Camille was the first to reach him, and though the lad was unconscious, his lungs yet fought for air.

"See what you've done, Camille," hissed Aigrette. "Had we gold we could make him well."

With tears in her eyes, Camille embraced Giles, and weeping, she whispered, "You win, Maman. I will go."

That night in her bed, Camille was awakened by someone slipping out the door, and by the glow of an ember or two yet remaining on the hearth, she could see that the Bear was gone. She eased out from the lower bunk, and only the harness and the remaining bundles lay where he had been. And she thought that perhaps even Bears needed to relieve themselves. After reassuring herself that sleeping Giles breathed peacefully, Camille crawled back under the blanket with Joie and Gai and quickly fell aslumber. She did not stir when the door opened again, but awakened later to see the Bear once more lying nigh the center of the room.

The next morning Henri found a small wooden case on the table, and when he opened it he gave a great shout, for it was filled to the brim with gold coins. "The bride-price!" he called out. "The bride-price has come, and, oh, what riches we have!"

Aigrette leapt from her bed and rushed to the board, while daughters scrambled up and to the table as well, Joie and Gai scuttling over Camille to do so. Camille sat up and glanced at Giles, to see him looking at her. He smiled his quirky smile and rose from his cot and made his way to the table, too, where he found Aigrette testing each coin by biting down with her teeth.

The Bear merely sat and watched.

"But wait, Maman," said Lisette to her mother, glancing at the Bear, "what if this is merely a glamour and nought but fairy gold, to turn to dross in the light of the sun?"

At Lisette's words a low growl rumbled in the Bear's chest, but Aigrette's eyes flew wide. "Here, here," she snapped, grabbing up the wooden case and scooping the gold from the table and within. She hied past the Bear to take it outside and into the sunlight, and he made no move to stop her.

Moments later she came dancing back in, holding the case of coins on high and crowing, "It's real. It is truly gold," for in the direct rays of the sun none of the coins had changed to iron or lead or other base metal or slag, or to rubbish of any kind.

The Bear sniffed as if to say, "You doubted?"

After a breakfast of gruel, the Bear sharing Camille's bowl, with father and mother and the sisters all chatting gaily and the gold heaped on the table, Camille sighed and looked about at her family. Only Giles seemed pensive, and tears stood behind his eyes, for he would not lose his dear sister. Wiping her own brimming tears with the heels of her hands, Camille smiled at her brother and murmured, "It will be all right, Frère." He grinned his crooked grin at her, but his heart wasn't in the smile.

Camille turned to her father. "And you, Papa, what will you do with the gold?"

Henri took a deep breath and slowly let it out, and ran his fingers across his greying temples. He glanced at the pile of coins and said, "Now we can afford a team of oxen or a horse to plow the land, and a milk cow for the girls as well, and medicine for Giles."

Aigrette shook her head and glared at Henri. "Your father always did think small, Camille. As for the gold, there's more than enough to build a fine house, enough to provide me—to provide all of us—a luxurious way of living."

"Just as the prince in his letter said," agreed Lisette.

The conversation turned to what things they could buy, and what dowries they could have, and what young men might come calling. Neither Camille nor Giles nor Henri joined in.

After breakfast, Camille stepped behind the burlap privy curtain to don the very fine travelling clothes. She slipped into the undergarments, the delicate silken touch caressing her. She pulled on the silk hosiery, and then the jerkin and laced it up, and donned the soft leather trousers and vest, the silken garments underneath to keep the leather from chafing. Then she pulled on the socks and boots, and they fit her feet quite well. She cast the dark green cloak over her shoulders and fastened it with the jade brooch she discovered at its throat. With her golden tresses lying across the velvety, forest green shoulders of the cloak gracing her slender form, taking a deep breath, she stepped from behind the drape, and gasps went up from the sisters. Giles stared at her wide-eyed, as if he had never seen her before, and both Henri and Aigrette reflected his look of astonishment. Even the Bear seemed o'erwhelmed, for he stood fourfooted and dipped his head low, almost as if he were bowing.

"Oh, Camille," said Colette, raising a hand to her cheek, "though dressed as a boy, you look like a fair lady true."

Camille blushed at Colette's words and the scrutiny she received from all. To cover her discomfiture, she turned to the Bear, and he *whuff*ed and nuzzled the harness and goods lying on the floor.

With help from Giles, Camille affixed the rigging about the Bear's massive frame, and then she fastened the bundles onto the straps. Her sister Felise stepped forward with a petite roll and said, " 'Tis raggings, in case your courses come upon you on the journey." Camille nodded and tied on this small bundle as well, next to the one which held her most precious possessions: a wood-and-fishbone comb, dried mint leaves to sweeten her breath, several chew-sticks to scrub her teeth, and a small piece of soap made of rendered animal fat and scented with clover blossoms.

At last, all was ready. And Camille hugged each of her sisters, Gai and Joie, Felise, Colette, all of whom said, "Merci, Camille," and finally Lisette, who stiffly received the embrace and gritted through clenched teeth, "It should have been me."

Camille then hugged her mother, who said, "Now we have gold," and then her father, who whispered, "I'm sorry."

Last of all she hugged Giles, who burst into tears without saying a word, but Camille said, "Fear not, Little Frère, for I believe all will be well," even though her heart was hammering in dread.

At another *whuff* from the Bear, Henri opened the door, and out into winter they all trod, where sunlight aglance across the snow cast diamondlike glints to the eye.

Sighing and forcing a smile and raising her hand in au revoir, Camille started trudging toward Faery, but the Bear growled and did not move.

Frowning, Camille looked back and said, "O Bear, do we not go this way? It is your own tracks in the white I follow."

Yet the Bear still did not move.

"Oh, my," hissed Aigrette to Henri. "Something has gone wrong. The prince will take back his gold."

Camille returned to the Bear's side. "What is it you want, O Bear?"

Giles frowned down at the glittering snow and then looked up at Camille. "The letter, Camille. Remember the letter?"

Camille looked at her little brother. "Y-yes. I do. But what does it—?"

" 'I await your answer,' " quoted Giles. " 'If it is yes, my ambassador will bear her to me.' Oh, Camille, don't you see, the Bear wants you to ride."

With uncertainty, Camille looked at the Bear. "Is that it, O Bear? You wish me to ride?"

"*Whuff.*" The Bear lowered his head.

Taking a deep breath and catching hold of the harness, Camille mounted up, Gai and Joie gasping in borrowed fright, Lisette frowning in disdain, while Felise and Colette and Père and Mère looked on in wonder at Camille, the golden-haired girl perched as would a lady riding sidesaddle upon a horse. Only Giles laughed in glee; but then the Bear began to move away, heading toward the twilight realm, and Giles' laughter died in his throat and tears sprang to his eyes, for his beloved sister was leaving.

Without turning, Camille waved adieu to her family, for she did not want them to see she was weeping; after all, she was all of sixteen and now on her own, and surely beyond such displays. Nevertheless, tears flowed down her cheeks to drop away in the cold. And she cast the hood of the cloak over her head to hide her teary-eyed face and to fend against the chill, while the Bear padded forward toward twilight.

Before the Bear had gone halfway, Aigrette turned and rushed back into the hovel to count once more the measure of precious gold, Lisette trailing after. But the rest of the family remained where they stood, watching, as Camille rode away to an unknown fate on the back of a Bear from Faery.

4
Springwood

Across a winter-fallow 'scape laden with crystalline snow went the Bear, with bundles strapped to his harness and a young girl mounted above. And Camille's heart hammered ever more frantically the closer to Faery they came. Even so, even though her mouth was dust-dry with fear, just ere crossing out of the mortal world and into the mystic realm, she managed to turn and wave to the cluster of kindred standing beside the little stone cottage where all of her life she had lived; yet even as they raised their hands to return her distant au revoir, the Bear crossed over the marge, and within ten strides or mayhap ten hundred, the hovel and family were gone. And though it was midmorn in the world behind, it was twilight in the numinous domain. Camille gasped in surprise, for though she had not known what she had expected, it certainly was not this, for they had entered a burgeoning forest, a realm where the gentle air of midspring wafted among newly leafed-out trees, a place where winter held no grip.

Camille cast back the hood of her cloak and shook loose her flowing tresses to cascade golden down her back. And she breathed in the scent of the woodland, fresh and full of new promise, where, somehow, in spite of the twilight, the shades of the forest seemed darker, and yet at the same time the hues were more vivid than any she could ever dream. Old were these trees, some of them, their roots reaching deep, their great girths moss-covered, their branches spread wide and interlacing with others overhead. Yet here and there was new growth—thickets of saplings and lone seedlings and solitary treelets, all reaching upward into the strange, crepuscular half-light. Yet, her eye was drawn to the old growth: oak, she could see, proud and majestic, and groves of birch, silver and white; maple and elm stood tall, with dogwood and wild cherry blossoms filling the air with their delicate scents. And down among the roots running across the soil, crocuses bloomed, as did small mossy flowers, yellow and lavender and white. Birds flitted here and there, their songs claiming territory and calling for mates. The hum of bees sounded as they moved from blossom to blossom, and elsewhere beetles clambered along greening vines and stems. Overhead, scampering limb-runners chattered, and down among the grass and thatch, voles and other small living things rustled. Somewhere nearby and hidden in bracken, a small stream burbled and splashed, as if singing and dancing on its way to the shores of a distant sea. Bright and dark and twilight were these woods, and full of wakened life, and Camille was filled with the marvel of it all.

While looking this way and that in the impossible task of trying to see the whole of it, Camille unclasped the brooch at her neck and removed the cloak from 'round her shoulders, for the air was mild and she would be shed of the warm garment. As she reached for a strap of the harness at hand to affix the cloak under, Camille looked down and said, "Oh, Bear—" but her words chopped to silence, for the Bear was no longer a pristine white, but an ebon black instead.

"Bear!" she exclaimed in wonder. "You've changed colors."

The Bear merely grunted, and padded onward across the sward and among the close-set boles of trees.

As they travelled on, the twilight brightened, as if day were coming unto this mystical land. Onward they went and onward, the day getting brighter and brighter, yet whenever they topped a clear rise and Camille looked back the way they had come, in the distance hindward twilight yet cloaked the land. Frowning, she looked ahead, and twilight seemed to reign there, too, as well as to left and right.

Full daylight came where the Bear now trod, the day nigh the noontide, and still there was twilight afar, seeming diminished no less than before.

Glancing up at the sun above, the Bear plodded a bit farther, to come under the widespread limbs of a great oak, and there it was he stopped. He looked over his shoulder at Camille.

"What is it, O Bear, that you desire? Should I dismount?"

"Whuff."

Turning full sideways, Camille sprang to the ground. She stretched her legs and walked about, for she was not used to riding. She came to the edge of a brook, and the bourne sang its rippling song as it tumbled o'er pebbles and rocks. Kneeling at stream edge, she drank long and deeply of the chill water, and rose up to her knees to find the Bear standing nigh. She wiped her lips on the back of her hand, then said, "Oh, Bear, that was perhaps the most delicious draught ever. Is all of Faery like such?"

The Bear grunted noncommittally, and then, moving downstream of Camille, he stepped to the brook and lowered his great muzzle and took a deep drink himself.

Camille stood and brushed off her knees, then straightened and filled her lungs fully with the cool, crystalline air. "Bear, what name has this place? Oh, I don't mean Faery itself, but this glorious woodland around."

The Bear raised his head from the bourne, water streaming down from his muzzle. He glanced about and grunted, and then lowered his head again.

"Well, then, let me see. Since your master is Lord of the Summerwood, then this cannot be his demesne, for here 'tis spring, not summer. This must be the Springwood instead."

The Bear again raised his head, and cocked it to one side as he looked at her, and then he gave a soft *whuff.*

"Does that mean *yes,* that I have guessed aright?"

Again the Bear *whuff*ed.

Camille clapped her hands together and laughed. "Oh, Bear, you are not much of a conversationalist, yet when you speak, I listen. But hear me now: my breakfast was sparse, and all of this travel and your constant chitter-chatter has made me quite hungry; you wouldn't happen to have some food in those bundles you carry, now would you?"

The Bear rumbled deep in his chest, and then turned and padded to the great oak, where he dipped his head low, almost as if in obeisance. Perplexed, Camille looked on as the Bear raised his head and canted it to one side as if listening to unvoiced words from the oak. But Camille could hear nought but the sibilant rustle of new-green leaves overhead. The Bear then turned and began circling the tree, snuffling along the ground. He stopped and scooped one powerful forepaw down into the soft loam.

He turned to Camille.

"*Whuff.*"

Camille stepped to where the Bear stood, and she looked into the foot-deep gouge, where, within, she espied a dark double-fist-sized growth of some sort.

"You wish me to dig that out, O Bear?"

The Bear *whuff*ed softly and looked into the hole as well.

Camille knelt and pushed away soft loam, and she reached with two hands and grasped the growth and pulled it up. Dark, it was, almost black and somewhat spongy, and it had an earthy aroma. Frowning, she said, "This feels somewhat like a mushroom, but I think it is not. Let us take it to the stream and wash it off, and then we shall see."

Moments later, with water yet dripping, Camille broke off a small piece, and just as the globular growth was dark on the outside, it was dark on the inside as well. Camille looked at the broken-off piece suspiciously. "Are you certain, O Bear, that this is safe to eat?"

"*Whuff.*"

Camille took a small nibble and gasped, "Oh, my. How delicious." She took another small bite, her eyes watering in joy.

Her face suddenly blossomed with enlightenment. "Oh, Bear, I think Fra Galanni spoke of these. This is a truffle, right?"

"*Whuff.*"

She broke the truffle in two, and gave the larger portion to the Bear.

"Fra Galanni named this the food of the gods, and now I see that he spoke true. He told me that a truffle's 'character' is somewhat like that of garlic laid over a penetrating earthiness, combined with a pungent sensation like a whiff of strong wine. Of course, I never knew what he was talking about, for, though I had eaten wild garlic, I had never had a strong, pungent wine, or wine of any kind, or aught I could say had an earthy taste, whatever that might mean. Yet now I suppose I know what he meant—these flavors in combination—though for the individual things he cited, but for garlic, I still have no idea of their essence."

With a snap and a gulp, the Bear's portion was gone, but Camille savored hers to the last, the Bear looking on somewhat avidly as she ate it in small bites. She cocked an eye at him. "If you want more, O Bear, I suggest you dig up another."

The Bear groaned and looked back at the tree, but made no move to comply. After a moment, he went downstream to a pool, and shortly had a fish to eat. Even so, now and again, he glanced up as if asking, "Are you going to finish all of that?"

They rested awhile, but then the Bear stood and *whuff*ed.
"Oh, is it time to go on? But it is so peaceful here."
The Bear rumbled low in his chest.
"All right, all right, O Bear, but first—" She stepped into the bracken to relieve herself, the Bear standing guard and looking everywhere but toward her. Camille then trod to the stream and washed her hands, and, after taking another deep drink, she once again mounted up.

Onward through the wondrous springtime woods they went, the midnight-black Bear and his slender rider Camille, and everywhere he bore her were marvels to delight the senses— birds singing, iridescent insects winging, the scent of loam and flowers and other growing things drifting on the air, the mild wafts caressing the skin. And Camille reveled in all.

"O Bear," she said, laughing gaily, "to think how I did dread coming into this place, for many are the tales of monsters and of peril dire, and yet I deem herein are no monsters, no peril; I think 'tis but a rumor fostered by the Fey Folk to hold us Humans at bay, else we would o'errun the—"

But the Bear roared at these words, as if protesting their untruth. And crying in fright, birds fled into the sky, and only the soft hum of an insect or two and a trickle of water broke the stillness left behind.

"Oh, my," whispered Camille, her heart racing at the thunderous outburst. "Mayhap I am wrong after all."

She rode in silence for a while. But then—"Is it that there is peril herein after all?"

"*Whuff.*"

"Monsters?"

"*Whuff.*"

At these answers, Camille's eyes widened in apprehension, and she looked about the splendid forest, seeking . . . seeking . . . she knew not what.

Onward they went, Camille somewhat on edge, for a nagging disquiet clutched at her heart. And now and again movement flickered in the corners of her eyes, yet when she jerked about to look, it seemed nothing was there. *Birds perhaps, or small, running things. Oh, Bear, why did you have to bring me such ill news!*

The sun continued to slip down the sky, and but for the fact that she rode through Faery on the back of a great black Bear within an enchanted forest, the day seemed normal to Camille, though far in the distance all 'round, twilight graced the land.

The sun set and dusk came, and, in the nearness to the fore, Camille could see a small flicker of fire. Toward this glow the Bear trod. As they moved among the trees, Camille thought she detected the patter of small feet running lightly alongside. *A bit of an animal hieing nigh, I suppose. Wait, it seems there's more than one. And— What was that? A giggle? Was that a giggle?* Camille listened intently and peered into the evening shadows. Yet she saw only darkness, and the sound was not repeated, and the footsteps pattered away.

They came to a wee glade in which a small campfire burned within a ring of stones. Spitted above the flames, a brace of rabbits cooked, fat dripping down asizzle. No one was there to greet them; no one seemed about. Nearby, a spring gurgled from the earth and ran down a slope to a lucid mere, cattail reeds ringing 'round.

In the tiny campsite, the Bear stopped and looked over his shoulder at Camille and *whuff*ed. Camille dismounted. Now the Bear nuzzled the harness; she unbuckled the straps, and at another sign from the Bear, undid one of the bundles: it was a bedroll.

"We are to spend the night here?"

"*Whuff.*"

"But there must be someone who kindled the fire and spitted the rabbits to cook; are we to camp with him . . . or with them, if there's more than one?"

The Bear made no reply.

Camille stamped her foot. "Oh, would you had more than a simple *whuff* to say, or more than that deafening roar."

Again the Bear made no comment, but instead looked back and forth between Camille and the rabbits over the fire.

"Oh, no, Bear, that's someone else's meal." Yet Camille's mouth watered at the aroma and sight of the well-cooked meat.

Camille looked out into the forest 'round, and she called aloud, "Allo, the woods! Is the owner of the camp nigh?"

No one answered.

Frowning, she turned to the Bear. "Do you know whose camp this is?"

"*Whuff.*" And the Bear looked at Camille and the bedroll on the sward, and then sat down.

Camille cocked a skeptical eye. "My camp, O Bear? Our camp?"

"Whuff."

Camille shook her head in disbelief. "And just who set it up? Fairies? Sprites?"

"Whuff."

Camille was taken aback by this answer from the Bear. *Wait, the footsteps. The giggle. But who could command—?* "The prince of the Summerwood, did he arrange such?"

"Whuff."

"And this is *our* meal?"

At another soft *whuff* from the Bear, Camille grinned and said, "Well, then, let us eat. I am starving."

"*WHUFF!*" agreed the Bear, loudly.

Camille plucked the spit from the fire and gingerly—"*Ow, ow*"—pulled the rabbits from the wooden skewer. She held one out for the Bear, and with a great crackling and crunching, he ate it bones and all. Then he sat and watched longingly as Camille daintily ate of hers.

It was delicious.

But she could only eat one hind leg and a fore, and she gave the rest to the Bear, and snap, crunch, it was gone.

She washed her face and hands in the rill running down, and scrubbed her teeth with a chew-stick, and then took to her bedroll, where she was lulled toward sleep by the ripple of water and the chirruping of small things nearby. But then she remembered the Bear's implied warning that in Faery were monsters dire and other hazards herein, and this momentarily startled her back awake. But then she recalled Lisette's words: *As for things of peril, Camille will have the Bear for protection, and a finer guardian none could want.* The last thing she remembered seeing was the great black Bear standing ward.

The next morning tendrils of a misty fog wreathed among the trees as Camille stepped down to the spring-fed mere, and though the water was chill, she doffed her clothes and parted the reeds and slipped into the limpid pool, gasping at the bite of the water.

Saving her precious soap for her hair, she scrubbed her skin with sand from the bottom. As she did so, again she heard the patter of tiny feet and the sound of a faint giggle. "Allo! Bonjour! Who is there?" she called, unable to see aught for the reeds.

Once more came a giggle, and then the sound of wee feet running away.

Camille sighed. *If the Bear is correct, 'tis small Sprites you hear, ma fille.*

Working swiftly, soon she had scrubbed herself clean and had washed her golden tresses. As she clambered out through the reeds and into the chill morning air—*Oh, no. How will I dry myself?*—she found a soft cloth for a towel lying next to her clothing, and looked up to see the black Bear ambling away.

And when she returned to the campfire, she found waiting a mug of hot tea and a meal of cold biscuits. They, too, were delicious.

Her hair, though combed, was still wet when once more Camille mounted up, and the Bear headed through the forest again. As they padded onward, she could hear rustlings in the surround. In the morning light, Camille looked left and right, fore and aft, seeking to see what made the swash and swish among the undergrowth. *Perhaps it's whoever set the fire and spitted the rabbits last night, and who made the tea in the morn, and who may have been watching me bathe.* Camille blushed at this last, yet she continued to search among the bracken and tall grass and the boles of the trees, where wisps of the morning mist yet threaded the greenery here and there. Finally, down within the early shadows, she thought she detected movement, for she caught glimpses of *somethings* or *someones,* small beings, perhaps, passing through the woods, though the sightings were so brief she could not be certain.

The morning light waxed, and the sun shone aglance through the branches of the trees and down, and though it was daylight where trod the Bear, the distant twilight yet clung to the forest afar.

Now Camille was certain she saw small beings keeping pace, for now and again one would pass through a shaft of sunlight, and it seemed they were riding small animals of some sort, lynxes she thought, though she was not certain.

Onward went the Bear and onward she rode, yet scanning the surround; and then she gasped, for in the near distance and passing among the trees and keeping pace on a parallel track was a small white horse or some such, yet out of its head rose a—*Oh, my, it is a* Unicorn! *Just like the one pictured on the tapestry in the sanctuary.* "They seek out unsullied maidens," *Fra Galanni had said, but then did not tell me what unsullied meant, though Agnès, votary of Mithras and gardener to Fra Galanni, told me it meant 'pure.'*

When the sun reached the zenith, again the Bear stopped. And this time they dined on true mushrooms, the kind Fra Galanni had named in the Old Tongue "le champignon de morelle, une autre nourriture des dieux," and Camille had to agree, for morels truly also must be the food of the gods. Still, the truffle of yesterday had seemed even better. But here in this place the Bear had found an excess of the mushrooms, and he and Camille dined extravagantly. "O Bear, are mushrooms and the like to be our everyday midday diet? Even though these are delicious, I think our palates will grow weary of such over time."

The Bear did not respond, but continued snuffling after the scent of mushrooms and gobbling down those he found.

After a rest and a drink from a nearby stream, onward they pressed, and Camille began to wonder just how far away the Summerwood lay, for the Springwood was yet all about.

In midafternoon they topped a rise and came to the lip of a wide, deep gorge. Along one side sheer rock fell into the depths, while along the other, numerous waterfalls cascaded over the brim and down. On the floor of the ravine far below, the Springwood continued, the new green leaves vivid in the light of the afternoon sun. A river wended along the bottom of the gorge and seemed to disappear into a great split at the base of the rock-wall face. Far to the fore and in the distant twilight, the slope of the gorge rose up to meet the crags of a rising mountain range, and Camille thought she could see snow lying high.

The Bear turned toward the cataracts and padded along the rim. He came to a pathway down into the chasm, and this he followed, descending toward the floor far below, the way quite narrow for the Bear, and the drop into the depths sheer. Gasping, Camille grasped the harness and cast her bent leg across the Bear, changing from sidesaddle to astride, for she thought it a safer way to ride. Now more firmly mounted, she did turn about to see if any wee folk were arear, those who perhaps were accompanying the Bear on the journey, but the way behind was clear of followers, and the path ahead clear as well. Looking up, she saw on the rim above the Unicorn standing in a shaft of sunlight, its coat a glorious white, as if the sun itself held the magnificent creature in awe, but it made no move to follow the Bear down into the deepness below.

The Bear came alongside a cataract plunging, the great downpour falling silently but for the rush of wind, the water to thunder into a churning pool far under. And as the Bear wended back and forth along a series of switchbacks, now and again Camille thought she could hear giggling, yet the ways before and behind seemed clear. But then as they came toward the waterfall again, the laughter came quite near, and Camille's eyes widened in astonishment, for swimming within and *up* the cataract was a trio of small laughing beings: nearly transparent they were, as of water itself come alive. Webbed fingers and long webbed feet they had, the latter somewhat like fishtails. Translucent hair streamed down from their heads, as if made of flowering tendrils of crystal. And they were female, Camille could see, for pert breasts and all-but-smooth cleft groins did they have. And though completely engulfed in lucid water, still did their laughter come ringing clear. And they swam, oh how they swam, defying the power of the cataract, as up and up they drove, until they were lost to sight. Camille in awe looked upward, yet seeking, but they were gone as if vanished. Then Camille laughed in joy, for momentarily the trio of two-foot-tall beings reappeared, standing on the lip of the linn high above, only to dive into the falls and plunge merrily past, their shrieks of gaiety growing and then fading as they hurtled nigh and at hand and down.

"Oh, Bear, oh, Bear, did you see and hear? Waterfolk. Waterfolk dear."

The Bear merely grunted, and, bearing Camille, followed the narrow way.

On down they went and down, down to the valley floor, and the sun sailed downward as well. When they reached the bottom of the gorge, shadows from the mountains ahead o'erspread the land. But to the fore and alongside the river a small campfire burned, and upon arriving at the stone-encircled blaze, they found pheasants roasting above.

That night Camille awoke to find the valley filled with wee dancing lights flitting among the trees, as of a tiny folk bearing lanterns and riding upon dragonflies. While the Bear had been nigh when she had gone to sleep, of him there was now no sign, though the back of her neck did tingle, as if an unseen observer stood somewhere in the darkness watching her. And even though she saw the Bear not, still she did feel safe, and she fell asleep again, while in the forest all 'round, dancing lights did weave.

After fording the river next day, up a long slope toward the far end of the valley they fared, making for the mountains ahead, Camille again riding astride. And as they went, the noontime came, and this day they dined on wild spring éschalots and the pale tubers of a sedgelike plant, all harvested by the Bear from the earthy banks of a stream, the gentle piquancy of the shallot bulbs complementing the mildly sweet and starchy taste of the nodules of sedgelike rootstock.

After their meal, up the long remainder of the slope they went and out from the valley, and as they reached the beginning of the mountains, they came to the end of the Springwood. In contrast to the land behind, that before them was snow-covered and ice-laden and bleak. It was marked by a border of twilight, a dusky wall rearing up unto the sky, only this seemed a darker, more sinister marge than the one they had crossed when they had first entered Faery, and the moment the Bear stepped into that bound his ebony color vanished, and once again he became an immaculate white. Within the ambit of that frigid realm a harsh coldness bore down upon them, and Camille donned her cloak and wrapped it tight about her and pulled her hood up and 'round, for they had come once more into the brutal clutch of cruel winter.

Camille looked at the way before them and gasped, for ahead stood a tangled and twisted wood, with barren, stark trees clawing at a drab, overcast sky. All was black and white and gray, no color whatsoever in the land. And there at the verge of this drear and lifeless place, the Bear paused as if reluctant to pass into the grim fastness beyond. But he roared in challenge, and clawed the frozen earth, and then pressed forward and into the wood.

And as they entered this desolate snarl, Camille took a deep breath and straightened her spine, though her heart was racing in dread.

5
Winterwood

Among the twisted trees they went, the Bear and his rider Camille, and all about was gloom and desolation and chill, a drear and silent wood. And now and again the Bear would pause and raise his head and sniff the air, but what he was seeking—water, food, habitation, friend, or foe—Camille knew not, though she suspected that what he sought was the scent of peril in the surround. After each pause, he would growl low over his shoulder at Camille, and she construed he warned her to silence, and for her part she did stay mum, as the Bear pressed on into what surely must be the Winterwood, or so Camille did think.

Forward they went into the fading day, the Bear following a narrow track through the dreadful demesne. Embedded in ice and snow and looming all 'round were harsh gray rock and jagged crags and stripped, barren trees—nought but cracked and splintered and tangled wood—and Camille shrank away whenever a clawlike branch seemed to clutch at her. Yet even though this was Faery, where strange and grim things were said to occur, Camille reasoned it was the Bear passing under or near the deadwood that made the limbs seem to reach out to grasp, rather than it actually being so . . . or so she did think. Still, she continued to flinch away when misshapen boughs reached forth with their fingers of twisted twigs as the day drew down toward night.

And just as the last of the dismal light was fading, a distant and terrible skriegh sounded, seemingly from far above, and Camille looked up through gnarled limbs to see high in the gloom a great and terrible creature of leathery wings and a sinuous body with legs ending in claws. "Oh," she gasped, breaking her silence. "A Dragon. A Dragon dire."

Yet the creature flew on to disappear beyond ice-laden peaks afar. But even after it was gone, Camille's heart continued to race, and a goodly while passed ere it came to steady rhythm again, if a beating heart within this tangle could ever be said to be steady.

Even after darkness fell, the Bear continued apace, and in spite of the dreadful realm they trod, Camille began to nod in weariness, and now and then she would jerk awake in startlement to peer about, only to nod again. It was when she nearly fell from his back that the Bear came to a stop at last, and neither camp nor fire nor cooking food awaited them this night in this ghastly place. It was as if their unseen attendants had abandoned them.

Stumbling about, Camille managed to loosen the bundles the Bear did indicate, and in one was food—jerky and cold biscuits . . . it would have to do.

"I am thirsty, O Bear," whispered Camille, her lips quite dry, for she had had nothing to drink since they had left the stream where they had eaten shallots and rootstock.

The Bear gave a soft *whuff,* and he sniffed the air and then led her to a frozen pool. With his great weight he broke through the ice and then backed away. Camille knelt and sipped at the frigid water, her face twisting in revulsion, for it tasted of brimstone, sulphurous and disgusting, but she drank of it nevertheless. When she raised up and moved away, the Bear, too, drank his fill, though he snuffled in loathing.

Back in the camp Camille fell asleep while wrapped in a blanket and eating, the partially consumed biscuit falling from her lax hand. Gently the Bear took up the remainder and finished it for her.

The next drab day, after a cold breakfast and another foultasting drink, and after Camille had relieved herself, again they went through the drear land, Camille weary of travel, weary of fear, weary of this dismal realm. And this day seemed even darker than the one before, the woods more tangled, the shadows deeper, the ice and snow more chill; it was as if they were now travelling within the malignant heart of the dreadful domain, with its shattered gray rock and dark, looming crags looking on with sinister purpose. Even so, she once again straightened her spine to sit up tall, for she would not be defeated by the grim Winterwood, no matter how baleful its frigid clutch.

On padded the Bear through the unremitting gloom and rocks and crags and gnarl, and still the sky darkened above, and somewhere off in the remote fastness a distant Wolf howled, answered by an echoing howl even farther away. Though Camille gasped in alarm, the Bear gave no heed to these callings, as onward they went.

They stopped nigh what Camille thought might be the noontide, though with the blackening skies above, she could not say of a certain just what time it might be. The Bear directed her to loosen the food bundle, and again they dined on jerky and cold biscuits. And once more the Bear found water to drink, water again tinged with a sulphurous tang.

Forward they pressed after hardly any rest, and as the dark day began to wane, Camille thought she could see ebon shapes scrambling through the tangle afar. But the sightings were too brief for her to be certain, and the crags and rocks and shadows and snarl alone had fooled her more than once. Even so, "Oh, Bear," she whispered, "does someone or something run alongside our course?"

The Bear paused and raised his head on high and sniffed. Long he stood, snuffling, but then without comment continued on. Camille wetted a finger and raised it to measure the flow of air, and yet all she discovered was the forward motion of the Bear. *Mayhap the air drifts the wrong way for the Bear to scent th— What's that?* Camille's heart hammered in her chest. *I thought I saw something large and looming in the dark by that tall crag, something staring, leering.* But the Bear had moved onward, and whatever it might have been had vanished behind a dead thorny tangle, and though she peered intently, she saw it not again. Slowly her heart calmed. *Mayhap it was nought but shadows in the murk, or a standing stone or twisted tree or other such.* Still she kept a sharp eye out, and now and again did she think she saw what might be dark forms running among the ice-laden twists and angular wrenchings of the tangled wood and the outlying crags and jumbles of shattered rock, but still she could not be certain.

Long did they travel as the day wore on, and toward night a wind began to blow down from the mountains above, and the pall o'erhead was riven into ragged, gray, wraithlike tendrils streaming across jagged peaks. In an effort to stay warm at the end of a day become blustery and chill, Camille wrapped her cloak about and huddled down within, abandoning her vow to remain unbowed within the Winterwood.

Night fell, and once again did the Bear pad onward as if trying to be quit of this terrible place. And once again did weary Camille nod and jerk and nearly fall from her perch. And in the windy cold, once again did the Bear finally stop for Camille to make camp and drink distasteful water and fall asleep while eating.

Wha-what? What was tha—?

Camille was wrenched from sleep by screams of dying and yawls of terror and howls of combat, and a great snarling and roaring. And just as she jerked awake in fear, a dark being crashed to the frozen ground beside her, his face torn off, his abdomen gutted. Shrieking, she scuttled back and away from this hideous dead thing, and looked up in the slanting light of a low gibbous moon to see a great battle raging, her Bear standing on his hind legs, ringed 'round by creatures with spears stabbing. And then she knew from her papa's stories—*Oh, sweet Mithras, they're Goblins!* And the Bear laid about with massive blows, his great claws ripping and rending, and blood flew wide and bones crunched, and Goblins fell 'round him slain. Yet the Bear was bleeding as well, his white fur stained with a scarlet gone black in the night.

Scrambling up, Camille looked for something to—

She was jerked from her feet and hauled into the air and clasped against a huge body, and a large hand slapped down on the top of her head, huge fingers grasping, curved talons clamping against her face. And a voice bellowed out above the Bear's own roars, "Stop now, or I'll snap the girl's neck like a twig!"

6
Deliverance

At the shout from the huge being clasping Camille, the Bear swung his great head 'round, his ashen eyes mad with rage, and for a moment it seemed he would charge. But instead he took one last swipe at the beringing Goblins, scattering them, and then he dropped down to all fours and stood, his fighting done. At another command, the Goblins again surrounded the Bear, their spears ready to stab.

And when the Bear was encircled, the creature grasping Camille shifted his clutch to her shoulders and turned her about and held her out at arm's length, and she gasped in dread and clenched her teeth to keep from screaming, for 'twas a huge, ugly Troll had her in his claw-fingered grip.

Hideous, he was, and massive, some nine foot tall or so. And in spite of the blustering wind, all about him was a terrible miasma, a stench like that of a rotting animal burst open after lying dead afield for a full sevenday in the glare of the hot summer sun. He was dressed in greasy animal hides. He gazed at her with yellow eyes, his green-scummed tusks revealed as he leered. "Ah, but what a beauty you are," he declared, and the foulness of his foetid breath caused Camille to gag and retch. "I am Olot, King of the Goblins and Trolls, and I have come for you, my girl, for I have been watching you, and although I have a queen, I will keep you as my mistress and—"

At this last the Bear roared in rage and reared upward, his great claws brandished. Goblins shrieked, and scuttled back, yet their spears were held at the ready. And Olot the Troll snatched Camille again to his breast, pressing her into his foul reek. But the Bear remained standing upright, fully as tall as the Troll. And in spite of all, Camille could feel the Troll tremble in fright.

And the light of the moon fled away, as riven clouds scudded across the sky, a pall of darkness falling. Yet within but a moment through a gap above, the argent light returned.

Still standing, the Bear roared and growled and swept his claws and bared his teeth and irately postured, but he did not attack. And it seemed the Troll knew what the Bear was saying, though it was no ordinary tongue. The Troll nodded and looked at Camille, and his yellow eyes narrowed in cunning and he turned Camille to face the Bear. "Hear me, then, Bear: you spurned my daughter, and you refuse to yield this tasty morsel to me." Olot clutched a dull amulet at his neck. "I have you in my power, just as did my child, and as did she, so will I do." The Troll grinned a tusky grin, and added, "If for nothing else than in retribution for the ten of my best you murdered."

In spite of her fear, Camille cried out, "But the Goblins were attacking the Bear. He was merely defending himself."

"Shut your clack, woman!" bellowed the Troll, shaking Camille like a rag poppet, momentarily dazing her.

The Bear roared at this handling of Camille, and took a stride toward the Troll.

Olot backed hindward a step and cried out, "Stay away, Bear, or else . . ."

The Bear stopped.

"What I plan for you, Bear"—here the Troll glanced at Camille and laughed—"is not for her to know. Go. I will follow. But hear me, my remaining Goblins will watch over her, and should aught happen to me, she will suffer a dreadful fate."

At a gesture from the Troll, the Bear dropped down to all fours and moved into the tangle nigh, and so, too, did Olot the Troll King go, leaving Camille surrounded by a dozen or so bandy-legged, yellow-eyed, snaggletoothed, spear-bearing Goblins.

And when the Troll and Bear were gone from sight, one of the Goblins leered and stepped toward Camille, and he reached out a skinny arm to paw at her with his talon-fingered hand, while the other Goblins sneered and laughed, though some glanced nervously in the direction the Troll and Bear had gone, as if to make certain that they themselves would suffer no interruption.

In the fluctuating light of the cloud-obscured moon, Camille gasped and shrank away as other Goblins crowded 'round, reeking and foul and filthy. Dressed in coarse-woven cloth and partly cured hides and standing some five feet tall, hideous they were up close, with their viperlike eyes and bat-wing ears and their overlarge noses with long gelid strings of snot dripping down. And they all wore black caps, and—

No, wait! Not black. For just as the night had turned the Bear's blood black, so, too, must these hats be crimson! Oh, Mithras, these are the Redcaps.

Flinching, Camille backed away, to come up against the jagged bole of a gnarled, dead tree, where she could go no farther. And the Goblin at the fore became bold, and with one hand began to pluck at her clothes as if to undress her, while with the other he fumbled at the cord of his breeks.

Lashing out, she shoved him into the ones behind, and then turned and scrambled up the twisted branches, seeking escape, while Redcaps japed and hooted and danced about the dead tree and made crude, suggestive gestures.

Reaching a high branch and clinging to the trunk, her breath coming in fear-driven huffs, Camille looked down at the cavorting Goblins below, as once again the moon broke through the clouds. And she peered across the twisted 'scape, desperately seeking the Bear.

Oh, my guardian, where are you when I do need you so?

And then, on a stony ridge and momentarily silhouetted against the gibbous moon, Camille saw what looked to be the great, hulking Troll shaking a fist at a man. But what would a man be doing out here in this dreadful place? And whence had he come? The moon fled behind another cloud, and she saw no more. In that short glimpse, she had not espied the Bear, though a large dark shape off to the left might have been him, yet it could just as well have been a boulder instead. Too, he could have been just this side or that of the ridge where Olot stood and hence would not have been seen.

And midst the jeers coming from the darkness below, and in the blustery wind, now and again from the direction of the ridge Camille could hear snatches of voices arguing:

"... slew ten of my ..."

"... attacking ..."

"... daughter ..."

"... never will I ..."

"... She will fail, and then the geas ..."

The tree trembled as if—

Camille looked down in the dimness, and just then the moon broke clear.

Jeered on by his mates, the Redcap who had pawed at her came clambering up the bole. Camille gritted her teeth and turned so that she could kick at him. In counter, he scuttled around the twisted trunk so as to avoid her strikes. Camille then moved to another gnarled branch to meet his maneuver, but again he scuttled counter and scrambled higher and, leering around the trunk, reached for her. And just as his long-fingered hand grasped her wrist—*thuck!*—a feathered shaft sprang full-blown from his left eye, the arrow point punching up and out through the crown of his skull.

Even as he fell away from Camille and crashed down through crooked branches, fury exploded below, wild Wolves slamming into and through and over shrieking Redcaps, tearing out throats, snapping necks, hauling down running Goblins from behind.

In a trice it was over, all Redcaps slaughtered and silence fallen within the wood, but for the bluster of the wind and a growl or two from Wolves making certain that every Goblin was slain.

"Ho, Lad," came a cry, "are you all right?"

In the moonlight a man with a bow strode under the tree and stood amid the Wolves.

Camille, her voice shaking with the residue of fright as well as in relief, called down, "I am well, O Sir. And I thank you for coming to my aid."

"Well, then, climb on down, Lad, and let's have a look at you."

Glancing again at the ridge, Camille saw neither Troll, nor man, nor Bear; they were gone from the light of the gibbous moon.

"Come, come, Lad," said the man, gesturing to the Wolves. "My companions are quite civilized."

As Camille turned about to clamber down the tree, her golden hair swung 'round as well, and the man below huffed in revelation and said, "I see I should have called you mademoiselle instead, my lady."

Descending, Camille said, "You may call me my lady if you wish, but only if I must call you my lord." As the man laughed, Camille climbed down the last few feet, then paused and looked at him. Tall and slender, he was, with pale, pale eyes—ice-blue perhaps, though Camille could not be certain in the glancing light of the moon. He was dressed in varied greys—cloak, leathers, boots, vest, jerkin—their colors much like those of the Wolves at hand. Around his head and across his brow, a silver-runed, grey leather headband held his silver-grey, shoulder-length hair in place.

Yet smiling, the man reached out a hand to aid her to step to the ground. As she took it, he said, "I am Borel. And you are . . . ?"

"Camille, Good Sir. Yet names can wait, for urgency presses, and I ask you and yours to aid my Bear." She looked at the grinning Wolves, with their lanky frames and long, lean legs, the pack standing and waiting as if for a command, a few facing outward on guard.

Once more clouds slid across the moon, and in the dimness Borel said, "Bear?"

"The one who is taking me to Lord Alain, Prince of the Summerwood."

"Ah. That Bear. And just why is he taking you to the Summerwood?"

The light brightened and Camille said, "I am to be Alain's wife."

"Ah, then, you are the one," Borel said, and he frankly eyed her face and form, appraising. And at last he said, "Now I can see why he was so smitten."

"How know you this?"

"He is my brother," replied Borel, "for I am the Prince of the Winterwood."

"Brother and prince you may be, Good Sir, yet again I ask, will you give aid to my Bear?"

Borel looked about. "Where—?"

"He is with a monstrous Troll—"

"The one we've been tracking," gritted Borel. He gestured at the slain Goblins and added, "Along with his Redcap band." Borel glanced up at the riven sky. "A storm is coming, yet we may have a chance. Where is this Troll now?"

"He was on a ridge yon," said Camille, pointing through the dead trees toward the cloud-covered moon. "He has my Bear, and I fear—"

But even as she spoke, there came a crashing from the direction of the ridge. Hackles raised, all the Wolves turned to face this menace, and Borel nocked arrow and stepped between Camille and the oncoming threat and drew the weapon to the full, aiming toward the sound of shattering wood. And then the Bear burst forth from the tangle, a thunderous roar bellowing. But upon seeing the Wolves and the man, he skidded to a stop, the roar dying in midbellow. Grunting, he sat down.

The Wolves relaxed, their hackles falling, and one or two of the animals set their tails to wagging. "Ah," said Borel, "you are safe." And he eased his bowstring even as Camille rushed 'round and forward.

Camille flung her arms about the Bear's neck. "Oh, Bear, I thought you imperilled."

The Bear merely grunted in reply.

Releasing him, Camille said, "Bear, I would have you meet Prince Borel, brother to Prince Alain."

"We've met," said Borel, slipping the arrow back into his quiver. "For as I said, Alain is my brother, and—"

The Bear growled low, as if in warning.

Borel pushed a palm out to allay the Bear and murmured, "As you wish."

Stepping to the arrow-slain Goblin and leaning his bow against the tree, Borel said, "Now about that Troll, has he any more Redcaps in his train?"

"I think not," replied Camille, looking about at the slaughter and shuddering. "My Bear slew ten of them, and you and your Wolves killed the rest. As far as I know, the Troll is now alone, but perhaps for some unknown man I saw standing with him on the ridge."

The Bear huffed.

Borel grunted as he jerked the arrow free from the skull of the dead Redcap, then began scouring it with snow to scrub away the dark grume. "I would be rid of this Troll who has invaded my demesne."

Camille looked about at the tangle. "My lord, 'tis a drear and dread realm you rule."

Borel glanced up from where he knelt. "The Winterwood is not all like this cursed sector, my lady, for herein not even the Ice Sprites dwell. Elsewhere, my principality is the most beautiful of the four."

"Four?"

"Aye. Spring, Summer, Autumn, and Winter: four seasons and four forests, ruled by four siblings: Celeste, Alain, Liaze, and me."

"You four rule all of Faery?"

"Oh, no, Camille," said Borel, rising, sliding the now clean arrow in among the others. "There is much more to Faery than just the Forests of the Seasons."

Taking up his bow, Borel turned to the Bear. "Just as did you come running this way at the sound of my Wolves slaying the Redcaps, this Troll, he ran the other way when he heard?"

"*Whuff.*"

Borel nodded, then said, "I suggest you travel on with your lady, for the Troll may double back to this place, and he is a formidable foe. Yet whether or no he does, we will be close behind, unless the oncoming storm does thwart."

"*Whuff.*"

Borel then faced Camille and bowed. "My lady."

With a curtsey, she replied, "My lord," as darkness fell once more.

In the dimness he laughed, and then, with an utterance somewhat between that of a word and a growl, he called to the pack. And off they sped, loping back along the track of the Bear and toward the ridge where last was seen the Troll. Moments later there came a long howl; the Wolves were on the trail.

The Bear nuzzled the bedroll and the harness with its bundles, and soon Camille had all packed and loaded. And once again she mounted up as the chill wind blew and foreboding clouds thickened above. And thus did the Bear and Camille set forth in the lees of the night, leaving behind a slaughter ground—twenty-two Redcap Goblins lying dead in blood-laden snow.

Given the blackness of the sky, Camille was uncertain as to whether dawn had yet come unto the Winterwood when spinning white flakes began to swirl down. She pulled her cloak and hood tighter about as the blustery wind strengthened into a frigid blow. More snow fell, and more, as the storm intensified, the wind did scream and hurtle stirring snow across Camille and the Bear. On they went and on, the blizzard worsening with every stride, until Camille could no longer make out the tangle and crags right at hand, as into the brutal blast they did fare. Across that howling morn did the storm savagely rave, as if trying to halt their flight from this frozen, drear realm. Finally the Bear paused, for he sensed Camille's violent shivering; and, groaning and hissing through chattering teeth, she dropped down. As the Bear shielded her from the direct blow, Camille struggled to fetch a blanket from one of the bundles, her fingers numb and perverse. Freeing the cover at last, with effort, she remounted. As she fought against the wind to wrap the flapping mantle 'round, she called above the yawl, "Oh, B-bear, g-go on, go on, for I would be r-rid of this d-dreadful Winterwood." And so onward he pressed, stride upon stride, as the storm strove to steal their heat away and leave them dead and frozen in that most appalling place. Yet stubbornly the Bear forged into the teeth of the shrieking gale, and Camille lost all track of time and place in the hurling white, and it seemed as if they went on forever. But as Camille thought to give up all hope of ever escaping this dire storm and dreadful wood, ahead a great dark wall loomed, and of a sudden they came to a twilight border. The Bear did not pause, but quickly passed through the tenebrous marge, to step into an extravagantly bedecked forest with a nip in the air and gloaming all about. And though a blizzard yet raged directly behind, it came not into this twilit place.

Surrounded by autumn and free of the storm, Camille shed tears of exhausted relief as the Bear moved away from the bound and deeper into the color-splashed woodland.

7
Autumnwood

Leaving the Winterwood marge behind, the Bear went onward, and he passed into a forest adorned in scarlet and crimson, and in amber and yellow, bronze, and gold, and in russet
and umber and roan. The gloam diminished as he went, until a
high blue sky shone o'erhead, with sunlight angling down
through the brightly festooned branches above. At last he stopped
in a small glade surrounded by great oaks with leaves all ver-
milion and saffron. Groaning and but half-aware, Camille slid
from his back and slumped to the loam; chilled to the bone as
she was, she had not the strength to do aught else. She lay back
on the yellowed sward, and as the day edged toward midafternoon, slowly, slowly the cold seeped from her, sun-warmth taking its place.

She slept for a while—how long she could not say, but when
she awoke evening was drawing down, and she sat up and
looked 'round for her Bear, to find him sitting nigh, no longer
white, but a grizzled reddish brown instead. "Oh, Bear," she
rasped, "you've changed color again." Her voice was hoarse
with thirst, for she had had nought to drink since yestereve
when she last sipped a sulphurous swallow or two within the
Winterwood. "Is there water nearby?"

"*Whuff.*" said the Bear, standing, and Camille groaned to her
own feet, her frame gone stiff from lying on the ground. The
Bear led her across the glade and to a rill beyond, and Camille
drank of its sweet, sweet run. Refreshed, she rose to her feet, and
she scented the odor of apples on the air. Just beyond the stream
stood a tree laden with the ruby-red fruit, ripe and ready for har-

vest. Her mouth watering, Camille stepped across the stream to come under the tree, but the bounty was too high for her to reach. The Bear padded across and reared up on its hind legs and, using its weight, jolted the bole of the tree with both forepaws, and apples fell down all about, while Camille squealed and ducked and covered her head with her forearms to shield against the fall. She then gathered in some of the precious yield and sat by the stream and ate her fill, the apples snapping with each bite, juice flying wide, while the Bear snuffled about under the tree and gobbled down the rest.

Their supper dealt with, Camille set about making camp, arranging her bedroll and laying the basis for a small fire, but she fell asleep before she could set it ablaze. Even so, when she awoke the next morning, warm coals yet glowed in the ring of stone she had laid the night before.

On that second day in the Autumnwood, in spite of the glowing remnants of a fire, there had been no prepared breakfast at the dawning, just as at the close of yester there had been neither a waiting camp with a burning fire nor a cooked meal of fish or fowl or game. Still they did not want for fare as deeper into the forest they went, for, although they were surrounded by woodland, there were runs of what seemed to be fruit orchards—apples, for the most, yet other kinds as well, many of which were unknown to Camille, but were delicious nevertheless: some sweet, some tart, some with a delicate flavor, but all delightful to the tongue. And there were small stands of laden nut trees— hazel and beech, and the like. To Camille's eye, these groves of fruit and nuts seemed to have been well cared for, for the limbs were trimmed and shapely, but pruned by whom, she knew not, for no cottages nor byres nor other such signs of crofters did she see.

Nigh the noontide of that day, as they topped a hill and emerged into the open, in the low vale before them Camille saw a meadow of ripened grain. The Bear plodded downslope and into the field, to pass among oats and then rye, while alongside and hidden among the teeming stalks, someone or something scampered, and once again Camille heard the trill of elfin laughter, but she caught no glimpse of who or what had made the sound.

When they emerged from the meadow to start up the far slope, then did she see sitting on the hillside with his back to a tree the figure of a man—or it looked to be a man—dressed in coarse-spun garb, as would a crofter be, and a great reaping scythe rested across his knees. As they approached, he stood, the scythe in one hand, the blade grounded; Camille gasped in apprehension, for the man was huge, seven or eight foot tall, and for a moment she thought the Troll had returned. But a Troll he was not as was clear when he doffed his hat, revealing a shock of reddish hair. And as the Bear padded by, the man, the crofter, the reaper of grain, bowed low in respectful silence. "Bonjour," called Camille, uncertain as to what else to say or do, but by no sign did the huge being respond to her call, and he remained bent in an attitude of obeisance. The Bear grunted in seeming acknowledgment of the individual's deferential bow, and the crofter then straightened and watched as the Bear and his rider passed without stopping, continuing on up the slope. And when they topped the rise at the far end of the vale to start down into the valley beyond, Camille looked back to see the man—if a man he truly was—once again sitting with his back to the tree and the scythe across his knees.

That evening, Camille stripped and bathed, this time in a chill, deep pool of a wide, slow-running stream, the Bear standing ward and looking everywhere but straight at her.

On the third day within the brightly hued wood, they passed along deep river gorges and high chalk bluffs and through thickets and mossy glens, the land rising and falling as they went. And whenever they topped crests or went along cliffs where Camille could look afar, in every direction but where they were she saw the bright woodland fade into distant twilight, just as the forest had shaded into silver-grey gloam in the Springwood and perhaps in the Winterwood as well, though where they had passed through that cold realm, only dismal darkness had ruled and twilight would not have been seen. But this was neither the Winterwood nor the Springwood, but the Autumnwood instead, and always in unexpected places did they come upon groves of fruits and nuts and fields of flax and barley and millet and other grains. And this day as well they crossed plots of loam bearing beans and peas, leeks and onions, pumpkins and squash, and carrots and parsnips, as well as vines of hops and grapes, none of which seemed to be growing wild.

And as they fared through the bountiful forest, with its generous stands and glens and glades and fields, so, too, did other denizens slip through the woodland as well, some running along limbs, others scuttling across the ground, some flying above—birds and animals and wee folk alike, or so Camille did ween. Of huge crofters, Camille had sighted none since yester; nevertheless, she believed that they were about, but chose to remain unseen; mayhap they were shy.

And thus did the grizzled Bear and golden-haired Camille travel and live off the land, eating berries from vines, and grain from the grasses, and vegetables from the loam, as well as fruit from trees. For in the Autumnwood 'twas harvesttime—eternal Camille did think. Still, she wondered whether the fruit and other such ever replaced itself, and if so, then how did it manage the feat, for without winter to rest and spring to renew and summer to ripen, how could harvest continue without all eventually becoming barren?

Ah, but this is Faery, where mystical things are said to occur. I will have to remember to ask Prince Alain about such, assuming that Alain is a bit like his brother Borel, and not some monster instead. —Oh my, I should have asked Borel what Alain was like. Ah, but he and his pack were after that terrible Troll and had no time for my girlish chatter. Oh, but I do hope Borel and his Wolves are safe.

In the eve, when they had camped and Camille's kindled fire brightly burned, in the darktide beyond the reach of the flickering light she could see eyes glittering and now and again catch a glimpse of movement: foxes and lynx and other night hunters, some, it seemed, with riders astride; too, there were moving glimmers among the trees, somewhat like the dancing lights of the Springwood, though here in the Autumnwood, the gleams seemed to proceed as if in solemn ceremony instead of in carefree joy. As the night wore on, now and again something large with a heavy tread would pass by in the dark unseen, and at these times Camille looked to the Bear, but he appeared unperturbed, and though her heart did beat with excitement, it did not gallop in fear.

Late on the fourth day within the Autumnwood, they came to another looming wall of twilight, and when they passed through the marge they came into the warmth of summer, and there the Bear did change color again, becoming a deep, dark brown.

Then did Camille's heart race in apprehension when they

crossed into this realm, for this was the Summerwood, the demesne of Prince Alain—

Someone whom I have yet to meet—man or monster or beast or Troll or something else altogether, I know not—yet someone I am pledged to wed.

And deeper into the Summerwood trod the dark brown Bear, a golden-haired slip of a girl on his back.

8

Summerwood

Reveling in the warmth of the Summerwood, Camille shed her cloak and vest, for although evening was drawing nigh, her green-silk jerkin sufficed. Through the duskingtide pressed the Bear, and stars began to dimly shine, growing brighter as he and Camille left the twilight border behind and as night drew down on the land. And a slowly cooling waft of air coiled among verdant trees and bore the fragrances of summer: of grasses and green leaves and mossy loam and oozing sap on the bark of wild cherry trees, of wildflower blossoms and reeds in water and the aromatic foliage of mint. All these and more did Camille distinguish drifting on the air, while crickets sang in the surround, and far-off frogs *breek*ed, and some thing or things scuttered alongside in the dark.

In the distance ahead, Camille espied the glimmer of a fire, and just as had been in the Springwood, here, too, did a camp await their arrival, this one with a quintet of quail roasting above the flames. Camille ate two of the birds, the Bear the rest, she carefully nipping the meat from the fragile frames, he snapping up his trio and crunching them down, bones and all.

The next dawning, Camille found awaiting a breakfast of scones and tea. And she reveled in this meal, for embedded throughout the biscuitlike pastries were tart, sun-dried fruit nuggets, contrasting with and yet enhancing the honey-sweetened taste of the tea. As she sipped her drink and ate, Camille could hear the Bear off among the nearby trees, snuffling and rolling over deadwood and pouncing on that which he found 'neath.

Grubs, mayhap, or beetles. Camille shuddered, and continued with her own fare.

Finished with breakfast, Camille fetched forth one of her chew-sticks and began cleaning her teeth. Yet now and again she paused and listened, for occasionally she thought she heard a small, piping voice somewhere nigh the Bear, and grunts from the Bear in response; but when she hearkened, the voice spoke not, and when she looked, she saw nought to account for whoever or whatever might be in converse with the Bear.

At last the Bear came padding back, and Camille broke camp as day washed into the sky.

On went the Bear with Camille throughout the Summerwood, the cool, green forest shaded by rustling leaves above, with shafts of golden sunlight streaming down through the gaps between. They crossed warm and bright fields and sunlit glades laden with wild summer flowers, where the air was filled with the drone of bees and the flutter of butterflies, all flitting from blossom to blossom to burrow in or to elegantly sit and sip. Occasionally a lone bee arrowed off into the forest, bearing its precious nectar and pollen treasures to cache in honey-burdened trees, leaving behind the butterflies to continue their vivid dance. And to Camille's wondering eyes, now and again, among the stir of airborne creatures, she thought she espied tiny, winged beings clad in gossamer green and darting thither and yon, perhaps teasing the butterflies—Sprites? Pixies? Hummingbirds instead? Camille could not be certain, for none flew nigh the treading Bear with the wide-eyed girl on his back.

Down into a river-fed gorge they went, the lucid water sparkling, green sward and willowy thickets adorning its banks. From somewhere ahead Camille could hear a cascade, and soon the Bear trod alongside falls pouring down amid a spray of rainbows into a wide, sunlit pool. And on the opposite shore otters played, a handful or so, sliding down the steep bank and into the glitter of water to disappear under, only to emerge and turn about and race ashore and scamper up to slide down again.

"Oh, Bear, do stop. This water looks warm, and I've had nought to bathe in but chill."

Grunting, the Bear looked at the sun standing nigh the zenith, and halted.

Moments later, Camille glided through the clement, crystalline water toward the play of otters. As she neared, she could hear the chime of laughter, and lo! the moment the otters splashed into the river, Waterfolk they became, with their tiny frames and long fishtail feet and along each side a translucent fin running from wrist to ankle. Their eyes were large and they looked at Camille and then playfully darted between her legs and 'round her back and up between her breasts. One paused before her, and then Camille could see that he was a male . . . they all were males.

Squealing, Camille fled back toward the shore on which lay her clothes, as Waterfolk swam over and under and about her thrashing legs and flailing arms and 'round her waist and across her bosom, brushing against her most private places and giggling.

Gaining the shore at last, Camille scrambled up the bank and to her clothes, flinging them on in spite of her wetness, while Waterfolk laughed joyously, and swam back to the opposite shore to shift their forms and resume their otter play.

"Bear! Where are you, Bear?" she called, looking about for her absent guardian, furious at the laughter behind.

A grunt came from higher up the embankment, and she saw the Bear sitting amid a patch of brambles eating dewberries, his muzzle stained purplish from the fare. Struggling with her boots, "You could have warned me," cried Camille, cross with embarrassment.

"*Whuff.*"

With a foot half in, half out of her last boot, Camille stopped and glared at the Bear. "Does that mean you *could* have warned me?"

The Bear grunted and pulled over another thorny vine and began to rip off the dark berries.

"Oh, you!" Camille stamped her foot into the boot, and, fully dressed at last, she glanced across at the Waterfolk otters and then began to giggle.

That evening, another camp awaited the Bear and the girl, with a brace of marmots roasting above the flames, and large leaves laden with dewberries sitting off to one side. Camille ate a leaf or two of the sweet blackberries, as well as a hind leg and a fore, the Bear eating all the rest.

Unlike the Autumnwood, with its mild days and chill nights, in the Summerwood Camille needed neither cloak nor vest by day, and only a thin blanket at night, and that but near the break of light. Yet just after the dawntide of the third day in the wood, from a grey sky above a very light rain began to fall, more of a fine mist blowing than a drenching pour, and Camille wrapped her cloak about to ward away the mizzle. By the noontide, though, the sun broke through, and ghostly vapor seeped up from the earth and coiled among the trees, like streaming wraiths seeking to escape the sun.

Even as the insubstantial vapor swirled about, they topped a hill, and there the Bear paused and grunted. "What is it, Bear? Why do you—?" Camille's words chopped short, and her heart suddenly sprang to her throat, for down below and shrouded in ethereal mist twining 'round, stood a great mansion midst widespread grounds. And Camille knew it could be nought but the manor of the Lord of Summerwood, the manor of her husband-to-be.

9

Mansion

As the Bear started downslope toward the huge manor, Camille tried to still her racing heart by studying the great house and the immediate grounds, that which she could make out through the rising vapor curling 'round.

Vast was the mansion itself, four or five storeys in height, though here and there it rose above even that, and broad and deep with many wings, and even courtyards within. Chimneys it had in abundance, yet Camille wondered why here in the warmth of the Summerwood fireplaces were needed at all—other than those required for cooking and perhaps those needed to heat bathwater. The far-flung grounds about the great chateau were surrounded by a lengthy and high stone wall, with gates standing at the midpoints, at the moment all closed. Inside the wall, in spite of the mist, Camille could make out groves of trees and gardens with pathways through, a small lake, and—

Is that a hedge maze?

She had read of such in Fra Galanni's library, but she had never thought to see one.

Several outbuildings ranged along part of one wall, presumably at the back of the house. What they contained, Camille could not say, though she speculated that perhaps one was a stable and another a carriage house and still another a smithy and—

Wait. If the Prince had horses, then why did he send a Bear to fetch me? Mayhap because of the dreadful passage through the Winterwood, where the Bear could protect me, and a horse could not. Regardless, I do not know how to ride . . . except Bearback, so to speak. Camille laughed at her bon mot, but then sobered quickly, for the Bear had come to the floor of the vale and now angled leftward toward one of the gates, and Camille's heart beat all the faster.

The Bear trod toward the great barrier, with its long brass bars running up and down through heavy brass braces across, the gate itself decorated with a copper bas-relief in the likeness of a great oak tree, verdigris making the leaves and trunk green; it was the same emblem that had been impressed in the wax seal of Prince Alain's letter, though that on the entrance was in low relief rather than intaglio. As they approached, the oak tree split in twain and the two halves of the gates swung inward and wide, yet Camille could not see aught of who might have opened them.

Onto the grounds of the vast estate they went, the Bear padding along a road of white stone wending within a gallery of oaks, their limbs arching overhead and intertwining to form a green leafy canopy above. As down this way they went, to the left and right through the spaces between the boles of the oaks Camille caught glimpses of the estate, with its gardens galore and white stone paths and long stretches of green sward. "Oh, Bear, how large this holding. Why, Papa's entire farm could fit in one small corner yon." On they went and across a stone bridge, with a wide lucid stream meandering under and flowing between high mossy banks; and black swans swam in the water, their long necks proudly arched. And still the road gracefully curved, the oaks standing honor guard, yet of a sudden the Bear emerged from the canopy and into the open beyond, and Camille's heart leapt upward again, for straight ahead across a broad mead stood the great château.

"Oh, Bear, I am wholly apprehensive," quavered Camille, burying her hands into fur and gripping tightly. "Remain my protector, please."

"*Whuff.*" replied the Bear quietly, and pressed on ahead.

As they went on toward the manor, Camille now saw just how vast a place it truly was. Left and right the building stretched away, and loomed upward as well. Pale grey it was, and made of granite, with a huge, deep portico upheld by fluted columns, the pillars granite, too. Here and there along the front, from second-storey rooms and above, leaded-glass doorways opened onto white-marble balconies, while all across and abounding, leaded-glass windows in white wooden sashes stood in white wooden frames.

Great Mithras, there must be two hundred rooms or more. Much to dust and sweep and clean, endless windows to wash, chambers to air, linens to— Oh, my, but I do hope that I don't have to—

Just then Camille heaved a quiet sigh of relief, for she could see that within the great portico the doors to the house stood wide, and flanking and extending outward from the portal stood servants arrayed in two long rows. Steadily trod the Bear, to come up the two steps and onto the wide porch. And servants silently bowed or curtseyed deeply as the Bear trod between, yet Camille knew not how to respond, and so she rode into the manse on the back of the Bear without saying a word.

Past the open, brass-studded, thick doors of oak and down a short corridor she rode, to pass beyond another set of open doors and across a broad landing, then down two steps into a vast front hall: its floor was of white marble, with an inlaid depiction of a great oak centered therein—the leaves of malachite, the bole and limbs a subtle mix of grey and red granite. A full four storeys above, the white plaster ceiling held a leaded-glass skylight depicting the same oak—a reflection of the one below. Two massive staircases—one left, one right—swept from a common landing outward and up, curving to a high balcony all 'round, and higher up still were individual balconies jutting out of the three facing walls, with recessed doors leading into chambers beyond. There were doors and archways ranged to left, right, and fore, both at the great hall floor level and the balcony level above; through the archways, Camille could see corridors leading away. Sconces for candles and lanterns were arrayed along on the walls around, but sunlight pouring in through high, front windows and the leaded-glass skylight above lighted the chamber brightly.

The Bear padded to the center of the great hall and stopped on the inlaid stone-oak; then, led by a tall, slender, grey-haired man dressed all in black, a flurry of servants—footmen and butlers—surrounded both Bear and girl. At a signal from the man in black, a footman stepped forward and placed a small stool on the floor, while another held out his hand and murmured, "My lady."

Camille swung her leg over and took his hand and stepped to the stool and then to the floor. At another signal, the footman whisked the stool away, while others unclipped the harness from the Bear.

The grey-haired man, who seemed to be in charge of all, said,

"Mademoiselle, my prince names me Lanval, and I will show you to your chambers."

Camille's heart lurched. "But my Bear: will he not accompany me?"

"No, my lady. There are other things my prince—"

The Bear growled low, and Lanval said no more.

Camille turned to the Bear and flung her arms about his neck and whispered, "Oh, my protector, will you come if I call?"

A soft *whuff* was his answer.

"My things," said Camille, releasing the Bear and turning to Lanval and gesturing at the harness and bundles.

"They will be delivered to your chambers," replied the man, "though I believe that you will find it quite well-appointed to serve the needs of a lady."

Up one of the long sweeping staircases Lanval led her, to the balcony above and thence through an archway into a corridor wainscoted in cherry wood with red-velvet walls above. Cherry-panelled doorways stood left and right, some open, others closed. Up a short flight of steps he led her, and turned right and right again, passing through richly carpeted and panelled hall-ways, all hued in a pale green, to come to a massive oak door, which, unlike the others, had the Summerwood crest thereon. Camille's heart beat a bit faster upon seeing the symbol, yet she breathed deeply and braced herself for whatever was to come.

"One moment, my lady," said Lanval, and he opened the door to a dimly lit room and stepped inside. Within instants, light flooded the chamber, and Lanval reappeared. "Your quarters, my lady," he said, standing aside and bowing.

Hesitantly, she entered, Lanval following after. Into a radiant sitting room they came, and though lamps and candles sat upon tables and stood ensconced along the walls for nighttime needs, all was illuminated by daylight streaming inward through a skylight above, its pull-cord shade now open. But it was the chamber itself that caused Camille to take in a deep breath, for it was luxurious: satins and silks of pale yellow and old gold and rich creams seemed everywhere, on lounges and chairs and love seats and the pillows thereon, though several of those were bright white instead. Filling the air with their subtle fragrance, yellow roses in yellow vases sat upon the oak-wood tables standing against cream-colored walls embel-lished with a gilded tracery. All was arranged for quiet conver-sation of pairs and trios and more. Camille saw to the left stood an archway and straight ahead an open door, and they led to rooms beyond.

Discreetly, Lanval showed her about the suite: he escorted Camille through the archway and into a small library with tall, book-laden shelves standing against one wall with a rolling track-ladder for reaching the top. Therein as well sat plush leather chairs and lanterns and candles for nighttime reading—though in this chamber as well, Lanval tugged the pull cord to remove the shade from the skylight high above to let in the light of day. Along another wall sat an escritoire and chair, with trimmed goose quills and an inkwell and blotters and talc and a trimming blade, as well as blank journals and foolscap and vellum and parchment with wax for sealing, all arrayed at hand or on the shelves above should she have the need to write. Camille looked about in wonder, and then stepped to one of the bookshelves and reverently ran her fingers across several of the spines of the leather-bound books thereon and whispered, "Oh, so very many."

They lingered but a moment, and Lanval then led her through a small doorway and into another shade-managed, skylighted chamber; therein stood a great bed, covered with a yellow-gold, satin spread, with pale yellow silk draping down from the canopy above, the curtains held back by yellow-gold, satin ribbons tied 'round the four massive bedposts. In this chamber as well were sitting chairs upholstered in yellow satin and cream silk. There, too, sat a wide vanity table and bench, an oval, silvered mirror on the wall above; a silver comb and brush and a hand mirror lay ready for use, with powders and rouges and soft brushes and cloths, and vials of fragrances at hand as well.

Lanval then pointed out the bathing room, with its great stone tub and stone basin chased in gold, and soft towels and facecloths and soaps and gentle bath oils and other such lady's fare. In this chamber, too, a skylight stood above.

Camille looked about. "Is it all gold and yellow and cream?" she asked. "—The rooms elsewhere, I mean."

Lanval smiled. "Nay, my lady. Elsewhere the rooms are of green and blue and red and white and other hues of the rainbow. These chambers, though, were intended to be a reflection of the gold of your hair."

"Oh, my," said Camille, and she glanced back toward the bedroom and the open doors to the rooms beyond.

Lanval cleared his throat. "My lady, the privy is yon." He pointed to a curtained archway connected to the bathing room.

Camille stepped to the arch and peered into the skylighted chamber beyond—a goodly sized room with a commode enclosing a chamber pot, and a table with a washbasin and pitcher thereon, along with soap in a dish; shelves and racks laden with cloths and towels and additional bars of soap ranged along the walls; therein, too, sat a lidded bucket for disposal of that which was used. As she surveyed the chamber, Camille could not help but to think back to her papa's stone cottage, with its burlap curtain on a rough hemp cord and the wooden bucket with its lid.

Sighing, she turned back to Lanval, and from her bedchamber he escorted her through a heavily curtained, gilded, glass-paned door, and Camille found herself on the central high balcony looking down onto the great entry hall below, now empty of all, including the Bear.

Camille turned to Lanval. "My lord—" she began, but Lanval raised a hand to halt her words.

"My lady, no highborn lord am I, but merely the steward of Summerwood Manor. Please call me Lanval."

Camille sighed. "But I am not highborn either, Lanval, for until a handful of days past, and even still, I was and am nought but a mere crofter's daughter."

"Nevertheless, my lady, highborn or low-, you are the betrothed of my prince"—Lanval's blue eyes did twinkle—"and from what I can discern of thy bearing and manner, he did choose most wisely."

At the mention of her pledged future, Camille did start, for somehow in the display of all the opulence she had managed to forget entirely the reason she had come to this manor, yet Lanval's words did jerk her back to reality.

Camille took a deep breath. "When will I meet the prince?"

Lanval looked down at the white marble floor far below, with its granite and malachite inlay. "It may be awhile, for he recently returned from a long journey." Lanval then smiled at Camille. "You, too, have journeyed far, and must needs bathe and rest." He stepped back into the bedchamber, Camille following, where he tugged on a yellow silk pull cord and said, "This will summon your handmaid. She is close by in her chamber, or mayhap in the servants' hall. Regardless, these cords are in each room of your suite, and should you have need, simply pull, and aid will be here in a trice."

"Handmaid? Oh, Lanval, what need have I for such?"

"My lady, you would not have the prince send her away, would you?"

"Oh, Lanval, would he do so?"

Lanval smiled. "I think not, my lady. Still, you must allow her to do that for which she was . . . intended. She will attend you, as well as show you the house and the grounds, and will speak of where breakfast is to be found, and other such daily matters. Yet I caution you to not ask of the prince, for he has made it plain it is a matter between the two of you."

Again Camille's heart leapt to her throat, for who but a monster or creature of some sort would have all keep silent in matters concerning himself, even unto his intended.

As they returned to the sitting room, there came a soft knock on the outer door, and Lanval called, "Enter!"

An ample young woman in a simple black gown stepped into the chamber. In her hands she bore Camille's goods, taken from the Bear's harness. Hastily, she set all upon a small table beside the door, then curtseyed and murmured, "My lady."

"This is Blanche," said Lanval, "your lady's maid."

Blanche looked to be no older than Camille, though she stood perhaps an inch or two taller. Fair was her skin, and black her hair, and her eyes so dark as to be black as well.

"Blanche," said Lanval, "the lady needs to freshen up after her long journey, and to shed her travelling clothes for something—"

"Oh, Lanval," blurted Camille, looking at the scant bundle holding her meager belongings. "I brought nought but a simple shift with me, one quite threadbare at that. Certainly nothing as elegant as these garments I now wear."

Blanche smiled knowingly, even as Lanval said, "Show my lady her dressing chamber, Blanche."

As Blanche clapped her hands together in pleasure, Lanval added, "My lady, now that you are in good hands, I return to my other duties. Even so, should you have need of aught . . ." He bowed low, and then turned and stepped to the door.

As he exited, Camille called after, "Merci, Lanval."

"My lady," said Blanche, a gleam of pleasure in her eye, "if you will but follow me."

Blanche led her mistress through a small doorway off the bedchamber and into a dim room, where the handmaid tugged on a pull cord, drawing the shade from the skylight above. And Camille drew in a great breath of incredulity, for revealed was a room perhaps even larger than the bedchamber itself; and it was filled with splendid clothes: gowns, dresses, skirts, blouses, chemises, shifts, jackets, lingerie, shoes, boots, gloves, cloaks, hats, ribbons, jewelry cases, and more. Camille gaped at the trove in disbelief, her astonishment reflected in the gilt-framed, full-length mirror affixed to the far wall therein.

"Oh, Blanche, these are marvelous, yet I wonder if they will fit."

Blanche laughed. "My lady, they were fashioned for you alone."

"But how? I mean, it's not as if someone came in the night and took my measure."

"Do not be too certain of that, my lady," said Blanche, grinning, pulling at the cord to close the skylight blind above and protect the clothes against sun damage. "And now let us to the tub with you."

That eve, served by Blanche, Camille, while abed, ate a delicious meal of biscuits and butter and jellies and tea and cream over berries, for the handmaid insisted that she needed rest after such a long journey. And so, bathed and scented, Camille sat propped against many pillows in her great, soft bed, the first ever she had not had to share with a sister or two. And in the middle of that vast expanse, with a bed tray across her lap, her meal half-eaten, Camille fell quite asleep, for it seemed, after all, Blanche was right.

The very next day, Blanche escorted Camille about the great manor, showing her all within, all that is but one floor of one wing—" 'Tis the quarters of the prince himself, when he's about, that is, and none but Lanval is permitted therein. —Oh, once a fortnight, maids are allowed, but only under Lanval's eye." Camille frowned, for she did not think those chambers would be forbidden to her, for, after all, even though she had yet to meet Alain, she was his betrothed, hence surely she would not be barred; yet she did not gainsay her handmaid.

All through the rest of the mansion they went, with its sitting rooms and guest rooms and ballrooms and rooms of other sorts, some small, some large, some vast. In one of the smaller chambers sat an elegant harp, with violins in cases nearby. Lyres and lutes and tambourines and small drums lay in the chamber as well. In the next room sat a harpsichord, and though neither

Camille nor Blanche could play, they sat on the bench and struck the keys and laughed at the plucked dissonance they made. Even so, Camille looked longingly at the music sheet on the board above the keys, and she wondered at the symbols thereon and yearned to be able to read the arcane notations and play. Elsewhere, in several ballrooms, other harpsichords sat, some on stages, others directly on the ballroom floors, others still on balconies above.

Guest rooms abounded, and they sampled a number, and each one they entered was furnished in elegant taste. And with but few exceptions, nearly all the chambers had fireplaces— "Seldom used," said Blanche, "given the warmth of summer."

"Yet the rooms are not overwarm in the summer sun," replied Camille, frowning. "And even though my chambers have no outside windows, still I believe I felt a drift of air therein."

"Oh, my lady, that's one of the wonders of Summerwood Manor," replied Blanche. "I am told by Renaud the smith that on the many roofs, great scoops with fins that catch the wind and turn their mouths into the blow, direct the air down through channels in the walls to the rooms within, and the air does flow onward and out other hidden channels beyond. Only on the hottest or stillest of summer days might it become uncomfortable, but then we all sleep outside." Blanche pointed up at a wide lattice in one wall, and then down near the floor on the opposite wall to another. "Have you not seen the grillwork in your chambers, my lady?"

"I thought it was just decorative," replied Camille.

Blanche smiled, and on they went, visiting the servants' chamber down below, butlers and maids jumping to their feet and bowing and curtseying. Camille merely nodded in acknowledgment, having been instructed by Blanche that such would be sufficient, and onward they went.

They visited the kitchens as well, and here Camille was given a sweet pastry to hold her until the noonday meal, even though she had eaten breakfast in her bed, served to her by Blanche.

Through a laundry room they passed, with its great tubs sitting on platforms, wood-fired heating chambers beneath, cold for the nonce, no laundresses in sight.

They came to a door which seemed about to burst with women's laughter. Blanche grinned, saying, "Follow me," and they entered into a sewing chamber filled with gaiety, a half dozen seamstresses laughing. Upon seeing Camille their voices stilled, though mirth yet dwelled in their eyes, and the women rose from chairs and curtseyed. Feeling as if she had interrupted a festive party, Camille did thank them all for fashioning so many lovely clothes for her to wear. And then she and Blanche withdrew.

Later on they entered a ladies' sewing chamber, with its tambour frames and sewing baskets and daylight streaming in, a place where fine fabric with cross-stitch and embroidery patterns laid thereon would be captured in hoops, and needles and thread and floss and yarn would pop and hiss through taut cloth, while quiet converse murmured about. Camille could not but think that the cheer of the seamstress chamber would be a better place to sew.

In one room they found a nursery with rocker, crib, and toys—cloth poppets, rattles, teething rings, and the like. "In a place such as this your children will sleep," said Blanche.

"My children?"

"Those visited upon you by Prince Alain," replied Blanche.

"Oh," said Camille, reddening, feeling quite naïve.

They stopped for the noontide meal, Blanche having deposited her mistress in an elegant dining room and then abandoning her. Camille sat alone at the foot of a great long table, feeling embarrassed at the number of servants waiting upon her—all those eyes looking without seeming to look, watching her every bite—the men ready to leap forward at her slightest need.

Somehow she managed to struggle through, and not a stray drop or crumb fell onto her lovely lavender dress. *Thank Mithras for Mistress Agnès and the etiquette lessons she taught to me. "I may be nought but a gardener, young lady, yet manners I do well know, and we wouldn't want you to embarrass Fra Galanni by acting like a pig, now would we? Here, then, I'll teach you about knives and forks and other such, including finger bowls, though 'tis unlikely you'll ever see any, much less use one."*

Camille dipped her fingers in the finger bowl and dried them, and, as if by some mystical means, Blanche reappeared, and they took up once again the tour of the manor.

In a grand chamber was a great library, one that made the small library in Camille's suite look to be no more than a shelf or two by comparison. Books abounded, along with scrolls and pamphlets and journals and other printings and writings. Camille studied the spines of several books, finding poetry, legends, fables, histories, and much more ere Blanche dragged her away, saying, "My lady, there will be time in years to come to learn all, and I would have you see a great deal of this manse." And so onward they went.

A game room they visited: in the center of the room sat a small table with facing chairs and holding an elegant échecs set of carven jade—pale yellow for one player, translucent green for the other—the pieces arrayed on an onyx-and-marble board. Tears welled in Camille's eyes as she remembered the wooden set her père had carved, the set she and Giles had used.

"Do you play?" asked Camille, taking up a spearman.

"Oh, no, I think not, my lady, at least I do not remember ever having done so." Her voice trembled as if in some distress.

Camille frowned. *How could one not know whether they had ever played échecs?* But she merely said, "Someday I will teach you, then."

There were other échecs tables scattered about, though the sets were not quite as elegant.

In one corner sat a large, round table with several chairs about, and thereon were a scatter of small, flat, very stiff paper rectangles. Camille took up several and studied the various depictions of vices, virtues, and elemental forces, and nobility and peasantry thereon. "What are these, Blanche?" asked Camille.

With her fingers interlocked and clasped tightly, Blanche said, "I only know they are used in a game called taroc, my lady, though some say there are arcane uses for such as well."

On other tables sat games of dames, twelve red and twelve black pieces on alternating squares of the damiers, the boards like those of the ones for échecs, though the playing pieces were round disks all.

Camille looked up from the games and found hanging above a broad fireplace the portrait of a slender young man dressed all in blue and standing on a grassy hill, the wind blowing his cloak about and ruffling his dark hair. He was quite handsome, with a long, straight nose and regular features; across his body he held a walking stick in his two hands, almost as one would hold a quarterstaff low. He seemed to be looking out of the portrait and straight across the room. Camille turned, and on the opposite wall above a white marble table was a second portrait, this one

of a striking woman in green, standing on another windy hill-
top, her black hair loose and blowing, her cloak and gown billowing in the wind; she was dressed as if for riding horseback, a
crop in her hand. She faced the image opposite. It was as if they
stood on adjacent hills in the same gusty blow, looking at one
another across a vale between.

"Who are they?" asked Camille.

"Prince Alain's sire and dam," replied Blanche, her face quite
pale. "They say this is how they met—him out for a walk, she
out for a ride."

"Does Alain look like his père . . . or mère?"

"Oh, my lady, please don't ask. I am pledged not to say aught
of the prince. It is his wish, for he would tell you himself."

Camille took a deep breath, and then asked, "Where are they
now, père and mère, that is?"

"No one knows, my lady. They vanished sometime back,
and all the hunters and trackers in Faery couldn't seem to find
them. 'Tis a sad thing for his brother and sisters and himself,
their parents gone missing."

"Prince Borel, and Ladies Celeste and Liaze?"

Blanche nodded, and in a pleading voice said, "Oh, let us go
from this room, for tragedy is like to overwhelm me." And so
they went onward.

Through hallways they trod, and here and there in the walls
were panels, and when asked, Blanche opened one and pulled on
a rope in the space behind, pulleys squeaking somewhere above;
a wooden box, open on the front, came into view. "It is used to
convey food or other goods from one floor to another," said
Blanche, smiling. "It is called a sourd-muet serveur."

"Oh, but how clever," said Camille. "It must save many a
footstep bearing loads up and down stairs."

"Indeed, my lady," replied Blanche, closing the panel and
then moving on.

They came to a chamber with a hardwood floor; at the far end
there was nought but a great oaken desk and chair facing toward
the door, with other chairs ranged about the walls. Blanche had
no knowledge as to the use of this room, though Camille
deemed it was for conducting the landowner's business; meet-
ings with smallholders, mayhap.

Still in another room sat a huge table of many shallow drawers running from board to floor, and therein lay maps and charts
of lands both within Faery and without, some sections marked

with warnings of dire creatures therein, other whole sections completely blank.

And thus did go the day, Blanche leading Camille thither and yon as they explored the whole of the house, all, that is, but for one floor of one wing, there where the prince did dwell. Camille was quite astonished at the size of it all, as well as o'erwhelmed by its opulence.

That evening, again she dined alone at the foot of a very long mahogany table, servants hovering in the candlelight and watching her every move like owls ready to pounce on a vole, even though they stood quite motionless with their backs to the wall and their eyes seeming elsewhere . . . more or less.

The next day Blanche took her out on a tour of the grounds, and they followed along white-stone pathways wending among the many gardens, with their chrysanthemums and roses and violets and tulips and entire spectrums of flowers that Camille could not name, their blossoms all nodding in a gentle summer breeze. They strolled past ornamental grasses alongside ponds of still water with flowering lily pads afloat. In some, golden-scaled fish swam lazily; in others, the fish seemed bedecked in many-colored calico. Streams burbled across the estate, lucid in their clearness, singing their songs as they tumbled over rocks. One stream was quite broad and fairly deep, and here did Camille see the black swans aswimming. She and Blanche passed by deliberate arrangements of large and small boulders sitting here and there, with vines growing between and spiralling up and 'round the rocks. And now and again to Camille's wonder, they came across stone sculptings and metal castings and various other imaginative placements: small figures of toads and frogs sat on the banks of ponds; stone mice and voles peeked out from 'neath the bases of boulders; here and there were scattered burbling fountains and slow-flowing basins in which birds bathed and mayhap other diminutive beings as well; small footbridges crossed over rills, stanchions for lanterns along the rail, and in places only large, flat stones spanned the running streams.

Everywhere they went, gardeners and groundskeepers and other such bowed or tipped their hats to the Lady Camille. As she had been instructed by Blanche, Camille responded with a nod, though she also added a smile.

They passed by a long queue of empty stables to come to a

smithy, where a fairly young and portly man with grey eyes peering out through a hanging-down shock of dark hair stepped forth and bowed low. "This is Renaud, my lady," said Blanche, "blacksmith and farrier."

"Smith I may be, Blanche, or at least I think so, for in these last several years, I have learned much about the blending and heating and hammering and shaping and molding and quenching of metals, bronze and brass in particular."

"Bronze and brass and not iron?" said Camille.

"Oh, no, my lady, not iron," answered Renaud. "There are those in Faery who cannot abide iron, and so we keep it out."

"No iron whatsoever? Not even for nails or horseshoes?"

"Wooden pegs make splendid nails . . . likewise brass. Brass for shoeing horses, too—shoes and nails alike—not that I am much of a farrier these days, for there are no horses at all in the stables."

Camille laughed and said, "Horses or no, it matters not, for I know not how to ride."

Renaud grinned and thrust out a hand of negation, saying, "Not true, my lady, for did I not see you riding to the great house yon on the back of the"—Renaud frowned—"on the back of the—"

"The Bear," supplied Blanche.

"Yes, the Bear," agreed Renaud, nodding at Blanche.

"Ah, but, Master Farrier," said Camille, "I would think that quite different from riding a horse."

Renaud smiled and said, "And so would I, my lady. And so would I. Still, I think you'll not get a chance to learn, for, ever since the Bear came, the horses are all gone away."

"Bear? My Bear? Why would that ever make a difference? He's quite gentle, you know."

"Aye. We know—you and I and Blanche and all folk here at Summerwood Manor—however, try telling that to a horse." Renaud sighed. "We simply had to send them away." He glanced over his shoulder to the red coals in the forge. "But now if you will excuse me, I have fittings in the fire."

Camille nodded, and Renaud rushed back into the smithy, leaving the ladies to go on.

At the noontide, in one of the many gazebos, servants provided Camille with a lunch of peeled cucumber slices served on a white, crusty bread. Too, there was golden honey and pale yellow butter, if my lady did so prefer; and all was enhanced by a sweet, tangy drink made of a yellow fruit from across the seas, or so did the handmaid believe. Camille did manage to have Blanche join her in this fine midday repast, though the black-haired girl barely ate a bite, belying her hale manner and her ample size.

After lunch, they came to the entrance of the tall hedge maze, and, in spite of Camille's importuning, here did Blanche balk. "Oh, my lady, I dare not enter. 'Tis a puzzle I must not essay, else I would be lost forever."

"Pish, tush," responded Camille. "The maze is here for the fun of it. Besides, in Fra Galanni's library I read about such labyrinths, and I've always wanted to experience one." Laughing, she took Blanche's hand and tugged, yet Blanche burst into tears and pulled loose and fled away.

Puzzled, Camille followed, coming upon Blanche sitting on the grass beside one of the many ponds.

Camille sat on the sward at her lady's maid's side. Calico-fish lazily gathered in the water nigh, as if waiting to be fed. "What is it, Blanche, that frightens you so?"

"I don't know," replied Blanche. "It's just that I can never go in there."

"Well, then, we shan't," said Camille.

Timidly, Blanche smiled at her mistress.

"Come," said Camille, standing and holding out her hand, "there is much more to see."

Blanche reached up and took the offered grip and stood and brushed herself off, brushing off Camille's white dress as well.

Through shaded arbors they strolled, the summer air mild within. In one of the arbors they came across an elderly gardener upon his knees in a freshly tilled plot, where he carefully worked seeds into the dark soil.

"What is it you are planting, Andre?" asked Blanche, stepping past the turned-over earth to stand in front of the man.

Concentrating upon getting the placement just right, Andre glanced up and then back to the soil, replying, "White camellias, Blanche, a tribute to the prince's most beautiful young mademoiselle."

"Oh, my," said Camille.

Andre looked back to where Camille stood, then scrambled to his feet and touched the brim of his cap, saying, "Beg pardon, my lady, but I didn't see—"

"Oh, Andre," said Camille, "there's no need to apologize. May I help with the planting?"

A look of doubt crossed Andre's face. "Oh, I don't know about that, my lady, for 'tis but common labor I do. Besides, the seeds must be put just so, and—"

"Trust me, Andre," said Camille, "for common labor I do quite well, especially planting, for I am a crofter's daughter."

"I mean not to gainsay you, my lady, but a crofter's daughter you no longer are. Instead, you are the mistress of this great estate and all the holdings beyond."

At these words, Blanche nodded in affirmation, but Camille said, "Nevertheless, I would aid."

"Oh, my lady," said Blanche, "you would soil your dress and—"

"Then I shall change," said Camille, "into one which has seen many a spring sowing."

A short while later, dressed in the shift she had brought from the stone cottage—her very best dress back there, though she did not say such to Blanche—Camille grubbed in the soil next to Andre, planting camellias in those places where he did direct.

After a pleasing afternoon of work, and a bath and another solitary dinner, that night Camille fell asleep while reading a book of poetry and sitting in one of the soft leather chairs in her small library.

When she awoke she was in her bed. How she had gotten there she did not know, but 'twas in her bed she awoke.

Past the silk canopy, through the unshaded skylight Camille saw night fading to dawn. Sliding out from under her light cover, Camille padded to her closet and quickly dressed, donning her travelling clothes, for they were suitable for what she had in mind. She stepped from her chambers and quietly slipped down the stairs and out the main door and ran lightly across the dew-wet grass, morning mist swirling in her wake, the sun not yet risen.

To the hedge maze she went and 'round to the entry, then, taking a deep breath, she stepped within. Along the shadowed path she trod, keeping track of twists and turns, noting openings left and right, and using the trick of which Fra Galanni had spoken—that of keeping her right hand always brushing along the right-side hedge-wall. She knew that in some mazes this was the key to finding the center . . . but this maze was not one of those, for she found herself back at the entrance.

Ah, then, another strategy is needed.

Camille once again followed the right-hand way, but at the first opening into another row on the left, she stepped across and entered, and moments later came to a dead end.

Back to the first row she went, and to the second leftward opening.

Again and again she repeated her tactic, exploring more and more of the maze.

Now rightwards she tended from leftwards, and the layout became clearer to her, and then she was quite certain where the center must lie, and toward this end she went.

As she came nigh the last of her journey, she thought she heard what seemed to be the soft sound of weeping.

Oh, my, it would not do to come upon a saddened someone unawares.

"Allo!" she called. "Is anyone there?"

Abruptly, silence fell.

Hesitantly, as the sun beyond the hedges lipped the horizon and day came upon the land, Camille stepped forward and 'round the last turn, to see—

"Oh, Bear, I have missed you so!"

10
Masque

With sudden tears springing to her eyes, Camille rushed forward and threw her arms about the neck of the Bear and hugged him fiercely, murmuring, "Oh, Bear, oh, Bear, where have you been?"

She stood a long while with her face buried in fur, the Bear sitting quite still as she did so. Finally she released him and glanced 'round, scarcely noticing the stone benches placed about the green sward and the statues of a man and woman on a low pedestal in the center. "Oh, Bear, are you lost? Is that why I heard you moaning?"

The Bear gave a low rumble somewhere between that of a *whuff* and a deep growl. At this Camille laughed gaily, saying, "Tell me, O Bear, is that *rrrumm* a yes or a no? Ah, *tchaa*, but never mind, for I shall set you free of this maze. You see, I know the way out. Come along."

With Camille strolling beside the Bear, down the shadowed way between hedgerows they went, Camille chatting gaily of her explorations throughout the manor and surrounding grounds, and her working with Andre to plant camellias, and the terribly lonely dinners she had eaten surrounded by dozens of servants. The Bear made no comment whatsoever, but merely padded along.

As they neared the exit, Camille heard voices calling, dozens of voices, and they all seemed to be crying her name.

"Oh, Bear, I wonder whatever could be the matter?"

Camille hurried forward, the Bear lagging behind, and she exited the maze to see servants scattered throughout the grounds, all calling "*Lady Camille*!" Nearby, she espied Blanche and Renaud. "Blanche, I am over here!" cried Camille. "Whatever is this clamor all about?"

"Oh, my lady, my lady," cried Blanche, as she rushed toward Camille, Renaud following, "we thought you had been kidnapped, or vanished into thin air, just like Lord Valeray and Lady Saissa."

"Valeray? Saissa?"

"Prince Alain's dam and sire," said Blanche, puffing up, Renaud right behind, just as the Bear stepped out from the hedge. The handmaid and blacksmith curtseyed and bowed in deference, even as Camille frowned and asked, "Is that the why of this fuss? You thought I had been taken? Stolen away or some such?"

Blanche gulped and glanced at the Bear and said, "Oh, my lady, when I discovered you gone from your chambers, I didn't know what might have happened to you, and now I find you at this dreadful maze."

"Not dreadful at all, Blanche," said Camille. "You see, therein I discovered my Bear." She turned and threw her arms about the Bear's neck.

"Not meaning to gainsay you, Lady Camille," said Renaud, running his hand through the dark shock of his hair, "but there is something terrible about that maze. Just like Blanche, I feel it in my bones, and, like her, I think if I ever went in there, I would lose myself forever. And if you take my advice, you'll not go in there ever again."

"Ah, fie," said Camille, releasing the Bear. "All is quite splendid within, and it's a marvelous puzzle to solve. Besides, someone must tend it regularly—a gardener, that is—for it is well trimmed."

"Aye, my lady," replied Blanche, "Andre does go in there, as do other groundskeepers and gardeners, but I think none else of the staff does."

Camille sighed and shook her head. Then, looking about, said, "They're still out there shouting my name."

"Blanche, you take care of Lady Camille," said Renaud. "I'll call off the hunt." As Renaud hallooed and went across the grounds to round up searchers, Blanche and Camille and the Bear headed for the mansion, Camille saying, "May I be served a breakfast out here, Blanche? In the gazebo where you and I had lunch? I have much to tell the Bear, and I would not lose him again."

"Certainly, my lady," replied Blanche. "But wouldn't you like to bathe, and change into something more apropos for dining and chatting with the . . . the Bear?"

Camille smiled. "Blanche, he has seen me at my worst: grimy and disheveled and exhausted. And we have dined together in quite trying circumstances—digging in dirt for food, eating in a cold nearly beyond enduring, drinking brimstone-tinged water. Nay, I think a meal in the gazebo just as I am and just as he is seems quite genteel to me. Don't you think so, Bear?"

"*Whuff.*"

"There you have it, Blanche. He and I agree."

"As you wish," said Blanche, curtseying and then starting toward the manor as Camille and the Bear headed for the chosen gazebo.

"Oh, Blanche!" called Camille after. "Have them bring plenty for the Bear."

In midafternoon, Camille and the Bear strolled toward the manse, she having told him of her explorations in full, and her concerns at not yet having met Prince Alain, and her fears that Alain would be a monster for none of the staff would tell her what he was like. "Of course, I have only spoken at length to Blanche, though Lanval would say nought of the prince, either. The only others to whom I have said more than a word are Andre the gardener and Renaud the smith. Andre talks only about plants and planting, and from Renaud, I've heard even less. From something he said I get the impression that, as a smith, he seems to be yet learning his trade, though for the life of me, I cannot recall why. Regardless, there is no one to whom I can pour out my hopes and fears as I can with you, dear Bear, and you'd gone missing these last few days. Where have you been, I wonder. In the maze hiding away? Oh, would that you could talk, I am sure you have many wonderful things to tell."

As she came nigh one of the many entrances into the great château, the Bear stopped. "Aren't you coming with me?" asked Camille.

The Bear gave a low rumble in his chest.

"Well, then, I take that as a no." Camille embraced the Bear and whispered, "Promise me, Bear, that you will not disappear again except in the most dire of needs, and that in some part of the day I will find you to unburden my qualms and to speak of my dreams."

A soft *whuff* was her answer.

Camille then turned toward Blanche, who stood waiting. "All right, Blanche. All right. I am coming to take that bath you insist I must have, and to change into something more lady-like."

Blanche curtseyed in homage, and the Bear watched as Camille moved toward the entry, and when she was gone inside, the Bear stood a moment longer, staring after, but then ambled away.

After the bath and changing into an elegant pale green gown with cream-hued garniture and trim, and pale green ribbons entwined through her golden hair, and matching green slippers afoot, Camille went looking for her Bear, having now remembered what it was that Renaud had said which caused her to believe he was yet learning his craft. Out into the gardens she went, Blanche standing on one of the balconies and watching after her.

As the sun sank into the horizon and dusk drew nigh, groundskeepers moved across the landscape, lighting candle-lanterns along the paths within the gardens, and over the bridges, and in the several gazebos. That eve the twilight was quite magical, oranges and pinks in the sky fading into lavenders and indigos.

It was as she was standing on a lantern-lit bridge over the wide stream and gazing at sleeping black swans huddled on the mossy bank, that she heard a quiet footfall behind, and a soft voice said, "Lady, I am Alain."

With her heart racing and blood thundering in her ears, Camille turned to see a tall and slender dark-haired man, his face concealed by a mask.

11
Alain

Camille gasped and drew back, but the man who had called himself Alain made no advance. Instead, somewhat as if he were pleading, palm up, he held out his hand. "Lady Camille, for reasons I cannot explain, I must wear this mask, such that I can never show you my face." Now he took a tentative step into the full, bright lanternlight, where the mask could wholly be seen. Fitted to the contour of his face, it was, and made of silk layered and stiffened, all but two panels of silk along his cheeks to the corners of his mouth, which gave way with his chin as he spoke. And it was blue, matching the blue of his silken shirt and breeks and hose, and silver-buckled shoes. Held on by a broad silk ribbon tied behind, from hairline to under chin it reached, with only his lips and his somber grey eyes exposed, and here Camille had to suppress a gasp, for ne'er had she e'er seen such a tortured look in another's gaze . . .

. . . *If the eyes are truly windows to the soul, as Fra Galanni said, then here is a soul in dire torment. . . .*

. . . Camille came back to what he was saying, noting that his entire body had become quite taut, as if bracing for some onslaught, or a defeat. . . .

". . . and since this was unknown to you, as well as to me, at the time of my proposal and your consent, though I will keep my pledge to your parents, I release you from your pledge to me."

Alain paused, waiting for a response, which did not come. And his body seemed to ease, and he said, "Nevertheless, I would have you stay awhile and see whether or no"—he reached up and touched the mask—"this presents a barrier we neither one can breach."

Camille took a deep breath and exhaled it, trying to calm her racing heart. And then she curtseyed and murmured, "My lord."

Alain bowed, and then stepped forward and offered her his arm. "Would you sup with me?"

Yet trembling slightly, Camille slipped her arm in his, and together they strolled along white stone pathways through blossoming gardens and to the great château, though neither said aught on that fleeting journey 'neath endless deep indigo skies.

They sat at opposite ends of a very long table, he at the head, she at the foot, and the distance between seemed uncrossable. When the manifold attendants had served the first course, a fragrant split-pea soup, with white bread and pale yellow butter at hand, at a gesture from the prince, the servers retired from the room.

Oh, my. Would that I had known that gesture. I wouldn't have had all those eyes watching me eat. Even so, how—?

"My lady"—Alain looked down the length of the long oaken board—"I would have come to you sooner, but I had just returned from an arduous journey, one where I did not sleep, and I fell into my bed and failed to awaken for two days, it seems, and spent the third merely shaking off the effects of such a trial. Else we would have met ere now."

"There is no need to apologize, my lord, for Steward Lanval said as much," replied Camille. "The Bear—is it your Bear?—regardless, the Bear and I had quite a journey as well, and he took the best care of me."

"I had known he would, for him I do well comprehend. Yet I am told that you were beset upon by Goblins within the Winterwood."

"Redcaps, my lord, the worst of the lot, or so I am told. And a Troll as well. Your brother, Prince Borel, and his Wolves came to our aid, rescued me, in fact, from a rather wretched end."

"If it does not distress you, I would hear of this rescue," said Alain.

"Would that I were a bard, my lord, for it is a tale well worth the telling, quite dreadful in the doing, but splendid in recount. Yet a bard I am not, but I will try my best to do it justice."

Alain canted his head and gestured for her to go on.

"We had stopped for the night, the Bear and I, there in the

Winterwood, and, in spite of the bitter cold, I had fallen quite asleep. . . ."

Camille's retelling lasted awhile, and when she came to the end, so did they come to the end of the delectable soup. Alain took up a small bell at hand and rang it once, and attendants appeared to whisk away the bowls and used utensils, and to serve the next course.

So that's what the bell is for. Lessons Mistress Agnès neglected to teach: the gesture and the bell.

Artichoke hearts came next, and Camille watched Alain down the full length of the table to see how, in sweet Mithras's name, this yellow-green thing could possibly be eaten. She managed to muddle through the consumption of the artichoke, though she felt she did it quite badly. That dish was followed by honeyed pheasant, with a fine sauce over a vegetable Camille did not recognize. Served with the course was a dry white wine, the first wine Camille had ever tasted, and it made a frisson run up her spine, and Alain smiled at her shiver.

Lastly, they were served a cherry tart, accompanied by a small glass of sherry, amber and sweet to offset the tart's sharp tang. And even though Camille was quite stuffed, she did manage a bite or two, as well as several sips.

And all through the meal, and after, they did talk—about her journey and the wondrous beings she saw: the Unicorn, the Lynx Riders, the meals waiting in camps, the Waterfolk, though here Camille omitted the telling of her encounter with the shapeshifting male Waterfolk otters. She spoke of the Bear and of finding him just this day in the maze. Through it all, Alain offered comments on the Springwood, Winterwood, Autumnwood, and the Summerwood, and he spoke of other parts of Faery, telling of various creatures dwelling therein: of Ice Sprites and Twig Men, of Spriggens and Cluricauns and Pwca and Pysks, of Bogles and Selkies, and of many more, some gentle, some harmless, some vile, some dangerous, some deadly, some ready to lend a hand, but all quite amazing to Camille.

It was quite late when they stood up at last, well past the mid of night. Even so, Camille was filled with excitement, with energy, though she had risen at dawn.

It was not until Alain came to her end of the table to escort her to her chamber, that she again became aware of the mask, and how tall he was—a full head above her own five-foot-three.

As they strolled along the corridors, he said, "On the morrow, what would you do, my lady? With me, that is."

Camille smiled. "My lord, the morrow is already here."

Alain laughed. "True. Even so, would you—? Ah, I have it, I will play the harpsichord and I would have you sing."

"Oh, my lord, I would not ruin your playing with—"

"Tush. Recall, I have heard you sing."

"You have?"

"Did I not say so in my letter?"

"Oh, but I thought that someone had simply told you I sang in the field."

Alain stopped and she as well, and he faced her. "My lady, you may think this forward of me but . . ."

Camille waited, yet the prince said no more. "My lord?"

Alain took a deep breath. " 'Twas in the twilight I first saw you, gathering the last of the harvest from a meager field. I sat in the wood at the edge of Faery and watched and listened to you sing; I was thunderstruck. And that day afield your brother fell ill, and you were the first to his side, and you aided him to breathe, and you wept over his distress. And then I knew that not only had you golden hair and a golden voice and beauty of face and form, but that you had a golden heart as well. And when I came back to Summerwood Manor, I could not think of aught but you."

Camille's heart raced at these words, and yet by no outward sign did she betray the inner chaos hammering at her emotions.

"I sat in my chambers for days," said Alain, "and you occupied my every thought. I wrote a paean to you, one I had not the daring to deliver, though I did spend more days at the edge of Faery hoping for a glimpse. Finally, Lanval told me that I was neglecting the demesne, and that I had better propose to you ere all fell to ruin. Yet it took me until the wintertime to gain the courage to ask for your hand."

Camille's emotions roiled, and she felt her blood rush to her face. To cover her confusion, she said, "You wrote an ode to me?"

Alain's fists clenched, and then opened, and he softly said:

> *"I ne'er was struck before that day,*
> *With love so sudden, so rare.*
> *How it happened, I cannot say.*
> *. . . Ah, golden was her hair.*

"My heart did pound, my blood did thunder,
My stunning so complete.
What spell was this I'd fallen under?
. . . Her face and form so sweet.

"I heard her sing, and then I knew
I would ne'er be the same,
A voice so pure, a song so true,
She put the larks to shame.

"Oh, my love, but I will die
If you come not with me,
For to my heart, you surely know,
You have the only key."

Alain fell silent.

Her face flush, blood pounding in her ears, Camille knew not what to say. Neither, it seemed, did Alain, and once again he took her arm and they went onward toward her chambers. As they reached her door, she softly said, "My lord, the ode was lovely."

Alain turned her toward him and said, "My lady, it pales to mere doggerel when compared to the truth of you, and I—"

Camille's gaze dropped from him, for she was unable to peer into such intensity.

He backed away a step. "My lady, I did not intend to alarm."

"I am not alarmed, my lord," she quietly replied. "I am instead nonplused, at a loss to know what to say, think, or do, for you are a noble prince, whereas I am but a mere farm girl, and—"

"Oh, Lady, it is not our station that makes who we are, but rather what we hold in our hearts."

"My lord, thou art truly a noble prince."

Alain quietly said, "This moment it is I nonplused, and knowing nought else to do . . ." He opened the door. As candlelight spilled outward, he bowed. "My lady. Your quarters. Sleep well."

Camille curtseyed. "My lord." She stepped into the chamber and closed the door after, and sighed and leaned back against the panel.

"There you are," said Blanche, rising up from one of the silken couches.

"Oh, Blanche," said Camille, pushing away from the door and twirling 'round and 'round the room, stopping occasionally to curtsey to the chairs and the love seat and couches, "I am quite giddy, for I had the most marvelous time." Then she rushed to the handmaid and embraced her.

Blanche grinned and returned the embrace, but then said matter-of-factly, "Come, come. We must get you ready for bed."

Camille frowned, for shouldn't everyone be swept away by her giddiness? "Bed? But, oh, I will never sleep."

Yet in spite of these words, a short while later Blanche tucked her in, and ere the handmaid could reach the door and ease out, Camille was fast asleep.

Midmorn was on the Summerwood when Camille at last awakened. And she sang as she bathed, then dressed for the day—a pale blue gown with pale blue organdy trim.

The sun was nigh the zenith when she took her breakfast of blackberry crepes in her now-favorite gazebo, the Bear snuffling through a somewhat heavier fare of syrup-doused pancakes and biscuits with butter. All through the meal, she told the Bear of the wondrous time she had had last eve, telling of the menu, of the splendid converse, and going so far as to recite as much of the paean as she could remember, inserting *tum-d'lums* where she knew not the words.

She spoke little of the mask, saying only that she wondered why the prince wore such, briefly speculating that mayhap he was disfigured in some manner, or perhaps he had a birthmark he did not wish for anyone to see. "Ah, but Bear, mask or no, birthmark or no, disfigurement or no, he was wonderful, and it was a marvelous eve."

All through her commentary, the Bear made no ursine remarks, but he did pause now and again over his breakfast to listen to her words. Finally, the meal was done, and as the Bear padded to a nearby stream to wash it all down with water, Camille sipped her tea and gazed about the estate and wondered where Prince Alain was.

Perhaps conducting the affairs of the demesne in that great room where sits nought but a wooden desk and chairs. Mayhap I should— Ah, fie, I would not intrude.

As the Bear came back from the rill, water adrip from his muzzle, so too did Blanche come across the sward. The handmaid waited for the Bear to arrive, then curtseyed and said, "My lady, Andre says that he is planting along the sunward wall, and though I think it is somehow not seemly for a lady of your standing to grub in the soil, he says if you would care to join him . . ."

"Oh, Blanche, much as I would like to, I would rather wait for Prince Alain."

"My lady, I think you'll not see the prince until late in the day . . . this eve, mayhap."

"Oh." Camille's face fell. But then—"Very well. Please inform Andre I shall join him as soon as I change."

Blanche sighed. "If you must."

"Bear, will you like to grub in the soil with me?" asked Camille.

"*Rrrumm,*" rumbled the Bear.

"Ah, feh. I take that as a no. Oh, well."

It was again in the twilight that Camille took herself once more to the lanternlit bridge, and there it was that Prince Alain found her. This eve he wore satins of pale jade green, his silk mask green as well, all in subtle complement to Camille's cerulean gown.

"My lady, would you care to sing for your supper? I will play for you."

A panic struck Camille, and she flushed. *Sing for the prince when he no doubt has heard bards and minstrels? How can I contend with such?*

"My lord, in a chamber, the one with the portraits of your père and mère, I saw sets for playing échecs. It is a pastime of mine. Is it one of yours?"

Pleasure sprang into Alain's eyes, and he grinned. "Indeed, ma'mselle, yet I must warn you, I am no rank beginner."

"Well, then, sieur, I must warn you also: neither am I."

Arm in arm they entered the mansion, where Alain called on a servant to run ahead and prepare the game room. And soon they came to the chamber wherein sat the échecs sets, the lanterns now lit.

"Choose a table," said Alain.

"This one?" said Camille, pointing to the board midway between the portraits, the board with the carven jade sets, one side translucent green, the other pale yellow.

Sadness filled Alain's grey eyes. "Oh, Camille, I did not think. . . ."

Camille flushed. *He called me by my name!*

". . . That table is reserved for my sire and dam. Here it was they oft vied with one another, using échecs to settle disputes between, or to contest for a prize of some sort."

Gaining control of her breathing, Camille glanced at the portraits and said, "Who had the upper hand?"

Alain laughed. "Neither, I think."

"Then, my lord, what say ye to this table here?"

"Ah, a splendid choice, my lady: onyx and marble." Alain took up a white and a black spearman, and held them behind his back, then thrust his clenched hands forward. "Choose."

Camille grinned. "I choose sinister," she said, tapping his left fist.

"Then I move first," said Alain, returning her smile and opening his hands: white in the right, black in the left.

As they sat down, Alain said, "And what shall we play for? What prize?"

"Name the stakes, my lord," said Camille.

"Ah, a dangerous request, that."

Camille blushed, though she knew not why. But Alain said, "Should I win, you will sing for me."

Oh, no! "And should I win?"

"Well, my lady, since you have asked me to name the terms, I *could* say, that should you win, again you will sing for me, yet I won't. Instead, I shall play the harpsichord and sing for you. In either case, the prize is a song."

"Then I shall just have to win," said Camille, "for I would have that song."

"As would I, my lady. As would I." Alain reached out and pushed a piece forward two squares. "White king's spearman advances," he said, and so the game began.

The prince seemed to play quite recklessly, his moves coming swift upon hers; Camille's play was more deliberate, as she studied any new alternatives following each of his moves. Yet Alain's play was anything but reckless, as Camille came to understand, for, as did she, he also studied the board assiduously between each of his moves.

They became completely absorbed in the game, and time passed, while moves were made and countered, with pieces captured, warriors falling, and queens slain in spite of heroic efforts of the spearmen. Kings fled, and towers toppled, and heirophants fell, doomed regardless of their diagonal flight. But at last Camille said, "I shall mate in three moves."

Alain pursed his lips and studied the board. Finally he said, "Ah, the spearman. I see." And he reached out and laid his king on its side. "And thus I fall, crushed."

Camille giggled and then sobered. "Well, now, sieur, you owe me a song."

"Indeed, ma'mselle, I do. But first, shall we dine? I am certain that Cook and Chef have our meal ready. We could eat it here and play a second game, for I would win a song from you."

Camille looked about the chamber. It would certainly be better to eat in this cozy room than at opposite ends of a very long table.

"Very well, my lord."

Alain stood and stepped to the pull cord, and moments later a youth appeared. "We would eat in here, Jules."

"Yes, my lord, my lady," said the lad, bowing, then fleeing.

"Ere they arrive with the food, Camille," said Alain, "let us play a second game."

He called me by my name again.

"My lord, how can we? Our first game was quite long."

"Ah, there is the beauty of it. We each must move within ten heartbeats, following the other's move."

"Ten heartbeats? But what if my heart beats faster than yours?"

"Ah, then, I shall count"—Alain laughed—"though perhaps faster for you than for me."

"Well, then, sirrah," said Camille, grinning, "it is I who shall keep the count for you, and you who shall count for me."

They rearranged the board, Camille now playing the white pieces.

"Ready?"

"Ready."

Camille pushed out a spearman. "One, two th—"

Alain's move answered. "One, two, three, four, fi—"

Now Camille counted. "One, two—"

But a mere handful of moves later, Alain said, "Fool's mate!" and laughed.

They set up the board again, moving swiftly, counting, laughing at blunders and coups, and even coups d'état as one or the other moved his own king very badly.

Before the servants came with the food, they managed to get

in five games altogether—three of which Alain won, two going to Camille, but it counted not a whit to either just who won, for only the laughter mattered.

This evening in addition to the various courses—celery soup; goose-liver pâté on thin, crisp wafers; beef ragout; strawberries on a sweet biscuit with cream poured over—Camille drank a very fine dark red wine, the first of her life.

And the meal was so very intimate, she sitting knee to knee across a small table from him. And now and again Camille looked at the portraits on each wall, wondering which parent Alain favored, under that pale green mask. He had his père's grey eyes, rather than his mère's very dark ones, nearly black, or so the portrait would indicate. It was his mother's black hair he had, his own dark locks falling to his shoulders. As to his mouth, it seemed to take on the characteristic of his père, though his lips were a bit fuller, like those of his mère. But nought else could Camille discern, other than there was no obvious malformation of his face, or so the fitted mask would seem to indicate.

After dinner, they were served a small glass of a very dark, nearly purple, fortified wine—port, Alain called it—somewhat fruity in its taste.

Ah, now I remember. Port-wine stain, Agnès had named it, the reddish-purple birthmark the child bore. Mayhap Alain has such on his face.

After dinner they returned to gaming, resuming échecs, playing a few more of the heartbeat games, laughter filling the room. But then they settled down to two more serious sets: Alain winning one, the other a stalemate.

Alain showed Camille the rudiments of taroc, and they laughed together at her attempts to shuffle the deck. But they did not play, for more than just two people were needed for the game, five or six being the best.

And all the while they talked: of music, of books, of Camille's learning to read and write, of Fra Galanni and Sister Agnès, and of many other things.

Again, it was well past mid of night when Alain delivered Camille to the door of her chambers, and there they lingered awhile, yet talking. But finally they parted, and once more she fell into her bed, her glad heart quite afloat.

The days blended together in a wondrous blur, Camille spending the noontime with the Bear, telling him of her evenings with the prince, confiding her most secret thoughts and hopes and dreams, as well as her deepest fears.

A bit later in the day, the afternoons found her with Andre the gardener, planting some new bush or flower, at times in the courtyards between the wings, or in the gardens beyond; or she spent the time with Blanche, learning more details of the great house, as well as becoming acquainted with the quite extensive staff, Blanche slowly introducing her to a few more each day, so as not to overwhelm her all at once with too many faces and names.

From dusk until just beyond mid of night she spent with Prince Alain: dining on fine meals with red and white wines, playing échecs and dames, visiting the great library and quietly reading poetry to one another. One evening he taught her to dance—a slow stately dance, with much pacing and pausing and turning and bowing and curtseying and touching of hands, several servants playing harps and drums and horns.

"Oh, Bear, I do love him so, and I do think he feels the same."

The Bear looked up from his great bowl of custard, pale yellow spread round nose and jaw and chin, and he cocked his head and rumbled low, as if to ask *How could he not?*

"Does *rrrumm* mean you think it so?"

"Whuff," said the Bear, and then stuck his nose back into the bowl and began lapping up more sweet custard.

"Well, then, it must be true," said Camille, spreading butter on toast.

That evening, as they stood up from the dining table, Alain said, "Lady, you have put me off long enough."

Camille drew in a sharp breath, but managed to say, "How so, my lord?"

"A nine-day past you lost a wager, and I would have you sing for me."

Camille's shoulders relaxed. "I seem to recall, my lord, you lost the wager to me."

"True, I lost the first game, yet you lost the second, and the third was a draw; hence, I owe you a song, you owe me one, and mayhap we will sing a duet."

Feeling trapped, Camille looked about the dining chamber, where they stood at opposite ends of a long table. "My lord, you surely have heard bards sing, and I am but—"

"No more excuses, Lady, for I would collect my debt."

Camille sighed. "Very well, my lord, yet I would not have just anyone hear."

Alain pursed his lips. "I have a harpsichord in a chamber next to my quarters, where none regularly come but Lanval."

Clutching the flowing skirt of her white gown to lift the hem a fraction, Camille curtseyed. "As you wish, my lord."

Alain bowed, and then paced to her end of the board and crooked his arm. She slipped her arm in his, and out into the hallways and to his wing and then to his floor they went, a place Camille had not yet been. Down a long oak-panelled hallway they strode, all the doors marked with the Summerwood sigil. Into a chamber he led her, much like her own sitting room, yet therein and just beyond the silken couches and chairs sat a cherry-wood harpsichord.

Alain sat on the bench and ran his fingers along the keyboard, plucked strings sounding in response.

"Now, my lady, what would you have me play for you, and you can sing for me."

Camille sighed. "Do you know 'The Sparrow in the Tree'?"

Alain laughed and clapped his hands. "Indeed I do, Camille. A splendid choice. How came you to know it, for it is quite obscure?"

"A votary of Mithras taught it to me. She said she learned it at court."

Alain grinned. "I think I recall from your singing in the field, but is this a proper pitch for you?" He struck a single key, sounding a note.

Camille nodded, and Alain played an introductory phrase, and when he looked to Camille, she began to sing:

"Tiny brown sparrow, sitting in the tree,
Scruffy little soul, just like me,
Would you be an eagle, would you be a hawk,
Or would you wish instead to sing like a lark?
Or would you have plumage bright and gay,
Or would you wish . . ."

Camille sang verse upon verse, chorus after chorus, the song telling of a maiden who wished a different lot in life, yet who found comfort in familiar things, and she finally discovered love, which set her free to fly as the transformed sparrow she then was. And all throughout the aria, Camille's voice soared to unrestrained heights and dropped to whispering depths, with tones so pure, so clear, so true, that tears ran down Alain's face from the sheer perfection and joy of it.

And as the song came toward an end, Alain's clear tenor voice joined with hers, and he caroled in flawless harmony and in melodic counterpoint to her ascendant soprano tones, he singing of the sparrow, she singing of the girl.

At last the song ended, and Alain sat long moments in silence, Camille not daring to say even a single word. Finally he looked up at her, his eyes glistening with unshed tears. "My lady, you take my breath away."

All the tension fled from Camille, and she expelled a trembling sigh and said, "My lord, I am giddy with relief that you find my singing to your like. Even so, now it is your turn to sing unto me."

Alain wiped his eyes with his fingers and then said, "Giddy? You are giddy?" He grinned, then sobered and struck a chord and said, " 'The Giddy Sea.' " He then played an introductory phrase, and lifted his clear tenor in song, all the while looking at Camille:

"What is this thunderbolt stop'd my heart
  And shook the breath from me
  And set my soul a-sailing
  'Pon a giddy sea?

"What is this pounding in my chest
  When you come into seeing,
  This wondrous surge from head to toe
  That floods my entire being?

"What is this burning in my blood
  That spins my head around
  And stuns me trembling helplessly
  As in your eyes I drown?

"Oh, should I ask the answer
  From all the gods above,
  When every eye can see
  That I've been whelmed by love?

" 'Tis you, my heart, my dearest heart,
  To me this thing hast done,

And left me yearning for the days
Our two hearts become but one.

"Oh, leave me not alone, my love,
  Upon this giddy sea.
  Instead let's make it giddier:
  Come sail away with me.

"Leave me not alone, my love,
  Come sail away with me.
  Oh, my love, my sweet, sweet love,
  Let us sail the giddy sea."

As the notes faded into silence, Alain looked into Camille's eyes and whispered, "Leave me not alone, my love, come sail away with me."

Camille slid onto the bench and said, "I think I shall go entirely mad if you do not kiss me now."

Alain took her in his arms and gently kissed her, and she answered with an urgency. Pent need broke free, his fire matching hers. Yet kissing, they stood, the bench toppling over, but they paid it no heed, so hot now the flames of desire. And then Alain swept her up and bore her through a doorway and into his bedchamber as Camille kissed his neck, his shoulder, his ear, as well as his cheek, silk caressing her lips.

He set Camille to her feet, and then slowly undressed her, kissing her mouth, her shoulders, her hands, her breasts.

He threw back the covers and lifted her up and laid her on silken sheets, and she watched as he undressed, all but the mask, and Camille's breath shuddered with confusion and desire, for his slender body was beautiful, and his need was plain to see. At this last she was somewhat frightened, yet wanting.

Then he blew out the candle, saying, "I'll not make love wearing this."

In the darkness, he lay down beside her, his hands caressing as she clasped him to her, her lips clinging to his, their tongues exploring. And though she didn't quite know what to do, she opened her legs when he gently moved between. There was but an instant of pain as he entered into her. And then for a moment he remained quite still, and she did not understand, but then he began slowly moving, slowly, slowly, gently. Joy, delight, desire, love: all thrilled through Camille, and she embraced Alain and began responding, her own tentative movements meeting his.

And still he moved slowly, ever so.

A joyous tension began to build, Camille's breath coming in gasps, though Alain remained silent.

And gradually, ever so gradually, the pace of his thrusts increased, hers matching, Camille completely lost in a closeness so total, a commitment absolute, in the wonder of two being one, and the joy of being complete.

And then—"Oh, my. I never. Oh, Alain. Oh, Love. I . . . I . . ."

Moaning, gasping, wild with desire, she wrapped her legs 'round and began kissing him frantically, finding no mask to interfere, her responses frenzied, urgent, needing, wanting, matching. "Oh, Mithras. . . . Oh, sweet Mithras. . . . Oh. . . . Oh. . . . Oh . . ."

12
Idyll

Drenched in perspiration, at last they disentangled and fell away from one another, each lying back in the softness of the bed in the absolute darkness of the chamber. But then Alain rolled onto his side toward Camille and reached out and touched her shoulder and slid his finger down her arm to find her hand and enlace his fingers in hers. "Oh, my love, I had not meant for this to happen until we were wed, yet I am quite glad it did." Camille squeezed his hand in silent agreement. Alain turned her hand over in his and kissed her palm, but then took a deep breath and expelled it. "Even so, at this time we cannot be formally married—the banns posted, the king notified, our union blessed by a heirophant. And the terrible thing is, I cannot tell you why, for to do so would bring disaster to all."

In the darkness, Camille frowned. "I do not understand, my lord."

"Please, Camille, when we are alone together, or within family, I am Alain, though I would rather you call me by that which you named me in the throes of our passion."

"My love," whispered Camille.

In the dark, Alain kissed her lips, a kiss she fervently returned. Then he captured her hand again and said, "Hear me, my sweet, I will not keep from you any secrets but this one, and only because I must, for this I do tell you, it would bring a calamity beyond reckoning were we to wed ere a terrible predicament is resolved. And I can but ask that you trust me till then, though given my silence I cannot say why you should. Yet this I do pledge: when the dilemma is banished, I will most ardently marry you, for then we can wed without bringing tragedy crashing down upon Faery, and you are my very heart."

Alain fell silent, and Camille drew his hand to her lips and kissed each one of his fingers. "My lord, my love, my prince, my heart, my own, would that I knew this quandary you face, for then I could share the burden. Yet if it is not to be, then I do so accept, for wedded or no, I do love you most dearly."

Alain drew her to him, flesh to flesh, and showered her with kisses, and he cupped each of her breasts and kissed curve and slope and aureole, and Camille could feel him quickening even as she responded, and passion flared anew, and they made love again, gentle at first, then afire.

Dawn was in the sky when Camille drowsily wakened. Faint light seeped 'round the edges of the curtained skylight above, the only window in the room. She turned and reached for Alain, yet he was not there, his side of the bed quite empty, the warmth of his presence nearly gone, the silken sheets growing chill in his absence. Camille sat upright and looked about, yet in the dimness, her prince was not to be seen. Where he had gone, she knew not—*Yet perchance he will soon return.* Yawning and stretching catlike, Camille then settled back, and moments later she was asleep again.

"Hruhmm!" A man cleared his throat.

"Oh, Alain—" Camille turned to face him, then bolted upright, barely catching the silken cover as it slid down. Clasping it to her bosom, "Lanval," she said.

"My lady," replied the steward, a sparkle in his eye. A white silken robe was draped over his arm.

"Oh, my, but where is the prince?"

"About his business, I deem," said Lanval. "He sent you this." Lanval placed the snow-white, satin robe upon the foot of the bed. "Do you wish to be served your breakfast here?"

"Well . . . —Oh, no! Blanche! She will have the hounds out after me, finding my own bed empty. My lor—um, Lanval, I believe I should hie there now."

A faint smile crossed Lanval's face, as he took up her gown from the floor to shake out the wrinkles and then draped it across his arm. He pointedly did not even look at the undergarments, petticoats and all. "Fear not, Lady Camille, for she knows of your whereabouts. In fact, will it set your mind to ease, I deem the entire staff knows."

Camille reddened then said, "Nevertheless, 'tis to my quarters I will go." She pointedly looked at the white robe at the foot of the bed. "If you will excuse me . . ."

Lanval bowed and said, "I will await you in the next room."

When he had gone through the doorway, Camille cast back the light satin cover and snatched up the robe. Quickly, she slipped it on and belted it closed, then stepped into her shoes and gathered up her undergarments, rolling all into a petticoat bundle, then turned to the bed to—

"Oh, my!" she gasped.

"My lady? Is aught amiss?"

"Oh, Lanval, I have ruined a sheet. I thought my courses ended a three-day past, yet . . ."

A smear of blood stained the bedding.

Camille looked up to see Lanval now at her side. A faint smile crossed his face. "My lady, I ween 'tis not your courses."

"If not, Lanval, then what?"

Lanval reddened. "I'd rather not say, my lady. Ask Blanche instead."

"Lanval!" said Camille sharply.

Lanval sighed and mumbled a few words, and to Camille it sounded as if he said, " 'S rngrn blth."

"What? I didn't hear."

Lanval took a deep breath. " 'Tis virgin's blood," he said, clearly this time.

"Virgin's blood?"

"Um, yes, my lady." Lanval, who in other matters seemed so sure, shifted about uneasily. "Harrumph! Did not your mère speak of such?"

"Nay, she did not."

For a moment Lanval seemed nonplused, but then he said, "Ask Blanche. She will explain." He took a deep breath, then plunged on. "Yet hear me, for this I do know: the prince will be glad of the sheet, though I think he will not call it ruin, but a testament to virtue instead."

Camille shook her head. "What do you mean, Lanval?"

Again the steward reddened, and he turned up his hands. "Ask Blanche," was his only reply.

Exasperated, Camille snatched her pristine white dress from his arm and sailed out from the chamber and down the hallways toward her own distant quarters.

*   *   *

"Is *that* what it means?"

"Yes, my lady," replied Blanche, scrubbing Camille's back.

Camille frowned. "Well, then, I don't understand how that can be a sign of virtue. It could be a sign of fear, or a lack of temptation or opportunity—I certainly had little opportunity, living as I did with a monk and a votary, and then isolated on Papa's farm. Too, it could be lack of desire or lack of someone to love. —Tell me: is it a sign of virtue when a man who has never made love before comes to the bed of a willing partner?"

"No, my lady. It is considered a lack of experience."

"Virtue for one, but inexperience for the other? —Fie! But this does seem somehow inequitable."

"Let me ask you this, my lady: would you rather have had Prince Alain as inexperienced as you?"

"Oh, no, Blanche. I can't imagine how awkward and fumbling such an encounter would have been."

"Then there you have it, my lady. —Now, duck your hair under."

When Camille came sputtering up from the water, Blanche asked, "My lady, did they not speak of this at the monastery? Of vices and virtues? Of men and women and love? Or did not your père or mère tell you of such?"

Camille shook her head. "At the monastery? No, Blanche. Instead they spoke of devotions to Mithras, and of the Devil and the good that men do. As for such talk at home, Papa always seemed to withdraw, and Maman simply glared at Papa and gritted her teeth and said, 'You'll find out soon enough, you will,' and, beyond that, she said no more."

As Blanche took up one of the rose-scented bars of soap, she said, "Well, my lady, now you know," and she began lathering Camille's hair.

"Inequitable or no, again I say, fie."

"Fie, my lady?"

"Yes. Fie." Camille's shoulders slumped and she sighed. "You see, Blanche, now I suppose I will never know whether or not I am virtuous, for I never faced temptation or opportunity or even knew love ere I met Prince Alain. Besides, it just seemed to happen . . . and I am glad that it did."

"So am I," said Blanche. "So are we all."

"All?"

"The staff, my lady. The household staff."

"Oh, my. Does everyone know? Lanval said all might."

Blanche paused in her scrubbing. "It is plain to every man

Jaques and woman Jille that you two were meant for one another. And the prince has so little joy in his life, it is good to see him laugh."

"Little joy? What mean you by that?"

"That I leave up to him to say," replied Blanche, taking up the pitcher from the washstand. "Now hold still while I rinse."

"Tell me of your père and mère, my love."

Alain hesitated, a black king in hand, and, in spite of the fawn-colored mask he wore, Camille thought she detected a frown from the look in his grey eyes. He then stood and stepped to the mantel and gazed up at his father's portrait, and turned and looked across the chamber at his mother's. "I love them both, I do, as do Borel and Celeste and Liaze. Every year, my sire and dam and their court would ride from woodland manor to woodland manor: a king's court rade."

"Raid?" asked Camille. "As in a loot and pillage raid?"

Alain smiled. "No, love: r-a-d-e. In this case it means to ride in procession, and my sire and dam's entire retinue would rade. To the Forests of the Seasons they would come, visiting each of us in turn." Alain paused, his eyes brimming in the lanternlight, and he whispered, "Those were splendid days."

Camille stood and stepped to Alain's side. "Love, if it pains you . . ."

Alain made a sign of negation. "I am saddened, Camille, yet I would speak on."

Camille took up his hand and kissed it, then held it gently as Alain continued:

"Some fifteen years back, by mortal reckoning, they disappeared, gone in the dead of night. They had arrived here at the manor no more than a fortnight ere then, and had intended to stay a fortnight more ere the king's rade would take them onward unto Liaze's manor in the Autumnwood.

"Yet of a sudden they were missing, my sire and dam, but their horses were still in the stables, and all of their goods were yet here, and so where and how they had gone was a mystery.

"We turned the house and grounds upside down in a search for them, yet nought did we find, not even the most remote sign of either.

"Hunters and trackers could come across no hint of a trail, not even Borel's Wolves. They had simply vanished into thin air.

Not even Ardu, the mage Celeste brought from the Springwood, could detect what had gone amiss, though he did say that an arcane spell was at work, one which he could not overcome."

Camille drew in a deep breath and whispered, " 'Twas magic?"

Alain nodded. "I even visited the Lady of the Mere, but she remained absent."

"Lady of the Mere?"

Alain vaguely gestured. "Not far from here. A seer. Yet she is wholly elusive. 'Tis said she only appears in circumstances dire. The disappearance of my sire and dam would not seem to be one of those events."

"Had they any enemies—your sire and dam—enemies who could have done this thing?"

"There was that trace of a spell cast, but neither the mages nor the witches we brought to Summerwood Manor could determine aught of it. And though 'tis said all kings have many a foe, none we know of has spells at his beck."

As Alain again mentioned magic, Camille shivered. Then she frowned. "And your sire is a king?"

"Aye."

"Who rules in his absence?"

"Faure: my sire's steward, Lanval's brother. And just as is Lanval, Faure, too, is quite honorable, and I ween would not do nor cause such a thing. Certainly not for power, for he is reluctant to steer the kingdom, and he urges Borel to take the throne, for Borel is eldest. Yet Borel declines, for he believes someday my sire will be found, as do my sisters and as do I. And as long as Borel and Celeste and Liaze and I refuse the throne, Faure must stand in my sire's stead."

Again Camille kissed Alain's hand. "Oh, love, surely they will be found someday."

The gloom of speaking of his lost parents weighed on Alain's spirit for a sevenday or so, but then he brightened, and once again Camille found joy in his eyes and a smile on his lips and laughter in his voice.

A moon passed, and then another, and Alain and Camille's ardor grew eve by eve, and their lovemaking became even more passionate. And Camille spent her noontimes with the Bear, and her afternoons with Blanche or Andre or the seamstresses, who allowed Camille to join them in their glad circle, where mirth oft rang; or she spent them with other members of the household staff, learning of their duties and deeds.

The evenings and nights she spent with Alain, and on a few of those, Alain conducted the business of the Summerwood Principality, and he had Camille sit at his side as he dealt with smallholders and merchants and hunters and the like, or a poacher or two, though within this part of Faery little changed, and so much could be handled by Lanval without need of intervention by the prince. Hence, for the most part, much or all of their evenings were free, and they took elegant meals and played échecs and dames, or they read in quietness to one another from the books and scrolls and tomes and journals in the great library. Alain taught her more dances: the quadrille, the minuet, and a right vigorous caper named the reel, which Alain said came from a land across a wave-tossed channel of the sea. Too, they oft sang—arias, or duets—Camille in her clear and pure soprano, and Alain in his flawless tenor. While she did not move from her quarters into his, she slept with him every night—sometimes with him merely holding her close or she embracing him, other times in amorous clench. Even though they bedded together, every darktide just ere dawn he would leave her side.

On one of those nights as Camille lay beside her sleeping love in the darkness complete and listened to him softly breathe, cautiously and with but a single finger she lightly traced his features, for she had never seen beyond the masks he wore, her touch tracing the line of his jaw, his lips, his brow, his cheeks, his nose . . .

They do not seem monstrous, disfigured. And regardless of any mark he might have, I would think him quite beautiful could I but see. She withdrew her touch. *Why does—?*

"Camille," his voice came softly through the dark, "please do not do that again."

"*Oh!*" Camille gasped. "I thought you asleep, my love."

"I was." Alain swung his feet out from under the cover and sat a moment on the edge of the bed. "Dawn is coming."

Camille kicked the satin aside and scrambled to her knees and embraced him from behind, her bare breasts pressing against his naked back. "Why, love, do I never see you in the day?"

Alain sighed. "What I do in the day is unavoidable. It's all part of the terrible problem with which I and others do grapple."

"Others?"

"My kith."

Camille rested her chin on his shoulder. "Borel, Celeste, and Liaze?"

"Aye. Even now they search their demesnes for those who might help. Should they find those with promise, they will bring them here."

"If they can help, then why can't I?"

"Oh, love, I can only say that one day you will know." Alain twisted about and took her face in his hands and kissed and then released her. He stood and moved away, and she could hear him donning his clothes in the dark. Moments later there came the *shkk* of a striker, and lanternlight filled the chamber, revealing Alain now fully clothed, his face concealed behind a pale yellow mask. He kissed her again, then said, "I must go, love," and then he was gone.

With a sigh, Camille settled back in the bed, his bed, but questions without answers tumbled through her thoughts, and she could not sleep. Finally, she arose and donned her own clothes, then made her way to her chambers. As usual, Blanche lay sleeping on a couch, but awoke at the opening of the door. Camille took a long, hot bath, Blanche yawning bleary-eyed as Camille soaked. Finally, Camille took to her own bed and fell asleep at last, as Blanche slipped away in the morn.

A sevenday passed with no resolution to Camille's manifold questions, and yet she loved Alain no less for his secrecy and silence. And still their adoration grew.

It was as Camille knelt next to Andre and dropped seeds into the soil and covered them over, that there sounded trumpets on the high hills above. Camille stood and shaded her eyes and peered afar even as the horns sounded again, and down the distant slope a procession came, riders ahorse.

"My lady," said Andre, now standing at her side, "methinks y'd better make ready to receive guests."

"Who is it, Andre? Do you know?"

"One of the siblings, I shouldn't wonder."

In that moment—"My lady!" came a cry. "My lady!" Camille turned to see Blanche running across the sward, her skirt held up to do so. "My lady, we must make you presentable; a rade, a rade has come!"

Reaching Camille's side and gasping for breath, Blanche said, "If I'm not mistaken, 'tis Celeste and Liaze, come to visit the prince. Oh, Lady, we can't have them see you like this, all grimed with dirt." The handmaid cast an accusing eye at the gardener, but he merely shrugged.

In that moment, topping the hill came another rider, only this one had a pack of Wolves padding alongside. Blanche drew in a sharp breath. "Oh, goodness, it's all three come."

"Aye," agreed Andre, "and there look to be strangers in their train."

Blanche tugged on Camille's arm. "My lady, now listen to me! We must go this instant, else they'll be here before you are presentable."

As Camille was drawn into the mansion by Blanche, footmen raced across the sward toward the distant gates. And inside the manor, servants and maids, all directed by Lanval, rushed to and fro, for there were rooms to be aired and beds to be made and banquets to be prepared, for indeed 'twas true: a splendid rade had come.

13
Siblings

"No, no, my lady," said Lanval. "You must stand here on the symbol of Summerwood Manor."

Freshly scrubbed and most hurriedly dressed in a pale jade-green gown with pale cream petticoats under, and in green shoes with pale cream silk stockings, and with pale jade-green ribbons wound in her golden hair, and a necklace of square-cut, pale yellow jargoons about her throat and a matching ring on her left hand, Camille had come rushing down the stairs and into the entry hall, where Lanval awaited her on the oak-tree inlay. She would have run right past him, but he stepped into her path.

Camille looked beyond him and said, "Oh, but I cannot stay here, for I wish to see them come. Please, Lanval, I have not before ever seen a rade."

Lanval sighed, though a hint of a smile crossed his lips. "Lady Camille, you need not my permission, for you are mistress here. Yet ere they reach the manor, I strongly advise that you return unto the oak and stand in the very center, for they, too, must learn you are the mistress here."

"Oh, merci, Lanval." Camille rushed from the grand entry hall and through the corridor and to the great front door. Once again lines of servants and maids and footmen stood aflank the open portal, awaiting the arrival of the visitors.

Camille stopped just within the shadow of the doorway, her eyes seeking the rade.

Lanval stepped to her side.

Endless moments passed, or so it seemed to Camille, yet of a sudden, emerging from the lane of oaks, two riders appeared, two ladies, followed by a small retinue and then a gap, where none came.

"Where are the others?" whispered Camille.

"Many stopped just inside the gate," said Lanval, "there to pitch camp and tend the horses, which will be stabled outside."

"Outside?"

"Outside the walls."

"Because . . .?"

"The Bear, my lady. The horses will not abide."

"Oh. I remember. Renaud said such. But what about these steeds that come?"

"They will be stabled without as well."

In that moment, grey shapes loped out from the shadows of the oaks, and another rider came, two or three more in his wake.

"Borel?" whispered Camille.

"Aye."

"Are the horses not afraid of the Wolves?"

"Nay, my lady. Methinks they simply believe them to be large dogs."

No more came from the lane, and Camille sighed in minor disappointment, for she would have liked to see the entire rade up close and in cavalcade.

As onward came the lead riders, "My lady . . ." said Lanval, canting his head toward the entry hall.

"All right, all right." As Lanval stepped outward, Camille hurried back to the malachite-and-granite inlay and stood in the very center, and she pulled at the top of her gown, wondering at its low cut and the bustier beneath, which thrust her breasts up and closer together, accentuating the cleavage. But then she stood straight and waited, for, out through the hallway and beyond the corridor of servants, she could see the riders arrive, their horses skittish and sidle-stepping and footmen rushing to aid.

Moments later—"My Lady Camille," called Lanval, now standing just inside the hall, "the Lady Celeste, Princess of the Springwood."

As Celeste stepped down onto the marble floor, Camille saw before her a slender, willowy, seemingly fragile lady with light yellow hair and dressed in pale green riding garb, the hue nearly the match of Camille's own jade gown. Celeste stepped to the granite root of the oak inlay and she and Camille curtseyed deeply to one another. Then Celeste straightened, her green eyes peering into Camille's eyes of blue. "Oh, Camille, you are so beautiful," she softly said, then stepped forward and gently embraced the girl, Camille returning in kind, and Celeste carried about her the faint fragrance of spring mint, which mingled with and somehow enhanced the subtle scent of roses clinging to Camille.

As Celeste released Camille and stepped aside, Lanval called, "My Lady Camille, the Lady Liaze, Princess of the Autumnwood."

Smiling, auburn-haired Liaze, dressed in russet garb, stepped onto the floor of the hall. Taller and appearing more robust than Celeste, Liaze strode to the root of the oak, her amber eyes sparkling. Again Camille curtseyed deeply, Liaze likewise, and then they did embrace, the air about Liaze faintly adrift with the fragrance of apples, and Liaze whispered, "My Lady Camille, I am so glad to meet you at last." Camille remained silent, for she had not been told nor did she know what to say.

As Liaze stepped aflank of Camille, Lanval called, "My Lady Camille, Lord Borel, Prince of the Winterwood."

Dressed in grey, Borel stepped in, Wolves padding at his side. He stopped at the root of the oak and bowed low, his silver-white hair cascading. Camille curtseyed in turn. And about him was the aroma of . . . what?—snow? frost? He stepped forward, and took her hand and kissed it, his ice-blue eyes again appraised her face and form, just as he had done in the Winterwood, and Camille felt her cheeks flush as his gaze lingered on her décolletage. "My lady, you are even more stunning than I thought when first we met. And once more I say, 'tis no wonder Alain was smitten."

To cover her embarrassment, "My lord," she said, unable to think of ought else.

"My Lady Camille," announced Lanval, "the Wizard Caldor, the Seer Malgan, the Witch Hradian."

Camille's eyes widened in alarm at these titles, and she looked up to see a tall, bald man in rune-marked blue robes step forward, a supercilious sneer on his face. He was flanked on one side by a reed-thin, sallow-faced man with lank, straw-colored hair, his hands tucked across and within the sleeves of his red-satin, buttoned gown, a man who whispered to unseen companions as he approached. Flanking the other side came a sly-eyed, leering crone accoutered in black, with black-lace frills and trim and danglers.

As they approached, Celeste murmured, "Fear not, Camille. They are here to help."

When the introductions were complete, feeling quite awkward and unlearned, Camille said, "You must be weary after your journey." She turned to find Lanval at hand. "Lanval, would you see the guests to their quarters?"

"Yes, my lady."

But ere they departed, Liaze said, "What say in a candlemark or so, we all get together for a game of croquet?"

Camille frowned in puzzlement. "Croquet? Shepherd's crook? Or do you mean the small cake?"

Liaze laughed. "No, no. 'Tis a game of long-handled mallets and wooden balls and wickets and the like."

Turning away to cover her embarrassment, "Do we have such, Lanval?"

"Indeed, my lady. I will have the wickets and stakes set on the lawn."

Camille turned back to Liaze. "I have never played such, yet I am willing to try."

"Oh, it was great fun, Alain," said Camille. "Would that you had been there to—"

"You should have seen her croquet Borel," interjected Liaze, grinning.

Celeste's green eyes twinkled. "Borel ended up chasing his ball down the center of the stream, your black swans highly upset at the intrusion."

Camille's hand flew to her mouth, but behind her fingers she grinned. "I didn't mean to drive it there, truly, Borel."

"Hmpfh," snorted Borel, yet he smiled. "Next time I'll send one of the Wolves, rather than jumping in myself. If truth be known, I didn't realize it was that deep."

The table rang with laughter, and finally Alain, masked this evening in white, shook his head. "Would that I had been there."

Celeste's gentle smile faded, and she softly said, "Perhaps soon, dear Brother, on the morrow or the next or the one after, for I have brought Caldor—"

"And I Malgan," interposed Liaze, "and Borel finally found Hradian."

Camille looked from face to face along the length of the board, yet a somber silence fell, and none said aught until Alain finally spoke: "After this meal is done, let us to the lavender room, where I shall play, and Camille and I will sing, that is if my love agrees." He then looked at Camille at the foot of the table, and all eyes turned toward her. Somewhat flustered, she canted her head in mute assent.

"This is the way, dear," said Liaze. She placed Camille's hand slightly higher up on the bow. "Yes. Now these three fingers go here, one above the nock of the arrow, two below. Good. Now then . . ."

They stood on the lawn in the afternoon light, a shock of hay some twenty paces away, a broad target of concentric rings fixed thereon.

"Well and good, Camille. Now draw the arrow . . . all the way . . . yes, now inhale full and exhale half, then aim . . . and loose."

Thnn!

The arrow missed target, haycock, and all, and flew past some twenty or thirty paces to skid through the sward. As Jules raced across the grass to fetch the shaft, Camille burst into giggles. "I think I'll never master this, Liaze. I seem to be all—"

Whoom!

"What was that?" Camille turned about, seeking the source of the noise. Beyond the mansion, a violet cloud rose into the air.

Liaze frowned. "One of the mages—Caldor I believe."

In that moment the Bear came dashing 'round the corner of the manor house and running toward the hedge maze. "Oh, my," cried Camille, casting aside the bow and lifting her skirts and starting out after. "They've frightened my Bear."

Later that day and after soothing the Bear, Camille saw gentle Celeste at a distance with Caldor, and they seemed to be arguing. Caldor made a violent gesture of negation, and, haughtily, he strode off. A time after, she saw Caldor and two attendants riding up the slopes and away from Summerwood Manor. What Celeste and the mage might have quarreled about, Camille could not say, for they had been too remote for her to catch their words, and Celeste did not enlighten her, though at dinner that eve . . .

"He failed, Alain. That's all." Celeste sighed. "Mayhap he is not as powerful as we've been led to believe."

"I think it was he who scared my Bear," added Camille. "And if so, then I, for one, am glad to see him go."

"I was hoping he would succeed," said Alain, softly.

Liaze growled. "So was I, dear Brother. So were we all."

Again a pall fell across dinner. But finally Borel said, "I hear you play échecs, Camille. If so, then I challenge you to a game."

" 'Ware, my Sister," said Celeste. "Borel is the best of us."

"Then I shall just have to be on my guard," said Camille, grinning. *Oh, my, she called me her 'sister.'*

"You were right, Alain," said Borel, as he turned his king on its side. "She is quite good at this." Then he looked at Camille. "I thought to win by dash and bold, but you outbolded me."

Camille turned up a hand. "Playing with Alain has sharpened my skills, for he has taught me much."

"I shouldn't wonder," quipped Liaze, casting a jaunty eye at Alain.

At Camille's blush, Liaze broke into quite infectious laughter, and all joined in but Camille, though she did grin.

That evening in bed, Alain said, "Pay them no heed, my love, for they do mean no harm."

"I know, Alain. Yet I seem to be the one who puts my foot in my mouth."

"Just one of the things I adore about you, for innocence becomes you, my dear."

"Innocent? Me? Come here, love, and we'll just see who is the innocent."

The next eve, it was Seer Malgan who rode away, his shoulders slumped in defeat, his retainers in his wake.

As Camille watched him go, she whispered to herself, "Well, whatever it is he tried, dear Bear, wherever you are, at least he didn't frighten you."

"Wands, cups, pentacles, swords, and trumps," said Celeste. "We shuffle and deal a card to each person about the table, and continue to deal the cards until they are all dealt out. Then we each look only at our own cards and estimate how many tricks we can capture— "

"Tricks?" asked Camille.

"How many other cards we can capture," interjected Liaze.

"How does one go about capturing cards?" asked Camille.

"Each person 'round the table in turn plays a card, until all have played one, and the highest card wins that trick, wins all those cards just played, that is."

"I see," said Camille.

"Now here is the best part," said Celeste. "The highest bidder has a secret partner, one she may not know about, but a partner nonetheless."

"How so?"

"The highest bidder names a king—the king of cups, or the king of swords, or of wands, or pentacles—and whoever has that king is the secret partner, none else knowing who might be the secret partner, not even the high bidder, until that particular king is played."

"But what if the high bidder has all four kings?"

"Then he or she simply names one of the kings and plays alone."

They sat in the game room, the five of them, at the taroc table, as Celeste explained the game to Camille. The others chimed in with advice at odd moments, all but Alain, who, behind his scarlet mask, seemed morosely quiet this eve. Still, Camille managed to concentrate on what Celeste was saying, for she hoped that the game would break Alain's glum demeanor.

Finally, the dealing and bidding and play began, and slowly Alain did become somewhat more cheerful.

After many hands were played—Camille being the secret partner but once, and that with Liaze—Borel reached the winning tally and took the first game.

Again they played, and again Borel won, and then the third game as well, though Celeste was close on his heels.

"Argh!" said Alain, and he took up a particular trump and held it to face Borel. "I think you must have Dame Chance on your side, brother mine, for never have I seen the cards run so one-sided."

Borel feigned nonchalance. " 'Tis simply my due, dear fellow."

Liaze grinned and said, "Mayhap, dear Brother, you keep a card or two up those floppy lace cuffs of yours."

As the others laughed, Borel feigned outrage, and thumped his elbows onto the table, his wrists upright, and the pearl-grey lace flopped down all 'round to reveal nothing hidden therein.

Alain tossed Dame Chance onto the table. "Shall we have another go?"

As they gathered the cards for the next game, Camille took one up—the one called the Naïf—and considered it, then held it out for the others to see. "These trumps—the choices of names and their depictions—are quite strange, one might even say arcane."

Celeste smiled faintly. "Arcane indeed, Camille, for 'tis said that one can see the future through the use of these cards, though not clearly."

Camille raised an eyebrow. "How so?"

Celeste pursed her lips and shook her head. "I am not certain, yet I believe one lays out the cards in a special arrangement and interprets each fall of a card, for by its suit and rank, its orientation, where it stands in the array, and other such signs it is said the future can be divined."

"Sounds like a mage art," said Liaze.

"Or the trick of a mountebank," said Borel, then gestured at the card Camille held, "or the belief of a naïf."

Camille dropped the trump onto the pile and frowned. "If a simple spread of cards can portend what is to come, would that not mean all is predetermined, that all that has ever been and will ever be is already set in stone?"

Celeste held up a finger. "Mayhap the fall of the cards simply shows a possible future, one that is potential."

Alain said, "I am not at all certain that I would like to know the future, predetermined, potential, or no."

"Why not?" asked Liaze, puzzlement in her amber gaze.

Alain pushed forth a hand, palm out. "For then I would perhaps try to change the outcome and make things even worse."

"How so, Brother?" asked Borel.

"Well, if one knew what the future held, say, defeat or even victory, would he try less hard, or instead more so, depending on what he knew? And if he changed his conduct because of knowing, and thereby changed the outcome, would he not thwart Destiny, and thus perhaps upset the balance of all?" Alain fell silent and looked 'round the table at pondering faces. Then he reached out and laid his hand atop Camille's and grinned, saying, "Besides, instead of knowing the future, I'd much rather be surprised."

Camille felt her face flush, though she knew not why. As she reddened, Borel laughed, and Liaze tapped him on the wrist with her closed, yellow fan, though she, too, smiled. "Pay these crude men no heed, Sister mine. And you, Borel, shut up and deal."

After dinner that night, to teach Camille a new dance they had Lanval gather up enough men and women of the household to make it more complete. The dance was called the Rade; it had much hand-to-hand, two-by-two graceful skipping and prancing about the floor in paired columns, as if travelling ahorse side by side, the women in one line, the men in another, hands between palm to palm. But they halted now and again, as if stopping to rest or water or feed the horses, or to take a meal of their own, or perhaps merely to stretch their legs, or simply to stop for pleasure, and here they stepped about in small circles in groups of four, two men and two women in each group, with much circling and bowing and curtseying involved. And the hall was filled with music and gaiety, for not often did such entertainment come.

That night in bed, Alain simply held Camille closely. "There is one more attempt on the morrow," he whispered. "That of Hradian the witch."

He said no more, and Camille did not ask.

The next afternoon, Hradian rode away, her shoulders sagging down.

The following day, in early morn, so did Celeste and Liaze and Borel go, setting out for their respective demesnes: they embraced Camille and whispered their farewells and then rode forth, defeat in their postures also. Whatever they had come for, whatever they had hoped for, it had not occurred, for all had said good-bye to Alain the eve before, unshed tears glittering in their eyes.

With the Bear at her side, Camille stood on the portico and watched as they made their way up the slope and beyond. And when she could see them no longer, she sighed and briefly hugged the Bear, then turned and went within, and Lanval closed the door behind. The Bear stood a long while after, looking at the far hill where they had gone. Finally he, too, took in a deep breath and let it out, then turned and went away toward the maze.

14
Journey

Over the next several months as mortals would count the days, more masters of the arcane came—some wearing rune-scribed robes, others dressed in splendid finery, still others in nought but rags. Some were haughty, some were meek, some were placid or wistful, and yet others muttered unto themselves and peered about in suspicion, and some were atwitch and flinched away from things only they could see. And when they came, Camille would watch Alain's expectations rise, only to plummet again, and she knew that whatever was afoot, it had to do with the dilemma he faced—perhaps related to the masks he wore, perhaps to the disappearance of his sire and dam, perhaps something else altogether—but of which he would reveal nought. Whatever it was, it seemed to be a secret everyone knew but her.

And yet, though each of these wizards and seers and sorcerers and witches and warlocks and other such magi came bearing promise—be they haughty or meek or given to fits or other strange oddities—each went away slumped in defeat.

Alain would fall into a state of dejection as well, and Camille would fret about him, yet by no manner did she allow her concern to show, hoping instead her cheerful normalcy would break his glum mood.

And as for the Bear, he would disappear whenever these enchanters came—*Ever since that terrible person Caldor scared him, I think he doesn't trust folk of this ilk. No wonder he's not about.* The next day, though, he would show up again, as if he knew when they were gone.

It was a great enigma as to what the magi might be attempting, and ordinarily, given a riddle, a puzzle, or a mystery, Camille would be delving for an answer. Yet because of what Alain had said in the past, and because she trusted him without reservation, she deliberately did not seek resolution, but instead set it apart, such that most of the time she did not think of it at all.

And so the months passed and visitors came and went, and the affairs of the estate carried on:

Camille and the Bear continued to take lunch together at her favorite gazebo, she speaking of this and that. Camille also spent time with various members of the household staff, planting or sewing or occasionally overseeing other tasks; in general, though, Lanval kept things in order, including the sending of the annual stipend of gold to Camille's family, along with her spoken message of love, for none in her family could read or write, and so a letter was not sent. And Camille and Alain took pleasure together, or, now and again, attended to the solemn affairs of the Summerwood Principality, and in all that time Alain had to deal with but one quite serious case. . . .

"My lord, I have come before you to see justice done," said the woman, down on her knees in the candlelit chamber, the prince sitting on his throne on the dais above, with Camille seated at his side. "They slaughtered my man."

At these words Camille gasped, though Alain glanced at Lanval, who nodded.

"Murdered Fricor outright and for no reason at all, but that of the skin of a cat," added the woman, bitterly.

"Killers seldom slay without cause, Lady," said Alain, his grey eyes gone flinty within the black mask he wore, "and you have named the skin of a cat. Who did this thing?"

"They, them, those without," spat the woman, jabbing a thumb over her shoulder. "Those outside this hall."

Now Alain turned to Lanval. "The accused are here?"

"Yes, my prince," replied the steward. " 'Tis Lord Kelmot and his sons."

"Bring them forth."

Lanval tapped a small gong, and at its sound two liveried footmen swung wide the doors to the throne chamber, and Camille gasped again, for marching inward came three tiny beings, no taller than a foot or so. And they were accoutered in brown leather breeks and brown leather boots, straps of leather crisscrossing their bare chests. Brown was their hair and hanging down their backs, with a strip of leather across each brow to hold it out of their eyes. Quivers of arrows were strapped to their thighs, and bows were affixed across their backs, and each one carried a spear in hand. In spite of their diminutive stature, quite savage they looked, and their strides conveyed a feral fierceness.

The woman on her knees scuttled aside. "Protect me, my lord," she wailed.

Yet the three tiny beings marched straight to the foot of the dais and looked up at the prince, their eyes widening at the sight of the mask, but the one in the center glanced at Lanval and received a nod of assurance.

And now Camille could see that ritual tattoos of swirls and lines adorned their arms and chests and faces; what they meant, she could not say, yet it added to their savage aspect.

"You slew her man?" asked Alain.

"Aye, my lord," replied the one in the center, his hand tapping the arrows at his hip.

"I told you," screeched the woman, then flinched as all three tiny beings glowered at her. "See, even now they would slay me, too, and I haven't done—"

A raised finger from Alain silenced the dame. "Lord Kelmot," said Alain, addressing the one who had spoken, "you slew him because . . .?"

"Because, Prince Alain, he slaughtered three of our lynx: at the first one, we said to him that he might have made a mistake. At the second one, we told him 'No more.' At the third one, we killed him."

"See, I told you!" wailed the woman. "All for the skin of a cat, all for—"

Again the prince silenced her with a raised finger. "My lady, the lynx is protected within the Summerwood. In fact, in all the Forests of the Seasons. Your husband Fricor, if I recall, was a poacher brought before me apast." Alain glanced at Lanval, who nodded. The prince turned back to the woman. "I told him at that time to forgo such ways, and it seems he did not heed. I deem justice here has been done by the Lynx Riders."

"Oh, but what'll I do?" moaned the woman. "Why should *I* have to go without for the disobedience of my man?"

Kelmot turned toward the dame. "You are the one who skinned the cats and scraped and cured the hides."

"And *cooked* and *ate* the meat," spat another of the tiny folk.

"And these were lynx!" exclaimed the third, then hissed and raised a clawed hand at the woman, who scuttled farther away.

"Ah, Madam," said Alain, "so then you are not completely innocent in this."

"Would you have me starve?" wailed the dame.

"None starve in the Summerwood," declared Lord Kelmot, "not with the bounty of the Autumnwood at hand."

Now Alain turned to Camille. "My lady, what punishment would you advise I should decree against this dame?"

Camille but barely contained her dismay at being asked to judge the woman, down on her knees and wringing her hands and moaning. Furiously, Camille thought, and then she said, "My Lord Prince Alain, I would have you give her a gold piece"—protests rose to the lips of the Lynx Riders, but Camille spoke on—"and banish her from all the Forests of the Seasons."

"No!" wailed the dame. "I would then have to work for my food and—"

"Silence, woman," said Alain. He gestured toward Camille. "So she has said; so shall it be. You are banished forever from the Forests of the Seasons. You may take with you only those things which you can carry." He then looked at tiny Kelmot. "My lord, would you and yours see that she is gone from these borders within a twelveday?"

"Gladly, my lord," replied Kelmot, then he glanced at Camille and smiled, revealing a mouthful of catlike teeth. "A most fair judgement, my lady."

And thus was justice done.

"Love," said Camille down the length of the table, "altogether a year and some months have passed since the Bear brought me here, and yet it seems but yester, for these have been the happiest days of my life."

"A year and some months? I didn't know, and I am quite happy, too."

Camille smiled, but silently added, *Save for the cloud which hangs over thee.*

"Speaking of the months that have passed, have you ever wondered about time?" asked Alain.

"Time, my lord?"

" 'Tis a great mystery to dwellers of Faery, for here it holds no sway."

"How so, my lord, for do not events occur, things grow, days pass in Faery? And if so, then what is that but a measure of time?"

Alain laughed. "Ah, Camille, you are too clever by far, yet this is what I mean: indeed things do grow and days pass, but nought in Faery becomes overly aged, with the attendant infirmities that does bring. People do not wither and die of time's rade, do not pass away into the dust of the years. All things in Faery simply are."

Camille frowned. "But Alain, people do grow old in Faery. Look at Andre; he is a man of age."

"Ah, but that is because he spent overlong in a place outside Faery, out in a mortal land where time does rule, and his age caught up to his years."

"Oh," replied Camille. "But what of those such as Jules? He is but a lad. Will he not age in Faery, not grow into his manhood?"

"Ah, there is the mystery of it, Camille. Jules will indeed age—though at a slower rate than in the mortal lands—up until he reaches his prime, and then he will not go beyond."

"All part of the magic of Faery?"

Alain nodded. "Indeed."

Camille paused and laid down her fork beside her plate. "Which reminds me, Alain: is the harvest eternal in the Autumnwood? If so, then how can that be? When grain is reaped, when crops are picked, what happens then? I mean, without winter to rest, spring to renew and seeds to be sown, and summer to ripen, how can autumn bring forth a harvest?"

" 'Tis another mystery, that, my love," replied Alain. "I think Borel's winter demesne does somehow allow *all* the Forests of the Seasons to rest, and that Celeste's Springwood somehow permits the renewal of all, as well as the sowing of—what?—not seeds, but rather *crop*. Too, my Summerwood somehow allows the ripening of the bounty that is to come, while Liaze's demesne takes from them all and provides an eternal harvest. Things plucked or reaped in the Autumnwood—or in the other Forests of the Seasons as well—simply seem to . . . reappear. —Oh, not instantly, but after some while, and not as long as anyone is watching; but one day it will be there, as if it had been there all along, somehow overlooked or unseen. Beyond that, I cannot say aught, for 'tis of Faery in the Forests of the Seasons we speak; I add, however, that elsewhere in Faery, across its far-flung realms, other conditions apply, some of them quite uncanny."

"My, but these are strange rules which govern this part of Faery and the life herein," said Camille, taking up her fork and spearing more of the delicious asparagus.

Alain said, "You speak of rules, my darling, as if there were many, but I know of only two."

"Two?"

Alain nodded and stood and walked to her end of the table. He leaned down and peered at her with his grey eyes through his grey silken mask, then he kissed her, and said, "The first rule of life is to live, Camille, but the prime rule of life is to love."

She reached up and pulled him down for another kiss, this one decidedly more lingering.

Alain then strode back to his end of the table and sat, and Camille said, "The reason I spoke of the year and some months that have passed, beloved, is that I would like to visit my family and see how they have fared, especially Giles. I think I would need but a sevenday at Papa's cottage, seven days to catch up in all."

Alain took up his goblet of dark ruby wine and sipped. He set the glass down and said, "I will arrange for it to be done."

"Would you not come with me?"

"My love, the Bear will be your escort, though I will send couriers ahead and have Borel and his Wolves accompany you through the Winterwood so that what happened there shall not occur again."

Camille hid her disappointment that he would not be with her and said, "Very well, my lord."

A handful of days later, after a night of passion and a tender and tearful adieu just ere dawn, in midmorn Camille set forth with the Bear from Summerwood Manor, she riding once more, he again laden with bundles, a cottage just beyond the far edge of Faery their goal.

As they came to the oakwood lane, Camille turned and waved au revoir to those who had gathered on the portico to see her off—Blanche, Lanval, Jules, Andre, Renaud, the seamstresses, and others of the household staff—all of whom Camille had come to love dearly. "I shall return in a moon or so!" she called, though whether they could make out her words, she did not know. And she faced front once again, tears streaming down her cheeks.

*   *   *

Across the Summerwood they went, as the sun traced an arc through the sky, and late in the day they came to the pool where the Waterfolk-otters had played, but they seemed wholly absent this eve, for none whatsoever were in sight. Even so, remembering, Camille did not shed her clothes to swim or bathe. At this place, as well, a camp awaited them, pheasant on the spit above the fire. Once more she and the Bear shared a pleasant repast, and then the bear waddled up to the dewberry briars on the hillside above and again sat among them and feasted.

The following day just after sundown, they came to the twilight border where the Summerwood ended and the Autumnwood began. Here another firelit camp awaited, with another meal on the spit above: several trout, altogether enough for Camille, though the Bear afterward rooted about 'neath fallen logs for whatever under there it was he ate.

The next morn they entered the Autumnwood, where the Bear's fur became grizzled reddish brown, and they passed back along the way they had come months agone, and they took sustenance from the plentiful harvest. As evening fell, no campsite awaited, for, in this realm, game acook above a fire was not needed, or so did Camille reason.

On the second day in the Autumnwood, as the Bear topped a hill, on another knoll in the near distance stood a white Unicorn. "Oh, Bear, look there's a Uni—"

With a toss of its tail, the Unicorn snorted and spun and trotted away, disappearing down the far side of the knoll. Tears welled in Camille's eyes, for now she truly knew what Fra Galanni had meant about being unsullied, and what Agnès meant about being pure; no longer having her virgin's blood, Camille was dismayed by the Unicorn's rejection, and it seemed somehow unfair.

On this day as well, at the top of a vale above a field of grain, they again had passed the huge man sitting with his back to a tree, a scythe across his knees; and, as before, he had gotten to his feet and bowed low as the Bear and Camille had passed.

In midafternoon of the third day within that demesne, they once again reached a twilit border, this one leading into the Winterwood.

The Bear stopped at the bound, and he whuffed when Camille asked if they would make camp at this place. She spent the dregs of the day finding a suitable stream to fill the waterskins she had insisted on bringing, for, as she had told the Bear, she would not abide again the brimstone-foul water of the ice-clad pools within the realm to come.

The next dawning Camille awakened to the cold nose of an animal nudging her cheek. "Bear!" she shrieked as she bolted upright, only to find a Wolf shying back. Laughter rang across the daybreak, for Borel and his pack had come. Yet chuckling, Borel said, "Best put on your cold-weather gear, Sister mine, for where we go 'tis quite chill."

Into the Winterwood they fared, into that tangle of twisted and broken trees, the skies above dismal, the light dim, ice and snow and shattered rock and crags looming alongside. The Wolves ranged fore and aft and on the flanks as well. Occasionally the Bear, his fur now white, paused and sniffed the air and grunted, but what he may have scented, if aught, Camille did not know. Even so, with a Bear and a Wolf pack and Borel—he armed with a long-knife strapped to his thigh and his bow in hand, arrows in a quiver at his hip—Camille felt quite safe.

"Still," she asked, "why do we come this way?"

"It is the most direct," replied Borel.

"And you say that other places in the Winterwood are quite beautiful?"

"Aye, Camille. Only in this region is the land cursed."

"Cursed?"

"Indeed. Cursed long past, but by whom, I know not. 'Twas all part of some enmity against my sire, I deem, mayhap by those responsible for his and my dam's disappearance."

"Oh," said Camille, as onward they went, the dim day growing old.

Just ere sundown they stopped to camp, and Borel set his Wolves on guard, then made a fire. Camille discovered that the water in her waterskins had frozen solid through, all but the one she had been using, and that nearly empty. But in a pan from one of the bundles Borel melted snow, and the water, although not sweet, was not brimstone-tinged either.

Beyond the stark mountains the sun fell, and night came over the icy realm. Something, some glimmer, plucked at the edges of Camille's mind, yet she couldn't quite capture the elusive thought, and it slid away unsnared.

She sat awhile talking to Borel, and ghostly tendrils of a spectral ice-fog coiled in among the broken trees to encircle the campsite . . . the icy wisps barely held at bay by the fire.

Of a sudden there came a thin wail, and Camille looked about, trying to locate the source. And then—

"What's that?" she cried, leaping to her feet and pointing.

Rising up from the snow-laden ground came creeping a nearly transparent hand, claw-fingered and grasping, followed by an equally lucent arm.

Borel snatched his bronze long-knife out from its scabbard and slashed through the emerging limb, but the knife slid right through with no effect whatsoever, and still upward came whatever it was, the transparent top of a head now showing, wearing a cap faintly tinged with red. And then its face broke through and a terrible cry wailed forth from its snag-toothed mouth.

"Oh, sweet Mithras!" cried Camille. " 'Tis a Goblin come out of the ground!"

The Bear roared and clawed at the being, with absolutely no consequence as it continued to emerge. Dodging the Bear's slashing swipes, Wolves, too, darted in and back, fangs gnashing through with no result.

"Borel, another!" cried Camille.

And behind them a second transparent Goblin came forth from the frozen soil. And another and another and another, all oozing up, all unkillable, all wailing, all—

"Mithras, oh Mithras," cried Camille, now knowing what had eluded her mind, "we've camped on the killing ground of months past; these are Redcap ghosts!"

Borel snatched up a burning branch from the fire and lashed it through the spectres crowding 'round, yet it, too, had no effect.

In spite of the fire, the long-knife, the roaring, clawing Bear, and the leaping, slashing Wolves, still the wailing wraiths crowded closer, for nought seemed to affect them at all.

And a wave of weakness whelmed over Camille, and she staggered back against a twisted tree, clutching it merely to remain upright; it was all she could do to not faint. And still the ghosts ghoulishly crowded 'round her, and she felt as if her very life was being sucked away on the shrill and ghastly keening. "We've got to flee," she called out, her voice feeble, but her legs would not obey. "Flee," she repeated, now mumbling.

But then a bitch Wolf stopped her leaping and slashing, and she looked at the spectres and cocked her head this way and that and listened to their ghostly wails; and then she raised her muzzle into the air and began to sing, her mournful howl cutting across the frigid night. And the nearest wraiths flinched away. Another Wolf began to sing, his voice joining hers. Ghosts reeled back. A third Wolf took up the refrain, and one more and another, and soon all nine Wolves, the entire pack, were singing in the night. And the spectres mewled in agony and clutched at their heads, slapping their hands over their ears, their own ghastly wails dwindling, dwindling; and even as Camille lost her grip on the tree and swayed and fell to her knees in the snow and then collapsed onto her side, ghosts about her began sinking back into the frozen earth, unable to withstand the mournful dirge of the Wolves driving them down and away. The last thing she saw was the Bear standing over her as blackness took her mind.

Camille became aware of a gentle jouncing, and she came to on a travois being drawn by the Bear. At her side walked Borel, his face haggard and wan. Dismal daylight seeped down from the gray sky above.

She tried to raise up but fell back, and feebly whispered. "Where, what—?"

"Be still, Camille. They nearly did you in," replied Borel.

"But how?"

"They say ghosts steal life from the living, as if trying to recapture their own, and they were primarily clustered about you."

"What of you, the Bear, the Wolves?"

Borel managed a weak smile. "Oh, I was leeched, yet not as were you, for even though my long-knife did them no harm, I ween 'twas their memories of blades apast kept most away from me."

"And the Bear, the Wolves? Did the wraiths steal the force of their lives?"

"Nay, Camille. It seems ghosts prefer pure Humans."

Camille's eyes closed and she whispered, "But I am not pure."

"What, Camille?"

Her voice was now faint, fading. "Ask the Unicorn."

When Camille next came to, she was lying on a bed of evergreen branches. At hand a warm campfire burned, and a brace of rabbits cooked above the flames. Dizzily, she sat up and looked about. The Bear, now black, sat nearby, as well as Borel and the Wolves, some of the latter alert and warding, others quite sound asleep. New green leaves swayed in a slight breeze above, and water ran down the slope and toward the valley below. While upslope and to the rear a wall of twilight loomed.

It was early morn, for the sun was just edging up over the horizon, and they were in the Springwood.

"How are you feeling?" asked Borel.

"Thirsty," said Camille, struggling to her feet. "And I need to relieve myself."

She tottered into the woods, and awhile later came out, and Borel had a waterskin and a cup waiting.

As she drank, the Bear came over and snuffled at her, and she gave him a hug. That seemed to satisfy him, and he padded to the opposite side of the fire and, grunting, lay down.

After quenching her thirst, she asked, "How long was I unaware?"

"But for a brief moment yester, a night and a day and another night all told," replied Borel. He looked back at the Winterwood behind. "I should have known that the curse on that sector would be more than just blighted woodland."

Camille also looked back at the cold and twisted and shattered forest darkly seen beyond the tenebrous marge. "This curse, can it not be lifted, the region returned to normal?"

Borel shook his head. "We have tried, just as we tried at—" Abruptly he fell silent.

"Just as those mages and witches and warlocks and other such tried whatever they tried at Summerwood Manor?" softly asked Camille.

Borel glanced across the fire and nodded. He then drew a deep breath and said, "Time to eat coney."

As they took the rabbits from the spit, Camille heard a heavy breathing, and when she looked—"Oh, goodness, my Bear is asleep."

" 'Tis no wonder," said Borel. "He dragged you here without stopping."

"Did you stop?"

Borel shook his head and bit into a coney leg. Around the mouthful, he said, "I did sleep last night though, when we reached this camp." He chewed a moment, and then glanced back at the path through the Winterwood. "I've a good mind to get me a sword of iron and lay those wraiths to rest once and for all."

Camille paused in her eating. "But Renaud the smith said that iron was not permitted in Faery. Is it not banned?"

"Not quite," replied Borel. "A few who sail the seas carry weapons of iron, of steel. It protects them from some of the monsters of the deep. They seldom bring it onshore however, and then but in direst need."

"What of a magic sword, Borel, an enchanted blade? I've heard tales of such weapons as being within the realms of Faery. Would one of those not lay these ghosts by?"

"Oh, Sister mine, enchanted blades are quite rare, and perhaps worth more than the wealth of all of the Forests of the Seasons combined. But you are correct, an enchanted blade would do the deed."

"*Rrhmm!*" suddenly chuffed the Bear and raised up his head and glared about, then settled back down to sleep.

Camille set a finger to her lips, and they ate the rest of the meal in silence.

They did not move on that day, but spent the whole of it resting, recovering, regaining vitality—through the full of the night as well.

The next dawning, Camille awakened quite refreshed, much of the effects of the spectres allayed. During a breakfast of biscuits and tea, she conferred with Borel, and they decided that she and the Bear would go onward, while he and his Wolves would return to the Winterwood. "But I and my pack will be here a twelveday hence and await your return, Camille, to escort you along the cursed way, and this time we'll not stop to rest in a place where phantoms lie."

As Wolves yipped and yammered and postured and circled and nipped and fawned, gathering for the return, Camille embraced Borel, then climbed upon the Bear, and down the long slope and into the sheer-walled valley she rode. She turned to wave adieu, but Borel and his pack were gone.

Down into the wide, deep gorge went the Bear and Camille, and far to either side rose vertical walls of granite, though here and there in niches and nooks high upon the steeps did trees manage to cling, their vibrant spring greens in sharp contrast to the pale grey of the stone. Far ahead and to the right, many separate waterfalls cascaded over the brim and down, thundering into streams below, which wended across the gorge, the runs to combine and combine again into larger flows, all to join together at last and course into a rift at the base of the rock wall on the far side. And all about Camille and the Bear, new branches and old held vivid green leaves, and spring blossoms bloomed amid the fresh grass growing across the leas.

In late afternoon they came alongside the pool at the base of the high cascade plummeting down the sheer wall at the far end of the vale, there where the switchback path led up the stone and out. As they started up the narrow way, Camille laughed in joy, for Waterfolk, nearly transparent, cavorted in the churn below, male and female alike, and they chased one another as if playing tag, and they raced and grabbed hold of ankles and wrists and waists, some nipping, some giggling, others kissing, while yet others paired off and engaged in—*Oh, my!*—Camille blushed and looked away, as on up the path the Bear did go.

Two days later, as the tide of dusk drew over the land, they came to the final twilight bound; the Bear padded on through and into a warm summer's eve within the mortal world beyond. And Camille gasped, for where her Papa's cottage once sat now stood a brightly lit mansion, with many carriages drawn up beyond; and lively music drifted across the field to fill the air with song.

15

Homecoming

The Bear, now a rich brown, growled and stopped. Camille slid from his back and looked across the field at the brightly lit mansion and the carriages and teams in harness. "Oh, Bear, it is not at all what we expected, is it?" Camille frowned. "I wonder who lives there and where my family has gone." She took a deep breath and let it out, and said, "Well, we'll not learn a thing simply by standing here. Let us go and see."

As Camille stepped away, "*Rrhmm,*" rumbled the Bear, and he did not move.

"What is it, Bear?"

The Bear raised its nose into the air and snuffled.

"Is it the horses? Or, instead, the men?"

The Bear gave a soft *whuff*.

"Ah, well, as for the horses, I know you do not wish to frighten them. And as for the men, I don't blame you, for, knowing the ways of mortals, they might take it in their heads to go hunting after you, my Bear, yes?"

"*Urrmm.*"

Camille frowned, for she did not know how to interpret that answer, one which might mean *No*, though in this case it might also mean something else altogether, such as *Let them try.*

"Never you mind, Bear, I'll go on from here, and see who lives there, then press on to wherever Papa and Maman have moved." Camille donned her cloak and tied a modest drawstring purse to her belt, a few coins therein—some gold, some silver, some bronze. She loosened a pair of bundles from the rig.

She hugged the Bear about the neck, and said, "In a sevenday, I'll meet you at this very place and you can carry me back to my beloved prince. You will remember, eh?"

"*Whuff.*"

She gave the Bear another hug, then shouldered her bundles and set out across the field, and the Bear watched her go.

Toward the mansion she went, and tall weeds and grasses swished 'round her boots and leather pants, thistles and burrs and bristly leaves clung to her cloak, and dust and weed pollen rose up 'round her in clouds. *Oh, my, but the land lies fallow, overgrown; Papa would be so disappointed at the new owners.*

On she strode through the oncoming nightfall, the music getting louder, and now she could hear voices and laughter, and she could see the window sashes were raised wide to let in the summer breeze, while yellow lantern- and candlelight streamed outward. When she reached the manse, she turned and looked for the Bear, but she saw him not in the gathering darkness. *Gone into Faery, I suspect.*

Faced with waiting rows of coachmen, she paused long enough to cast her hood over her head, then took up her bundles and rounded the end of the mansion. Past idle drivers and horses and carriages she went, some of the conveyances quite elegant, a few of these with footmen as well. On toward the portico she strode, and as she came to the front landing, "Ho, lad," called out one of the drivers. "If they toss you a bone, save a knuckle for me." Others laughed at his jest, but Camille paid no heed and stepped onto the porch, where the door stood open as well.

"Here now, boy, and just where do you think you're going?" demanded the doorman, stepping into her path. "Off with you, and be quick about it. We want no beggars, no bindlestiffs here."

"But sieur, I would ask: who dwells herein?"

The doorman puffed up his chest and raised his chin; clearly he was pleased at being called sieur by this ignorant boy. He brushed the gloved fingers of his right hand down across the brass buttons of his uniform and, above the sound of music and laughter and gaiety drifting through the open windows and door, he said, "Not that it's any of your business, mind, but Lord Henri and Lady Aigrette rule here. Now begone, lad." But then he gave a wink and added, "Though y' might slip around th' back and ask Cook for a bite. Dust yourself off afore then, and don't let the old lady catch y', eh?"

Even as Camille's eyes widened in surprise that her mère and père owned this fine mansion, "With whom are you speaking, Claude?" came a haughty voice, and a tall and quite bald, black-clad majordomo stepped into view and looked down at Camille and sniffed in disdain.

"Just this beggar-lad, sieur. I told him to be off."

The majordomo pulled a handkerchief from his sleeve and flicked it at Camille. "You heard him, boy. Begone, and swiftly, else I'll set the dogs on you."

Even as she opened her mouth to reply, "Camille!" came a glad cry, and Giles rushed out and threw his arms about her, and she dropped her bundles and clutched him tightly.

"What are you doing, Master Giles?" demanded the major-domo, horror in his voice. " 'Tis a beggar-boy! A vagabond! You know not what *diseases*, what *vermin* he might carry." And he reached out to pull Giles away.

"Oh, Pons, this is no beggar-boy," cried Giles in glee, casting off the majordomo's hand, "this is my sister!"

Yelling "Papa! Maman! Camille is here!" the eleven-year-old grabbed Camille by a wrist and dragged her inward past the astonished doorman and the dumbfounded majordomo.

"My bundles!" cried Camille, her cloak hood falling away, her golden hair spilling out.

Quickly recovering, "I'll bring them, ma'amselle," said the doorman, snatching up the goods and starting after. But at a gesture from haughty Pons, the doorman paused, then servilely followed the majordomo into the manse, trailing far behind the excited lad and Camille.

Down a hallway went Giles, calling, "Papa! Maman! Camille, Camille has come!" They came to a doorway on the right, leading to a small sitting room. Therein Giles found his mother and several matronly ladies, all dressed in fine ball gowns.

"Maman, Camille has come," said Giles, pulling Camille in after.

Aigrette stood, her eyes flying wide in shock, and she rushed forward. Camille held out her arms for an embrace, but it was Aigrette who now grabbed her by the wrist and jerked her away from the door. With Giles trotting after, down the hall Aigrette dragged Camille, the mother angrily muttering, "What would everyone think of me, should anyone see you like this, all dusty and running with sweat, and is that field weeds and burrs and such I see clinging to your cloak? What were you thinking, Camille? Gave you no thought to me?"

She rushed Camille by an entry to a grand ballroom, and in the swift glimpse Camille caught as she flew past, she saw the chamber was filled with people in finery, stepping out a dance to the music played by musicians on a modest platform beyond. On down a hallway and up a back stair Aigrette scurried, Camille in tow. "We've got to get you out of those horrible clothes and scrub that grime from you. No fille of mine is going to come into this house looking like a scruffy beggar-boy."

"Maman, aren't you glad to see Camille?" asked Giles, still following

"Of course I'm glad to see her," snapped Aigrette, and suddenly her eyes widened in revelation, as if she had just then stumbled across a wonderful idea that only she knew. "Oh, yes, indeed, I am quite glad she has come at this very time." And Aigrette laughed to herself.

A few more steps down a hallway she went, then shoved Camille into the sitting room of a small suite. "Here, Camille, these are Joie's quarters, or Gai's, I am uncertain which."

"They're Gai's," said Giles.

Aigrette turned on Giles in exasperation. "You go and find one of the maids to help Camille, and be quick about it. And tell no one else, you hear?"

"Yes, Maman," said Giles, and turned and bolted away.

As the lad rushed out, Aigrette opened a door; it led to the adjoining suite. Growling, she slammed it shut and opened another; a bedchamber lay beyond. Stalking in, she gestured at an archway. "Yon is the wash chamber. Now get you out of those filthy clothes and scrub yourself down." She opened yet another door, and Camille could see it was a small dressing room, with gowns and such hanging, and shoes on shelves nearby. "And put on a gown suitable for the grand ball below." Aigrette gestured. "One of Gai's should fit, for you are of a size. And do something about that hair. I shall return anon." She rushed back out, nearly running into the doorman—"Out of my way, oaf!"—but standing to one side was the majordomo. "Oh, Pons," barked Aigrette, "come with me, for I have a very important task for you, and a most splendid task at that." Together they vanished down the hallway.

"Ma'amselle?" called the doorman, peering in. "Your bundles?"

Nearly in tears, Camille stepped into the sitting room and gestured at one of the chairs. The doorman set the goods on the seat, then touched the brim of his cap and quietly withdrew.

With the help of Milli, the maid that Giles had found, within a candlemark, Camille was dressed in a dark blue gown, with pale blue petticoats under, dark blue shoes on her feet. At her mother's insistence, underneath was a bustier to accentuate her cleavage. Her hair was artfully woven through with blue satin ribbons matching the blue of the gown. Though she had yielded to her mother's dictates in all else, Camille stubbornly refused to wear the gaudy, cut-glass tiara, saying that the ribbons were quite enough.

Hissing in fury, Aigrette slammed the diadem down on the dressing table. "You think of only yourself, Camille, but very well, stubborn child." Then she slipped the cord of the blue fan about Camille's wrist, a small fold of paper attached. "Now here is your dance card. Pons filled it out at my instructions. Treat your partners well, for they can do me, do us, much good. —Now let us be gone from here and to the ball."

As Camille glanced one last time in the mirror, "You are quite beautiful, my lady," said Milli. "The men, their eyes will look nowhere else, while the women's eyes will all fill with green."

"Merci, Milli; I am glad you—"

"Come, come, you look well enough, Camille," impatiently said Aigrette. "Let's have no more of this prattle; my guests are waiting."

Out the door and along a hallway they went, to come to a balcony at the head of an elegant, curving stair leading down into the grand ballroom. Aigrette snatched Camille's hand and kept her from going on. Waiting below was Pons, watching for them to appear, and at a signal from Aigrette, he rapped the marble floor with a long staff. The music stopped; the dancers paused; a stillness fell over all.

"My lords and ladies and honored guests," rang out the majordomo, "the Lady Aigrette presents her daughter, the Lady Camille, Princess of the Summerwood!"

Camille was thunderstruck, for she did not consider herself a princess of anything, much less the Summerwood. And a great intake of air swept throughout the room, as men and women looked up to see, standing high above, the beautiful golden-haired girl in the sapphire-blue gown.

Though Camille was bewildered, Aigrette was in her glory, as down the staircase she descended, arm in arm with Camille, Aigrette's chin held high in queenly dominance, the mother of a princess no less. Ah, yes, she was indeed glad that Camille had come to visit, as all dutiful daughters should.

As Milli had predicted, the eyes of all men were irresistibly drawn to Camille, and the eyes of all women narrowed and perhaps even filled with envy, and some did fill with despair, for Camille was stunningly beautiful, and it is doubtful that anyone whatsoever even noted that Aigrette was at this splendid creature's side.

And pressing forward through the crowd came Giles, hauling Papa Henri in tow, with Felise and Colette right behind, then the twins—Joie and Gai—and finally Lisette, the eldest of the sisters coming last of all.

As moths to a light, Camille was surrounded by young men, each one demanding a dance, and man after man offered her glass cups of punch and begged for a stroll in the garden out by the wishing well.

During a pause in the music, Camille leaned over and whispered behind her fan to Giles, "Wishing well?"

"Papa's old well out back," he murmured. "Maman had a stone wall put 'round, with a roof above and a winch and a bucket across, all to replace the old wooden trapdoor and the pail on a rope we used to cast down and flip over to draw water. And she had gardeners plant violets and such, and vines . . . all to hide the fact that it was once nothing more than a farmer's clay-walled cistern."

Camille looked at her mother, now surrounded by a group of older women, all of whom Camille had been introduced to, none of whose names she remembered. Her mère preened among them, and even though she was standing quite still, it appeared as if she were strutting. And as Maman spoke, the older women cast glances toward Camille, and now and then one would break away to urgently talk to a young man or two, presumably a son or sons.

Playing two violins, a viola, a cello, a harpsichord, and a tambourine, the six musicians struck up again, and Camille's next partner came and fetched her, this one quite old and fat and short and leering; Lord Jaufre, he named himself, and, in spite of his obvious bulk, Camille could hear the creak of a corset as he bent to kiss her hand, managing to slobber all over her fingers. And all through the dance, he talked of his hounds while peering quite closely at her bosom.

And she danced the minuet, and then the quadrille, and then more dances after, all with different partners as listed on the dance card dictated by her mother—young men, old men, tall and short, stout and slender, all quite wealthy men, or sons of the very rich. And though she glided about the floor with these various partners, Camille could not think of aught but Alain, for he had taught her each of the dances, and she did miss him so.

And so she stepped and curtseyed and turned and paraded 'round the chamber and paced hand-to-hand with old roués or handsome rakes, or whirled about in a joyous fling with robust and laughing young men, but she would have given it all up, and gladly, just to be sitting quietly with Alain again at distant Summerwood Manor.

Midmorn of the next day, from one of the guest rooms where she had been quartered, Camille descended to find five of her siblings and Papa breaking fast at a long, walnut-wood table. She served herself buffet-style from a sideboard, selecting from scrambled eggs, rashers, hot biscuits and butter and jellies and jams, and tea.

She took a seat beside Giles and said, "You are looking quite fit, Little Frère, less given to searching for air."

Giles nodded. "I still have a bit of trouble breathing at times, though mostly not."

"The doctor claims his former ill health had something to do with thatch," said Papa Henri, "especially thatch that has gone to mold, though what mold or even thatch has to do with aught, I cannot say."

"Maman says the doctor is a fool," said Lisette, "and that it had more to do with dampness and wind whistling through chinks than with any dark mold."

Giles made a face and shuddered. "Even so, I still have to take that awful medicine."

"Well if you ask me," said Colette, "I think it was all due to ill vapors, and somehow they've gone away."

"Regardless," said Papa, "be it mold, thatch, wind, damp, or ill vapors, clearly Giles is much better, and whether it is due to our new home or the medicine, who can say?"

Camille leaned over and embraced Giles. "Papa is right, and I am so glad for you."

They ate in silence for a moment, Camille looking about, and then she turned to her father at the head of the table and asked, "Papa, this mansion is quite splendid. Who built it?"

"Hundreds of workmen from Rulon," said Henri, "and in but nine months or so."

"Maman drove them mercilessly," said Colette.

"Had she a whip, she would have lashed them," said Joie, Gai at her side nodding, the twins in total agreement.

"They were lazy," said Lisette, glaring about at the others as if in challenge.

"Lazy?" exclaimed Giles, taking up the cast gauntlet from across the table. He gestured about. "Papa says they did the impossible, completing this mansion in but the time they did."

"Only because of Maman," retorted Lisette.

"Only because of Maman for what?" demanded Aigrette as she swept into the room.

" 'Tis only because of your efforts, Maman," said Lisette, "that the mansion was started and finished when it was."

"Indeed," Maman replied as she took her place at the foot of the table. "Had I not kept after those idlers, we would still be living in your père's hovel." She rang the small handbell.

Giles leaned over to Camille and said, "They tore it down, you know—Papa's old place."

"Good riddance," snapped Maman Aigrette, though at the opposite end of the board a look of sadness touched Papa's eyes.

An attendant came into the room, and under Aigrette's sharp instructions, he readied and served her a plate, though he did have to return to the sideboard several times to get the best of the scrambled eggs, the portions quite small, and then the correct jellies in small dabs as well, for the waists of Maman's gowns were quite tight, and she would have them so. When at last she dismissed the servant with a haughty wave, he left in obvious relief.

"Where is Felise?" asked Camille, glancing toward the door.

"Probably yet abed and enjoying Allard's attentions," replied Colette, wistfully.

"Allard?"

"Her husband."

"Felise is married?"

"Indeed," said Maman, raising her chin and peering down her nose at Camille. "And she married quite well, I might add."

"Oh, but not as well as you, Camille," said Colette, "you being wedded to a prince and all."

Lisette muttered something under her breath, and Giles said across to her, "Fear not, dear Sister, for you might on a day snag some unwitting soul."

Colette and the twins burst into laughter at the lad's gibe, with Giles grinning in the face of Lisette's glower. Camille hid her own smile behind her napkin.

Even though he kept a straight face, Papa said, "Now, now mes filles et fils, let us have no—"

"Giles!" snapped Maman. "You will treat your sisters with respect."

"But, Maman—" began Giles, only to chop to silence as Aigrette glared at him.

Even as Lisette's scowl at Giles turned into a smirk, "What's all the laughing about?" said Felise, coming into the room, an anticipatory grin 'neath the freckles on her face, her complexion a bit flushed and glowing, as if she had just been engaged in some strenuous activity.

Giles laughed. "I said to Lisette, that—"

"*Giles!*" snapped Lisette and Maman together, and the lad fell silent, while the twins and Colette stifled giggles.

"Good!" said Camille, setting a small bundle to the table. "Everyone's here, and I have gifts for all."

As Felise filled a plate and took a seat, Camille unwrapped the bundle. "Here, Papa, here, Giles, these are for you." She passed a small case to each, and inside each was a folding knife and a hone. As they reverently took out the knives, Camille said, "Renaud tells me these are fine blades, made of the very best bronze. And the handles are mother-of-pearl from the tropical seas of Faery. Too, your birthstones are set in the pearl: a diamond for each of you, since you are both April-born."

"*Ooo,*" breathed Giles, as he unclasped the dark-metal blade. Then he looked up at Camille, his eyes glittering. "Are they magic? Enchanted?"

Camille smiled. "Perhaps you could say so, for the more skilled you become through practice, the better will your carvings be."

Giles beamed. "Oh, Camille, that's marvelous." But then his face fell. "—Hoy, now, wait a moment. That's no real enchantment at all, is it?"

Camille grinned and tousled his hair and said, "No, Giles,

but now you and Papa can whittle to your heart's content, and you won't have to trade a single knife back and forth." Giles brightened again and returned her grin.

"Merci, Fille," said Henri. "This will be used to make a fine échecs set."

"Just what I was thinking, Papa," replied Camille. Then she unwrapped six rings, some set with glittering gems, while others held semiprecious stones. Amid murmurs of appreciation as she passed them to the recipients, Camille said, "These are birthstone rings: tourmaline for Joie and Gai; for Felise, saphir; sardoine for Colette; rubis for Lisette; and for you, Maman, héliotrope, also known as bloodstone."

Even as the others tried on their rings and *oohed* and *ahhed*, Aigrette looked disdainfully at the bloodstone-set band and sniffed in dismissal and laid it aside and said, "I expected something finer from a princess, Camille. After all, with your wealth and position . . ."

Stricken, sudden tears brimming, Camille said, "Oh, Maman, can't you just merely be happy for once?"

Giles reached over and touched his hand to Camille's and whispered, "No matter what Maman says, dear Camille, these gifts are quite splendid."

Felise held up her beringed finger in the rays of light streaming through one of the windows, the blue sapphire glinting, "*Ooh*, it catches the sun and transforms it into a star. I shall have to show it to Allard, when he wakes up and comes down."

"Let us see what our rings will do," said Gai, glancing at her twin, and they turned the pale green tourmalines into the light.

"Oh look, now and again they glint blue," said Joie.

In the sunlight, Lisette's ruby burned with fire.

Colette's opaque sardonyx ring did not transform the light, though the stone was quite elegant and different from the others, its bands of brown and tan and white clearly beyond the ordinary. "Oh, my," she said, "how striking. Perhaps I'll pretend that it came from some mysterious suitor and make Luc jealous."

Maman, unable to resist, pushed her red-and-green bloodstone across the table and into a sunbeam streaming onto the walnut wood, but her stone was opaque as well, and though the red flecks within the dark green stood out brilliantly, the stone itself did not break the light, and she huffed and returned to her rashers and eggs.

"Where did you get these, Camille?" asked Felise.

"From Alain," replied Camille. "When we decided that I would come for a visit, the prince asked me what birthdays each of you had and then selected the gifts specifically to match the months I named."

Aigrette's eyes widened, and she reached out and took up the bloodstone ring. "These are from the prince himself?"

"Yes, Maman."

"Well, then." Aigrette slipped the band onto her finger and held her hand up so that she could see it. Then she resumed eating.

Camille sighed heavily, but Giles said, "Maman, when you believed the gift was from Camille, you thought it quite insignificant; but a gift from the prince himself, well now, that was different. Yet, in between your assumption and the revelation of the truth, the ring itself did not miraculously transform. Tell me, Maman—"

"Don't talk to me like that!" snapped Aigrette.

Giles fell mute, but he turned to Camille and grinned.

A silence descended 'round the table, but finally Camille looked from sister to sister and asked, "So you have suitors?"

A babble broke out, all sisters talking at once:

"Luc and I are engaged, and—"

"I'm married, Camille, to Allard—"

"I believe that Javert is getting quite serious, though whether to me or Gai, I cannot—"

"Oh, Camille, you should have been here when the men first began to come to call. They would take us out to the wishing well and toss in coins and—"

"They still do," called Gai, her voice rising above the others. "Just last eve, Philippe tossed in a gold coin and wished for a kiss from me and—"

"—and she gave him much more than just a—" interjected Joie, suddenly breaking off and glancing at Aigrette, even as Gai jabbed an elbow into her twin's ribs. Amid quiet titters, conversation stilled.

Maman cleared her throat and said, "As to Phillipe, his prospects are quite dismal. Instead I suggest that one of you consider Lord Jaufre—"

"Maman!" cried Gai. "He's old and fat and always trying to slobber a kiss on me."

"And all he speaks of are his hounds," added Joie.

"And he pants and sweats," added Gai, "and whenever he gets a chance he presses against my bosom."

"Well," said Lisette, first glancing at her mother, then looking at the pair, "you let others kiss you, and, I suspect, caress you as well, perhaps even fondle."

"*Lisette!*" cried the twins.

"Maman," interjected Felise, "Lord Jaufre is an old roué. I wouldn't wish him off on even one of his dogs, much less a sister of mine."

Aigrette glared down the table. "I will not have you speaking this way of our houseguest; why, Jaufre could come down the stairs at any moment and overhear these slurs."

"He knocked on my door last night," said Colette, "and asked me if I was in bed. I didn't answer. I didn't let him in, either. After a while he went away."

"The old seducer," growled Felise.

Maman rapped a spoon against the table. "Now listen and listen to me well: by one of you marrying Lord Jaufre it will increase our fortune considerably." She gestured at Camille. "Besides, having another royal personage in the family will raise our status as well."

"*Maman!*" cried the twins and Colette. Camille shuddered in revulsion as she remembered her dance with Lord Jaufre, and she could not imagine anyone desiring him as a mate. Lisette also shuddered at the prospect of being wedded to that old roué, but she nodded in agreement with Aigrette.

But then Papa said, "Aigrette, it will not happen, not only because our filles will not have it so, but neither will Lord Jaufre. I think he is here to eat our food and drink our wine and seduce anyone he can, and nothing more."

Aigrette seethed in fury and through clenched teeth said, "Henri, be silent!"

None said aught for a while, but then Felise asked Camille, "What does Prince Alain look like?"

"Well, he's a head or so taller than me, and slender, yet quite well built, with black hair and grey eyes and full lips and gentle hands . . . he plays the harpsichord."

"Is he handsome?" asked Colette. "My Luc is quite beautiful."

"Beautiful?" said Joie. "I would not describe him that way."

"Well, I think it so," snapped Colette.

Papa smiled at Colette and said, "That's all that matters,

Letty. If you think him beautiful and let him know, it will fill his heart." Henri then glanced at Aigrette.

Aigrette huffed, and spread butter on a biscuit.

Colette smiled at her father, then turned again to Camille. "Is he handsome: your Prince Alain?"

"My Allard is quite handsome," said Felise. She smiled at Colette. "Do you remember how splendid he looked at the wedding?"

Gai clapped her hands and turned to her twin. "Oh, and what a grand wedding that was."

Joie nodded in agreement and said to Camille, "There were spring flowers and guests galore, and a heirophant came from Rulon to bless the union."

"It was quite lovely," admitted Lisette.

"Oh, Maman, when it is my turn, I do hope to have a wedding just as beautiful," said Colette.

"And, for me, a groom as handsome as Allard," added Joie.

For a moment silence fell, all but Camille remembering that day. But then Colette said, "I wish you had been here, Camille. Still, you did not answer my question: is Prince Alain handsome?"

Camille shrugged. "I don't know. I have never seen him without a mask."

"What?" cried several at once. *"A mask?"*

Aigrette dropped her knife aclatter to the table. "You mean you have never seen his face?"

"No, Maman."

"What prince would wear a mask? Why, he could be a robber, a thief, an outlaw, to always go masked like that."

"No, Maman. He is no outlaw, but truly *is* the Prince of the Summerwood."

Frowning, nevertheless Felise came to Camille's defense. "Maman, mayhap he is simply disfigured—a scar, a wen, a gape, the aftermath of pox, or some such."

"Perhaps a birthmark," added Papa.

"Ooo," said Giles, his eyes wide in speculation, and he peered 'round the table and whispered loudly, "What if there's nothing under the mask but just a bony, skeleton skull?"

Now the twins' eyes flew wide in alarm.

"No, Giles," replied Camille. "Not true, for every eve I see his lips and his eyes, and although I have never seen his visage, I have felt the contours of his face, the flesh of his cheeks and jaw, brow, nose, chin, and, of course, his gentle mouth. No, Giles, there is no"—Camille grinned and raised her hands in mock fear—"*ooo*, bony, skeleton skull under the mask."

"Oh," Giles said, his face falling in disappointment, underneath which hid a grin.

"This mask, does he never take it off?" asked Lisette.

Camille blushed. "He does not wear it in bed."

"And still you have not seen his face?"

"The room is quite dark, Lisette."

"How strange," said Henri. "Still, do you love him? And more importantly, does he love you?"

"Oh, yes, Papa. We are madly in love with one another."

Papa turned up his hands and shrugged and said, "L'amour est tout."

"Indeed, Papa, love is all," replied Camille.

Maman merely muttered under her breath, but what she said, none at the table did hear.

"What was your wedding like, Camille?" asked Felise, glancing at Lisette, whose eyes narrowed.

Nonplused, Camille remained silent.

"Come, come," demanded Maman.

"We have not yet had a wedding," Camille admitted.

Again Aigrette dropped her knife. "What? No wedding?"

"No, Maman. No wedding, though we are pledged to one another."

Aigrette glowered at Henri. "And he has taken you to his bed, this masked prince?"

Camille nodded mutely.

Lisette smiled a wicked smile and raised her chin as if in victory.

"And no banns have been posted, no king notified, no monk, no heirophant has solemnized aught?" asked Aigrette.

"No, Maman," Camille meekly replied.

"What would Fra Galanni say, Camille? Living as you are without proper sanction."

"I don't know, Maman."

"Aigrette," said Papa softly. "No banns were posted when you pledged to me, no messages sent, no heirophant sought, no formal wedding at all."

"*What?*" exclaimed several daughters simultaneously, turning to Maman.

"You and Papa were never properly wedded?" said Gai.

"We are all bastards," declared Giles, grinning.

"Be quiet, all of you," barked Maman, glaring in outrage at Papa. "What your père and I have or have not done is neither here nor there. It is what Camille has not done that is at the crux of the matter."

"How so?" now challenged Camille, regaining some of her spirit. "We are pledged, and Alain himself has vowed that as soon as he resolves a vexing problem, then we will wed."

"What is this problem?" asked Lisette, smugly grinning.

"I don't know, Lisette. Only that it is dire."

Lisette raised an eyebrow. "Indeed?"

"Indeed," replied Camille, her ire rising.

Lisette smacked a palm to the table. "Indeed, indeed. Here is a prince who wears a mask he never removes, and there has been no wedding ceremony, for what monk or heirophant would sanctify the wedding of a so-called innocent girl to a man who wears a mask? Why, it is as Maman has said: he may be a well-known pirate or thief or brigand or other kind of foul looter . . . after all, where does his wealth come from? Perhaps we ought to gather a warband and go after this pirate and haul him to prison."

Both Camille and Maman gasped in alarm, and Maman said, "Oh, no, Lisette, we cannot do such a thing."

"Why not, Maman? After all, there may be a reward on his head. Perhaps even dead or alive."

Even as Camille's face turned pale, Maman raised an admonishing finger. "No matter what the reward, be he a pirate or no, and no matter the source of his fortune, think on this, Lisette"—she turned to the others—"think on this, all of you: we would be much the poorer should his annual tithe of gold stop. Would you have us lose that ever-running stream of wealth?"

"Maman," said Giles, "you think only of riches, when you should treasure Camille instead."

Now Aigrette glowered at Giles. "But it *is* Camille I am thinking of, and—" Abruptly, she stopped, and a calculating look swept into her eyes. "Camille, you should remove his mask."

Camille shook her head, remembering what Alain said when she merely ran a finger across his features. "Maman, he said he could not show me his face."

"Ah, but did he ever say you could not see it?"

Camille cast her mind back to that very first evening in the lanternlight on the bridge:

"Lady Camille, for reasons I cannot explain, I must wear this mask, such that I can never show you my face."

"No, Maman. Only that he could not show me his face."

"Well," crowed Maman, leaping up from her chair and stepping to the mantel and pulling the stub of a fat candle from its holder and picking up a small box of matches as well. "Here, Camille, take this candle with these matches, and when he's asleep in the bed you share, you can light it and see his face. Thus will not he have revealed his visage to you, for you will have seen his face for yourself without him having had the slightest hand in it. After all, once he sees that you love him in spite of his disfigurement or scar or birthmark, or the fact that he is a notorious pirate or such, he will then discard the mask and a proper wedding can take place, thus assuring that you will inherit his wealth if he should die on you. After all, should he fall dead and you not be married, then you would be left without any claim to his riches—be it pirate gold or not—and then what would happen to us?"

Even as Camille shook her head in refusal, her sisters were stricken pale. Papa's eyes gazed at the fine things throughout the room, and his lips drew thin. Only Giles seemed unaffected by this potential future, and he looked at Camille and shrugged, saying, "I can live in a cottage again."

"Oh, Giles," whispered Camille, "what of your aversion to thatch?"

Once more Giles merely shrugged, but this time he said nought.

Throughout the remainder of the week, Maman never let Camille have respite from the vision of something happening to Alain and she being left without a sou, her family cut off from the annual stipend, and Giles becoming sickly again.

And yet, every evening there was a ball, with Maman quite haughty in her newfound wealth and position, strutting about like a petty lord, showing her bloodstone ring to any and all who would look, telling them that it was but a trifling bauble sent to her by the prince as a minor show of his regard. And every night Aigrette had Pons announce Camille as the Princess of the Summerwood, though she and the entire family knew it was not yet so. Camille grew quite weary of such—her mother's harangues and of the balls, and the unwanted attentions of many a would-be lover, including the fat old roué Lord Jaufre, who knocked on her door several nights running, asking if she needed company. The only company she desired was that of her Prince Alain, and oh how she longed to return to Summerwood Manor to share quiet evenings with him.

And thus did the seemingly interminable round of exhortations during the day and unwelcome dances at night drag on.

But finally the week of the visit was up, and at the dawning of the following morn, Camille dressed once again in her travelling clothes and made ready to meet the Bear. But even as she slipped down the stairs, Maman stopped her at the door, and she handed Camille the fat candle stub and a full box of matches, saying, "We wouldn't want the plan to fail should one of the matches not light."

Sighing, reluctantly Camille tucked the candle and box into her drawstring purse, and then with a cold embrace from Aigrette, across the field she fled. And even before she reached the twilight border, the Bear stepped into view, and Camille ran crying to him and threw her arms about his great neck and sobbed into his fur, "Oh, Bear, I missed you so. Take me back to Summerwood; take me back to my prince."

"Whuff."

Camille tied on her bundles, and climbed onto the Bear's broad back, and into Faery they went.

Hindward, in the mansion—"Loose the dogs! Loose the dogs!" cried Lord Jaufre, ponderously thudding along the halls and hammering on bedroom doors.

"What? What is it, Lord Jaufre?" cried Aigrette, running up the stairs and meeting him halfway, the fat old roué puffing down to gather the servants, even as Henri came yawning after to stand at the top of the stairs, his negligee-clad daughters behind, as well as three half-dressed young men, one of them Allard, the husband of Felise, the other two coming after, both having been covertly invited by Joie and Gai to be their overnight guests. Giles was at the top of the stairs as well. Kneeling and peering through the balusters.

"A Bear! A Bear! I saw it from my window!" cried Jaufre. "Lady Camille was out for an early walk, and she was carried off into Faery by a great and savage brown Bear! We've got to break out the bows and arrows, the spears and lances, and don our Bear-hunting gear. We must saddle the horses, loose the hawks, and call out the dogs, and go after her . . . even though it means crossing into that dreaded realm."

It took Henri until nearly breakfast to convince Jaufre and the three young men that the Bear was nought but Camille's riding steed.

And then, as Giles grinned and Colette and Felise tittered, and Aigrette and Lisette looked on in disapproval, Henri eyed the two young men upon whose arms Joie and Gai adoringly clung. "Well, now, mes jeunes hommes et jeunes filles, what have you four to say for yourselves?"

16
Candle

"Welcome home, my lady," said Lanval, a great smile on his face.

Handed by footmen, Camille slid from the Bear's back and onto the footstool and then stepped onto the inlaid stone oak, and all the staff, now assembled in the great entry hall, bowed and curtseyed, every face beaming in joyous welcome.

Camille smiled and curtseyed in turn, then said, "Oh, it is so good to be back."

Footmen unladed the Bear, and Camille said, "Oh, Bear, it is nearly dusk, and I must make ready to see my Alain." And she hugged the Bear, and then turned and ran up the stairs, calling out, "Blanche, Blanche, to me."

Dressed in a full white gown with white petticoats under as well, white stockings on her legs and white shoes on her feet, and a strand of white pearls at her throat, and a white-pearl ring on her finger, she stood on the bridge in the lanternlight, while black swans slept below.

Onto the bridge stepped Alain, dressed all in deep indigo blue. And he took her in his arms and kissed her—deeply, longingly, hungrily—and she returned his kiss in kind.

"Oh, my love, but I missed you so," he said, and then he kissed her again.

When they finally broke apart, "I love you, Alain," murmured Camille, pressing his hand to her cheek.

They stood a moment in silence, then Alain said, "Come, let us stroll awhile."

Hand in hand they roamed the gardens, passing among azaleas, their white blossoms stark in the moonlight, and roses, blooming pink and red and yellow. Tiny, violet moss flowers glittered like onyx in the night.

"I think I'll never go away again, or at least not to visit my mère."

"Why so, love?"

"Oh, Alain, she made the visit quite terrible."

"But it should have been enjoyable instead."

"It wasn't."

"Again I ask, why so?"

"Mainly because you were not there, my love. And every night she presented me with an already-filled dance card, and I was to charm those partners for Maman's advantage. And, *ugh*, every night I had to dance with Lord Jaufre."

"Who is Lord Jaufre?"

"An old roué, that's who. I had to fend him off at every turn, as well as a number of others, rakes all."

Alain smiled, his grey eyes dancing behind his indigo blue mask. "Though I can hold them accountable for being boors, Camille, I cannot fault them for their splendid taste in women, for you, my love, are quite fetching."

"Oh, you," said Camille, tapping him lightly on the arm with her white fan.

They came to the hedge maze, and this night it was illuminated by lanterns within. "I thought we might step therein," said Alain.

Camille took one of Alain's wrists in her two hands and, turning backwards and tugging, said, "Oh, let's do, Alain," and, laughing, she pulled him into the maze.

Along the labyrinthine rows she went, haling Alain after, laughing at dead ends and twice-trod paths and at finding the entrance again, Alain enjoying her play.

When they came to the entrance for the third time, Alain said, "Love, would you have me show you the way?"

"Ah, *tchaa*, sieur, think you I know it not?"

Alain shrugged, and Camille said, "I have been toying with you, my lord. Come. Follow me."

And straightaway she led him to the statues in the center, missing not a turn.

"You, my dear, are a devious wench," said Alain. "I shall remember the next we play at any game."

"Games, my lord? Would you play at any game with me?"

He took her in his arms and said, "There is but one game I would play here and now."

"Then, my lord, play away."

"They are my sire and dam," said Alain, now reclining on the grass, his arms wrapped about Camille, she in nought but petticoats, he in but his shirt and mask. Her white gown lay on a stone bench at hand, while his breeks lay on the sward amid the scatter of shoes. No moon stood in the night sky, though a spangle of stars wheeled above.

Camille looked at the pale marble likenesses. "Though handsome, I think I rather like the portraits in the game room more. Even so, these are quite admirable. If they had color, they would be quite lifelike, though color would ruin the beauty of the carving itself. Who shaped them and when?"

"My sire engaged a sculptor from the mortal lands, a man from Latium, I believe. It was long past, ere I was born. I know nought else of the carving, though perhaps Lanval could find some records if you so desire."

Camille shook her head, saying, "I was just curious."

They fell silent for long moments, and then Camille said, "Oh, my," and then giggled.

Alain looked up at her, behind his mask a question in his grey eyes.

"I was just thinking, love," said Camille, "of your parents standing there and watching as we, well . . ."

Alain laughed and said, "If it would make you more comfortable, we can move to the other side to continue this tryst." Even as he said it, Camille could feel him quickening to the idea.

She sat up. "My love, as much as I desire, the bed will be much softer than grass and ground, and the bed as well will not further stain my petticoats should you, as an alternative, suggest that."

Alain's mouth pursed downward in mock disappointment, then turned upward in a grin. "Then it's off to bed we go," he replied, releasing her and sitting up. "But first, let us dine, for although love alone is quite satisfying, other needs of the body intrude."

"Though your eves were not as you wished, did you not find relief in the day? Did you not catch up on all the news with your sisters, your sire, your brother?"

In the dark, Camille sighed deeply. "Some. I did enjoy talking with Giles and Papa. Felise was quite taken with her husband Allard—a rather handsome fellow, and pleasant enough. Colette is engaged to Luc, but I didn't meet him, for he was away in Rulon on business. The twins—Joie and Gai—ah, they are such fun, as is Giles. But in spite of the small amount of agreeable times I had, Maman and my sister Lisette made much of my day unpleasant as well."

"How so?"

"Because every day my mère and I argued over—" Abruptly, Camille fell silent.

For a long while Alain held her hand in quietness, yet she spoke not. Finally he said, "Argued over what?"

Camille took a deep breath then said, "Over the fact that you and I are not yet wed."

Alain cuddled her in his arms and murmured, "Oh, Camille, you are my life, my love, my heart, and though we are not formally married, we are as wedded as any two could ever be. You are truly my wife, beloved, and I will love you forever."

Camille sought his face in the darkness and kissed him deeply. And then she lay with her head on his chest, listening to the beat of his heart.

At last he said, "When the geas, the curse, is lifted, then will we formally wed."

Camille felt her heart clench, but she managed to resist a shudder. *Geas? Curse? So that is the problem. Ah, me, there is magic involved here, and I know nought of such. In fact the only true magic I've even heard of concerning the Summerwood was when Alain told me of that trace of a spell left behind when his parents disappeared. —No, wait! On wind-borne words did I hear that terrible Troll Olot say something about a geas. But what would that have to do with Alain? Of a sudden, Camille's eyes widened in startlement at an unexpected thought: Oh, my, perhaps Alain was the man I saw standing there on that ridge with the Troll. But why would he have been in the Winterwood? —Oh, Camille, that matters not. What is of importance is that my beloved is cursed. And what could it be, this curse? Oh, Mithras, what could it be?*

Over the next several days, Camille spent time in the great library reading of magic and spells, of curses and geases, and of numerous other things arcane. Many were the legends and tales, and several fables told of heroes and heroines who, through their wits, resolved dilemmas dire. And one or two of the legends spoke of mysteries which required a lad or lass to solve a problem on their own by revealing an answer that was staring them in the face all along.

What if this is one of those? What if it is I who have to find an answer, something plain to all others but me? Most certainly, the folks here at Summerwood, Alain's kindred, the mages and witches and warlocks and such, they all know what's afoot; indeed, everyone does know but me.

Every day, on she read, gleaning for clues as to what she might do on her own to resolve whatever curse, or geas, lay over Summerwood Manor. And she said nought to any as to what she was about, not to Alain, not to Blanche, not even to her beloved Bear.

Every night she and Alain played échecs or dames or croquet by lanternlight, or sang to one another or read poetry or danced. And they made love tenderly and passionately and even wildly at times.

And she shared with him all the details of her visit to her parents—both the joys and the disappointments—speaking of everything but the discussions pertaining to Alain's masks and her mère's idea concerning the stub of a candle and matches. These she kept to herself, for a glimmer of a notion was taking place in her mind.

The resolutions to many of the fables are quite simple at base. What if my mère was unwittingly right concerning Alain not being able to show me his visage, but rather my seeing his face for myself? What if he has given me the only clue he can, and now it's up to me to act? What if my seeing his face on my own would break the curse which hangs over my beloved? Mayhap it would return his parents to the Summerwood from wherever it is they've vanished. But even if that is not the case, mayhap my mère is right, and by my seeing Alain's face he could abandon his masks altogether.

Camille dithered, not knowing if she were right or wrong, not knowing whether such a simple act would bring about the alleviation of the curse . . . or perhaps make it worse. And then one day, her heart beating frantically, she took up her drawstring purse in which was held the fat candle stub and box of matches, and she went along the corridors to Alain's quarters and slipped them into the bedchamber. There she secreted them away, then slipped back out and ran lightly down the hall, praying to Mithras that none would see.

Several nights running, she waited until Alain was asleep, but she could not summon the courage to fetch the stub from its hiding place and light it. Two nights, though, she held it in her hands, and yet put it away unlit, for she felt as if it were somehow a betrayal of his trust.

But then one night—*It is such a simple plan, just like the ones in the fables; what, pray tell, can go wrong?*—she struck the match and set the wick aflame and in the glimmering light turned toward her beloved Alain . . .

. . . and gasped . . .

. . . and tears sprang to her eyes . . .

. . . for he was beautiful, so very beautiful: no scars, no wens, no gapes, no pits, no birthmarks, no—Camille smiled through her tears—no, *ooo*, bony skull; his features were completely unmarred by anything whatsoever, lest marred by beauty instead. And he lay innocently sleeping.

She sat on the edge of the bed next to him, Alain on her left, the candle in her left hand the better to see, and somewhere a wind began softly to moan. And she sat beside him a long while, studying his beautiful face, as if to store up the sight of it for all time. And still there came the sound of the wind slowly rising, as if a storm brewed.

Long did she look, but at last, unable to resist, Camille leaned over to kiss his sweet lips, and as she did so, a great blob of hot wax spilled from the hollow of the fat candle stub and splashed onto Alain's bare chest, and he bolted upright and looked at her in horror. "Oh my love, what have you—? What have you done? The curse, the geas. Now I must—" But his words were chopped off, and there came the moan of a great wind rushing throughout the manor, a wind filled with screams of the living, a wind filled with screams of the damned. A churning darkness came over Alain, as of shadows alive swirling all about his form, and within the dimness his shape began to change, to alter. Camille stumbled up from the bed and hindward, her own mouth gaping wide in shock. And the raging wind shrieked along the halls and hammered upon the doors, the very walls shuddering under the thunderous blows. And all about Alain, blackness swirled, and then he was gone, the huge brown Bear now in his place. And he roared in rage, and Camille reeled back, a soundless scream trapped in her throat. His ashen eyes mad with fury, the Bear rose up and raised a massive claw as if to strike her. Camille shrilled in terror and cowered down, throwing up an arm in futile protection, the candle falling from her grasp to roll and lie on its side. In the flickering shadows the Bear loomed above her, his deafening roars bellowing out over the howl of the wind, and in that moment Camille knew that she was going to die at his claws, just as had the Redcap Goblins. But then the Bear turned and dropped to all fours and crashed out through the door, and the howl of the wind yawled as if in victory, the wails within shrilling in terror. The shrieking wind rose in screaming crescendo, up and up and—

—Of a sudden the terrible wind vanished and a profound silence fell as the candle guttered and went out, leaving nought but blackness and weeping Camille trembling in the still room behind.

17
Desolation

Yet weeping in the darkness, Camille fumbled her way to the mantel, to find the lantern there and a striker. A yellow glow illuminated the sleeping chamber, the bed curtains torn where the Bear had ripped his way free, the satin covers ajumble.

Sobbing and barefooted and in nought but a negligee, Camille stumbled across the broken-down door and into the corridor beyond, and there she found more wreckage: hallway and alcove furniture lay atumble; plants were overturned, their pots shattered and dirt strewn along the passage; tapestries lay where they had been ripped from the walls, along with paintings, frames broken and lying askew.

"Lanval!" she cried out amid the wrack as she made her unsteady way along the hall. Down a stairwell she went, only to find devastation there, too.

A profound silence filled the manor.

"Lanval! Blanche!"

No one answered, the stillness oppressive, broken only by her anguished cries of distress. On into the darkness she struggled, lanternlight revealing nought but ruin.

"Lanval! Blanche! Anyone!"

Camille began to run, and as she ran she called out for someone to answer, someone to be alive in the ruin, and everywhere she went, every room she burst into, every corridor she fled down, every hall and chamber she entered, there was nought but total disarray, terrible damage done by the terrible wind that had howled throughout the manor:

Chairs were overturned; tables displaced; pottery smashed—wreckage and litter and shatter.

Books and papers and pamphlets and journals were strewn about the great library, and many of the freestanding shelves had toppled, their volumes and tomes and manuscripts and scrolls flung wide.

In the large kitchen, pots and pans were scattered, some dented nearly beyond recognition, and dishes and cups, bowls and saucers and platters were smashed, shards of porcelain and glass cutting into Camille's bare feet as she stumbled through, and she left bloody tracks in her wake as she ran onward, calling out for someone to answer.

Like webs of strange spiders, yards of cloth and yarn and thread draped about the sewing chamber, though most was on the floor. Baskets were smashed, and tambours lay broken, some yet clinging to remnants of embroidered scenes.

The game room was in a shambles, with the taroc cards and dames and échecs sets strewn, and the portraits of Lord Valeray and Lady Saissa lay up against overturned tables. Camille wept to see such ruin in that special place she had come to love, and though she did not right the whole of the chamber, she did re-hang the portraits.

And everywhere, candles were smashed, as well as lanterns, the oil running to pool, or to soak into precious carpets.

But nowhere did Camille find anyone: no Lanval, no Blanche, no Jules, no Renaud, no Andre, no Cook, no seamstresses, no footmen, no member whatsoever of the household staff. And certainly no Alain, not even as the Bear.

The entire manor was utterly deserted of everyone but Camille.

She was alone in the shards of her own doing.

She was alone amid the wrack.

She was completely alone.

Completely.

Alone.

It was as if the wind itself had—

Camille gasped in revelation and burst into tears anew, for running through her mind, running through her mind, running again and again—*The screams. The screams. All those I love, those I love, the wind, the screams, the raging wind, oh Alain, gone, all gone, carried off by the wind.*

And I did not go with them.
The screams.
The wind.

Dawn came.
But Camille did not see it.
Exhausted by grief, by guilt, by ruin, she had fallen asleep upon her own bed amid the wrack of her suite. But even in sleep she now and again sobbed, though tears failed to come, for they were exhausted as well.

The sun rode up in the sky, finally to shine down through the shattered skylight above. A breeze gently blew, and it set the ruin of the skylight shade to swaying.

tick . . .
tck . . .
clk . . .

"Alain!" she cried, starting up, not knowing where she was. Not knowing what had awakened her.

tck . . .
clk . . .

And then she saw the wreckage, and memory came crashing in.

For three days Camille lived in the ruin of the manor, and much of those three days she spent cleaning, sweeping, uprighting, straightening, and other such onerous chores. But the mansion was vast and she could only deal with a small part of the whole, yet it gave her something to do while she tried to decide her course. The silence was oppressive, though now and again something sounded: a creak of settling, a pop of a beam, a clatter of some precariously balanced thing finally falling, and other such noises. And at every sound, Camille would run to see if someone, anyone, had returned or had come to call, yet no one was ever there.

Perhaps I should go to the Autumnwood and find Liaze, or to the Winter- or Springwood, where Borel lives, or Celeste. They would know what to do. But I know not where within their demesnes they dwell. And, oh, the Winterwood is cursed, at least a part of it, where dreadful things do lurk.

Should I instead try to make my way home, make my way back to Papa's mansion? But once there, then what? Wait for Alain to appear? Wait in a place where Maman and Lisette would do all they could to make my life wretched. And, oh my, if Alain does not come, the tithe of gold will stop, and Papa will lose the mansion, and poor Giles will fall into ill health again. —No. I did this thing, and I will do all to set everything to rights.

It was as she was straightening Alain's suite that she came across a grey mask, and as she held it, only then did she realize—

Oh, but what a fool I have been. Alain's eyes and those of the Bear are the same ashen shade of grey. I should have guessed. I should have known. One was never about when the other— Camille, you were and are an utter imbecile! And as you once thought, the man on the ridge with Olot the Troll that terrible night in the Winterwood: that had to have been Alain! What did Olot say just before he and the Bear went to the ridge? "Hear me, then, Bear: you spurned my daughter, and you refuse to yield this tasty morsel to me. I have you in my power, just as did my child, and as she has done, so will I do." Surely that meant his daughter had laid a spell upon Alain, for he was already a Bear when Olot set his own bane; hence, it must have been the daughter who cursed him so. —Oh, Mithras, now I recall more of Olot's wind-borne words of that terrible Winterwood night: ". . . she will fail, and then the geas . . ." Those words could only mean that I would fail, that I would seek to see Alain's face, and should I ever do so—

Camille burst into tears. Furiously she went about straightening Alain's chambers, her thoughts awhirl.

I am the one who brought about this ruin. Oh, but why didn't Alain ever tell me? Then I wouldn't have— Camille, you ninny, he couldn't tell you, else the curse would have struck regardless. That's why the mages and seers and sorcerers and witches were here at Summerwood Manor. To break the Trolls' two curses, and—

Of a sudden, dread filled Camille's heart. *With Alain gone, the Bear gone, everyone gone, the Troll is free to come after me. I must decide what to do and be away from here.*

Camille began assembling a travelling kit: a waterskin and a bedroll came first, each fitted with a sling. Then into a rucksack she packed spare clothes, some dry food, some salt and pepper and additional seasonings, a cooking pot, flint and steel and tinder, soap, raggings, a tiny lantern, and other such necessities.

I shall find Liaze, and then we will get Borel and Celeste, and then . . . and then . . . — Then what?

Camille frowned in concentration. *Then what? Then what? Then what will we do? What can we do?*

As she took up a small bronze knife—like the ones she had given Papa and Giles—she paused and looked at it, and opened and closed the blade.

Ah, then, that is what we can do: raise a warband and find this Olot and his daughter and make them tell us where Alain and all the others have gone. A warband, that's it.

She slipped the knife into the kit and again paused and looked about. *What else do I need? —Oh, if for some reason I must travel far, I will need—*

Moments later, Camille rifled through her jewelry boxes and took brooches and rings and necklaces and bracelets and other such jewelry of significant value. Then she went to the steward's office, and in Lanval's desk she found a small lockbox, which she bore to the smithy and broke open using Renaud's great bronze hammer and a chisel. From the box she took up a handful of gold coins, yet she paused. *It won't do to flash a gold piece just anywhere, nor the jewelry either. There may be thieves about, and— Oh, but I did send that poacher's woman away with nought but a gold piece. I should have specified silver and bronze.* Camille added silver and bronze to the coinage, then she buried the lockbox in Andre's compost pile.

Yet thinking of thieves, she went to the seamstress chamber, and there she sewed jewelry and coins into the lining of her all-weather woolen travelling cloak and behind a panel in the rucksack. And she stitched together a money belt to wear under her jerkin.

Night fell, and she spent it in one of the abandoned stables, sleeping in straw, where perhaps Olot and his Goblins would not think to look if they came that eve.

The next morning, she took breakfast in the manor, eating rapidly so as to be away without delay.

I wonder if there are enough folk in the Forests of the Seasons to raise a warband? Perhaps that great man with a scythe has kindred elsewhere. I know of few living in the Summerwood: a handful of smallholders who came on business, that poacher's wife—now gone—and the Lynx Riders and those of us here at the—

Camille paused, a biscuit partway to her mouth.

The Lady of the Mere, a seer, and she lives not far from here, or so Alain did say. Perhaps she can help. But wait; Alain also said, ". . . she only appears in circumstances dire." Then he said the disappearance of his sire and dam would not seem to be one of those events. Since that is the case, what chance have I that she will be about, even should I find the mere? I mean, if the disappearance of a king and queen was not enough to cause her to show . . . —Ah, fille, if you do not try, then you will never know.

Bearing her rucksack and bedroll and waterskin, Camille spent the day walking through the woodland surrounding Summerwood Manor, her path spiralling ever outward in a pattern she hoped would swiftly bring her to the Lady of the Mere. And from time to time she called out for aid, yet no one answered, though birds and small animals flew and scuttled away from this creature disturbing their lives, a doe and a fawn fleeing as well.

As twilight fell across the land, adding its silvery light to that of the ever-present twilight of Faery, Camille made a small camp on a hill rising above the forest, and she was dismayed to see the manor standing what seemed to be but a stone's throw away, yet, in truth, it was full mile or two off. Even so, she cried herself to sleep that night.

For three days did Camille search without success, for she knew not how far or which way the mere of the lady did lie. Too, she could have easily passed by a small pool without ever knowing it was there. And Camille's spirits fell into a pit of despair at the futility of her quest.

And on the eve of that fourth day of fruitless searching, with her head in her hands she sat on the remains of a long-fallen tree and quietly wept.

"Why do you weep, Lady Camille?" came a voice.

18
Mere

Startled, Camille gasped, her tears stemmed. And she looked up to see a Lynx Rider stepping out from the tall grass, his cat following. Reaching nearly to his knees, a brace of voles dangling from the rider's belt, and he carried his bow in hand. He stopped before Camille, and she thought from the markings on his face, she knew him.

"Lord Kelmot?"

Kelmot bowed. "At your service, my lady." Then he turned and signalled the lynx, who sat, and began licking a paw and washing its face and ears.

"May I aid you, my lady?" asked the tiny lord.

He smiled, again revealing a mouthful of catlike teeth, and as close as he was, in spite of the failing light, Camille could see that his eyes were catlike as well—yellow and with a vertical slit of a pupil.

"My lord, I am most desperate," said Camille, "for I seek the Lady of the Mere, and I know not where I must go."

Kelmot took a deep breath. "My lady, I can take you there; yet heed: none seek the Lady of the Mere unless somewhat dire is afoot, and even then she may not appear."

Camille burst into tears anew, and though Lord Kelmot was nonplused, his lynx merely looked up from its grooming, and then went back to washing itself. Finally, Camille regained control of her weeping, and though tears yet welled in her eyes, oft to break free and stream down her face, she haltingly told him of her disastrous attempt to put an end to the curse, speaking of the candle and her mother's urgings, of Alain's remark concern-

ing the geas, of her readings in the great library, and her hesi-
tancy to light the candle within the darkened room but then
succumbing, and of the wax falling onto Alain, and the wind
and the screams therein, and of Alain becoming the Bear, and
the disappearances of all in the thunderous blow, and of the
wind itself vanishing, leaving nought but destruction in its
wake, and of her search for anyone yet within the manse, but
finding all were gone.

Full night had fallen when she came to tale's end, a waning
half-moon high in the sky, and Kelmot, now seated on the
ground, looked up at her and nodded as if unto himself. "Ah, so
that was it. The night my sons and I came to the manse because
of the poacher's wife, Steward Lanval told us the prince would
be wearing a mask, yet he did not tell us why; but now you, my
lady, have; 'twas all because of a curse." The tiny Lynx Rider
then frowned and shook his head. "There is great magic at work
here, and none I know has such at his command, most certainly
not a Troll, for they are not natural wizards. Tell me, my lady,
was there about him some token, some item of power?"

Camille thought back to the only time she had seen Olot,
there in the Winterwood. Slowly she shook her head. "Nay,
Lord Kelmot, I think no— Oh, wait. There was about his neck
on a leather thong an amulet of sorts. But it was quite insignificant, or at least seemed so."

"An amulet?"

"Yes. Small and round and dull, almost as if made of clay."

Kelmot gasped and then looked about as if seeking eaves-
droppers. "It must have been one of the Seals of Orbane," he
whispered. "I thought them long-lost or long-gone."

"My lord?"

Kelmot took a deep breath and let it out. "Orbane was a great
wizard, yet evil grasped his heart. As to that which you thought
was but a clay amulet, it was a seal holding within a great and
fearsome power; there were seven seals in all, each one capable
of invoking a terrible curse when broken—speak the curse,
break the seal, and such will it be."

"Though you numbered them seven, I saw but one. What of
the other six seals?"

"Two were destroyed when we trapped Orbane in the Castle
of Shadows in the Great Darkness beyond the Black Wall of the
World. The missing five: we thought them gone, used up by Orbane or perhaps lost. But it seems we were wrong, for nought

else I know of has the power to do that which you described—
the wind, the vanishment, Prince Alain cursed to be the Bear in
the day. Too, it would explain how Olot, and indeed his daughter, could cause such great harm, and it's just like a Troll and his
spawn to use such for their own vengeful ends. Most certainly
they had at least two of the seals: the daughter one, the sire another. Wherefrom, I cannot say."

Camille frowned. "Lord Kelmot, you say Alain was cursed to
be the Bear in the day, but on our journeys he was the Bear in
the night as well; even so, at Summerwood Manor, he was Alain
at night, and not the Bear."

In the moonlight, Kelmot shrugged. "Mayhap at night he had
a choice as to which he would be; while in the day he had
none."

Camille frowned and added, "Then again, perhaps it is only
Summerwood Manor where he could become Alai— No, wait.
He was also Alain when he was on the ridge with Olot in the
Winterwood, or at least I think it was Alain."

"And that was nighttime as well?"

"Yes."

They fell silent for a moment, but the lynx suddenly stood
and faced away, its ears twitching.

"Something is amiss," said Kelmot. He called the cat to him
and mounted. "I will see." And up a tall pine went the lynx,
Kelmot riding.

After a while, down they came. Kelmot pointed and said,
"Yon lies the manor, and toward it across the grounds I saw
black shapes scuttling: Goblins, I ween."

Camille's heart lurched. "Oh, my. I was right. Olot sent his
Redcaps to fetch me."

"Fear not, Lady Camille. I and mine will handle these inter-
lopers." At a word from Kelmot, somewhat between a spit and
a growl, the cat bounded into the tall grass.

"But wait, my lord," called Camille after, "what of the Lady
of the Mere?"

"I shall return," came Kelmot's cry, and then he was gone.

Moments after he vanished, Camille heard a forlorn calling,
and she looked up to see silhouetted against the glowing half-
moon, five great birds winging away; they were the black swans
of Summerwood Manor, and two were missing from the flight.
Distressed, Camille sat for long moments, certain that the Goblins had slain two of the swans out of hand.

Even so, weary as she was, at last she nodded off to sleep. How long she was aslumber she did not know, yet something awakened her, but what, she could not say. Still, she had a foreboding, as if something evil were afoot. She glanced all about in the silvery light shedding down from above, yet no Goblin or aught else did she spy. And she glanced up at the moon, now three-quarters down the sky, and of a sudden she gasped, for another black silhouette crossed the half-lit face, yet no swan was this, but a sinister knot of darkness, streaming tatters and tendrils of shadow flapping in the wind behind. And though Camille knew not what she had just seen, shudders ran up her spine.

In the last candlemark ere dawn, Camille was awakened by a soft call. Riding his lynx, Lord Kelmot had returned. "Hurry, my lady," said Kelmot, dismounting. "The Lady of the Mere: if there, she is only present between the first sign of dawn and the full coming day."

As Camille rolled her bedroll by the light of her small lantern, the diminutive Lynx Rider said, " 'Twas indeed Goblins at Summerwood Manor, my lady"—Kelmot touched his bow—"yet they no longer live."

"Were they Redcaps?"

"Aye. Just as you suspected."

"You slew them all?" asked Camille, pausing and looking at the wee person, wondering how such a small one could be so deadly.

"Not alone," replied Kelmot. "Other Lynx Riders came at my call, for Goblins in Summerwood are an abomination—especially Redcaps—and we will not abide their presence. —And, yes, we slew them all, though something or someone with them fled—escaped—something dark and sinister, though I know not what or whom."

"I think I saw it," said Camille, "flying across the moon. A dreadful thing of streaming shadows."

Kelmot nodded.

Camille looked across at the wee Lynx Rider. "The swans: they flew across the moon as well, but two were missing."

"Goblin-slain," said Kelmot.

Camille sighed. "I had feared it so."

"We took revenge," said the tiny lord. "The Goblins all lie dead."

"Oh, but I do hope their ghosts will not haunt my beloved's mansion," said Camille, tying the last of the knots.

"Fear not, my lady, for even now my riders are fetching others to come, other dwellers of Faery, those who can see that the bodies are burned and the spirits banished."

Camille stood and shouldered her bedroll and rucksack, and Kelmot mounted up, and through the woodland they went, Camille pressing hard to keep pace with the Lynx Rider.

Light had seeped well into the sky when they finally came to the marge of a woodland glade. There it was Kelmot stopped. "Straight ahead, Lady Camille, that's where you'll find the mere and perhaps the lady as well."

"Aren't you coming with me?"

Kelmot shook his head. "Nay, Lady, for, if she appears at all, she will not do so if more than one stand along her shore. Yet I will wait for you here. Now hurry, for day is nigh upon the land."

Taking a deep breath and exhaling, Camille said, "Merci, Lord Kelmot."

"Go," he replied, glancing at the oncoming light of day.

Camille hurried into the glade, and in its midst she came upon a crystalline mere of still water. Vapor rose from the surface, tendrils of mist to waft upward and twine out over the mossy banks, or to curl among a small cluster of reeds along the near shoreline. Across the limpid pool stood a huge oak, its great limbs shading above, its large roots reaching into the water. In the base of the oak Camille could see a hollow, and her eyes widened in revelation, for within the darkness therein sat a robed, hooded figure.

Of a sudden, Camille realized she was totally unprepared, for she had not considered what she would ask of the seer.

Oh, why hadn't I— Stop it, you goose of a girl! Now think!

Thoughts swiftly raced through Camille's mind. *As a seer, she can tell me of the future. Perhaps I should ask, Where will I find Alain? But wait, what if it is not my fate to find him, but someone else's instead? Then it would be a wasted question, a lost opportunity. What if instead— Oh, my, I remember what Alain said about knowing the future: that one would perhaps try to change the outcome and thereby thwart Destiny, and thus perhaps upset the balance of all and make things even worse.*

Nonplused, Camille glanced at the sky; the sun would break the horizon in but moments. She took a deep breath and asked, "Where can Alain be found?"

And still the sky brightened, for, despite Camille's desperation, the oncoming day did not falter, and her spirit fell, for only silence reigned. But at last a whisper came across the mere, and Camille's heart leapt with hope, but then fell, for the lady said, "What service have you given me?"

"Service, my lady? How can I have performed a service when I knew you not?"

"You must serve me in some manner: a favor, an aid, a duty."

"Then, my lady, this I pledge on my heart: if there is aught I can do for you, then so I will."

"Any service? Ponder well ere you answer."

Camille glanced at the horizon. The sun was nigh at hand. Only moments remained ere it would rise. Though frantic, Camille considered deeply then said, "I will do no service which goes against my conscience."

A sigh came across the mere, yet whether in satisfaction, relief, or disappointment, Camille did not know. Yet the lady murmured, "Well answered, Camille. Now riddle me this:

"I open the eyes of the world,
So wide-awake I be,
I close the eyes of the world,
Name me, I be three."

Silence fell, and in desperation Camille again glanced at the ever-brightening horizon. Then, of a sudden, she knew, and she smiled and said, "You are dawn and midday and dusk."

"Indeed, I am," came the whisper.

"Oh, lady, please, where can Alain be found?"

Long silence reined, but at last: "East of the sun and west of the moon is where your prince does lie. And this I will tell you for nought: a year and a day and a whole moon more from the time you betrayed him is all you have to seek him out, and you have already wasted seven days. Take my two gifts and go, and go alone, but for one of my gifts. Unlooked-for aid will come along the way."

"But I would have the aid of Borel and Celeste and Liaze," cried Camille. "The aid of Lord Kelmot, too."

Only silence answered.

"But I don't know where east of the sun and west of the moon might be. Oh, please, my lady, tell me where I should be bound."

But the figure remained silent.

Frustrated, Camille circled 'round the water to confront the Lady of the Mere, yet when she came to the massive oak, all she found was a strange burl in the dark hollow at the base of the tree, a gnarled stick leaning against it.

"Where are you, Lady?" called Camille, tears stinging her eyes. "I am in desperate need."

But an onset of chatter of a nearby bird was all that answered her anguished cry.

All 'round did Camille turn, seeking the seer somewhere in the glade or among the trees of the Summerwood. And then her shoulders slumped in defeat, for she knew she would not find the lady, for the glowing limb of the sun had risen above the horizon.

And still, nearby, a bird chattered.

"Oh, Lady," groaned Camille, leaning her head against the oak, "you were no aid at all."

Suddenly the bird fell silent.

"Was she here?" came a query.

Camille looked down. Lord Kelmot and his lynx now stood at her side. "The sun had risen," said Kelmot, dismounting, "so I came to find you. And again I ask, was she here, the Lady of the Mere?"

Camille nodded. "She was. And she told me Alain lay east of the sun and west of the moon."

Kelmot blanched, his catlike eyes widening in alarm. "Oh, my lady, how dreadful."

Sudden hope blooming, Camille asked, "Know you of this place?"

Kelmot shook his head. "Nay, I do not."

Camille frowned and turned up her hands. "Then why did you say—?"

"Camille, that the Lady of the Mere was here at all means that dire events are afoot, and we must gather a warband and find that place east of the sun and west of—" Kelmot's words abruptly stopped, for Camille had pushed out a hand to halt his speech, and she was shaking her head. "What?" he asked.

"She told me that I must go alone," said Camille. "That unlooked-for help would come along the way."

"Were those her exact words?"

Camille's brow furrowed. "Her exact words were, 'East of the sun and west of the moon is where your prince does lie. And this I will tell you for nought: a year and a day and a whole moon more from the time you betrayed him is all you have to seek him out, and you have already wasted seven days. Take my two gifts and go, and go alone, but for one of my gifts. Unlooked-for aid will come along the way.' " Camille's eyes widened in remembrance. "Oh, two gifts. But where—?"

Camille looked about the glade, seeing nought but things natural to the Summerwood: the sward, the water of the mere, the cluster of reeds within, a small patch of briars nearby, a silent bird in among the thorns, and the trees 'round the marge of the mead. Then she looked in the hollow of the oak. Nothing therein but the strange burl and the gnarled sti— *Wait!* Camille reached in and took up the stick. It was a walking staff, and it had a carved festoon of flowers winding 'round the shaft and up to a dark disk just below the grip at the top.

"This is surely one of the gifts," said Camille, showing the ornate find to Kelmot.

"No doubt," agreed the Lynx Rider. "But she said there were two."

A flurry sounded nearby, and the bird in the thorns—a sparrow—chattered frantically, alarmed by Kelmot's lynx, the cat, belly low, now creeping through the grass toward the briars. Yet the bird did not fly.

Suddenly Camille gasped. "Lord Kelmot, call off your lynx!"

Kelmot frowned, but spat a hissing word, and the lynx flattened in the grass, but did not take its eyes from its would-be prey.

Camille strode to the briar patch, Kelmot following, and all the while the bird chattered. " 'Tis a wee, black-throated house sparrow and trapped," said Camille as she worked her way inward. "Oh, my, but he is injured, his wing caught on a thorn. Mithras, it has stabbed right through a wing joint."

Kelmot stood outside the briars. "What has the bird to do with aught?"

As Camille carefully eased the bird's wing from the thorn, she said, "Remember the words of the seer, Lord Kelmot: 'Take my two gifts and go, and go alone, but for one of my gifts.' From her words I deem one of her gifts is a companion."

"Ah, I see," said Kelmot, nodding in agreement. "Alone, but

for one of her gifts. Yet, Camille, what makes you think this bird is that gift?"

"Well, there is this: I heard not the sparrow until after the Lady of the Mere was gone. Ere, then, I deem he was absent." The sparrow now in hand, Camille worked her way out from among the briars. As she stepped forth, she glanced at the lynx, and then frowned at Kelmot. "Will you, can you, keep your cat away from the bird while I tend to him?"

A look of indignation crossed Kelmot's tiny face, yet he said, "Most certainly, Lady Camille." He turned to the lynx and spat-hissed a word or two.

Now it was the cat who looked offended, and it turned its back to them all: Camille, Kelmot, and the sparrow.

Kneeling at her rucksack, Camille took a small jar from within, and, making soothing sounds, she applied a daub of salve to the injury. "I think he may never fly again," she said, sadness tingeing her words as she carefully folded the wing shut.

Kelmot frowned and asked, "Think you this sparrow will be a willing companion?"

"Let us see," replied Camille, setting the sparrow on her shoulder.

Now free from Camille's gentle grip, "*Chpp!*" chirped the bird in alarm, and it tugged on one of Camille's golden tresses, and, pulling, it leapt down into a high vest pocket, tugging the end of the lock in after. Then it peeked back out over the verge at the disgruntled lynx.

Camille smiled and whispered, "Tiny brown sparrow, sitting in a tree, scruffy little soul, just like me, would you be an eagle, would you be a hawk—"

"My lady," said Lord Kelmot, "mayhap you are correct in that this is the second gift, but I would have us search more, for in events dire enough for the Lady of the Mere to speak, one cannot be too cautious."

Camille sighed, but nodded, and back to the oak they went.

Long did they look—in the hollow and about the base of the oak and in the limbs above, Kelmot and the lynx climbing to do so, 'round the mere and in among the cluster of reeds, and across the sward—yet they found nothing else that seemed to apply to the words spoken by the seer, and all the while the sparrow rode in Camille's vest pocket, occasionally chirping quietly, its gaze, whenever possible, on the cat. Finally, Camille said, "Lord Kelmot, the staff and the sparrow: I deem they are the gifts, for there is nought else here."

Kelmot sighed, but nodded in agreement. "Even so, though I know not where is a place east of the sun and west of the moon, I would go with you, but for the words of the Lady of the Mere."

Camille sighed. "I was going to ask Borel and Celeste and Liaze to accompany me, and when you came to my aid, I would have asked you as well, Lord Kelmot. Yet, 'Go alone,' she said, 'but for one of my gifts.' " Camille smiled down at the sparrow. Its tiny brown eyes peered into her eyes of blue. "*Chpp!*"

"Scruffy little soul, will you go with me?"

"*Chpp!*"

She laughed and turned to Kelmot.

"It appears I have a companion, though I know not where to go." Camille frowned and then said, "Tell me, Lord Kelmot: would anyone in the Forests of the Seasons know where this place east of the sun and west of the moon might be?"

Kelmot shrugged. "Mayhap, yet I know not who."

"What of Witch Hradian or Wizard Caldor or Seer Malgen? Would they not know?"

"Oh, Lady Camille, there is that about each of them I do not trust, and I would not like to place the fate of Prince Alain into the hands of any one of the three, for they might lead you astray."

"Why so?"

"Hradian strikes me as false in some manner, my lady, she with her sly eyes. Malgen seems quite unsound. And Caldor is a pretentious ass, perhaps a mountebank. In fact all three could be such. If so, any or all would send you astray, and a year and a day and a whole moon beyond would find you at no good end."

Camille nodded, for Kelmot's opinions as to the nature of these three magi echoed her own. "Tell me, my lord, which way lies Autumnwood?"

"Yon," replied the Lynx Rider, pointing. "But I thought you were not now going to ask Prince Alain's kith for—"

"I'm not," said Camille. "If none of the siblings are to accompany me, then that means I should not go into the Autumnwood, Winterwood, or Springwood, for surely Alain and Lanval and Blanche and the remainder of the staff would not have vanished into any of those three demesnes, for if they had, then Borel or Celeste or Liaze would make certain that all could return to the Summerwood. Hence, I shall go the opposite way, for

surely a place east of the sun and west of the moon must lie
elsewhere. Besides, if I went therein, Liaze and Celeste and
Borel would insist on coming with me, and as you know—"

"—You must go alone," said Kelmot. "Even so, by the same
reasoning, Lady Camille, I can lead you to the far marge of the
Summerwood and by the swiftest ways, for surely Prince Alain
and his staff are not within these bounds either, but somewhere
in Faery beyond."

"In Faery?"

Kelmot nodded. "Indeed, for I ween that nowhere in the mortal world could there be a place lying east of the sun and west of
the moon."

A faint smile crossed Camille's face. "Only in Faery, indeed."
Camille took up her kit and the staff. "Let us be gone, then."

And together they went, the Lynx Rider on his cat, Camille
striding at his side, with a sparrow in her upper vest pocket.

A day and a half later—"Shall we press on, Scruff?"

"*Chpp.*"

"Au revoir, Lord Kelmot," said Camille.

"Be safe, my lady," he replied. "And this I advise: ask the
traders, the travellers, the merchants, the mapmakers, and the
elders in particular, for they are most likely to know where such
a place might be. Go with my benediction: may you find that
which you seek."

Camille nodded, and, gripping the garland-carved stave in
hand, she stepped through the wall of twilight and into another
realm of Faery beyond.

19

Grass

Grass: hip-deep, thick-stalked, jointed, and green, with nodding heads of seeds. Camille had stepped through the twilight border to come into a vast sea of such, stretching away toward snowcapped mountains in the distance afar. To left and right the verdant plain extended to the horizon and beyond. Far off to the right as well, dark clouds rose into the sky, building in the afternoon warmth.

Now that the lynx was beyond the twilight, flapping and scrambling, one wing held awkwardly, the sparrow managed to clamber out from Camille's vest pocket and to her shoulder.

Camille glanced at him sidelong. "What do you think, Scruff? Left? Right? Straight?"

"*Chp.*" The sparrow cocked his head and peeked 'round her chin to look into her eye.

Camille grinned. "Ah, but you are no help. For me, I think we'll go straight ahead, for to the left I see nought but grass forever, and to the right I deem a storm is brewing. Aye, straight ahead we'll go; perhaps if foothills lie along the mountains, we can climb a tall one and be high enough to see some sort of town or farm or the like, if one is nigh, a place where we can ask directions."

And so she set out toward the mountains, travelling generally westward, she thought, yet in Faery, in spite of the moon and sun and stars, none could be sure of directions, or so she had been told by her père, though how he would know, she could not say.

Across the early afternoon she walked, trudging—*swish, swash*—through the heavy grass, her rucksack and bedroll and

waterskin slung, her festooned stave barely aiding. At times she
came to hidden swales, dips in the land, and down she would go
into the dint, where the plants were taller than she. It was
difficult travel, for the grass did sorely impede, dragging against
her as it did, slowing her considerably.

Of a sudden in midafternoon, *"Chp!"* chirped the sparrow,
and, pulling on a lock of Camille's hair, down into the high vest
pocket he fluttered, where he chattered frantically and tugged
on her tress.

"What is it, Scruff? What is the matter?" Camille looked all
'round, yet she saw nought but empty plain. But then a shadow
glided across the tall grass, and she glanced up to espy a red-
tailed raptor soaring in the sky above, sweeping to and fro in a
hunting pattern.

"Ah, I see. First a lynx and now a hawk. Perils dire, eh,
Scruff?"

Yet she received no answer from the sparrow, the wee bird
silent and hiding in a pocketful of golden hair now that the
hunter was near.

"Peril to you, indeed, Scruff, but peril to me? . . . I think not,"
said Camille, smiling, as she strode onward.

Suddenly, the hawk stooped, its wings folded, only the tips
guiding, and just ere striking the grass, it flared. Camille continued
to watch as she walked onward, and sometime later, up struggled
the raptor, and in its talons it bore the remains of an animal—rabbit, marmot, or what, Camille could not say. "Well, Scruff, there
is life herein after all—hawks and small game though it be."

When the raptor could no longer be seen, once again Scruff
scrambled to Camille's shoulder, as across the plain she went.

In the far distance to her right—north, she thought—the dark
clouds now towered into the sky, and lightning stroked the
ground and flashed from cloud to cloud, at times illuminating
the darkness from within. Distant thunder rolled across the
grass, a mere grumble from afar. And rain fell down in long grey
streaks, like wind-driven brooms sweeping o'er an endless plain.

"Oh, Scruff, let us hope the storm does not come this way to
drop its bounty on us, for there is no shelter for as far as the eye
can see."

But Scruff made no comment, and Camille pressed forward,
glancing now and again at the remote storm, too far away to be
of immediate concern. Too, it seemed to be moving away, or so
Camille hoped—northward, she believed.

On she went and on, the mountains seeming no closer, and when the sun stood in late afternoon, regardless of the distant storm, she stopped awhile to rest and to take a meal, stamping down the grass all 'round to make a space to sit. Then she plopped down and set the sparrow to the ground beside her.

"Some nest, eh, Scruff?" she asked, as she rummaged through the rucksack for hardtack and jerky. But the sparrow was busily nipping seeds from the felled grass, and pursuing an insect or two, and he answered not.

As she ate, Camille wondered if only hawks and small game and insects dwelled in this grassland, for she and the sparrow had so far seen nothing otherwise. And there was no smoke on the horizon to indicate a dwelling or community.

Time passed, and Camille fetched a cup from her rucksack and filled it with water. After she had drunk, she again filled the cup, but this time she offered it to Scruff. The sparrow hopped to the rim and dipped in his beak and raised his head to swallow, then did so again and again until his thirst was quenched, then he hopped into the cup itself and fluttered and flounced in the water. Laughing, Camille said, "Oh, Scruff, I suppose I'll not drink from that vessel again, at least not until it is washed. Yet I know how you feel, my sparrow, for would that I, too, had a bath. But I couldn't very well bathe in front of Lord Kelmot, now could I? Nor you in front of his lynx. And since you and I have been on our own in this land of grass, we've not come across a stream or pool. Mayhap we'll find one when we reach the foothills, or the mountains beyond."

The sparrow hopped out from the cup and fluttered and shook, though awkwardly with its injured wing. Camille again applied salve from the jar on the injured joint. "Oh, wee Scruff, but I do hope you'll be able to fly again someday."

Finally, she packed all away, and once more they started across the grassy plain, the storm in the north receding.

When darkness fell, Camille made a fireless camp mid the grass, and, in spite of furtive rustlings in the nearby surround, she fell quite soundly asleep.

By midafternoon of the following day, although she had kept up a steady pace, the mountains seemed no closer, and the foothills, if any, were not in sight. And still Camille had seen no significant life, but for the hawk of yester. Oh, not that she had seen no other life whatsoever, for there were insects, aye—beetles and hoppers—and worms and grubs as well, all unearthed by tiny Scruff during their pauses for meals. Yet they had seen no farms, no towns, no habitation of any kind there on the broad, green plain, and yet it seemed that such should be—

Of a sudden, Scruff chirped and grabbed a tress and dove for the cover of the vest pocket. Camille looked into the sky, yet no hawking bird of any sort did she see. But Scruff repeatedly tugged on her hair and chattered in alarm, and so Camille slowly turned about, her gaze sweeping across the grass, searching—

There! What is—? Riders! Far off. Coming this way.

And still Scruff twittered madly and tugged on her lock, as if trying to pull her within the vest pocket as well.

Camille frowned and glanced down at the bird then up at the riders again, apprehension now in her gaze. "Very well, Scruff," she said, and knelt down. "I will wait until I see what they look like, and then decide whether or no I should stand revealed and ask them for direction or aid."

But Scruff yet chattered and pulled on her tress, and Camille crouched a tiny bit lower.

On came the riders and on, and now she could see—

"Oh, my, those are not horses."

Hairless were the steeds, scaled instead, glittering green, with pale undersides, and long, lashing, whiplike tails, the mounts an impossible crossbreed of serpent and horse, as only in Faery might be. And the riders—

Camille flattened herself in the grass, lying lengthwise to present the least target, praying to Mithras that none would run over her.

—the riders, too, were serpentlike, or so they seemed . . . either that or they wore hideous gargoyle masks, and armor scaled much like the serpent-horses they rode.

And the ground trembled as onward they came, and Camille flattened herself even more, taking care to not crush Scruff, the bird now silent with dread so near.

And then riders thundered by, the steeds hissing and blowing and grunting with effort, the ground shaking as they passed. And riders sissed cries as onward they plunged and away, the shuddering earth slowly subsiding. Yet Camille did not rise, but instead lay with her face buried in grass. And the tremble of the ground became a quiver, then a shiver, and then was still once more. And yet Camille could hear a blowing, as if nearby—

Crack!

"Oh!" Camille emitted a squeal and scrambled to her knees. *Crack!*

She whirled about and saw coming toward her on his serpent-horse one of the riders, a long, lashing whip in hand. And again Camille screamed, for it was *not* armor he wore, but gleaming scales covered his body, and it was *not* a mask, but a gargoyle-like face instead.

The whip lashed out—*Crack!*—the panting serpent-horse jerking its snakelike head up, flinching at the report, yet coming onward. And as Camille sprang to her feet, the rider's dreadful face leered at her, his long, forked tongue licking out as if to *taste* her scent. Hissing laughter sissed as he slowed his steed and drew back his whip for a strike.

Cringing inside, but bracing herself and raising her meager staff in defense, Camille prepared for the blow, yet the rider's eyes widened, and, gasping in alarm, he wrenched the reins about, the serpent-horse squealing in pain. And jabbing long, thornlike spurs into the steed's side, away he galloped, shouting out something to his now-distant and on-riding band as he fled across the plain after.

"Wh-what?" Camille blurted. And she looked down to see Scruff peering out from her pocket and watching the rider hammer away. "Ah, Scruff, is he frightened of nought but a wee little bird?"

Of a sudden Camille's legs gave way, and she fell to her knees in the grass, her whole being shaking with released dread, her breath coming in gasps.

Scruff looked up from her pocket. His tiny brown eyes upon hers. "*Chp!*" he chirped, as if to ask, Why are you trembling? They're gone, you know.

Camille burst out in hysterically giddy laughter, and it was long ere she gained control.

The next day Camille awakened to an empty waterskin, and she walked all that morning, her thirst growing. And still she saw no sign of habitation, nor did she espy any of the serpent-like riders, though she did wonder if they were the reason why there seemed to be no homes.

In midafternoon, far to the south, or so she believed it to be, another storm built, and she hoped it would come this way, as on toward the mountains she trudged.

But by the time night fell, the storm had taken its gift beyond the horizon and away. And Camille had come across no rill, no mere, no water of any sort at all.

In the noontide of the next day, her lips cracked, her throat parched, Camille watched as another distant storm swept over the grassy plain, this one toward mountains far off to her left.

"Oh, Scruff," she rasped, "would that the rain come our way and drench down on us instead of falling on ground so removed. And we have happened upon no streams at all, nor springs, nor ponds, nor lakes. Where do you suppose all the water—" Of a sudden Camille slapped a hand to her forehead. "Ah, fie! And me a farmer's daughter. Of course!" Camille plopped down in the grass, and as Scruff awkwardly fluttered to the ground beside her, she pulled a stem loose at the lowest stalk joint and chewed on the pale end revealed; she was rewarded with a drop or two of moisture. Another stem she pulled and chewed, and another stem, and another, while Scruff dug and scratched in the soil and snatched up insects.

Long did it take Camille to fairly quench her thirst. "Ah but, Scruff, what will you drink?"

As if recognizing the name she had given him, the wee sparrow looked up to her, a wriggling grub in its neb, then hopped across the litter of long grass stalks lying 'round Camille and laid the succulent tidbit at her feet. She burst out laughing. "No, no, my friend, merci, but all the juicy grubs are yours to, um, drink. For me, until we find a pool or stream, it will be these water-bearing stalks of grass."

In all it took Camille a sevenday to reach the foothills, and by this time she was completely out of food, but where she came to the slopes, there she found a stream, and she and Scruff reveled in the luxury of water, drinking and bathing, both.

Her stomach growling, she looked back at the grassland, where it seemed no one at all dwelled, for no settlement of any kind had she seen, not even from the tallest of hills did she espy any. As to life therein, in the days past, several rabbits had scurried away, and raptors had soared in the skies—three redtail hawks and a dark falcon—much to Scruff's anxiety. The riders had appeared once again, thundering down the grassy plain, though the second time she saw them, they were quite distant and did not draw nigh. Whether they were the same serpent-folk, she knew not, nor did she care to know.

And with the lack of friendly dwellers in the grassland, she had decided that she would cross the mountains, for there was a col ahead, perhaps a pass through the range. And so Camille spent the next nine days snaring game—five coneys and two fat marmots—and she thanked sweet Mithras that Giles three years past had taught her how to rig a snare. And though she was quite hungry, she began by baiting her first four traps with pieces of a dug-up wild carrot she otherwise would have eaten whole. The first animal she caught, she cooked and ate nearly all, for she had gone some three days without a substantial meal. Most of the remaining game she used for jerky, cutting and seasoning the thin slices of meat and laying them on racks made of branches set well above glowing coals. Scruff was quite pleased with the suet she spared from rendering the fat from the meat. As the slices slowly dried in the heat, she grubbed for more roots and foraged for berries and nuts and other edible vegetation—pausing occasionally when the times came to turn over the meat strips to dry the opposite sides. And thus she spent the days, storing up food for the trek to come, now that her initial stock was gone. And even as she did these things, still she begrudged the time. "Oh, Scruff, our journey will take even longer should we have to live like this off the land."

Scruff cocked his head and *chp*ed as if to ask, What is so hard about that?

Camille laughed and said, "Well, my cocky little friend, if we both could survive on nought but a few bugs and a handful of grubs and a worm or two each day, then perhaps it wouldn't be very difficult at all. Yet alas, worms and such are not to my taste; besides, it would take—*ugh!*—a great heap of the slimy little wigglers to keep me going. Merci, Scruff, but the worms and bugs are all yours."

When Camille deemed she had enough food to last for a fort-night or so—more with careful rationing—she made ready to set out. But even as she packed her rucksack, a torrential downpour came, and Camille and Scruff huddled under a blanket swiftly rigged much like a tent on a rope tied low between saplings; still, in spite of her all-weather cloak, she became thoroughly drenched by blowing rain and water dripping through, though she did manage to keep the wee sparrow dry by huddling over him. Yet Scruff chirped mournfully, and shifted his distressed wing a bit, as if he were in pain. "Ah, Scruff, 'tis the dampness, eh?" As she had done every day, Camille applied a tiny bit of salve to the injured joint, then she slipped Scruff inside her jerkin, hoping to yield up some warmth to him.

All day it rained, and water rushed down through the foothills from the steeps of the mountains above, and the knoll she camped on became surrounded by a hurtling flood.

The following day the sky cleared and the water slowly subsided, and Camille and the bird basked in the warm rays of the sun as her clothing and blanket and rope and other gear dried out. The sun shone the next day as well, and they lazed in its warmth again, for they were yet trapped by rushing water. Scruff seemed quite pleased to do nought but peck about on the ground; Camille, though, fretted, for now they had lost three days to the storm, and she was anxious to get on with her search for a place east of the sun and west of the moon, wherever it might lie. *Whether or no I am even going in the right direction, I cannot say. Oh, would that this land had someone in it other than those dreadful serpent-folk, someone whom I could ask. But there isn't anyone. Oh, Alain, Alain, where are you? Where are you, my sweet love?*

The day after, with Scruff perched on her shoulder, Camille waded through the runnel of water yet surrounding her hillock and at last began her trek up a long vale and toward the high col ahead.

Up and into the high valley she strode, the land rising before her, pines growing along the slopes, as well as silver birch and aspen, the leaves of the latter trembling in the faint wind.

All morning she hiked upward, wending among the trees as she climbed up toward the pass. She stopped in the noontide to take water and food—rabbit-jerky, for the most part—while Scruff dug about for grubs and beetles, as well as pecked away at the grass seeds Camille had thought to bring. But the pause was short, for she felt the need to go forward, and so she took up the sparrow and onward they pressed as the sun rode down the sky.

Twilight was drawing across on the land when she at last reached the crest.

"Time to make camp, Scruff," she said, as she angled toward a small aspen grove in the throat of the col.

But even as she reached the stand of white-barked trees, a tiny voice squeaked, "Who dares tread in the domain of Jotun the Giant without paying a proper toll?"

20
Giant

"Wh-what?" Camille looked about in the dusk, yet she saw no one. "Who is there, s'il vous plaît?"

Again the voice squeaked out. "Jotun the Giant. And still I ask, who dares tread in my domain without paying the proper toll?"

Now Camille turned about and about, seeking to see the speaker. On her shoulder, Scruff, drowsy in the twilight, emitted a soft "*pip*" as Camille faced a small pine among the aspens.

"Stay away from me, you beady-eyed sparrow," piped the tiny voice. "I am not for you to taste! And you, mademoiselle, control your bird, or I shall have to stomp on him!"

In spite of not seeing this Jotun the Giant, Camille laughed. "Scruff? Why, he wouldn't hurt a fly. —No, wait. That's not right, for he would indeed eat a fly."

"See! I told you!"

"Stay calm, sieur," replied Camille. "Scruff will behave. Besides, he is nearly asleep, and quite well fed, I assure you."

"All right," grumped the wee voice, somewhat mollified, "but see that you keep him in hand, for I might stomp you by mistake. —And now about the toll."

"Toll?"

"Are you planning on going through my pass, Mam'selle um . . . ?"

"Camille. My name is Camille. And, yes, I seek to go beyond this range, and I hope to find someone to tell me where might be a place east of the sun and west of the moon. Would you happen to know, by the way?"

"First things first, Lady Camille," replied Jotun, still unseen. "My toll."

Camille sighed. "I can pay. What will you have? A bronze, a silver, a gold?" The moment she said it, Camille gritted her teeth in silent admonition, for though she had the coins, still she should not have admitted such to a total stranger.

"Pah! What need have I for bronze or silver or even gold? Instead I would have something of more value."

"And just what might that be, M'sieur Jotun the Giant?" asked Camille.

"Have you any pepper?"

Pepper. And here I thought it might be jewels he would demand. "I have a wee bit, m'sieur."

"Fine-grain or coarse or peppercorns?"

"Coarse-grained, sieur."

"Then it's one grain to pass through my col; for another grain I will give you directions to guide you beyond; or three grains in all, and I will conduct you through the range myself and to a town beyond."

"Done!" said Camille, unslinging her bedroll and rucksack and setting both down and laying her staff aside. "Would you have me pay you now?"

"Indeed," piped Jotun. "Else how would I know you have the fee?"

"Very well," said Camille, and in the fading light she rummaged through her goods and drew forth her small lantern and unscrewed the brass oil-keeper-cap from the wick and struck a match and lit it. Then she found her pepper tin, and asked, "Have you canister or some such to store it in?"

"Of course," replied Jotun. "Right here."

"Where are you?" said Camille, looking up, yet unable to locate the speaker.

"As I said, right here," querulously replied Jotun. "On the pine."

Camille held up her lantern the better to see, and her eyes widened in wonder, for stepping forth along a needled branch came a tiny being but an inch or so high. Dressed all in green, a miniature man he seemed. Brown hair, he had, that much Camille could discern, but as to the hue of his eyes, she could not say, for in this dim light they were entirely too small to see any color in them at all. In his hands he held a very tiny canister.

"M'sieur Jotun the Giant?"

"Yes," he replied.

Camille burst out laughing.

Jotun frowned. "Why do you laugh, mam'selle?"

Camille managed to gasp out, "It's just that you name your-self a Giant, when it is plain to see you are a Twig Man, or so my love did describe such as you."

"Twig Man, ha!" scoffed Jotun. "I merely take on this shape as necessary, for, you see, this way it is much easier to find food and such to meet my needs. —I would change into my true form, but I am afraid it would frighten you quite witless."

"Oh, m'sieur, no need to change," said Camille, yet giggling. "I'll simply take your word for it."

"All right, then," said Jotun. "Now about the pepper. Will it be one grain, two, or three?"

"Oh, three certainly," said Camille, opening her pepper tin. "I would have you lead me across these mountains to a town beyond."

She held out her tin, and Jotun searched through the contents as if examining a great pile of gemstones, and he stirred the pep-per with a twig now and then, and one by one he carefully se-lected three large flakes. "The best of the lot, I think," he murmured, stowing away the grains in his own wee canister.

"Have another," said Camille, yet holding out her tin, "and tell me what you know of a place east of the sun and west of the moon."

"No, no, mam'selle," said Jotun, "no more pepper. Three grains I asked for and but three will I have. They'll last me quite awhile as it is." Camille started to protest, but Jotun added, "As to this place you seek, I've not heard of a site so strangely lo-cated, nor do I know where it might be. And so another pepper grain would gain you nought, and I would not dupe you so."

Camille sighed. "It would have been but by chance alone had you known of such; even so, I had to ask."

"Perhaps some of the wise folk in Ardon will know," said Jotun.

"Ardon?"

"The town on the far side of the range."

"Ah," said Camille, "a town will be nice, for I would sleep in a bed again. Yet for now, Jotun, 'tis a camp I must make, and then we'll have a meal—if you would join me, that is. I have some rabbit- and marmot-jerky and some nuts and dried berries and roots—wild carrots and parsnips, in the main . . . a bit of wild onion, too. What say you?"

"Is the jerky peppered?"

Camille nodded, adding, "And spiced with other seasonings as well."

"Ah, then, there is a nice glade within the grove, where a fire will not be easily seen. Still, with me about, you wouldn't have to worry overmuch concerning brigands and such."

As Camille gathered up her things—"Brigands?"

"The Serpentmen from the grass plains below sometimes come up this way"—Jotun puffed out his wee little chest—"especially when I am elsewhere. They pursue any poor folk caught within their demesne. You were fortunate that they did not see you, for they are quite cold-hearted, I say."

"Oh, but they did," said Camille. "—See me, I mean; or at least one did." She held out her hand. "May I carry you to this glade of yours?"

Jotun stepped to her palm, and she set him to the shoulder away from the sleeping sparrow. Holding on to a tress, he directed her toward the center of the grove. As she wended through the trees, Jotun said, "The Serpentmen saw you? And you got away?"

"Aye."

"Well, then, you are most fortunate. The last one that tried to cross over from the Summerwood was slain. A woman, I believe, or so it seemed to me, as I watched from here on my mountain. I would have helped her, but they were done and gone ere I realized it was a woman."

Camille sucked in air through clenched teeth. *Was it the poacher's wife, I wonder? Oh, and it was I who sent her to her death. I shouldn't have suggested that she be exiled from—*

"How did you escape?" asked Jotun.

"I don't know," said Camille, glad for the diversion. "The Serpentman may have actually run away from my sparrow."

Jotun snorted. "Unlikely."

"Well, then, I cannot explain it."

"What exactly did you do? —Oh, wait. Here we are."

Camille set Scruff to a nearby branch, the sparrow peeping an irritated chirp or two at being so disturbed ere falling back to sleep. Camille cleared a patch of ground, then gathered up fallen branches and suitable stones for a ring. Within half a candle-mark altogether she had a small fire ablaze.

She shared out the jerky and some of the dried berries; Jotun took but a tiny portion of each, a mere nip by Camille's standards. As they settled down to eat, again Jotun asked, "What exactly did you do to evade the Serpentmen?"

Camille shrugged. "As they rode past, one of them must have espied me, there where I hid in the grass. As the others raced away, that one turned and came back, him with his long, cruel whip. He came at me, ready to strike, but then he fled away. I looked down and from my high vest pocket"—Camille tapped the one near her left shoulder—"Scruff was peering out. It seems he hides there when danger is nigh. Regardless, the Serpentman cried out in fear and galloped away, and that's all I know."

"He just fled?"

Camille nodded, and took a bite of jerky.

"And you did nothing else at all whatsoever?"

Camille turned up her hands.

They sat without speaking awhile, placidly chewing before the small fire, Jotun savoring the tiny jot of spiced meat. At last they finished their meal, and Camille yawned sleepily. "I must rest, for I am weary, having walked uphill all day." She rolled out her bedroll, but as she did so she said, "Oh, I remember, but I don't see how it could mean aught." She reached over and took up her garlanded walking staff. "When the Serpentman came at me, I thought I might fend off his whip with this." In the light of the fire, Camille thrust the stave out before her, holding it like a quarterstaff.

Tiny though they were, Camille saw Jotun's eyes widen in revelation. "Where did you get that?"

"It was a gift from the Seer by the Mere."

"Lady Sorcière?"

"I do not know her name."

"That is who she is," said Jotun, "or so I do believe. Ha! It is no wonder the Serpentman fled. It was the staff he ran from . . . perhaps believing you were the lady herself." Jotun laughed. "Ah, but what a gift it is you bear, for many know of that staff, and some fear it. Certainly the Serpentman did. —How came you by it?"

"It is a long tale, sieur. Perhaps I can tell it on the journey to come." Camille yawned again.

"Oh, pardon, Mam'selle. I did not think. On our journey will be most acceptable." Jotun stood. "Sleep well. And worry not in your slumber, for if danger comes in the form of Serpentmen, or aught else for that matter, I will stomp them flat."

Camille laughed and took to her bed, and in the flickering light of the dying fire she was asleep in but moments, a smile yet lingering on her lips.

"Shall I change now?" Jotun piped in his tiny voice. "But I warn you, you might find it quite fearsome."

"No, no," said Camille, grinning. "I like you just as you are, my wee friend; that way you can ride on my shoulder, just as does Scruff—he on the left; you on the right. Or would you prefer a high vest pocket?"

Jotun sighed. "As you wish, Mam'selle, and the vest pocket high on the right will do, for there I think it will be easier for me to listen to your tale."

"My tale?"

"How you came to be on this strange quest of yours to find such an odd place as might lie east of the sun and west of the moon. Also, tell me how you came by Lady Sorcière's stave."

"Ah," said Camille, taking Jotun up in her palm and letting him scramble into the pocket. She slung her bedroll and rucksack over her left shoulder and set Scruff there as well, then began the trek through the high-walled pass. As she strode forth, she said to Jotun, "I am a mere farmer's daughter, and I thought I would always be, yet one winter's night as a blizzard was howling there came a loud knock on our door . . . ."

"There it is," said Jotun, pointing down the slope at the lights of the village in the near distance. "I will leave you here, for I do not wish to frighten the townsfolk with my presence. And, Camille, I have so enjoyed your company these last thirty days, coming across the mountains as we did, especially your singing. And I will always be your friend, and I cannot but wish you the best of fortune in finding your Alain. I do believe that Lord Kelmot was right seek the advice of merchants and travellers and traders and mapmakers and such—especially the elders, for they are most likely to know where lies this strange place you seek. Let me down here, for I would say my au revoir now."

Camille smiled as she set the wee mite to the slope, though tears stood in her eyes. "Oh, Jotun, would that I could take you with me, but Lady Sorcière, if that is her name, said I must go alone, though unlooked-for help would come along the way, and it certainly did, else I would have wandered about in those mountains for who knows how many years? Merci, my little Twig Man, for guiding me through, else Scruff and I would not be here now."

"Go," said Jotun. "Else I will be blubbering giant tears, and to see a Giant cry is a terrible thing. So go and go now; your destiny awaits."

With Scruff asleep in the high vest pocket he had claimed as his own, Camille turned and started down the slope. As she went she heard Jotun call down after, "Though I will always treasure the days we spent together, I only wish you had let me change, for we would have been here much the sooner."

From behind there came a great *whooshing* outpush of air, icy cold, as if all the heat, all the power, had been sucked from it. Camille turned and gasped, for looming up toward the stars themselves stood a giant of a man. Fully two hundred feet or more he towered upward in the night, and by light of the waning gibbous moon, Camille could see he was dressed all in green and had brown hair, and she knew his eyes were brown, as she had discovered Jotun's eyes to be in the sunlight of thirty days past. The Giant waved down to her a sad good-bye and then turned and strode away over the mountains, heading back the way he had been borne.

"Oh, Jotun, you really were, really are a Giant," whispered Camille to herself. "Only in Faery," she added, as she turned and made her way down the long slope and toward the village below.

21
Staff

As Camille savored her first hot meal in more than a moon, she glanced about the common room of Le Sanglier, the only inn in the village of Ardon. Illuminated by lanterns set in sconces along the walls, the chamber, though modest, was rather large for such a small thorp, or so Camille judged. Perhaps that in itself held out the promise that travellers and traders oft came this way. The room had but one fireplace, unlit, on the far wall to the left. A handful of oaken tables, with chairs about, sat here and there—one of them occupied by four men drinking ale and playing cards. More or less in room center there were two long tables, common benches on either side, also made of oak. A modest bar sat nigh the back wall, three or four stools in front, two of them occupied by elderly men who spoke across to the innkeeper as he washed earthenware mugs. On the back wall stood two doors, and Camille knew they led into the kitchen, for it was from there the servingwoman—the innkeeper's wife, it seems—had fetched Camille a trencher filled with slices of roast beef smothered in gravy, with bread and cabbage and beans. Camille herself sat at one of the smaller tables, there along the front wall, and to her right beyond the foyer stood an archway leading into a vestibule, where a set of stairs led to the rooms above. It was the first inn Camille had ever seen, and her gaze roamed here and there, taking all in.

As she studied the wild boar's head mounted over the fireplace, one of the doors to the kitchen swung open and out bustled the matronly innkeeper's wife, bearing a tray laden with a teapot and cup and small pitcher of milk and a small pot of honey. "Here you are, mam'selle, freshly brewed."

"Merci, madam," said Camille, smiling. "And madam, if you are not too busy, I would ask you to sit and tell me: do you have any travellers or traders staying at your inn? I am trying to find a place, and I know not where it lies."

"Oh, Mam'selle, just call me Jolie; everyone else does."

Camille took up a piece of bread. "And my name is Camille." She took a bite and chewed.

Jolie smiled and called to her husband to bring her a mug, then sat down in the chair across and poured Camille a cup of tea. When her own mug arrived, she waved her husband away, and then poured herself some tea, adding milk and a bit of honey. She took a sip then said, "This place you seek, Lady Camille, has it a name?"

Camille shook her head; she swallowed her bite and said, "East of the sun and west of the moon is all I know it by." Camille sliced off a bit of beef.

Jolie frowned. "I have not heard of such, and— Oh, my, but is that a bird you have in your pocket?"

Camille grinned and nodded and said around the chew of beef, "Scruff. A sparrow. Asleep for the nonce. He is my travelling companion."

Jolie shook her head. "A young fille like you, out on the roads alone with nought but a wee sparrow for company. It is quite dangerous, you know, what with villains and thieves about, Spriggans and such, ghosts of Giants they once were—the Spriggans, I mean. Tell me, aren't you afraid to go about without a strong guard at your side, a knight or some such?"

"I have no choice. I must travel alone, though I can accept help along the way."

"Alone?"

"Aye. Lady Sorcière so bade me."

Jolie's eyes widened at the mention of that name; even so, she took it in stride. "A quest it is, then?"

Camille nodded, chewing.

"I take it you are bound for this place east of the sun and west of the moon, but where did you come from?"

Camille vaguely gestured. "Through the grass and over the mountains, I came from the Summerwood."

"Oh, my. All the way across the land of the Serpentmen and then through the les Montagnes Sans Fin?"

Camille frowned in puzzlement. "Why do you call them the Endless Mountains?"

Jolie shrugged. "Although I've never entered the chain, it is said that the range is only one hundred miles or so across this side to that, yet I am told the ways within are so twisted that one could travel endlessly and never make it through. The merchants mostly go around."

"Around? But the chain seemed quite long to me; the way through quicker."

"Ah, but there is a twilight border somewhat down the road"—Jolie pointed . . . south, Camille thought—"and beyond that marge one can go 'round, for there are no mountains there. No Serpentmen plains either."

How can that be? —Ah, I know: 'tis Faery. Camille sighed. "Well, I went through, and endless they did seem. It took thirty days altogether; and even with careful rationing, I ran out of food on the last day, though Scruff had no difficulty in finding a meal."

Jolie *tsked* and shook her head, saying, "You were fortunate, for even with a guide who knows the way, they say one will travel three or four times the distance—days and days and days of travel, just as you did, simply to get from one side to another."

Camille nodded, saying, "Indeed, 'tis true. —And I was guided by one who knew the way."

"Who?"

"Jotun."

"Jotun the Giant?"

Camille nodded.

"A fearsome sight, is Jotun. We all run a distance away when he comes nigh."

"But he is quite gentle," protested Camille.

"That he may be," replied Jolie. "But he once stepped on a herd of sheep. Squashed them flat; killed them all dead, there in their wee little pen, when Jotun, unthinking, took a step backward, and his heel came down upon them. And now when he comes about, we all run to a safe distance."

"Ah, then, that's why he did not come to the village," said Camille. "He believes you are afraid, you know."

"That we are, indeed. That's why we run somewhat away, just in case he loses his balance and takes an unplanned step, or even stumbles and falls. You are to be commended for your bravery." Jolie frowned. "Even so, I do not understand. Jotun the Giant can cross over the mountains in but a day or so, and yet it took you thirty?"

Camille sighed. "I did not realize he was a Giant."

"How could you not know he was a Giant, that big fearsome thing?"

Suddenly Camille realized that the folk of Ardon might not know that Jotun could take on another form, and she did not know whether it was a secret he wanted her to keep.

Before Camille could answer, "Jolie!" called one of the card players.

"One moment, Camille," said Jolie.

As Jolie went to serve the man, Camille continued to eat, and she wondered how she would answer Jolie's question without betraying Jotun's secret, if indeed a secret it was. But when Jolie came and seated herself again and took up her tea—"Did you see the Serpentmen?"

Camille nodded. "A band rode past me, and one saw where I lay hidden. He came back, his long whip in hand." Camille pointed to the staff leaning against the table at her side. "My stave saved me. He recognized it as Lady Sorcière's and fled away."

"Oh, my," said Jolie. "You were most fortunate." She looked at the staff. "May I?"

Camille nodded and handed the stick to her.

Jolie examined the stave. "How beautiful. And though I don't recognize these blossoms, the garland is so lifelike." Of a sudden Jolie's brow furrowed. "But here down by the tip there are no carved flowers, and the vine itself looks a bit withered, and the very bottom flower seems withered as well. I wonder why the carver made it so?" She looked at Camille and shrugged, then peered at the stave again, adding, "I suppose we'll never know. Ah, but the rest of the staff is quite beautiful." After another moment or so, she handed it back to Camille.

Camille frowned and peered at the bottom flower. Indeed it did look shrunken, as if it were dying. The vine curling on down to the tip did seem shrunken, too.

Jolie took up the teapot and poured a bit into each cup, saying, "These need warming. —Now about your question, Camille . . ."

Camille set the stave aside.

". . . there is one traveller in the inn. He's over there playing cards with some of the locals. Losing too, I might add. I asked him if he knew of such a place as you seek, but he said he did not, nor did the other players. And when I fetched ale, I asked my husband Bertrand and those two at the bar, and they did not know either."

Camille sighed in disappointment. "Jolie, are there any mapmakers in town?"

Jolie shook her head.

"Then what about folk who might know where a land or town or village or dwelling or aught whatsoever lies east of the sun and west of the moon; do you know of any? Former merchants, travellers, hunters, elders, anyone who might know?"

"Well, I know everyone in Ardon, and I think none have travelled that much. Even so, it is a small hamlet, and you can easily ask each one. 'Twould only take a day or three to do so."

"Oh, my," said Camille. "I do hope that every town I come to I don't have to ask every dweller within."

Jolie smiled and laid a sympathetic hand atop one of Camille's.

In that moment, Bertrand called, "Jolie, th' lady's bathwater is hot out back, so as whenever she's ready. And as to the laundry . . ."

"Ah," said Jolie, turning to Camille, "as to your laundry, just leave it for me." Then she grinned and looked at sleeping Scruff. "I take it the little tyke rides on your shoulder, there where I see the white dripping on your cloak."

Camille blushed. "I usually clean it off each evening myself, but I was so hungry I didn't stop and—"

Jolie laughed. "Never you mind, fille, I can do it quite well."

Of a sudden, Camille remembered the coins and jewelry sewn into the lining of her all-weather cloak. "Oh, Jolie, I will clean my own cloak, if you will but show me to the tubs."

Jolie argued, but Camille insisted, and so to the bathing room they went, which also doubled for the laundry. When they were alone, Jolie said, "If it's coins and such you have in the lining of your cloak, *pish-tish*, travellers come here all the time with such, and I've not broken a confidence yet."

Camille sighed, and handed Jolie the all-weather garment and then each of the others as she disrobed to bathe, not bothering to hide her money belt.

That night in her room ere climbing into bed, again Camille examined the staff. *My goodness, the bottommost blossom seems even more withered. Whatever can that mean?*

*   *   *

The next dawntide, Camille was awakened by Scruff gently pecking on her cheek and chirping, heralding the light of the new day. Camille stumbled out from the bed and fetched a bit of the remaining grass seed yet stored in her rucksack. She made a small mound on the floor and set Scruff down. Eagerly he took to the seed, and Camille flopped back into bed. In moments she was deep in slumber.

In midmorning there came a tap on the door. Yet half-asleep, Camille groped her way to the panel. It was Jolie, the laundry fresh, the leather pants and vest scraped and wiped down clean. "Break of fast awaits your pleasure, Camille, though the day is well on its way." Jolie swept from the room.

Camille groaned, and looked about for Scruff. He was pecking away at some kind of insect safely ensconced down between two floorboards. Camille poured water from an ewer into a basin and splashed some on her face, then she set the basin to the floor, where Scruff then took a full bath, fluttering and flouncing in the water, ere hopping out to shake himself off.

In moments Camille was dressed. "Come along, Scruff, it's time to eat. She took up her stave, then paused, and once again looked at the bottommost—

Goodness, it seems to have recovered. Now how can that be? Was it just a trick of the light?

The bottom blossom no longer appeared withered, but fairly fresh instead, though the blossom above it seemed fresher still.

Shaking her head in puzzlement, Camille set still-damp Scruff to her shoulder and headed for the common room. Jolie had Camille take her morning meal at a table in an arbor out back, where Scruff could scratch for grubs and insects and worms. Too, Jolie arranged for some millet seed to augment the little bird's fare.

After a breakfast of rashers and toast and eggs, Camille took Scruff up, and through the village she went, stopping at dwellings and businesses and barns and such and asking the folk she found if anyone knew of a place east of the sun and west of the moon.

Long she spent at some of these stops, for folk there wanted to know of the news. Camille could only tell them of various happenings in the Summerwood, and of her Alain gone missing—though she avoided speaking of the curse. She spoke of her trip across the grassland and escaping the Serpentmen, then of her travel through Les Montagnes Sans Fin. Each and every one she met that day said she should have gone around—" 'Tis much safer that way, you know."

As evening drew nigh, Camille had only talked to a portion of the villagers; she would have to resume the next day.

Oh, I should have asked them who is the oldest person in the hamlet, for Lord Kelmot advised me that especially the elders might have the lore. I'll do so on the morrow.

Camille returned to Le Sanglier.

After she took her supper that eve and had gone up to her room, Camille sat in the bed and by lanternlight examined the walking staff. Again the bottommost blossom was withered. Frowning in puzzlement, Camille set the stave aside and blew out the lamp and pulled the covers about her chin. Moments later she fumbled for the striker and lit the lantern once more. She rummaged through her rucksack and pulled out a spool of thread. Breaking off a piece, she wrapped it around the cane, tying it tightly just below the withered flower. Again she blew out the lamp; it was awhile ere she slept.

Dawn came, and Scruff chirped and pecked lightly on Camille's cheek, waking her. It was only after she washed her face that Camille remembered the stave. She took it up and where a flower should have been, there was nought, though the thread was yet tightly affixed. She closely examined the place where the flower had been. *Oh, what's this? A tiny indention on the carved vine itself, as if it marks the place from which the blossom fell . . . But these are* wooden *flowers.*

She looked on the floor for a tiny chip of wood or a grain of sawdust, something to be the blossom fallen from the stave. Yet she found nought.

Then she took up the stick again and looked down the length of the vine carefully. She found more tiny indentions along the part that appeared to be withered. Scruff chirped insistently to go out for his early feast, and Camille murmured, "In a moment, Scruff." She counted the tiny dimples. *Sixty-one. There are sixty-one wee dints.* Still Scruff chattered. Camille sighed and said, "All right, my wee hungry friend, it's to a meal we go."

Swiftly she dressed, and down the stairs and out into the arbor she took Scruff. As he scrabbled about after his morning meal, Camille puzzled over the staff.

*   *   *

Again that day, Camille spoke with villagers, and none knew where lay a place east of the sun and west of the moon. They did tell her that the oldest person in the hamlet was probably Vivette, or mayhap Romy: they were sisters, perhaps twins, and it seems they had built the first house in this place, and anchored by their dwelling, the hamlet of Ardon slowly came to be as others settled in as neighbors.

Gradually, stopping at each door, Camille worked her way toward the cottage of the sisters, but none of the villagers on the way could answer her question as to where the place she looked for might be. As to the sisters, they lived in the last dwelling along the outbound lane, and there did Camille finally come.

Her knock on the door was answered by a beautiful maiden, a jot taller than Camille and a deal more buxom, and she had dark blue eyes and black hair twined with flowers down to the middle of her back.

"Yes? . . . Oh, you must be Camille. The whole village is talking of you, my dear, and of your quest. Come in. Come in. We've been expecting you. —Romy! Romy! Camille has finally come."

As Camille stepped across the threshold and into a parlor, she said, "You are . . .?"

"Vivette," said the damsel, just as another beautiful, dark-haired, and buxom maiden entered, her eyes blue as well.

"Oh, but I was expecting someone, er . . ."

The sisters looked at one another, somewhat bewildered. "Someone . . .?" said Vivette, pausing, waiting on Camille.

"Well, older," blurted Camille.

Again the sisters looked questioningly at one another, and Romy said, "Well, there isn't anyone older in Ardon than us."

"But you're not, um . . ."

Enlightenment filled Vivette's eyes. "Ah, I see. Wrinkled, you mean. Age-bent."

Camille shrugged and grinned apologetically.

"Oh, la!" said Romy. "It's just that we've never been in the mortal lands, where I understand time does terrible things."

Only in Faery, thought Camille, and smiled as Vivette said, "Sit. I'll put on a kettle. Romy has some wonderful petit fours. And perhaps we can fetch up something for that cute little sparrow of yours."

On Camille's shoulder, Scruff emitted a *chp!* as if to say, Cute?

Camille spent an afternoon at tea with them, and though the sisters did have much lore, neither did know of a land or district or town or building or aught else that fit what Camille sought. They did, however, bid her to seek the aid of the Lady of the Bower. "She lives somewhere across the twilight boundary down the road," said Vivette. "Just where, I cannot say."

Camille looked at Romy, but she shook her head and shrugged.

"This Lady of the Bower . . ." said Camille.

"A wisewoman," said Vivette.

"With knowledge arcane," added Romy.

"And you know not where she lives?"

The sisters looked at one another and then to Camille and shook their heads. "But she's somewhere beyond the marge," said Vivette.

"It's just that we don't go there," said Romy. "The Spriggans, you know."

"I do not care for ghosts," said Camille. "Especially the ghosts of Redcaps, but any ghost of anyone or thing, I would rather avoid."

Vivette frowned. "Ghosts?"

"The Spriggans," replied Camille. "Jolie at the inn said that Spriggans are the ghosts of Giants."

"Oh, la, Camille, that is but an old wives' tale," said Vivette. "They are not ghosts at all, but rather ugly little things who can inflate themselves to enormous size to make you think they are Giants; yet instead they are quite cowardly."

"Thieves, they are," added Romy. "They'll steal you blind and flee to hidden caves, where they ward their ill-gotten gains."

"Though cowards all, some say they are quite dangerous," said Vivette, "able to call up great winds and storms."

"If you have any valuables," said Romy, "I would advise avoiding their realm. Either that, or you could wait for a knight-errant to escort you through."

"Knight-errant?"

"Yes," said Romy. "Travelling sellswords, they are. Now and then one comes through. They are quite gallant and brave, and would make splendid travelling companions across perilous realms."

"When might one come by?" asked Camille.

"Perhaps in a moon or two," said Vivette. She glanced at her sister and then leaned forward and whispered, "We usually entertain them."

Romy giggled and twirled a finger in her dark hair. "It seems they tell one another about us."

"In a moon or so," said Vivette. "Perhaps more than one will come. Then you can have a brave companion to escort you beyond the twilight. Of course, they tend to stay here awhile, and so it might be a fortnight or two ere they'll be ready to take to the road again."

"I think I cannot wait," said Camille, "for I must find my Alain, and if the Lady of the Bower can aid me, knight or no, I have no choice but to go on."

The sisters looked at one another and *tsk-tsk*ed, and Romy said, "Well, then, you must go."

Once again that evening, Camille examined the walking stave. As before, the bottommost flower looked withered. "Ah, Scruff, how can this be? At break of day it was quite healthy. But now . . . Besides, the flower is wooden, carved. How can such wither?" Scruff answered not, for he was quite sound asleep, tucked away in the shadows of the bed canopy. Once more she counted the tiny dints on the carved vine. *Sixty-one: the same as this morning.* Again she counted them. *Sixty-one.* She set the staff aside, and disrobed, making ready for bed. As she was washing her face, she glanced across at the stave. *I wonder how many flowers?* Swiftly she finished her ablutions, and then took up the stave again, but this time she counted the blossoms, including the withered one. *Hmm . . . Three hundred and five.* Once more she counted them, and then again; the tally remained the same. An elusive thought tugged at her mind, yet she could not quite grasp it. This night as well, she tied a thread about, just below the last blossom. Then she blew out the lantern and crawled under the covers. "Lady Sorcière, what does this mean?" she asked aloud in the dark. But no answer came.

Sixty-two and three hundred and four; one blossom less, one dint more. "Did you know that, Scruff? One blossom less, one dint more."

"*Chp-chp-chp-chp . . . !*" Scruff chattered, yet it seemed more likely he complained of being hungry, rather than responding to her question.

"All right, all right, you demanding little beggar, it's off to break our fast we go."

Down the stairs she went, and out into the arbor. She set Scruff to the ground and then took a seat at the table. And though her gaze was upon Scruff chasing insects, it was plain she did not see him, for she was deep in thought: *A blossom withers each day, sixty-two altogether. What can it—? Oh, sweet Mithras!* Swiftly Camille tallied up how many days she had been on her quest. *Two days and a half it took to go from the Lady of the Mere to the twilight border along the grassland; seven days on the grass; some nine days in the foothills gathering food; ah, three days trapped by rain; a day walking up to the col; thirty days across the Endless Mountains; and two full days in Ardon, not counting today, which has just begun. That sums to, um . . . fifty-five days altogether. Fifty-nine if I add in the time I searched for the Seer by the Mere . . . Lady Sorcière. That doesn't tally to sixty-two. Oh, then there is this: sixty-two dints and three hundred and four blossoms, that sums to three hundred and sixty-six; that's how many blossoms the staff must have started wi—*

"Your break fast, Camille," someone called.

Her concentration broken, Camille glanced up to see Jolie coming out to the arbor, a laden tray in hand. As Jolie set the tray to the table and began parceling out the dishes and such thereon, she asked, "Have you had any luck with your query? The whole village wants to know."

Camille sighed. "Non, Jolie. It seems no one in Ardon knows the—" Suddenly Camille's eye widened in revelation, and she snatched up the stave. "Three hundred and sixty-six! A year and a day!"

"What, my lady?" asked Jolie, taken somewhat aback by Camille's outburst.

"Don't you see, Jolie? Alain disappeared sixty-two days ago, the same number as are dints on the stave, the same number as the flowers that have withered. If I add up all the dints and the remaining blossoms, it comes to three hundred and sixty-six: a year and a day. 'A year and a day and a whole moon beyond,' that's what Lady Sorcière said. The withering blossoms are— But wait. What about . . .?"

Jolie, entirely confused, watched as Camille again carefully examined the staff. A moment later, Camille pointed to the dark disk at the top of the garland. "That must be the moon, Jolie.

—Oh, my, this is a calendar, a marking stick, keeping track of the days."

"I remember calendars from when I lived in the mortal lands," said Jolie, yet bewildered, for she had no idea whatsoever what three hundred and sixty-six had to do with Camille, nor a whole moon beyond, for that matter. Jolie shook her head. "But there are no calendars here. Not in Faery. Time touches not this place."

"Ah, but the sun does rise and days do pass," said Camille, "and moons do wax and wane. Oh, Jolie, I now know I cannot wait for a knight-errant, but instead must be on my way, for the days are truly numbered."

"Well, you'll break your fast ere you go," snapped Jolie, "for I'll not send you out on the road astarve."

Two candlemarks later, with her staff in hand and her bedroll slung, along with her replenished rucksack and waterskin, and with wee Scruff perched on her shoulder, Camille set out down the lane, a twilight border somewhere in the distance ahead. The entire village turned out to see her off, many calling out "Bonne fortune" and "Bonne chance," but others cautioning her to beware of brigands and thieves and ghosts and other such evil beings. The last to bid au revoir were the sisters Vivette and Romy, and they embraced Camille and kissed her, Vivette saying, "I do hope you find your Alain," and Romy adding, "Seek the Lady of the Bower, and 'ware the Spriggans."

A full two days later—with another pair of blossoms withered and gone—in early midmorn, Camille and Scruff came to a looming, twilight border and stepped into yet another realm of Faery beyond.

22

Everted

"Oh, Scruff," said Camille, a tremor in her voice, "I am not at all certain I like this place."

She and the sparrow had stepped through the twilight to come into a dismal mire, bogland left and right of the road, with cypresses and black willows and dark, gnarled oaks twisting up out from the quag, some trees alive, others quite dead. And from these latter, long strands of lifeless gray moss hung adrip from withered branches, as if the parasite had sucked every last bit of sustenance from the limbs, hence not only murdering the host, but killing itself as well. 'Round the roots and boles of the trees and past sodden hummocks, scum-laden water receded deep into the dimness beyond, the yellow-green surface faintly undulating, as if some vast creature slowly breathed in the turgid muck below. Ocherous reeds grew in clumps and clusters, and here and there rotting logs covered with pallid toadstools and brownish ooze jutted out at shallow angles from the dark muck, the swamp slowly ingesting slain trees. And from within the bog there came soft ploppings and slitherings, but what made these sounds, Camille could not see. And the road itself twisted onward, into the shadowy morass ahead.

"Well, Scruff, there's nothing for it, but that we must go on, for somewhere in this realm the Lady of the Bower dwells, though I do hope it is not in this quag."

"*Chp!*" answered the sparrow, its head turning this way and that, its tiny body slightly atremble.

Forward stepped Camille, the tip of her walking stave striking the soft earth of the road: *plp . . . plp . . . plp . . .*

She had taken no more than a half dozen strides when a whirling cloud of whining gnats and blood-sucking mosquitoes came buzzing out from the mire to swirl about and attack any and all exposed flesh, and to attack wee little Scruff as well. Swiftly, from the rucksack, Camille donned her gloves, and she slipped Scruff into her vest pocket, then drew her cloak about and pulled up the hood. For the most part this thwarted the blood-mad insects, though Camille then had to enwrap her face and forehead and neck in a scarf, leaving only her eyes exposed. Still, the most voracious mosquitoes managed to pierce the cloth and suck life regardless. And the gnats buzzed about her eyes, dancing motes gyrating in air. And though Camille brushed her hand back and forth before her face, it did little to drive them away.

The day was warm, and Camille began to swelter, enwrapped as she was. And this seemed to bring on more mosquitoes, more gnats, and in addition there came biting flies. But still she trudged on, sweating beneath her garb, a whining cloud all about. Yet the insects could not penetrate the leather of her pants and boots and gloves, nor the cloth of the all-weather cloak, and so, uncomfortable as she was, still Camille shed nought to be cooler. In the darkness beneath her cloak, Scruff had gone to sleep, though the wee bird was overwarm as well.

Just ere the noontide, and above the whine of insects, Camille thought she heard someone wailing, and the shrill of an animal too. And as she rounded a bend in the road, ahead she saw a bent crone holding the end of a frayed rope and tearing at her hair and howling. In a boghole at hand, a swayback nag grunted and wallowed and squealed in panic, mired up to its ribs in the muck.

As Camille approached, she called out, "Madam, may I help?"

The crone turned, and her eyes widened in fear. "Keep away," she croaked, cowering back and making an arcane gesture.

"Madam, I shall not harm you."

"Then why is your face hidden if not to rob me of my goods and steal my mare?" snapped the crone, now belligerent.

Rob her? And she dressed in nought but rags and her horse mired belly deep. "I am no brigand, madam," said Camille, casting back her hood. "I but wear this because of the—" Of a sudden, Camille realized that the mosquitoes and gnats and biting flies were gone. She unwrapped the scarf and tucked it away in her rucksack.

"Why, you're just a chit of a fille," said the crone, cackling in glee, revealing the stained snags of but three widely spaced teeth: two above and one in between below, her gums empty otherwise. But then like quicksilver her demeanor changed once again, and she held up the frayed end of the rope for Camille to see and gestured at the floundering nag and began to wail once more.

By this time Camille had reached the crone, and the stench from the churned-up quag was dreadful, much like rotten eggs. Near to gagging, but now breathing through her mouth, Camille looked at the poor animal, its shabby white coat splattered with mud, and she said, "Fear not, madam, I'm sure we can get your horse out from there."

"But how?" wailed the crone. "The rope is too short to reach my mare, and she's too stuck to come closer."

"We'll think of a way," said Camille, looking about. "Perhaps we can use that broken limb yon to snag the end of the rope I see yet attached to her harness."

The old crone laughed merrily and danced a bit of a jig, and she called out in a singsong chant, "How clever you are, 'tis easy to see, my beautiful young fille, to fetch out my filly for me." And then she smiled slyly and added, "But not clever enough, my tender sweet, else you'd release the bird ere he dies of heat."

Camille's eyes widened in surprise. "How did you kn—?"

"Never you mind. Just do as I say." The crone's tone was quite matter-of-fact.

Camille opened her cloak and wakened Scruff, his little beak wide and panting. He seemed quite exhausted, but after many sips of water from Camille's cup, he recovered somewhat, though not quite to his usual chipper self.

"I was protecting him from the mosquitoes," said Camille.

"Sometimes the cure is worse than the ailment," angrily barked the crone, her mood changing quicksilver again.

"But the blood suckers seem to be gone now," said Camille. "Mayhap it is the stench."

"What stench?" asked the crone a bit fearfully, the whites of her eyes showing as she looked about as if to see the very odor manifest itself as some wraithlike being.

Camille sighed, and then fetched the fallen limb. After several unsuccessful tries, with the crone sneering in derision behind her and ineffectually telling her just how to go about it, at last Camille managed to snag the rope and draw it from the watery muck. She tied that end to the one the crone held, and, calling for the mare to come forward, together they pulled, but the nag seemed to drag against them.

The crone hurled down her end of the rope and began to snivel and moan. "This isn't working," she blubbered, then snarled, "You need to come up with a better scheme."

Camille took a deep breath and looked at Scruff, the sparrow now pecking after something tiny with legs. "Have you any grain, or a carrot or apple or some such we can use to lure the animal forth?"

"Do I look as if I have a garden or orchard hidden in my fashion wear?" snapped the crone, flouncing her tattered clothes.

Camille gritted her teeth, yet she managed a smile. "Nay, madam, you do not. And neither do I have aught in my rucksack to use as a lure."

"Well, then, dearie," sneered the crone, "that's no plan at all, now is it?"

"Madam, perhaps I should simply leave you and your horse to your own devices."

At this the crone wailed, and once more the nag began to flounder.

Gritting her teeth, Camille whipped off her gloves and cloak and dropped them onto her rucksack, her vest following swiftly after. "There's nothing for it but that I must wade in and push from behind, while you pull from the front. But I'll not do it in my clothes."

The crone was astonished. "You would wade in for me?"

"More for your horse, I believe," replied Camille, plopping to the ground and jerking off her boots.

Camille shed her clothes quickly, snatching her jerkin over her head and stripping away her breeks, both jerkin and breeks turned inside out in her haste. At the sight of such, the crone's mad eyes widened and spittle flew from her gaping mouth, and as Camille disrobed, the crone danced about and in her crackling singsong she chanted:

> "For some 'tis like a terrible shout,
> When all are worn the wrong side out,
> Including cloaks to withstand the weather,
> And breeches and vests made of soft leather,

As well as a fine silky-smooth jerkin,
And two leather gloves made for working."

With each thing named, the crone shuffled her feet and hopped up and down and took up the associated garment, and if it was not then inside out she turned it such and laid it down just so.

"But not a pair of good sturdy boots;
These you must wear upon the wrong foots.
They quail before the horrible sight,
And many will run in headlong fright."

With this, and jigging to and fro, she set the boots side by side, with the left one on the right, and the right one on the left. Then wild-eyed she looked at Camille, the girl now completely undressed, and the old woman crooned:

"Even when night lies on the sward,
Wrong-side-out stands sentinel ward,
Much like iron for a wicked few,
Better than iron for me and you."

With that her chant was finished, and she twirled 'round and 'round and crowed madly at the sky.

"Madam, take up the rope, for I am ready," said Camille, and she gingerly stepped into the dreadful-smelling mire, then waded forward with purpose, slogging through the slime and water and churned-up muck and the squishing sludge beneath. Nearly to her armpits in the reeking quag, and pushing a turgid wake before her, Camille struggled to the rear of the nag. She turned and put her shoulder to the beast's hindquarters and called out, "Pull!" while at the same time shoving with all her strength. The animal leapt forward, and Camille fell flat on her face into the evil-smelling slough and plunged completely under. Up she came, spluttering and wiping her eyes, and on the shore the crone hooted and pointed at Camille with one hand while slapping her thigh with the other. The nag, now free, stood on the road behind her.

And even as Camille, grinding her teeth, pushed toward the shore, a sluggish wave preceding, the crone leapt to the swayed back of the animal and called out to Camille, "Be thankful for my gift, and remember what I told you!" She dug in her heels and away trotted the nag.

Gift? What gift? And what did she tell me, other than the ludicrous babblings of someone quite daft?

When Camille scrambled onto dry land, she looked down the road after the crone and mare, but they were nowhere to be seen.

Where . . .? —That broken-down nag simply wasn't that fast, was it?

Sighing, Camille turned back toward her inside-out clothes and noted for the first time just how they were arrayed: with the reversed-left-right boots standing, and the wrong-side-out cloak upon the ground behind them, the hem toward the boots and the hood away; the inside-out breeks were stretched out on the cloak, legs toward the boots, with the inside-out jerkin just above and dressed in the wrong-side-out vest; the inside-out gloves lay on the ground at the ends of the jerkin sleeves. It was almost as if all the garments had been laid out to represent a person. Shaking her head at the old woman's madness, Camille wondered just how in sweet Mithras's name she would ever get clean enough to don the clothes again. She looked down at her slime-slathered, muck-laden body, and that's when she discovered the leeches.

The bogland echoed with a prolonged scream, followed by some well-chosen words.

After wafting floating scum aside, Camille washed herself in fairly clean water from a pool she found along the opposite berm; then using some of her coursing rags, and a bit of the salve from the jar, she finally stanched the bleeding. With that done, she turned her clothes right-side-out and dressed. In spite of the scent of blood in the air, no mosquitoes nor gnats nor biting flies came to call. "Perhaps, Scruff, it's the dreadful stench of the churned-up quag. Then again, perhaps not. Another mystery of Faery, eh?" She knelt and opened her rucksack and looked behind the secret panel; just as with her money belt, all was there. "Well, Scruff, at least the old crone wasn't a thief," said Camille as she closed the rucksack again, "though I was a fool for undressing and wading into the mire without thinking that she might be. Why, she could have run off with everything I own, and I could have done nought about it. And this after the warnings in Ardon that thieves and such lie along this road. Indeed, I was a fool."

Camille slung her goods and took up her stave and set Scruff to her shoulder, and smartly down the road she went, completely free of blood-sucking mosquitoes and whining gnats and biting flies, though they swarmed in the sloughs at hand.

Slowly, so slowly, the road ascended, and the mire to either side diminished. In early afternoon, Camille paused for a meal, and she augmented Scruff's diet of slaughtered insects with a bit of millet seed. But soon she pressed on at a quick-march pace, for she hoped to be free of this dreadful and dismal quag ere the setting of the sun. And still the land continued its gradual rise, the swamp slowly retreating, though here and there stagnant pools did yet lie, where clouds of gnats and mosquitoes and biting flies swarmed, though they bothered not Camille and Scruff.

Toward evening, at last Camille emerged from the bogland and came into a forest, the road now wending among the trees, the land rising here and falling there and running level for stretches. As twilight drew down on the land—

"Oh, Scruff, did you see?"

—flickering among the trees there sped a flash of white.

Is that a rider? The old woman on the swayback? Ah, no, it moves entirely too fast to be that broken-down nag.

Then the white flash was gone.

Camille continued on a bit more, and she came to the edge of a rugged hill country.

"Enough walking for today, Scruff. Night draws nigh."

Scruff didn't answer, sound asleep on her shoulder as he was.

Camille stepped into a small clearing just off the road, and therein she made camp. And she fell aslumber while eating her meal beside a very small fire.

"Oh, Alain," Camille murmured, as he ran his hands up under her blouse and slipped them about her waist. Whatever else she might have dreamed, only that one thing did she remember when she wakened chill in the night, her cloak gone, her jerkin pulled out from her breeks, her money belt gone as well. Gasping in alarm, she sat up, and, by the light of the waning half-moon and the yet-glowing coals of her fire, she saw that her rucksack and Lady Sorcière's stave and her waterskin and bedroll were gone as well. Even as she started to call out to Scruff—the bird fast asleep on a nearby branch—in the silence of the night, she heard soft laughter, and the sound of some one or ones scrabbling off through the underbrush in the deep moonshadows, fleeing with the ill-gotten gains.

"Oh, no you don't," gritted Camille, and she leapt to her feet and took up Scruff and slipped him into her high vest pocket, the sparrow chirping softly once or twice at being handled in the night. Then, following the furtive sounds, Camille quietly ran after the one thief, or several.

Through the rugged hill country she followed, scrambling up steep slopes and down angled slants and across rocky streams. And now Camille knew that there were more than just one, for as they had gotten farther away from her meager camp, they became boisterous, laughing away at their ill deed, and jabbering at how easily it was done, no longer attempting to be quiet.

The moon slid down the sky as through winding canyons and across shale-laden hills and past thickets and briars they led her.

But at last they scrambled up a boulder-strewn slope, where high on its flank Camille saw the glowing mouth of a cave, lit from within by a fire. And she gasped once more, for in the light streaming outward she then saw the forms of the thieves: six altogether there were, and small, three or so foot tall at most, with spindly arms and legs. Their clothing was quite ragged, and, when one turned to look at another, by the firelight glowing forth Camille could see that he was wholly ugly.

"Goblins?" she whispered to herself, wondering. "Or perhaps— No wait. Spriggans, they are. Just as Vivette and Romy described."

"Ho, we're back!" cried one as he stepped inside, Lady Sorcière's staff in hand.

"With booty, too," called another, Camille's cloak draped over his arm, with a third Spriggan and three more following, each bearing an item of hers—money belt, waterskin, bedroll, and rucksack.

A babble of voices responded, and then Camille knew that this was a den of thieves.

"What will I do, Scruff?" she whispered. "There seem to be many within."

But Scruff answered not from the vest pocket, sound asleep as he was.

Using the boulders as cover, Camille crept up the slope. She came to a place where she could see in, and by firelight reflected 'round a turn in the cave, she saw a gaggle of Spriggans gathered, some of whom pawed through her rucksack, casting clothing and food and such aside, while others examined her remaining goods. One at the rucksack crowed and lifted up a necklace; he had found the hidden pocket. Another poured out the coins from her money belt, and still another tested each ducat with his teeth.

Just like my mother. The image flashed through Camille's mind, and she was immediately ashamed for having thought it. She cast that image away, and watched as one unrolled her bedroll and shook out the blanket, while another poured out the water from her waterskin and jiggled it up and down to see if aught of value was within, while others fumbled along the lining of her cloak, searching for more wealth. *Oh, sweet Mithras, what will I do without my goods?*

Once again, one of the Spriggans crowed; he had found the treasure sewn in the lining of the cloak. As he drew a knife to slit the cloth, another called out for attention, this one with a tattered black hat atop his head. "To the pile," he said. Whatever he meant, Camille could not guess, but the result of his words was plain, for they rerolled her blanket and poured the coins back into the money belt and returned the goods to the rucksack, including refilling the secret pocket with its coinage and jewelry. And then they took up all and trooped deeper into the cave, disappearing 'round the turn.

"What will I do?" she asked sleeping Scruff. "I have not even my staff as a weapon. Oh, would that I had a sword." She remembered Borel's words, and added, "A sword of iron would lay these by, though I know not how to use one. —Or would that I had an enchanted sword, one even better than iron."

A memory tugged at Camille's mind. "Better than iron," she repeated. " 'Better than iron for me and you,' that's what the old woman said . . . that, and 'remember my words.' Oh, Scruff, do you think it so? Durst I trust the mad babblings of a daft old crone. Yet did she not also say 'Much like iron for a wicked few'? Ah, but are these Spriggans among those for whom it is true; are they ones for whom such will be a terrible shout? —Oh, but I do need my goods."

Taking a deep breath and deciding, swiftly Camille stripped off her clothes and turned them wrong-side-out. The she redonned all, and as she slipped on the turned vest she murmured to Scruff that it was necessary, the sleeping wee bird now on the inside; she pulled on her boots: left on right, right on left. Lastly she turned her gloves, and slipped them on as well.

Then, clenching her fists and gritting her teeth, up and into the cave she went.

The moment she entered she felt a slight tingle, and from somewhere beyond the bend the babble of voices stilled, and then a loud voice called out: "Who dares enter the cavern of the giants?"

Camille nearly turned and bolted, but she heard a great sucking in of air, and many throats huffing and puffing, and remembering the sisters' words and praying to Mithras they were true, on inward she went.

"Fee, fum, fie!" came the booming voice . . .

In that moment Camille stepped 'round the turn to see a large firelit chamber, overcrowded with tall, ugly beings jammed from wall to wall, fully twelve or thirteen feet high and quite broad; and as Camille stepped into the light, the one in the fore, the one with a tattered black hat atop his head, boomed out:

. . . "I'll grind your bones to make a—"

"*Eeeeee* . . . !" came a collective scream as the great tall beings saw Camille's inside-out garments. And they bolted every which way, as if fleeing a peril beyond comprehension.

Pthbthththth . . . came a great roar of flatulence, much as would a hundred buffoons' air-filled, pig's-bladder-cushions prolongedly break wind were they all simultaneously sat upon. And the chamber filled with a terrible stench—worse even than that of the nag-churned quag—and had Camille eaten a full supper, surely she would have lost it right then and there. Breathing through her mouth to keep from gagging in the ever-worsening air, she watched as the beings shrank and shrank and ran about in panic, and struggled to fit into crevices and cracks and holes. Quickly they returned to Spriggan size, and they squeezed through the fissures and clefts, and down the small tunnels beyond they did flee.

And left in their foetid wake on a great pile of treasure and other goods lay Camille's stolen gear.

Yet gasping in the befouled air, swiftly Camille took up her cloak and put it on wrong-side-out. She grabbed her rucksack and money belt, pausing just long enough to make certain that her jewelry and coinage were yet within. She slung them over her shoulder by their sling straps, and snatched up her bedroll and waterskin and slung them as well; then she scooped up Lady Sorcière's staff, and, leaving all else on the glittering mound behind, she turned and strode from the chamber and toward the bend and the entrance beyond, all the while thinking, *Go slow, go slow. Don't let them see you are as frightened as they are. Slow. Don't run.*

But when she reached the mouth of the cave, she could no longer withhold her fright, and down the slope she ran in the moonlight, fleeing back the way she had come. And as she climbed up the far hill beyond, from the mouth of the cave behind a voice screeched out, "Thief! Thief! You terrible, wicked thief, you'll not live to see the dawn!"

Without replying, on upward pressed Camille and over the crest and beyond, as a chill wind sprang from nowhere to curl all 'round.

Onward she fled, the wind becoming more brutal, and it lashed tree limbs and hurled grit as if to punish Camille. And the night darkened, with racing clouds filling the sky. They slid across the moon, and Camille had to slow, for in the resulting gloom she could but barely see.

A deluge of frigid rain began falling, and it was then Camille remembered the words of Vivette: "*Though cowards all, some say they are quite dangerous, able to call up great winds and storms.*"

The blow strengthened, the cold rain thickened—*Is this a storm called up by the Spriggans?* Camille did not know.

Onward she pressed through lashing limbs and driven rain and the howling wind, the gale worsening with every stride.

I must find shelter, she thought, *but where?*

Camille was by then thoroughly turned about, and she knew not whether she went away from the Spriggans or toward them or even circled 'round.

And she was chilled to the bone and stumbling about in the darkness.

Around her feet frigid water began to rise, and she sought higher ground, but every way she turned, it seemed, she went to ground even lower. And fighting the blow and the icy rain she became exhausted, benumbed, barely able to stand, battered on all sides by the now-thundering wind and hammered by the frigid downpour.

Still the water rose: up to her knees it now came. Freezing, dully Camille realized her peril, yet she had not the wit to conceive even a simple plan, so terribly cold was she.

And then something blocked her way. Camille turned and

stumbled but a step, only to be blocked again. Once more she turned, and once more she was blocked.

Barely able to think, Camille shook the water from her eyes. Something but dimly seen, something perhaps white or grey, stood directly before her, barring the way. Above the scream of the wind, someone or something turned and nickered in her ear.

Horse . . . blocking.

Camille started to slump down, but again came the nicker, and from within the pocket of her inside-out vest she heard a frantic chirping.

Scruff.

Dimly, she realized he was telling her something, but what? She clutched at the large animal and pulled herself upright, and one thing penetrated her mind:

Save Scruff.

And then at last, pummeled by howling wind and hurled ice—the rain had turned to sleet—with her inside-out-gloved fingers, she clutched the mane of the creature and managed to crawl onto its back, all the while instinctively clasping Lady Sorcière's staff.

With Camille hanging on and leaning forward, the animal set off through the shrieking wind and the battering ice hurtling through the air, and Camille knew not where the creature was taking her nor did she have the will to care or the wit to do naught but cling.

A time later—a candlemark, a day, a fortnight, a moon? Camille could not even form the thought—she felt gentle hands pulling her from the mount and bearing her into somewhere. Her ice-laden clothes were taken from her, and she was put in a brick-warmed bed.

She roused long enough to hear Scruff chirping, and she saw in the candlelight the fair face of a red-haired maiden hovering above, who whispered, "Sleep, Camille; here you are safe, for I am the Lady of the Bower."

23

Bower

Camille fell into chills and fits of shivering, alternating with spells of torrid fever. She was drenched in cold sweat one moment, then hot and parched the next, and dry coughing racked her frame. Lucid moments she seemed to have, but then babbled quite madly, yet most of the time she was seized by unconsciousness, for surely it could not be called sleep. Days passed with her in this condition, but finally her illness broke, and then she truly slept. And at last she awoke to sunlight and Scruff off chirping elsewhere, and the sound of someone moving about and quietly humming.

She was in a soft bed within a small room, and the day shone through a window; slender shadows wafted to and fro, made by long and hanging-down branches beyond, swaying gently in the air. Past the foot of the bed, an open doorway led to another room, and 'twas from that place the sound of humming came, the sound of chirping as well.

Camille tried to sit up, yet—"Oh, my"—she fell back, quite dizzy.

Footsteps neared, and in the doorway stood a lithe, redheaded woman. Her face was narrow, her eyes emerald-green and aslant, her skin alabaster, tinged with gold.

"Ah, Camille, you are awake." She smiled, her mouth generous, her teeth white and even.

Again Camille tried to rise, and the woman stepped forward. "Let me help." And she plumped pillows and aided Camille to sit, then propped her up in place.

"How do you know my name?" asked Camille, her voice faint.

The woman smiled. " 'Tis a gift I have."

Camille started to ask another question, but the woman held out a staying hand. "One moment, Camille." She stepped from the room, and Camille could hear water being poured and the stirring of a spoon in a cup.

But then from beside the bed: "*Chp-chp-chp-pip . . . !*"

"Scruff," said Camille, glancing over the edge at the tiny sparrow, who had hopped into the room. "I'd take you up, but I'm afraid that I'd fall out on my head."

"*Chp-pip-pip-chp-chp . . . !*"

"Take this, Camille," said the lady, stepping once again into the room, cup in hand. " 'Tis a tisane of mint to restore the heart and mind."

Camille received the cup and inhaled deeply, the keen aroma refreshing.

Still, Scruff chirped insistently, and the lady took him up on one of her long, slender fingers and set him to the bed. The sparrow hopped across the cover to come before Camille, then he cocked his head and peered at her, as if examining a patient.

"Oh, Scruff, I think I am well," said Camille, "or at least on the mend."

Apparently satisfied, Scruff scratched up a small mound of cloth and settled down, as if nesting.

The woman laughed, and Camille smiled and sipped the minty tea.

"Camille, indeed you are on the mend, though 'twas touch-and-go for a while."

"How long have I been sick?"

The lady frowned. "A sixday or seven, I deem. I am uncertain as to which. Time means so little to me."

"A sevenday?" Camille sighed and looked to see Lady Sorcière's staff leaning in a corner. "More blossoms withered," she glumly said.

The lady arched an eyebrow, but Camille said nought.

A momentary silence fell between them, but then Camille said, "I'm sorry, my lady, but I know not who you are."

The woman smiled, her tilted green eyes aglitter. "Many know me as the Lady of the Bower, yet my name is Lisane."

Hope flooded Camille. "Lady of the Bower, Lisane, it is you I came seeking."

"I know."

"You know?"

Lisane sat on the edge of the bed. "Aye. You did come seeking answers, yet I speak not with just anyone."

Camille's face fell. "But I sorely do need your help."

"Camille, fear not, for well did you pass the test."

"Test?"

"Indeed, for I tried you sorely, yet you showed me an uncommon patience and goodness of heart."

"Tried me?"

"Aye. A test to see if you were worthy of my aid."

"How so? —I mean, how did you test me?"

"Oh, la, Camille, I was the crone with the horse."

Camille's eyes widened in shock. "You were the crone?"

"Indeed." Lisane made a small negating gesture. " 'Twas but a minor glamour I cast 'pon me and Thale, though he did not like playing the part of a broken-down, swayback mare."

"Thale?"

"The one who rescued you nights past." Lisane gestured. "Look without. You will see him."

Camille raised a bit and peered out through the cote window. Past hanging-down willow branches, there on a sward a splendid white creature cropped grass; horselike, it was, but smaller and with cloven hooves and a pearlescent horn jutting from its forehead, a thin spiral groove running up from its base to its very sharp tip.

Camille gasped. "A Unicorn."

The Lady of the Bower nodded. " 'Twas he who saved you." Lisane gestured at nesting Scruff. "You and your tiny sparrow."

"Saved us? Saved me? But I thought Unicorns would have nought to do with those who are impure, sullied, those of us who are no longer maidens, who no longer have our virgin's blood. To have a Unicorn rescue me is a wonder, then." Camille shook her head in rueful memory. "I was spurned by one once; with a flick of its tail it turned and trotted away."

Lisane frowned. "How so?"

"It was as I rode the Bear to visit my family—"

"You were upon the back of a Bear when you were so-called spurned?"

Camille nodded.

Lisane laughed. "Ah, then, 'twas the presence of the Bear that caused such."

"But I was told that when one loses her virgin's blood . . ."

"Oh, la, Camille, 'tis not virgin's blood which draws the Unicorn, but rather purity of heart. —Gods know, were it virgin's blood, then long past Thale would have left me. 'Tis but an old wives' tale you did hear."

"Oh," murmured Camille, her heart suddenly lighter. Then she grinned and said, "In this case, 'twas an old fra's tale, bolstered by a votary of Mithras."

Lisane shook her head and faintly smiled. "I oft wonder if fras and votaries and heirophants and other such have the faintest notion of Truth."

Again a quietness fell between them, but then Lisane frowned. "What is it you do seek?"

"A place east of the sun and west of the moon. I was coming to you in the hopes you would know where it might be."

Slowly Lisane shook her head. "I know not where this place lies, but mayhap the cards will know."

"Cards?"

"Aye. I use them for divination. That's how I knew you were coming. Oh, not you specifically, but that someone sought me and was on the way, or so the cards did say. That's why Thale and I were waiting along the road. We would have fetched you the following morn, yet the storm intervened, a thing the cards did not see."

Camille frowned, then cocked an eyebrow. "These cards, they are taroc?"

"You know of them?"

"Only as a game, as well as what some people say: that there are those who can read the future within an arcane spread."

Lisane turned a hand over in a small negative gesture. "They do not foretell the future, Camille. They speak not to what *will* be, but rather what *might* be, and then only if the reader has interpreted them wisely and true, and only if the acts they portray are not contravened by actions unshown."

"Hmm . . . Sounds much like the pronouncements of fras and votaries and heirophants," said Camille, grinning.

Lisane laughed gaily. "Touché, Camille. Touché."

Camille's smile faded, and she looked into the now-empty cup. "How long ere I can go onward?"

Lisane sighed. "A sevenday or so, mayhap."

"Seven more days?" Camille tried to struggle up in protest, but, nearly swooning, she fell back. Then she whispered, "Oh, but I must not tarry."

"Hush, hush, Camille. You cannot press on as you now are.

Heed, you were most seriously ill—the ague, I believe—and it took much out of you."

"The ague?"

"Aye. Mayhap caused by ill vapors of the mire, mayhap by the boghole you waded into, and for that I am most sorry. Mayhap 'twas brought on by a biting fly or mosquito, for 'tis said that some carry ill vapors in their sting, though the charm I cast should have protected you from their bites."

"Charm?"

"Aye, the gift I bestowed upon you when I played the crone."

"Ah, then that's the reason!" exclaimed Camille. "I wondered why the pesky pests left us alone, whereas upon our entry into the clutches of that mire they did anything but." Camille sighed and shuddered, adding, "Would that you had cast a charm against leeches as well."

"Leeches?"

"Aye. From the boghole."

Lisane shook her head in rue. "Mayhap 'twere leeches gave you the ague, for surely they carry the worst of ill offerings a mire can bestow."

Camille reached out and laid a hand upon Lisane's. "Berate not yourself, Lisane, for perhaps it wasn't the swamp at all made me ill, but instead was the icy storm."

"Mayhap," replied Lisane, yet her arching of an eyebrow spoke otherwise.

They sat wrapped in their thoughts for a moment, each looking beyond the window to where a Unicorn cropped grass. Finally, Lisane said, "You did babble of an encounter with Spriggans, and, if so, 'twas they who caused the blow."

"I wondered," said Camille. "Vivette and Romy said they could bring on storms."

"Aye, indeed they can," said Lisane. "Given its fury, I thought it might be Spriggan-sent, and then did Thale go seeking you."

Camille smiled. "Not only did Thale save me from the storm, but it was you who saved me from the Spriggans within their cave."

Lisane's eyes widened in shock. "You were in their cave?"

Camille nodded. "They stole my goods, but I retrieved them, yet wouldn't have were it not for your words spoken as a crone. Ah, but you should have seen them run about in panic when I stepped within their vault wearing inside-out clothes. Better than iron."

"Better than iron," Lisane echoed. "Even so, 'twas a dangerous thing you did, venturing into their den."

"Dangerous or no," said Camille, "I could not let them keep my belongings. And were it not for the words of the crone— were it not for your words—they would have."

Lisane sighed. "I thought you would set camp wearing inside-out clothes, for then they would not have taken your goods."

Camille's eyes widened in realization. "Ah, I see: 'Even when night lies on the sward, Wrong-side-out stands sentinel ward.' Oh, Lisane, ere I came unto the Spriggans' cavern, I thought the crone's words—your words—nought but the babblings of a mad old woman."

A slight smile fleetingly crossed Lisane's face. "Ah, me, mayhap I should have made my warning more plain . . . Still, I knew not for certain the Spriggans would come upon you, only that they might, or so the cards did say."

"The taroc cards."

"Aye."

"Then this time they did say true."

Lisane nodded.

Camille squeezed her hand, and Lisane grinned and squeezed back. Then she stood. "I have some broth warming, and 'tis time we began putting some strength back into you. Too, I would hear your full tale. —But first . . ." Lisane felt of Camille's forehead, then smiled and opened the window, swinging it inward, allowing fresh air to waft through. Momentarily, Thale looked up at this movement, then resumed cropping grass.

Two days later, Camille was finally strong enough to venture outside. It was then she discovered that Lisane's small two-room dwelling was wholly within the massive trunk of a great willow tree more than a hundred feet tall, its long swaying branches hanging down all 'round, though sunlight clearly shone through.

"That's why they name me the Lady of the Bower," said Lisane, "for does it not look as such?"

"Oh, it's much more, my lady," breathed Camille. " 'Tis a place of wonder."

Camille walked about the massive girth. There was but one door into the trunk, and it a bright yellow hue; two windows looked out on the world—one in each chamber. Both the door and the windows had willow-bark shutters, such that when they were closed, the trunk looked entirely whole, and nought could be seen of the dwelling within.

Shaking her head at the marvel, "Indeed, 'tis truly a wonder," said Camille as she came to the sward, where Lisane sat on a blanket.

Lisane smiled, then poured tea, and they sat and sipped the drink, while tasting small, sweet cakes. Scruff chitted and scratched about for insects, and Thale stood nobly by.

After a while, Camille said, "Lady, I think it is time I returned your bed to you. I will sleep on the pallet in yon chamber where you have been."

Lisane shook her head. "Nay, Camille. I oft arise in the night and read the cards by candlelight. I would not disturb your sleep. Think no more of it."

Camille started to protest, but Lisane pushed out a shushing hand and passed Camille another small cake.

And as the day slowly went by, Camille took in fresh air and basked in the sunlight, warming in the rays. Finally, Lisane said, "I shall read the cards for you this eve."

Of a sudden Camille's heart clenched, for though she was not yet well enough to venture onward, she felt a pressing need to go.

Lisane glanced up at Camille. "Remember, with all the cards, though I might name them he or she, they could just as well be the opposite: female instead of male; male instead of female."

Camille nodded, murmuring, "I will remember."

"Remember as well"—Lisane tapped the remainder of the deck—"there are four cards yet to come, but not until after the reading of the wheels, for they will speak to the whole, and I would not have their influence ere then."

On the table in the candlelight, upon a silken cloth spread o'er the oaken plank, a great circular array of cards lay, rings within rings, concentric, the cards facing outward, away from the center, or inward toward. Camille sat on one side of the table, her eyes wide in wonderment; the Lady of the Bower sat opposite, and she slowly shook her head in dismay. "There are so many swords, Camille, so very many swords, here about the center."

"Is that to the good?"

"It means great conflict."

"Do you mean combat, fighting, bloodshed?"

"Mayhap. Yet it can also mean confrontation, a great physical effort, a testing of wit, any number of things. Think of conflicts, Camille, and how so very many different kinds there are: conflicts of the heart and mind and body and spirit and soul; conflicts from within and without. Why, this illness from which you are on the mend, it, too, is a conflict of sorts."

"Oh."

Long did Lisane study the array, Camille silent, waiting. Finally, Lisane took a deep breath and closed her eyes, then circled her left hand widdershins above the wheel of cards, followed by her right hand, circling deasil. She then opened her eyes and said, "This is what I see," and she began speaking of the meanings of the cards and their relation to one another, and as she spoke, she touched each card: her right hand for those upright—facing inward—and her left hand for those reversed—facing out.

"Here at the beginning are the Two Lovers, upright. I can but think the card bespeaks of you and Alain. But flanking are the upright three of swords on one side and the upright four of swords on the other, and here is the Tower, upright. Respectively they mean separation, isolation, and disaster. Immediately at hand is the three of cups, reversed, signalling a reversal of circumstance, and what was good now causes pain. It is directly followed by the nine of swords, and upright it means despair, anxiety, misery. Camille, this is what has been."

Lisane looked across at Camille, who nodded, tears brimming. Lisane reached out and patted her hand, then spoke on:

"Here is the two of cups upright; it indicates harmony between two souls, yet I think this card does not represent you and Alain, for its position in the array seems to point to two souls you do know, yet mayhap in truth do not."

"How can that be?" asked Camille, a puzzled frown upon her face.

Lisane shrugged. "I cannot say, yet these cards flanking, this one upright, the six of cups, signifies friends, while this three of cups reversed speaks of a test or tests, the double-edged nature of intuition, and since it is reversed, your intuition, or mayhap your first thought, may be wrong."

"Oh," fretted Camille, her worried gaze upon the cards, "But I hope that does not mean something ill."

"Camille, in this case it merely means you should not always take things at face value."

At this, Camille relaxed a bit, though apprehension yet lurked in her gaze.

And on Lisane spoke, touching cards, explaining, as she moved 'round the array, coming ever closer to the center. Finally her reading of the wheels—the rings within rings—came to an end, though she was not yet finished, for some specifics remained and four cards were yet to come.

Camille shook her head and pointed at three of the cards. "I don't understand. The King and Queen and Page of Swords all reversed, all against me. Enemies unknown?"

"You do know the King, yet not *as* a King. Who he is, I cannot say."

"Hmph. Neither can I," replied Camille. Then she pointed at another card in the array. "And you say this represents me? The Naïf? Why so?"

"Ah, Camille, you are quite guileless and trusting, which is both to your good and ill; yet, remember, there will come a time when guile will win the day."

Camille turned up a hand. "I am who I am, Lisane. If that means I am guileless, then so it is I am."

Lisane smiled faintly in reply, then frowned at the cards. "I have never before seen this arrangement of Hermit and Fortune and the three of wands and pentacles: the Hermit, aiding, and see how the threes point; and the pentacles might indicate treasure; and the Wheel of Fortune aiding as well. I know not what it means, unless it is three recluses or mentors tied to destiny."

"Haven't I already met two? The Lady of the Mere, and the Lady of the Bower?"

Lisane laughed. "Indeed. Even so, I think this hermit or these hermits yet lie along the way."

Lisanne paused, her brow furrowing. "Camille, here you are greatly opposed by two beings unrevealed: by the Magician, and by the Priestess, who in this array appears to be but an acolyte of the Mage; yet the Mage is somewhat off center—not directly engaged in your immediate quest; even so, I believe he is somehow responsible; the acolyte, though, seems more involved in the events, albeit from behind the scenes."

Baffled, Camille looked at Lisane, and the Lady of the Bower shrugged. "As I say, the cards speak but arcane messages, yet one thing seems clear"—she touched a card with her right hand— "this one will aid, the Minstrel, for he is surrounded by good omens; even so, he is not the ultimate key to your quest, yet he is someone who can greatly help. He represents wisdom.

"And here is the card of Strength, and I believe can you find the one who is represented by the Minstrel, he will lead you to Strength."

"Do you know any minstrels?"

"Oh, Camille, the one so represented does not have to be a true minstrel, but someone with much wisdom, much lore."

Camille shrugged. "Nevertheless, my question remains: do you know any minstrels, especially those with much wisdom, much lore?"

Lisane shook her head. "No minstrels, directly, though I do know a bard. An Elf. Rondalo. He is one of the Firsts."

"Firsts?"

"Those who dwelled in Faery from its inception. Yet he may not be the one, Camille, the one of the card, for as I say, this card may not represent an actual minstrel, but someone altogether different. Recall as well, no matter how named or depicted, any of these cards can represent a male or female—one or the other or both, or perhaps neither."

Camille cocked an eyebrow at this last, but nodded. Then with her right hand she touched the Minstrel and said, "Know you others of wisdom and lore? Other Firsts?"

Lisane pursed her lips. "Raseri the Firedrake: he was one of the Firsts as well. Tisp the Sprite, yet she is quite whimsical and not given to lore which touches not on her life. Adragh the Pwca, but he is quite dangerous, yet then again, so are all those I name; even so, Adragh is one to avoid. Then there is Jotun, but him you have already met, and though he helped you across the Endless Mountains, that lies in the past, and I think he is not the Minstrel to come. —Oh, Camille, there are many who have much lore, and only by your own efforts"—Lisane gestured at the array—"is such likely to come about. Heed, the cards only indicate that which *might* be, not that which is certain."

"Well, then," said Camille, nodding, "it seems I should continue in the manner I started: seeking mapmakers and travellers and merchants and traders and the elderly, for they might know of the place where I can find my Alain and tell me how to get there."

Lisane turned up her hands and then said, "Now for the last four cardinals—first the two which speak of things to be nigh the end."

"Cardinal premier," said Lisane, and she turned up a card and laid it directly before her, just outside the array; the card pointed toward the center. Even so, she sucked in air between clenched teeth, saying, "Devil; upright."

"Cardinal deux," she then said, and this time she laid the card directly before Camille and just outside the array, and at sight of the card, Camille blenched. "Death; reversed," said Lisane.

"Oh, Lisane, these can't be good, especially Death."

Lisane shook her head. "Certainly the Devil upright is a terrible omen, for it means ravage, violence, vehemence. Yet at the same time it also means a dweller without, someone not allowed in." Lisane fell into long contemplation, and Camille thought she would go mad in the silence. But at last Lisane reached out with her left hand and touched the Magician. "Perhaps this one."

"But what about Death?" asked Camille. "Isn't it even worse?"

Lisane shook her head. "No, Camille. Death reversed can mean death just escaped, partial change, or transformation. Even so, it can also suggest great destruction as well, and coupled with the Devil upright"—Lisane took a deep breath—"I deem it signals a disaster you cannot avoid."

Tears welled in Camille's eyes. "Should I forgo my search, then?"

Slowly Lisane shook her head. "I think not, Camille, for the cards only say what might be, not what is certain to come. Were it my quest, I would go on"—with her right hand she touched the Lovers—"for true love can overcome much."

Camille nodded, and then Lisane said, "Now for the last two cards."

Calling out "Cardinal trois" and "Cardinal quatre," Lisane dealt two more cards and placed one to the right and the other to the left, just outside the wheel, and at the sight of these, both she and Camille gasped, startled, for they were the Moon and the Sun, both upright. Lisane touched the Moon on the right— "Somewhere between concealed enemies and danger"—and then she touched the Sun on the left—"and a promise of bliss"—she looked at Camille—"somewhere between the hidden and the revealed does your true heart lie."

A fortnight altogether it took Camille to recover well enough to travel onward. "I shall leave on the morrow," she said to Lisane that eve.

"I shall greatly miss you," replied Lisane.

"And I you," said Camille, reaching out to squeeze Lisane's hand.

They sat in silence before the great willow, twilight drawing down on the land.

"Would that I had been of more help," said Lisane after a while.

"Oh, Lisane, you nursed me back to health; without you I would have died."

"Mayhap," said Lisane. "But mayhap without my test in the mire you would not have fallen ill."

Camille shrugged. "That we'll never know. Yet there is your reading: just knowing that there is someone out there who can truly aid me has lifted my heart, for now I do have hope."

"Let us pray that hope is enough," said Lisane.

Once more silence fell between them, but then Lisane said, "Thale has agreed to bear you to a town, where you can continue your quest."

"But I know not how to ride aught," said Camille, "much less a Unicorn."

"Did you not ride the Bear? And did you not ride Thale from the wrath of the Spriggans unto here?"

"Yes, but—"

Lisane smiled. "Fear not, Camille, for a Unicorn will not let fall one who is pure of heart. You do not need to know how to ride, for Thale will bear you securely."

They sat until lavender twilight turned to star-laden cobalt night, and then went inside. But ere she crawled into bed, Camille took up Lady Sorcière's stave and by candlelight counted the days:

Two hundred eighty-seven blossoms remain; seventy-nine dints where blossoms once were. A fortnight lost to illness. Oh, Alain, will I find you ere all the blossoms are gone?

In the silvery light of the onset of dawn, Camille and Lisane hugged and kissed one another, tears standing in the eyes of each. Then Camille mounted up, Thale whinnying and tossing his head as if anxious to be away. Lisanne stepped forward and handed up Camille's goods, and then she lifted up chirping Scruff, who, until he was safely perched in his customary spot on Camille's shoulder, seemed to think he was being left behind. And when all was settled in place, "Seek the Minstrel,

Camille, whoever he or she might be," said Lisane, and then she stepped back.

"I shall," replied Camille, and with a final au revoir, she rode away on the back of a Unicorn, leaving the vast willow behind, it with its dwelling within.

Lisane watched until they were gone from sight, then she turned and went inside to once again lay out the cards to see if aught had changed. She found on the table awaiting her—

What's this? Gifts from Camille? Fourteen silver pennies: one for each day of her stay. But what need have I for coin? . . . Ah, but this white-pearl ring, a symbol of purity . . .

Lisane took up the ring and slipped it onto a finger, where it softly shone in the oncoming light of the newly arriving morn.

Two days later in the waning afternoon, Thale halted just within the edge of the forest. Down a long slope beyond, and across a narrow bridge above a swift river, stood a modest town of five hundred dwellings or so.

Quietly, Thale whickered and Camille dismounted. She embraced the Unicorn about the neck and said, "Merci, mon ami, not only for bearing Scruff and me here, but also for showing me that I am not sullied for having loved and been loved."

Camille stroked Thale's muzzle one last time, and he blew softly into her hand, then he looked up at Scruff and snorted.

"*Chp!*" protested the sparrow, but Camille laughed.

Tossing his head, again Thale whickered, his pearlescent, spiral-wound horn agleam in the slanting rays of the sun.

Camille sighed and turned and started down the long slope. When she looked back the Unicorn was gone, and on down toward the town she went to whatever lay within.

24

Images

As Camille crossed the narrow footbridge over the river, sounding above the shush of swift-running water she heard a clarion call, and along the road just beyond the buildings lining the far bank came a great, enclosed red coach, eight horses hauling. A driver and another man, both in red coats, sat on a high seat at the fore, with luggage strapped atop the roof behind. Standing on a footboard arear, and hanging on to a rail, were two lads—footmen—also wearing red coats. Again came the clarion call, and 'twas the man beside the driver sounding the trump, announcing the arrival of the great red coach into town. Here and there, through gaps between buildings, Camille saw folks stepping out from their dwellings and businesses, all to watch as the coach rumbled in, with some of its passengers lowering sashes and leaning out to see to what place they had come.

"Oh, Scruff, travellers. Mayhap one will know of that we do seek, or even perhaps of the Elf Rondalo, the bard Lisane did name." Camille hurried on across and along the pathway between a pair of buildings and to the main thoroughfare. When she reached the street, a short way to the left she saw the red coach now standing, horses fretting in their traces, while the driver held tightly to the reins, his foot on the long brake lever. The footmen had alighted to the ground and now handed passengers out, while the man who had sounded the trumpet tossed down luggage to a pair of youths below. Standing on the walkway, a woman welcomed passengers—seven altogether, five men and two women—and directed them into a substantial, two-storey building.

"Mayhap an inn, Scruff."

As the wayfarers trooped inside, Camille hurried toward the structure; nearing, she saw hanging from eyelets a signboard naming the place as L'Auberge du Taureau Bleu, its namesake— a blue bull—depicted thereon. "Ah, Scruff, have they a spare bedchamber, here we will spend the night."

Reaching the inn, Camille stepped in the foyer and waited patiently amid the bustle of rooms being assigned and luggage being claimed and people declaring just how good it was to be out of the coach at last.

"I need a bath," said one of the women.

"Me too," murmured Camille to Scruff. "If there is one thing I did come to appreciate at Summerwood Manor, it was the taking of daily baths, a luxury quite unavailable, it seems, when one takes on a quest . . ." She glanced sideways at the sparrow, who peered with beady eyes back at her. "But not unavailable to you, my wee little friend," Camille added in afterthought, "you who can bathe in nought but a cup, or flop about in fine dust."

In that moment—"Ma'amselle, you are next"—she was called forward by the lady of the inn.

"If you'll come with me, my little poppet," slurred the portly man, leering at her, and then at the serving maid as she delivered another bottle of wine, "perhaps then I'll remember."

"Ah, non, m'sieur," declined Camille, sighing and stepping away, for he was the last of the passengers. She had asked all the others, some hesitant to respond, peering at her suspiciously. What would a fille like you want with such? some had asked, while others simply shook their heads and kept on eating.

Camille finally returned to her own table, and as the serving girl set a plate of bread and cheese and scallions and beef before her, Camille said. "Ma'amselle, would you know where the driver of the coach might be? It occurs to me that he may have travelled far in his life and seen much."

"Call me Lili, my lady. And you are correct: Louis has travelled far, and he might know of this place you seek." She made an apologetic gesture. "I could not but help overhear. As to Louis's whereabouts, I would suggest you try L'Auge d'Or."

"Where might this Golden Trough be?"

Lili pointed. "Down the street, just across from the stables. That's where Louis and the others go after they see to the horses. But rather than waiting for the morrow, ma'amselle, you should ask him this eve, for he and his coach with its passengers will be off just after first light."

"How often do coaches come through?"

"Lili!" called the innkeeper.

Lili glanced over her shoulder at the man, then took up her tray and said, "Once every fortnight or thereabout, at times more often, at other times less, though Louis comes through but once every six moons or so, for he makes quite long runs. Pardonnez-moi, ma'amselle, but I must go."

"Merci, Lili."

The serving girl grinned and curtseyed, then hurried away.

Louis, a stocky man with shag of brown hair hanging down, peered deeply into his tankard of ale, then shook his head. "Non, I know of no such place. But if you ask me, this is not a town where you are likely to find an answer to where it might be, ma'amselle. Too small and out of the way, this village, more of a hamlet to my way of thinking." He took a swig, and then fixed Camille with his dark brown eyes. "If I were you, I'd go to a notable city, where you are more likely to come across those who can aid you: mapmakers, loremasters at the academies, merchants who import goods from afar as well as the folk who bring those goods, traders and travellers and other such world-wise sorts. Too, you'll find Elves and Dwarves and other Fey, as well as those of us who are of the common salt, and surely among such an assortment, your answer will be found."

"Sieur, I am newly come unto Faery, and I know little of cities herein. I would appreciate any advice you might have."

"Well, my coach is bound for Les Îles, a city of some noteworthiness."

"The Isles?"

"Aye. So named for it is built entirely on a number of islands at the confluence of four grand rivers. 'Tis these rivers which make it one of the great trading centers of Faery."

"Might there be minstrels there?" asked Camille.

Louis laughed. "Oh, yes, minstrels galore, for there are more inns and taverns and theaters there than you can shake a stick at. Many minstrels on street corners, too, singing for a copper or three, minstrels in the parks as well . . . perhaps even this bard you name, um . . ."

"Rondalo," said Camille.

"Yes. Mayhap he would be there as well, though if he is a true bard, 'tis not likely will you find him on a street corner, but in a great inn, or a music hall, or such."

"Ah, then, I shall go, if you have room in your coach."

"I do, for it will bear ten, and there are but seven now." Then Louis took a deep breath and frowned. "About the fare, ma'amselle, it is quite expensive to travel so far."

"Expensive?"

"Albert," called Louis, "the fare from here to Les Îles, how much?"

Across the common room, Albert, the coachman's aid, the one who had sounded the trumpet, consulted a small book. "Twelve silvers," he called back.

Louis waved his thanks. "There you have it, ma'amselle: twelve silvers, or a gold and two, or the equivalent in bronzes, or however you can manage your funds. —Oh, and you are responsible for your own meals and lodging along the way. It is, as I said, quite expensive in all."

Camille smiled. "I can pay. Yet would you charge me for my sparrow?"

"You travel with a sparrow? A true sparrow?" Louis held thumb and finger some three or four inches apart.

Camille nodded. "He is in my chamber at the Blue Bull and quite sound asleep, I believe."

Louis grinned. "For the sparrow, nought, but mind you, I would not have him disturb the other passengers."

Camille grinned in return. "I assure you, sieur, he is quite well-behaved."

"Then, Ma'amselle, um ah . . ."

"Camille."

"Then, Ma'amselle Camille, you must be on hand just after break of fast on the morrow, for we leave in the early morn."

Camille stood. "I shall be ready, sieur, and merci. The advice you have given is quite good."

Louis raised his tankard in a toast to Camille, then quaffed all down.

After she and Scruff broke their fast, Camille settled her bill with the innkeeper. And just as the red coach pulled up in front of the Blue Bull, through the open door, Camille saw an ample, black-haired woman hasten past, her head down in her hurry.

As Camille took up her gear from the floor before the counter, suddenly her eyes widened in recognition. *Blanche!*

Camille turned and called out. "Blanche! It's Camille!"

Quickly, Camille ran to the door and out. The woman, bearing a small basket, hastened down the street.

"Blanche!"

The woman hurried on without pausing.

Camille rushed after, calling out, "Blanche! Oh, Blanche!"

Just at the doorway to the stables, Camille caught the woman by the arm, and, startled, she turned. With Scruff scrambling to retain his perch, Camille fiercely embraced the woman. "Oh, Blanche, I've missed you so, and—"

"Ma'amselle," said the woman, struggling, pulling away, looking with apprehensive eyes at this madwoman with a chattering sparrow on her shoulder, "I know you not."

"But Blanche, it's me, Camille. Do you not recogni—?"

"Is aught amiss, wife?" came a deep voice. Wearing a leather apron and holding a horseshoe in one hand and a hammer in another, a portly, dark-haired man stepped out from the very first stall.

"Renaud!" Camille started toward the smith, but he threw up a staying hand.

"I am sorry, mademoiselle, but you have me at a disadvantage. And my name is Georges, not Renaud."

"Nor am I this Blanche you name me," said the woman, edging past Camille to stand behind her husband.

Camille could not believe what they said, for her eyes told her differently. "But you *are* Renaud and Blanche! Don't you know me? We are good friends, and we all lived together at Summerwood Manor for more than a year, until just"—Camille glanced at her stave—"some eighty-two days past."

"Nay, mademoiselle," said the man. "You have mistaken us for someone else. We have lived in Lis for nigh seventeen years, as time would be measured in the mortal realm, and have never been elsewhere in all those days."

"Then you are twins to those I know," declared Camille.

The woman's eyes widened. "Oh, ma'amselle, is it true? Twins? We did not know." She turned to the smith. "Oh, Georges, mayhap we have kith after all."

"How can you not know whether you have kindred?" asked Camille.

A horn sounded. Camille stepped to the opening and looked toward the inn. Passengers were boarding.

"*Chpp!*" chirped Scruff, as if to call Camille's attention to the coach.

The man sighed. "We have no memory beyond our village life here."

Camille frowned. "No memory?"

The woman's dark blue eyes filled with sadness. "It is as Georges has said, for it seems that one day some sixteen years past we were simply here. Neither of us knew how we had come, or where from, or even who we were—"

Again the horn sounded, and again Scruff chirped in response.

"—only that we were man and wife. And so I took the name Clarisse"—she turned toward the man, and smiled into his eyes of brown—"and he, a master smith, it seems, took the name Georges. But in truth, as anyone in Lis will attest, we have not set one foot from this town in all the days following, and so, ma'amselle, you are mistaken in thinking we are those who we clearly are not. But if we have twins at Summerwood Manor, mayhap 'tis a link to our unknown past. We should go, Georges, to wherever this Summerwood Manor lies."

The horn sounded for the third time, and the red coach began to roll.

"I am sorry to tell you this," said Camille, "but a trip to the manor will gain you nought, for no one lives there now; they have all gone missing."

"Missing?" said the woman, her face falling.

The man, the smith, looked at Camille's rucksack and stave and waterskin and bedroll and said, "Mademoiselle, if you are to go on that coach . . ." He gestured.

Groaning in frustration, Camille turned and stepped into the road and held up an arm to the oncoming coach. It slowed.

"I am searching for my love," said Camille over her shoulder to the pair, "somewhere east of the sun and west of the moon. When I find him, together we will seek all the others, those who vanished as well. And when we find them, then perhaps we will resolve the dilemma of exactly who you are."

The red coach rolled to a stop. One of the lads jumped down and opened the near-side door and lowered the drop-step. "Ma'amselle."

Camille looked up at the driver, and held up a golden coin and two silvers. "The lad will take it," said Louis. "Your luggage, too."

Camille gave the footman the coins and her bedroll and rucksack. He tossed the goods up to the lad atop, then handed her into the coach and closed the door after. Once inside, Camille

turned and leaned out the door window. "I shall return, I promise. —And, oh, do you know of a place east of the sun and west
of the moon, or know you a bard named Rondalo?"

The woman who called herself Clarisse and the man who
named himself Georges shook their heads *Non*, then each raised
a hand in au revoir, the smith calling out, "Bon voyage, and may
you find what you seek."

With a *chrk* of tongue and a crack of whip, Louis urged the
eight horses forward, and the red coach surged into motion.

Inside, even as the passengers stared at this fille with a sparrow on her shoulder, Camille found a place among them. Judg-
ing that Camille was a bona fide passenger, the others
introduced themselves, though Camille remembered not a single name, for her thoughts were quite occupied o'er the paradox
of Blanche and Renaud.

Of a sudden Lisane's words came back to her: *"Here is the
two of cups upright; it indicates harmony between two souls . . .
its position in the array seems to point to two souls you do
know, yet mayhap in truth do not . . . your intuition, or mayhap your first thought, may be wrong."*

*How did Lisane know? Rather, how did the cards know? Yet
I would swear those two are indeed Blanche and Renaud, for I
could not mistake them—each of the same shape, the same
hair, the same eye—*

"Non!" Camille blurted aloud. "Not the same eyes! Hers
were dark blue, not black! His were brown, not grey! They are
truly not my dear Blanche and Renaud."

At her outburst, the other passengers looked at Camille as if
she had gone quite mad. But one, a rather gaunt and pasty-
complexioned man, made a sacramental gesture and said,
"Mithras knows, my dear, the eyes are the windows of the
soul."

And toward distant walls of twilight the red coach rolled on
and on.

25
City

Forty-two days altogether did Camille and Scruff spend in the company of the red coach, forty-two days and six twilight crossings to go from the village of Lis to the city of Les Îles. Two of those days had been lost because of broken wheels, and another day while waiting for a fresh team. An additional handful of days were lost owing to a daylong drenching downpour that had turned the road into a mire, and the horses had been hard-pressed to go but a mile or two to reach the very next town. There Louis lay over until the road had dried out enough to press on.

All along the way—from Lis to Les Îles—Louis had often stopped to water and feed the horses and to allow the passengers and coachmen alike to stretch their legs and relieve themselves among the trees or within thickets or beyond rock outcroppings. At times on steep slopes to lighten the load and ease the haul, Louis had called for the passengers and footmen—Girard and Thoreau, both fourteen, both quite skinny, both madly smitten with Camille—to disembark and walk up the long hills, at other times to walk down; when this had occurred, Gautier, the obnoxious stout man—the one who had invited Camille to his bedchamber—complained that he had not spent good coin to slog all the way to Les Îles; and while the others had suffered his diatribes in silence, Scruff had chattered scoldingly, as if telling him to move along, and quietly, if you please.

They had passed through a succession of woodland hamlets and small towns, where they had taken meals and spent overnight in a variety of lodgings—from quaint to primitive to homelike. At each of the those stops, Gautier would imbibe entirely too much wine, and would then single out Camille and make quite lewd remarks; she had found ways to avoid him, though occasionally she was then afflicted with Eudes, the gaunt, pasty-faced man; he would find her and expound upon the evils besetting the world—mortal and Fey alike—and call for rigorous abstinence in all things, for surely that's the way Mithras meant it to be, except, of course, for the purpose of bearing young, which no doubt Mithras desired. Much of the time in these various towns Camille had gone about and had spoken with the elders and others, but none knew of the place she sought, nor knew of the bard she named, and none had any maps whatsoever of Faery and in fact thought the notion quite odd. The red coach would leave next morn and press onward, and Camille's spirits had fallen with each day, for nought would stay the withered blossom vanishing from the stave.

As to the other passengers, in general they had been pleasant, though at times they had complained of the jolting, or one or two had debated long and at times loudly with the pasty-faced disciple of Mithras over Truth and Devotion and the Meaning of Life.

Occasionally, Louis had told the passengers that there would be no town to stop in for a midday meal, and that he planned on pausing somewhere along the road for such, and he had bidden each of them to arrange for a small luncheon to carry on board. Gautier had always managed to acquire a bottle of wine to imbibe during these pauses, and then only the glares of all the passengers had quelled his lascivious remarks.

Along the route, some passengers had reached their destinations, and they had alighted and gone on their way with hardly a fare-thee-well. Occasionally new passengers had gotten on the red coach to travel the road to a village or town or sometimes just to a distant stead.

And so did passengers come and go, some pleasant, some silent, some quite loquacious.

During one part of the journey, they had come into a rather darkling forest, and Scruff had chirped and had grabbed a tress of Camille's hair and had taken to the high vest pocket. There Louis had whipped up the horses, and they had flown through the region, jouncing and rattling bones, Gautier complaining loudly. Sometime later, although the horses yet sped, Scruff had emerged and had scrambled to his usual perch, and in but moments Louis had slowed the coach, allowing the lathered horses to plod. Shortly after, he had stopped for a while, allowing the passengers to stretch their legs, while he and Albert and Girard and Thoreau wiped the horses down and fed them a bit of grain, as well as bore buckets of water to them from a nearby stream. Of the woodland hindward, Louis had said nought, though the lads—Girard and Thoreau—kept eyeing the way aft.

It was during the very last leg of the journey that Camille and Scruff and stout Gautier had been alone in the coach, and Camille had had to forcefully rebuff more than one advance, Scruff chirping and pecking at the man's fingers whenever a hand came near. At the very first rest stop, Camille had asked Louis if she and Scruff could ride on the seat beside him. Louis had taken one look at the stout man, and had called for one of the footman to give over his seat to her. Girard and Thoreau had played some kind of finger game to see which would do so, and black-haired Girard had shouted in victory, and, even as he had helped Camille to a seat beside him, he beamed broadly at Thoreau, while fair-haired Thoreau had glumly climbed into the coach following after the stout man.

And so it was that Camille and Scruff were sitting high on a bench at the back of the red coach when Les Îles came into view.

"Oh my, Scruff, but look."

The coach rumbled along the road high atop a riverside bluff, the river itself quite broad, five miles or so in width, a high, precipitous bluff opposite as well. And Camille saw spread out below them, there in the green flow of water, a city of red tile and white stone built on a series of sheer-walled, granite-sided islands all connected together by wooden spans and swaying rope-and-board bridges. Some of the islands were small, others quite large, yet about each were docks and piers, with boats of all manner moored in the stream or securely berthed in the slips; other boats as well could be seen plying the river. Wooden ladders and steps, or those carved in stone, rose some fifty to one hundred or so feet from the docks to the streets above, streets which bustled with commerce. Here and there, among the white stone buildings with their red-tile roofs, stands of trees grew; perhaps these were the parks Louis had spoken of, parks where minstrels sang and played.

"Oh, Girard, how many islands in all?" asked Camille, turning to the lad.

Girard, who had not spoken a word to her the full of the trip and who blushed madly whenever Camille had looked his way, with his voice breaking between that of a child and a youth, managed to say, "Nineteen, I think, or twenty, if you count that little one there." He pointed downriver, and Camille saw a tiny isle set off quite a distance by itself with but a single dwelling thereon. No span connected it to the others, and Camille could see no ladders, no stairs, no dock along the facing sheer side.

Once more Camille looked directly at the lad. "Who lives there?"

Again Girard blushed. "Um, they say it's the River Lady, though no one I know knows for certain."

"River Lady?"

"Mm, hm. Eternally grieving, rumor tells, though I don't know why."

Camille frowned at the islet, then scanned for other isles. Across and upstream, a great cascade poured over the far-side bluff and down, its sound a distant roar. Farther upstream and along a curving-away turn, Camille could see a great notch in the near-side bluff, and there another river issued out into the main flow. Downstream the bluffs curved away beyond seeing, but just at the far bend, on the near side yet another river poured through a notch, though not a tributary as large as the ones upstream.

"Girard, I can only see three rivers; Louis said that the city was at the confluence of four."

Red-faced, still Girard managed a sheepish grin. "Same mistake I made when I first saw this place, ma'amselle. The fourth river—"

"—Is the river itself," said Camille, laughing. "How obtuse of me to not see it."

"Then I suppose that makes me, um, obtuse, too," said Girard glumly.

"Oh, forgive me, Girard," said Camille, reaching out and taking his hand, which she found to be quite moist. "I did not mean to imply such."

Releasing the lad's hand, Camille turned her attention once again to the isles. "What are those great cages I see sitting along the docks?"

"Um, see the ropes leading up to those booms above? They winch cargo from the docks up to the city, or cargo from the city down to the docks. Sometimes people, too, those who can't or won't use the steps."

"How clever," said Camille. "But for me, I believe I'll take the stairs."

"You won't have to if you don't wish to, L-lady Camille," said Girard, pointing ahead. "You can cross over on a bridge, if you wish. It'll cost you a copper."

In the near distance, a long rope-and-board bridge spanned from the bluff to the nearest isle.

"Of course, if you wish, you can take the ferry over instead," Girard added, "though it'll cost more, depending on which isle you're ferried to."

"I'll take the bridge," said Camille, "for I would walk the length of the city."

"Bridge!" Girard called to Louis. Then he said to Camille, "Louis would stop there anyway, but I just wanted to make certain. And as for walking the length of the ville, it'll take more than a day."

"Know you of any good inns, somewhere near the midmost isle?"

"Well, there's the Green Toad, but not for a lady like you. Then there's—no wait, that's quite bawdy, too. —Oh, I know, the Crown and Scepter, but it's quite expensive and a bit out of the way. Still, a fine lady like yourself, ma'amselle, well, uh—"

Camille smiled as Girard stuttered to a halt. "Thank you, my friend," said Camille, squeezing the red-faced lad's still-damp hand. "The Crown and Scepter it is. Where might I find such?"

"Just stay on the main street across the isles, till you come to that big one yon. Then make your way along the road following the downstream bluff. It'll be on your left midway along the rim."

The red coach rumbled to a stop at the near end of the span. Like a flash, Thoreau slammed open the coach door and leapt out to hand Camille down, the fair-haired lad smirking at Girard, who was left to retrieve Camille's goods from the roof and toss them to Thoreau, then clamber down from the footmen's bench to deal with the stout man.

"Stupid boy," Gautier snarled at Girard. "You don't think I'm going to walk that, now do you?"

Girard sighed and closed the door; the man would be taken to the docks below to catch the ferry across to whichever isle he paid the ferrymen to take him, where, no doubt, he would ride a cage to the top.

Camille was relieved that she wouldn't have to cross the bridge with Gautier, and she thanked Girard and Thoreau and Albert and Louis, and would have given each a bronze, but Louis pushed out a staying hand, saying, "Non, ma'amselle, the gold and two silvers paid it all." Camille then bade adieu, and shouldered her bedroll and waterskin and rucksack, and took her stave in hand—one hundred twenty-three blossoms gone, the one-hundred and twenty-fourth blossom withering—and, as the red coach rolled on, with Girard and Thoreau on their high bench arear and looking back at her, she set out across the bridge, Scruff on her shoulder, the rope-and-board span jouncing a bit underfoot, the sparrow chirping that it was time to eat.

Never had Camille seen so many people bustling to and fro; to her eye the streets seemed utterly jammed; how anyone avoided collisions, she could not say, yet they managed to do so. People rushed thither and yon, bearing baskets, pushing carts, towing small wagons, all laden with goods. Others were there as well: shoppers, hawkers, a group of street urchins dodging in and out among the grown-ups, laughing, playing at some game. Merchants stood in doorways and invited passersby in. Playing a lyre and a lute and a drum and a fife, a quartet of strolling musicians winnowed among the mass. These and more did Camille see, and to her eye it was all quite confusing: much like a thousand motes of dust dancing in a beam of sunlight, and as with them, she couldn't seem to pick out from the crowd any given mote.

"I feel quite like a minnow, Scruff, about to swim against a tide of spawning salmon." Even so, she paid the bridge tollkeeper a copper penny, then plunged into the mass, trying to master the intricate ballet.

Camille made her way along the teeming street, foot traffic flowing about her, and though she did not know the dance, it seemed the others did, and so she progressed slowly along the way without crashing into anyone, or rather without them crashing into her. And as she went, instead of a faceless mob, she began to see individuals: tall, short, rotund, slim, breathless, sweating, rushing, casually ambling, standing still, elegantly dressed or wearing rags, some selling goods from carts or open-air stands.

"Oh, Scruff, that must be a Dwarf." Camille paused and watched the bearded, short, broad-shouldered being cross athwart the street to disappear down a byway. "I think he was no taller than I am."

Camille continued onward, and she came to a footbridge arching across to another island. Ahead, she saw a group of Dwarves—five or six—coming her way, and she stood aside to study them as they passed. Indeed, she was nearly a full head taller than any, each of them somewhere in the range of four-foot-six or so. Yet they were very broad of shoulder, and they all wore leather vests with small, overlapping plates of bronze affixed thereon. *Oh, 'tis armor they wear. Is this a warband, or do all Dwarves go about accoutered so?* At their belts they wore daggers, but no other weaponry did they bear. All were bearded, and all seemed to be male. And they spoke to one another in a rather guttural and harsh-seeming tongue.

After they passed, Camille continued onward, her gaze now on faces and forms. Most were Human—"*Common salt,*" *Louis would say*—while others were Fey. She saw someone child-size, three foot tall or so, brown and shaggy and quite ugly. *Spriggan?* Her heart gave a lurch. *No, not a Spriggan, but what? Mayhap one of those Alain called Pwca, yet then again, mayhap not.* Onward she went, making her way along the crowded street, passing across bridges, progressing toward the big island, where Girard had said the inn would be. As she came nigh the midmost isle, she encountered two bearers carrying a small, silk-curtained litter, and Camille heard high-pitched giggling coming from within, sounding much like the giggles she had heard in the Springwood an eternity past, or it seemed that long ago. Still, she did not see who or what made the laughter.

Finally, as the sun lipped the horizon, she came upon the Crown and Scepter, a rather modest but quiet inn sitting a bit back from the sheer drop to the water below. The clerk looked somewhat askance at Scruff riding on Camille's shoulder, and he shook his head and grinned, saying, "We get all sorts here, ma'amselle."

"Maps?"
Camille nodded.
"Of Faery?"
Again Camille nodded.
It was the next morn, and Camille had decided to start the day speaking with any mapmakers in the city. And so, after

breaking fast, she had asked the serving maid, who referred her to Huges, the desk clerk.

"Well, now," said Huges, "I'm not certain there is such a thing, the way Faery keeps changing, and all."

Even as Camille's heart sank at this news, a second man, sitting at a desk behind the counter, quill in hand, looked up from his ledger sums. "Huges, that's an old wives' tale. Faery doesn't shift about like a tassel in the wind."

Huges raised an admonishing finger. "I only repeat what I hear, Robert."

"Well, then, let me ask you this: how long have you lived here in Les Îles?"

Huges turned up his hands. "Why, I've been here almost as long as has the Crown and Scepter."

"Ah, then, a good long while, wouldn't you say?"

"Indeed."

Robert smiled. "We agree. Now answer me this: how often has this part of Faery changed in all that time?"

Huges frowned. "Why, not at all."

Robert touched his temple with the feathered plume. "And what would you conclude from that? —I mean about Faery changing and all."

Huges's jaw jutted out stubbornly, and he snapped, "Perhaps the 'scape of Faery doesn't change much around here, but elsewhere, now . . . well that may be a different story altogether."

Robert sighed, then looked across at Camille. "Ma'amselle, I suggest you visit the docks, for perhaps they know of mapmakers and chartsmen and other such."

"Merci, sieur. I shall do so."

A fortnight later, her legs weary from climbing up and down ladders and stairs on the sheer-sided steeps of the isles, Camille had located many folk who had charts—boatsmen; traders; merchants, three of whom did sell maps—yet none knew of the place she sought.

Then she began seeking out minstrels and bards, visiting the parks where some played or orated, stopping on street corners to talk to others, walking alongside strolling musicians, and haunting taverns and theaters and music halls to speak with any she found. And she asked if they knew of a place east of the sun and west of the moon, and she also asked after Rondalo.

And all those she queried shook their heads or turned up

their hands, though one had heard of the Elven bard, but had never met him.

She continued to visit the docks, for every day boats and travellers came and went, but it seemed a hopeless cause, for none knew of such a place, nor of a bard so named.

And another moon elapsed, and more blossoms withered away.

Oh, my Alain, one hundred ninety-nine blossoms remain; one hundred sixty-seven gone. Will I find you ere all are faded away?

In the lanternlight, Camille, having taken a late meal, trudged up the steps to her chamber. But at the top of the stairs, she heard Scruff chirping frantically even though it was night and he should have been well asleep. Fearing fire or some such, Camille rushed to her door and inside. Light from the hallway lantern shone dimly into the darkened room. "*Chp!-chp!-chp! . . .*" — Camille could hear Scruff chattering from the direction of the bed, and in the dimness she could faintly see his wee form fluttering and flopping about on the covers. Swiftly, Camille lit a lantern and then quickly stepped to the agitated bird. "What is it, Scruff?" Camille knelt at the side of the bed, eye level with the sparrow, and she held out a finger, but Scruff ignored the offer and, fluttering awkwardly, he hopped to the floor and toward an open window, where a faint breeze stirred the curtains.

Camille frowned. *I do not remember leaving the sash ajar.*

Now she looked about the room. *Oh, no!* The chifforobe stood open, the drawers pulled out, the contents of her rucksack were strewn about, her cloak lying on the floor. As Scruff chattered up at the open window, Camille rushed to the scattered goods. The rucksack was empty, the secret pocket lay open, all the contents gone. She turned to her cloak; the lining was slitted; the jewelry and coin that had been therein was gone as well. And her money belt no longer lay in the bottommost drawer.

"Oh, Scruff, we have been robbed."

The clerk called the city watch, and two men showed up, but there was little they could do, except take a description of the stolen goods—coin, jewelry, money belt. They did, however, *tsk-tsk* and admonish her for not taking better care of her valuables; and when she replied she thought the inn quite safe from thieves and such, they smiled and told her she was nought but a gullible girl.

When Camille suggested it might be Spriggans at work, they both denied that such were in the city. "We keep watch at the bridges and throw the buggers into the river below."

After the watchmen had gone, the clerk cleared his throat. "Ahem, ma'amselle, but does this mean you cannot settle your debt to the Crown and Scepter?"

Camille burst into tears.

"Ma'amselle," said Robert the very next morn, "you can work in my kitchen, though it will take some while to pay off what you owe."

"How long, sieur?"

"Three moons, mayhap a bit more."

Camille's heart sank. "Oh, but that's nearly one hundred days in all, one hundred blossoms withered."

"Eh?" Robert cocked an eyebrow.

"There is another way," said Huges, "one where you'll erase your debt much quicker, mayhap in two fortnights or less."

"Huges . . ." said Robert, a note of warning in his voice.

"Oh, sieur, I would be most grateful," said Camille. "Where is this job?"

"At the Red Garter," replied Huges.

"Red Garter?"

"A brothel," growled Robert.

"And what would I have to do?" asked Camille in all innocence.

"You really don't know, do you?" said Robert.

As Camille shook her head, Robert glared at Huges and said, "It's just as well you don't, for the Red Garter is no place for the likes of a young fille as you."

"Robert, it is hers to decide, not yours," said Huges.

"What would I have to do?" repeated Camille.

"Have you lain with a man?" asked Huges.

Camille reddened, but nevertheless replied, "With Alain, my beloved, he whom I do now seek."

"That's what you would have to do with the clientele of the 'Garter. And given your face and form and golden hair, men will gladly pay good coin to couple with you—"

Shocked, Camille blurted, "You want me to lie abed with strangers and do *that*?"

Huges nodded. "Many a lonely boatman and merchant and trader comes to Les Îles, and I would think one such as you would be in great demand; as I say, your debt would be wholly discharged within two fortnights, perhaps in but one." Huges glanced at Robert, who stood in grim-lipped silence. "Much less than the three moons Robert offers."

A fortnight compared to three moons. Yet to couple with strangers, any and all who can pay? But what if on the morrow, someone comes to the city who can tell me where to find my Alain? And if I work here at the Crown and Scepter, how will I even get about to ask, given that I am tied down by having to do kitchen labor? Yet if I work at the Red Garter, a place frequented by travellers and merchants and boatmen, could I not find one who knows whereof I seek? But to lie with strange men, would my heart remain pure? Would Thale ever bear me again? Would I ever—?

"Of course, my uncle would have to approve," added Huges, breaking into her thoughts. "Perhaps even try you himself."

"Your uncle?"

"He owns the Red Garter"—Huges smiled—"it is a play on his name: Gautier."

Camille shuddered and turned to Robert. "Sieur, may I work in your kitchen while I consider what to do?"

Robert smiled. "Indeed, ma'amselle."

That evening, Camille and Scruff were moved into cramped quarters in the attic, and the following day, Camille began washing dishes and aiding the cook and bearing out garbage to cast into the waters below. It was the best Robert could offer, for, though he sympathized with Camille, her manual skills were those of a crofter, and there were no farms in Les Îles for her to earn her keep while working off her obligation.

Even so, Camille struggled with her dilemma: one hundred days versus as few as fourteen; her virtue versus mayhap finding Alain. She spoke to no one about her quandary, though she did tell of her loss.

Many of the kitchen staff did commiserate with her, telling of cutpurses and robbers and muggers and such, some blaming the burglary on a shadowy thieves' guild, while others declared that it must have been those wretched urchins who had stolen her wealth, while yet others blamed it on Bogles in the night, or

Knockers or River Selkies, or even mayhap—Mithras forbid—creatures of the Unseelie.

The cook did ask how she could have been so innocent as to leave her valuables unwarded, and at this Lisane's words echoed in Camille's mind: ". . . *you are quite guileless and trusting, which is both to your good and ill* . . ." Even as tears brimmed in her eyes, Camille answered the cook as she had Lisane. "I am who I am, sieur. If that means I am an innocent, then so it is I am."

Some four days after, as she was washing dishes she began singing to make the work go swifter, a habit from her days in the cottage of her père. And as she sang, the cook stopped what he was doing and stood rapt, listening, along with the kitchen help and serving girls, and the common-room staff as well. And soon Robert came to the door of the scullery, drawn thereto by her voice, and, as did the others, he, too, stood spellbound. As Camille turned to take up another dish: "Oh!"—she abruptly stopped—"M'sieur, I did not— Is my singing disturb— I'll be quiet."

"No, no, Camille," protested Robert. "I would have you sing. Why did you not tell me you have the voice of an angel?"

"But, m'sieur, I—"

"How many songs do you know? And have you sung before an audience?"

"Oh, sieur, sing for others? I am no bard nor minstrel."

Robert snorted. "Minstrels, bards, what would they know of how an angel sings?"

In moments, Robert had taken Camille's apron from her and had given her a towel to dry her hands. And he drew her into the common room and quietly spoke of her working off her debt much swifter if she would sing therein—two times each eve, and for a candlemark or so each time.

It took less than a fortnight for the word to spread across Les Îles: a golden-haired girl with a golden voice was singing at the Crown and Scepter, and 'twas said she sometimes sings to a wee little bird.

And every night the common room was crowded, come to see and hear the beautiful maiden who sings to a sparrow. They had come for the novelty, but they stayed for the voice. Accompanied by nought but a flute and a drum and a fife and a harp—four

musicians she had met in her search—she held the crowd enthralled; and her songs were such that one moment they were
laughing, and the next they were in tears.

And every night, after every performance, ere she and the
musicians took up the coins cast upon the stage, she would ask
the audience if any knew of a place east of the sun and west of
the moon, or of an Elven Bard named Rondalo.

The answer was always *Non*.

Camille's debt vanished virtually overnight, much sooner
than the fortnight or two offered by Huges, and Robert moved
her into a suite of rooms. Seamstresses came and fashioned
gowns, and from the music halls came managers who offered
her unheard-of sums if she would but sing for them.

Camille politely declined, for she yet felt beholden to Robert.

But Robert now knew of her quest, and he bade her to sing in
the largest hall—Le Magestreux—at least three nights of each
seven, ". . . for the Crown and Scepter can still highly profit
from the other four."

And so she did.

And there, too, in the grand music hall did she ask the over-
flowing audiences did they know of the place she sought as well
as where might be the bard? And still no answers came.

Days passed, and blossoms withered and vanished—two hundred ten, two hundred twenty, and more—and each day
Camille's desperation grew, and she felt as if she needed to be
doing something, anything, other than remaining there in Les
Îles . . . yet what? She had no answer, and there came times in
the depths of the night, her despair so deep, she fell asleep while
weeping.

Camille continued to trek to the docks and through the city
seeking strangers. Too, she hired a group of urchins to be her
eyes and ears, and to ask her two questions of strangers as well.
But all the queries—hers and theirs—were met by shrugs,
though many of those asked did now seem to know of Camille
and her continuing quest.

But then came one night . . .

Camille took up Scruff and reached high to set him on the
branch of a potted tree there upon the brightly lit stage. She
stood silent for a moment, and a hush fell over the audience, and
then came a run of tweeting notes from the fife, and Camille

turned as if just discovering the wee brown bird, and she began to sing:

> *"Tiny brown sparrow, sitting in the tree,*
> *Scruffy little soul, just like me,*
> *Would you be an eagle, would you be a hawk,*
> *Or would you wish instead to sing like a lark?*
> *Or would you have plumage bright and gay,*
> *Or would you wish . . ."*

As Camille came to the second verse, the drum softly took up the rhythm, adding its beat to the chirping fife. At the third verse, the flute joined in, and at the fourth, the harp, and still Camille sang verse upon verse, chorus after chorus, her song telling the well-known tale of the maiden who found comfort in the familiar, yet who wished somehow to experience something new and unpredictable, a maiden who would finally discover love, which would set her free to fly as the transformed sparrow she then was. And in singing this song, Camille's voice soared to heights that caused the audience to gasp, and it dropped to depths but a whisper, her tones pure and clear and true.

And as the song came toward an end, a clear tenor voice from the audience joined with hers, and Camille nearly faltered—*Alain?*—and she looked to see who caroled in flawless harmony in melodic counterpoint to her soaring soprano. In the shadows beyond the footlights she could just make out a tall, fair-haired stranger standing midway up the right-hand aisle, someone she had never before seen, yet someone somehow familiar. The audience broke into spontaneous applause, quickly quelled, for they would not miss even a single note or word, as the stranger sang of the sparrow, and the golden-haired maiden sang of the girl.

And the harp and fife, and flute and drum fell silent, for here was perfection needing no accompaniment.

And as he caroled, the stranger walked forward to sing up to Camille, and she to sing down to him.

At last the song came to an end, and both Camille and the stranger fell silent, as did the entire hall, some in the audience weeping quietly in joy, others sitting wholly stunned.

But then Scruff emitted a loud *"Chp!"* and as if that were a signal, the hall erupted in great glad shouts and thunderous applause and calls of *"Bravo! Bis! Plus!"* and *"Camille!"*

The stranger leapt onto the stage, and he took Camille's hand and bowed to the audience as she curtseyed. As they stepped back from the footlights he smiled at her, the sapphire gaze of his tilted eyes sparkling within his narrow but handsome face, his alabaster skin somehow glowing as of a hint of gold. Tall and lean, he stepped forward with her again, and bowed as she curtseyed, and as he did so he glanced sideways at her and said, "My Lady Camille, I am Rondalo, and I hear you have been looking for me."

26
Bard

Hand in hand, they fled the music hall, escaping well-wishers and ardent admirers alike, Rondalo whisking her away into the shadows cast by a waxing gibbous moon above. He hied her down side streets, Scruff asleep in the special shoulder-pocket of her new-made gown. Finally, well clear of the devotees, Rondalo slowed to a stroll and reluctantly released his grip.

Catching his breath, he said, "My lady, I did not know any other than Elvenkind could sing as do you."

Somewhat breathlessly, Camille replied, "And I thought none but Alain could sing as well as you."

"Alain?"

"He is my love," said Camille, not noting how Rondalo's face fell at such news.

"The one I seek," added Camille.

"Lost, run away, kidnapped, vanished?"

" 'Tis a long tale, sieur," said Camille. "One I pray you can help me resolve."

"We have all night, my lady," said Rondalo, "and I know just the place where your tale shall trip gently from your treasured lips unto my unworthy ear."

Rondalo swirled the wine in his glass and peered within. " 'Tis quite a tale, that . . . one worthy of a saga or song, did we but know the end."

They sat in soft-glowing candlelight in a small, out-of-the-way restaurant on the downstream rim of the great isle. Faint dawn glimmered through windows. In a distant booth, the restaurateur slept.

"Regardless, Lady Camille, I know not where lies this place you seek—"

"Oh," said Camille, despairing.

"—but I know someone who might help."

Hope bloomed.

"Who? Where?"

"Nearby," said Rondalo, gesturing outward. "As to whom, mayhap you know her as the Lady of the River, though her true name is Chemine. She is my dam."

"Your mère? But I thought you were one of the Fir— Oh, my, now I know who you remind me of: Lisane, the Lady of the Bower."

Rondalo laughed. "A distant cousin, Lisane. Yet how do I remind you of her?"

Camille turned up a hand. "The same tilt of eyes, the same slender face, the same tipped ears, the same alabaster skin with an aura of gold."

Rondalo grinned and looked into his wineglass and shook his head. "My dear, those are but Elven traits."

"Lisane is an Elf?"

Rondalo looked up at her. "Indeed."

Camille dropped her gaze. "I did not know, for she said nought."

"Undeniably, you are newly come unto Faery."

Camille nodded. "There is much in this realm of which I have not the faintest inkling. Still, if your mère, Chemine, the Lady of the River, can aid, I would be most grateful."

Rondalo looked downstream toward the distant small isle. "We will go thither this eve, for first light comes, and I deem you need rest."

Rondalo cast coin on the table, and they slipped out without waking the restaurateur.

They strolled in silence along the bluff toward the Crown and Scepter, while the river below slipped gently through the waning night, and just as they reached the riverside door, full dawn finally came, and, with small, sleepy peeps followed by insistent chirps, Scruff awakened and scrambled to Camille's shoulder and demanded they break fast.

Rondalo was yet laughing when he bade au revoir, and that he would see her in the eve.

*   *   *

It was late afternoon as Rondalo and Camille, with Scruff on her shoulder, stepped from the bridge and onto the high riverside bluff.

"I thought we would be taking a boat to the isle," said Camille.

"Non, Camille, there are no docks, no cliffside stairs, no scaling ladders to my dam's abode."

"Then how—?"

"You will see," said Rondalo, smiling.

They followed the road a distance, past a large paddock and a busy set of stables, where, since no horse was allowed in the city of Les Îles, those of the red coach as well as those of other travellers were looked after. The road went onward a way, but then turned and ran down the face of the bluff through a series of heavily buttressed switchbacks to the ferry slips below. Rondalo and Camille did not follow this way, but instead at the high turn they did leave the road and entered into the galleries of the woodland beyond; therein they made their way among the trees overlooking the river far under.

"Tell me, Rondalo, are you one of the Firsts? I mean, Lisane said you were, yet it would seem that your mère had to precede you herein. Would that not make you instead one of, say, the Seconds?"

Rondalo smiled. "She was in labor the moment she stepped into Faery, and swiftly was I born . . . or so it is she tells me."

"What came before?" asked Camille. "That is, where did your mère live ere then? Whence came she?"

Rondalo shrugged. " 'Tis said that long past there was no Faery, until shaped in the tales of the Keltoi, a wandering race of true bards, every man a king, and they finally came to settle on an emerald isle somewhere elsewhen. How they did so—created Faery, that is—it is not at all certain. Some claim that as they told their glorious tales to one another, they spoke with such silver tongues, with such subtle mastery, that the gods themselves listened intently, and what the Keltoi told, the gods made manifest. Thus was Faery fashioned, twilight borders and all, and the moment my dam stepped into Faery was the moment I was born."

Camille frowned. "Has no one asked these men of the emerald isle? It should be easy enough to find the truth of the matter."

Rondalo shook his head. "Alas, the true Keltoi are no more, vanished from the worlds, and only their stone circles and dolmens remain."

"Then what of their descendants? Cannot they shed some light?"

" 'Tis said that many of those have silver tongues and some have golden pens, yet they are no wiser as to how Faery came to be than I."

"Then mayhap your mère will know," said Camille.

"Alas, my dam has but one memory of aught ere I was born, and that a grievous one: the death of my sire."

"Oh," said Camille, and fell silent.

The sun was just beginning to set, high white clouds turning golden in the foredusk sky, when at last they stood on the bluff straight across from the solitary isle. As Camille gazed at the distant white cottage within the walled grounds atop the sheer-sided river mesa, she said, "Now that we are here, how do we proceed?"

Rondalo grinned. "I will show you." Pulling Camille after, he stepped through the long shadows cast by the trees to come to a great white boulder. And on the side away from the river, he placed his hand to the stone and whispered a word, and lo! a silver-bound, oaken door appeared. At Camille's gasp, Rondalo said, "Fear not, lady, for my dam tells me 'tis but a simple glamour."

" 'Twas not a gasp of fear, Rondalo, but one of wonder instead, for glamours are strange and marvelous: they turn beautiful Elves into crones, Unicorns into nags, and doors into stone."

"And sometimes just the opposite," replied Rondalo, smiling.

In spite of the illusion, the door was locked, but Rondalo produced a silver key, and in but moments, by the light of a newly lit lantern found on a peg just inside, they descended a long, spiral stair down into stone depths below. At last they came to the bottom, and a tunnel stretched into darkness before them, and along this way they went, their footsteps echoing hollowly down the long, granite corridor.

There it was that Scruff peeped drowsily a time or two within the shadowy hall, and Camille carefully slipped him into the high vest pocket, where, after another peep or two, the sparrow settled down to sleep.

As they continued on, Camille asked, "Who made this?"

" 'Twas here from the first."

"A Keltoi creation, eh?"

"Them or the gods."

Finally, they came to the foot of another stair spiralling upward into the darkness above, and up this way they went nearly three hundred steps altogether. They came to another door, this one locked as well, but the silver key opened it, too.

As Rondalo blew out the lantern and hung it on a peg, Camille stepped outward into the early twilight beyond, for dusk was drawing down o'er the land, and she came into a splendid garden, flowers everywhere. A pillared gazebo sat centermost, beyond which stood a white-stone cottage. Pathways wended among blossoms. "Shall we?" asked Rondalo, offering his arm.

As Camille slipped her arm through his she looked back toward the door, yet 'twas nought but a stone boulder she saw, like the one on the shore opposite.

Through the gloaming they trod along one of the pathways, but as they circled 'round the gazebo, a gentle voice said, "Would you pass me by?"

Rondalo laughed. "Mother, I saw you not."

" 'Tis no wonder, son, for what man would have eyes for aught but the beauty who walks at your side?"

Even as Camille blushed, Rondalo said, "Mother, may I present Lady Camille; she has come for your aid. Lady Camille, my mother Chemine, the Lady of the River."

Camille curtseyed low, and Chemine rose and curtseyed as well. She was tall and graceful and had an ethereal quality about her, yet a quality of sadness as well. Her eyes were grey-blue and held a tilt, and her skin, like that of Rondalo, was alabaster touched by gold. Her hair was fair, though a trace of copper shone here and there among the flax.

"Come and sit and have some tea. I have been waiting for you."

"You have been looking into the water again, eh, Mother?"

Chemine canted her head and made a small gesture toward a stone bowl, which seemed to be filled with ink.

Rondalo turned to Camille. "Mother is a Gwaragedd Annwn, or as mortals sometimes say, a Water Fairy, though 'tis a misnomer, for the Gwaragedd Annwn are of Elvenkind rather than of the Fairies."

"I've heard of Water Fairies," said Camille, setting her cup aside, "yet I thought they were creatures such as those I saw in the Spring- and Autumnwood. Small, they were, nearly transparent, a long, graceful fin running from wrist to ankle. —Oh, and they can change into otters, or at least so did the males, as I discovered while swimming unclothed."

Rondalo laughed, and Camille blushed, and Chemine smiled and said, "La, child, those were Water Sprites. A curious folk, and playful. But not the so-called Water Fairies of lore, the Gwaragedd Anwnn."

"Why do they name you so? —Water Fairy, I mean."

Chemine glanced at Rondalo, then said, "We have certain power over water."

"And that would have something to do with, um"—Camille glanced at the bowl—" 'looking into the water'? And, by the bye, is that ink?"

Chemine smiled softly. "Not ink, but incanted water instead. And through it I can see far, though not without limits."

"Indeed, Mother, I brought Camille here so that you might see for her."

Chemine set down her own teacup and turned to Camille. "What is it, child? What would you have me espy?"

Chemine looked up from the ebon water. "There is a strong spell here, barring the way. I can see nought of this place you seek, nor aught of your true love."

Tears welled in Camille's eyes. "Is there nothing you can do?"

Chemine shook her head. "The only other time I could not see what I sought was when I and others of the Firsts were after the terrible Wizard Orbane; yet he is now beyond the Black Wall of the World, and so it could not be his hand at work, else we would know of it, or so I do deem."

"What of Lanval or Blanche, or any of the others?"

Chemine's eyes widened. "Blanche and Lanval?"

"My friends at Summerwood Manor. They've gone missing as well."

Chemine reached out and took Camille's hand. "Mayhap you had better tell me the entire tale. Perhaps therein will lie a clue as to that which might help."

Wearily, Chemine slumped back. "Again I cannot see. Whatever happed to your Alain might have happed to them as well.

The great wind you spoke of . . . a powerful spell, I deem, one that might have borne them all to this place east of the sun and west of the moon, and I do not know nor can I see where it is."

Silence fell over the three in the gazebo, now lanternlit in the night. But then Camille asked, "Can you look at all the places in Faery where you *can* see, and by elimination find the place you cannot?"

Chemine sighed and shook her head. "Child, it drains me to see through the black water, and to look over all of Faery to find the place I cannot see would take much more than I have to give. What you ask could perhaps be done, but certainly not in the time you have left, nor in a thousand thousand times, for the Faery I know of is quite extensive, and, in truth, the whole of it might be without end."

Camille sighed. "Then I suppose I'll have to keep asking, especially among those with much lore." She looked at Chemine. "Tell me, is there among the Firsts, someone with deep knowledge of that which has gone before, someone who might know?"

Chemine looked first at Camille and then at Rondalo, and suddenly she burst into tears. In spite of her weariness, she leapt to her feet and rushed into the garden. Rondalo sprang after, and when he caught her he held her in his arms as she quietly wept. After long moments she gained control of herself and sent him back to the gazebo. And Rondalo and Camille sat watching as Chemine paced the grounds, as if trying to come to a difficult decision. Finally she came and took Camille by the hands and haltingly said, "There is one who might help, for he is eldest in all Faery, the First of the Firsts. He has travelled far and knows much, yet he is a murderer."

"*Murderer?*" blurted Camille.

Rondalo sucked air in through gritted teeth and clenched his fists and said, "Name him, Mother," yet he was braced as if he already knew the answer.

"You know who he is, my son."

"Raseri," hissed Rondalo.

Camille frowned, for she had heard that name somewhere before.

Rondalo turned to Camille. "He is a—"

"—A Firedrake," said Camille. "Lisane named him during the reading."

Again tears streamed down Chemine's face. "He slew Audane."

"Audane?"

"My heart, my love, Rondalo's sire. He was to me as your Alain is to you."

"Oh, I am so sorry," said Camille, embracing Chemine.

Moments passed, and finally Chemine regained her composure. Gently disengaging from Camille, she turned to Rondalo. "You must guide Camille to Raseri."

"What? To my enemy? To the one who slew my sire? He of monstrous guile and loathsome treachery?"

"My son, we have no choice. If Camille is to find her Alain, she must speak with the eldest in the land."

"But Mother, I swore that if I ever went to his lair, I would take my sire's sword and slay him."

"Then leave the sword behind."

"Break my oath?"

Chemine sighed. "No, I would not have you break an oath sworn upon the sword of your sire."

"Then what you ask cannot be done," said Rondalo.

They sat in silence a moment, but then Camille said, "Would it break your oath to guide me to a place from which I could go on alone?"

"But Camille, I would not have you face that monster without someone at your side."

Camille smiled and gently touched the sleeping sparrow, and, as he gave a tiny "*chp*," she said, "Scruff will be with me, a gift of Lady Sorcière."

Long did they debate, Chemine saying that this might be Camille's only chance, and Rondalo admitting that he would not break his oath if he but guided her nigh, yet he would not abandon her to face Raseri alone, foul murderer that the Drake was. Yet Camille would not be swayed, arguing that without Rondalo's help, Alain and the others would be lost forever; and as for facing Raseri, it was a risk that she and mayhap Scruff were willing to take.

A glum silence fell over them all, yet at last Rondalo agreed, saying to Camille, "Your persuasion is almost as golden as your singing."

At this, Chemine raised an eyebrow. "You sing?"

"Oh, Mother, you must listen," said Rondalo. "Let us to the cote, and you take up your harp, and then you will hear."

Camille glanced at Chemine's weary posture and started to demur, but Chemine said, "Music is restorative. Besides, it will break this somber mood fallen o'er all our hearts."

*   *   *

It was mid of night when Camille and Rondalo took their leave of Chemine. She embraced them both, and said to Rondalo, "Let not this child sing to Goblins and Trolls." And to Camille she said, "May you find what lies east of the sun and west of the moon, and may it be your true heart."

Then she took up a sheathed sword and handed it to Rondalo. "Just in case, my son. Yet draw it not until the mountain comes into view, and then only if you believe you need go on, for, heed! you must not break the oath sworn upon your father's blade."

Rondalo nodded, his look grim, and he said nought as he buckled the weapon on.

Then Chemine kissed each and stepped back, and Camille and Rondalo went through the silver-bound door in the stone and down to the tunnel below.

As they started along the passageway, to break the brooding silence, Camille asked, "What did your mère mean, 'Let not this child sing to Goblins and Trolls'?"

Rondalo looked at her. "You do not know?"

"No."

"Then heed: 'tis said because of their own hideous, froglike croakings neither Goblins nor Trolls can abide the sound of sweet singing, for what they cannot have, they revile. The sweeter the singing, the greater their fury, and with a voice as pure as yours . . . I dread to think of what they might do. Regardless, that's what my dam meant when she spoke to me, but in truth was cautioning you."

"I did not know."

"I ween she suspected as much," said Rondalo.

They reached the end of the long corridor, where the spiral stairway led upward, and Rondalo paused and said, "My dear, you should not venture about Faery without someone of knowledge, someone of lore at your side."

"Would that I could," replied Camille, "but the Lady of the Mere said I must go alone, but for one of her gifts—Scruff, I believe. She did say unexpected help would come along the way, and it has. Even so, I deem Scruff and I must see this Raseri alone, but let us not argue that point again."

Rondalo sighed, then began the ascent.

They climbed up the long spiral to come to the glamoured door in the boulder, and they stepped out into the woods along the high, riverside bluff. The waxing moon rode high in the sky, and by its gentle light they passed among the trees of the forest along the rim, aiming for Les Îles.

As they came to the road, Camille said, "Tell me, Rondalo, if it pains you not overmuch, how did your père die?"

"I am not certain, for it did occur ere I was born. I only know that he was slain by Raseri."

"What does your mère say?"

"She knows not how it came about either, for her own memories ere coming unto Faery are all but nonexistent. All she says is that my sire Audane was her true love, and that he was slain by the villainous Raseri."

"And you have the sword of your père?"

"Aye. 'Tis all of his that I do have. 'Twas one of the few things my dam bore with her into Faery, the sword in her hand, with me in her womb straining to get out."

They walked in silence for a while, passing by the stables and paddock where horses slept in the night. Just ere coming to the rope-and-board bridge, Camille said, "Mayhap 'twas grief drove your mère's memory from her, yet if your tale about the Keltoi is true, then mayhap that's where your mère's story begins, with the death of Audane and the birth of you. Mayhap there *is* no story before that. Mayhap that's all the Keltoi told, or all of that tale the gods did hear, hence 'twas but a fragment they did make manifest."

Rondalo did not reply as they made their way across the span and into Les Îles.

"Ah, Camille, I shall miss you greatly," said Robert. Then he frowned. "What should I do with the gowns?"

Dressed for travel, her rucksack and waterskin and bedroll slung, her stave in hand, Scruff on her shoulder, Camille said, "Perhaps another singer will come along who can use them."

"And mayhap you yourself will return one day," said Robert, hope glimmering.

"Perhaps," said Camille, "and merci for all you did, Robert."

She turned toward Rondalo, he, too, ready for travel, and he said, "Shall we?"

With a final au revoir, Camille and Rondalo departed, and they made their way through the bustle of Les Îles, Camille's troop of urchins laughing and darting among the stir, yet keeping pace with their patron. At last they reached the final bridge, and here did Camille stop and call the children together. With a smile she said adieu, then flung a handful of copper pennies high into the air, scattering them widely, and with wild whoops the urchins dove after.

Even as the children scrambled for the coins, Camille and Rondalo stepped onto the bridge and went out of Les Îles. Soon they came to the stables, where two riding horses and one pack-horse stood waiting, and though Camille had protested she knew not how to ride, still she realized a deal more blossoms would wither away if she walked than if she rode. And so she mounted up, and off they went, away from the river and into the forest at hand, setting forth for a grim range of mountains somewhere in the far distance beyond, for deep in the foreboding fastness therein a murderous Firedrake did lair.

27
Firedrake

Two hundred sixty-five blossoms gone, the two hundred sixty-sixth awither. Oh why does it take so long to—

"Yon," said Rondalo, breaking Camille's thoughts.

"Wh-what?"

"Yon is the firemountain, wherein the Dragon does lair," said Rondalo, pointing, his breath blowing white in the cold mountain air.

Camille's gaze followed his outstretched arm to where tendrils of smoke from a truncated mountain rose into the early-morning sky.

Their horses plodded onward through the snow, rounding a great looming frown of stone, and slowly more of the firemountain came into view, the whole of it a dark ruddy color streaked with ebony runs. Finally, just above a long and sheer rise topped with a ledge, there gaped a black hole.

"Is that it?" asked Camille, her heart hammering in sudden dread.

"Aye," replied Rondalo, his voice grim.

They had been on the way some thirty-five days, travelling toward this place, and at last the goal was in view, there where a monster laired.

Thirty-five days of pleasant company. Thirty-five days of sleeping in forest campsites and crofters' lofts and hunters' cabins and in wayside inns.

Back trail some two days and a dawning ago, a mountain village lay; 'twas nought more than a dozen or so stone-sided, sod-roofed dwellings scattered along a narrow mountain road, with tiers of farmland carven in the slopes below. The villagers had spoken in a guttural language Camille did not know, for it was neither speech in the Old Tongue nor in that of the new. But Rondalo understood and he did converse with them, translating for the benefit of Camille. And when the villagers had discerned whither the twain were bound, their warnings were stark and forbidding.

Gjøre ikke . . .

[Do not go into the mountains, for there a deadly Drake does abide.]

[We have no choice but to do so.]

[Many a brave and foolish warrior has gone, armed and armored, ready for battle, seeking fame, seeking glory. None have returned, and their names are not remembered.]

[We seek neither fame nor glory, but knowledge instead.]

[Knowledge of what?]

[Where lies a place east of the sun and west of the moon.]

The villagers had looked at one another, yet all had shrugged, for none had known where such a place might be. After a moment an eld and toothless woman had gazed up at the ice-clad mountains and said, [Only the north wind would know.] Then with faded blue eyes she had looked beyond a col leading deeper into the fastness and added, [Or mayhap a Dragon dire.]

[That is what we are hoping for, and that is where we go.]

[Then we will see you no more.]

The villagers had then turned their backs and walked away, for what profit was there in speaking unto the dead?

And so Camille and Rondalo, after spending the night in an abandoned, roofless ruin of a stone hut, had ridden out the next dawntide, and no one had watched them go.

And now, on the morn of the third day after, their goal was in sight.

Camille reined her horse to a halt and dismounted. "I will go on from here alone."

Rondalo sprang down from his horse and stepped to her. "I cannot let you face Raseri single-handedly. It is entirely too dangerous."

"I have Scruff, and what of your oath? I would not have you battle a Dragon, Firedrake that he is."

"I shall keep my oath, and do battle with that foul murderer, but only after he has answered that which you need to know."

"No, Rondalo. The Lady of the Mere said I must go alone"—

Camille gestured at her shoulder, where Scruff perched, his feathers fluffed up against the cold—"Scruff and I, that is."

"These past thirty-five days you have not been alone, Camille. And I have come to cherish you, mayhap more than you know."

Camille blushed, remembering:

It had occurred in a wayside inn, just a fortnight past: After they had sung for the patrons, the innkeeper had sent a second bottle of wine to their table, and both Camille and Rondalo had overly imbibed. That was when Rondalo had leaned over and kissed Camille, and she, so very lonely for Alain and craving his intimacy, had fervently responded. It was only when Rondalo had paused and looked into her eyes that she caught her breath and saw deep within his gaze an ardor burning bright, and she was thrilled. But then, shocked at her own behavior, in a confusion of emotions, she had fled away from him and to her quarters, and in the next days they had ridden in uncomfortable silence, saying nought beyond the needs of the moment, or when making camp, or planning the morrow's journey. And during this time Camille had wondered if there were room in a single heart for more than one love. As she had done so, unbidden there had come to mind the image of the Unicorn Thale, and this had made her wonder as well of virtue and purity and other such, and whether or no she had lost that which she once had.

But that was then and this was now, and Camille said, "I cherish you too, my friend, and no more than would you have me face Raseri, so would I not have you face him as well."

Rondalo grasped the hilt of the sword at his waist and flashed it into the sky, calling out, "By the blade of my sire I—"

But then he fell into stunned silence, his eyes upon the gleaming bronze. And then he cried out, "Mother!" his voice slapping from vertical stone faces to echo among the peaks.

Camille stepped backward in startlement, for she knew not what was amiss, until Rondalo's shoulders slumped and he said, "This is not my sire's."

"Not your—?"

"Nay, for his is silver-bright, and hammered runes of power run the length of the blade."

And now Camille remembered Chemine's words as she had

handed the sheathed sword to Rondalo: *"Just in case, my son. Yet draw it not until the mountain comes into view, and then only if you believe you need go on, for, heed: You must not break the oath sworn upon your father's blade."*

Camille said, "Your mère knows you well, Rondalo. Yet she also knew I would need go on alone. And so she did that which had to be done to assure that it would be so, for you must not break your sword-oath."

Tears sprang into Rondalo's eyes, to run down his face. "Oh, my dearest Camille, I . . ."

"I know, Rondalo. I know."

Rondalo wiped his cheeks with the heels of his hands, then cleared his throat and said, "Remember, look not into his gaze, else he will glamour you."

"I remember," said Camille, untying leather thongs from behind her saddle. "You told me often enough of the powers of Drakes, and so I think I will not fall unto a Dragon's wiles."

"They are quite crafty, quite cunning. Treacherous, too."

"As I said, I shall remember. But you, Rondalo, must remember too that I shall take off my cloak and whirl it 'round my head if all seems to be going well. If at night, I shall swing my small lantern back and forth." Camille glanced up toward the dark hole. "From here, you should be able to see either."

Camille then took down her waterskin and bedroll and rucksack, the stave affixed in loops she had thought to sew thereon. She settled the sling straps over her shoulder and pulled loose the walking staff, the two hundred and sixty-sixth blossom awither. Finally, a tremor in her voice, she looked at Rondalo and said, "I now go."

Rondalo stepped forward and he kissed her on the cheek. "I shall wait here a sevenday, and if you return not"—his eyes turned hard as flint—"I will fetch my sire's sword and the Drake will not survive."

Leaving Rondalo and the horses behind in the fastness of snow-clad peaks, Camille crossed fields of ice and barren rock and snow, rubble and scree and schist half-buried in the winter white, Scruff shifting about to keep his balance as Camille scrambled across the boulder-laden 'scape. On she went, the trek difficult, and she paused now and again to take a drink and offer water to Scruff as well.

It was nigh the noontide when she came to the barren, dark

ruddy slopes. She paused briefly to feed Scruff a scatter of millet seeds and to take a meal of her own. Then on she went up the bleak sides, her staff aiding in the climb as she angled cross-slope for the ledge above the vertical rise, the ledge the Dragon's doorstone.

As she gained in height, she looked back into the fastness she had left behind, yet she saw no sign of Rondalo among the jumble of rock. Still, she knew that he was there somewhere, lost in the background, her gaze unable to find either him or the horses.

On upward she went, the sun sliding down the sky, and though a shoulder of the slope stood in the way she knew she must be getting close. Of a sudden Scruff grabbed a lock of her hair and leapt down into the high vest pocket, the tiny sparrow chattering frantically and tugging on the tress.

With her heart thudding in her chest. "Ah, then, I was right. Peril indeed is nigh, eh, Scruff."

Still the bird chattered, and still did Camille climb, yet when she rounded the turn to abruptly come to the broad ledge, Scruff fell silent.

Camille stepped thereon, and midmost yawned a black hole. And it was vast.

Timorously, Camille moved toward the gape.

"WHO COMES?" boomed a great voice, echoing hollowly.

"Oh!" Camille blenched and cried out at the thunder of sound, her heart leaping into her throat.

"IS THAT YOU I TASTE, RONDALO, FAINT THOUGH IT IS? COME TO YOUR DEATH? COME TO MEET YOUR FATE?"

Again Camille flinched, yet she managed to say, " 'Tis I, Camille, and though I did journey with Rondalo, instead I have come for your aid, O Raseri, your help to find my Alain."

As Camille peered into the darkness, trying to see, the voice drew closer and boomed, "ALAIN? PRINCE OF THE SUMMERWOOD?"

"Oh, yes, and I am so glad you know of him, know of my beloved. He is lost, and I—"

"Camille, my love," came a gentle response, and stepping forth from the darkness—

"Alain, Alain, oh my love." Sobbing, Camille rushed forward, and he took her in his arms.

"Shhh, shhh," he said. "I would not have you cry."

"Oh, Alain, my sweet Alain, I have found you at last and I have been searching for so very long, and—"

Camille felt an insistent yanking on a lock of her hair, and she could hear Scruff chattering madly. And she looked down at her pocket where the tiny bird jerked and pulled at her tress.

And from the corner of Camille's eye . . .

. . . from the corner of her eye . . .

. . . from the corner she saw . . .

. . . a great scaly foot with claws like sabers resting against the stone.

With a gasp, Camille drew back, and there before her 'twas not Alain, but instead—

"RRRRAAAWWW!"

The Dragon's roar was deafening, and he was monstrous, looming upward some twenty feet or more, his gleaming, sinuous body stretching back into the blackness of his lair. Like the stone of the mountain itself, he was a dark ruddy color, splashes of ebon blackness glittering here and there. Vast leathery wings were folded along his sides. And as he slithered forward, emerging from his den, Camille stepped backward in terror, the vertical precipice of the ledge coming near.

"YOU, RONDALO'S CAT'S-PAW, COME TO GULL ME WHILE HE PLANS SOME HEINOUS ATTACK. TREACHEROUS MAIDEN, YOU WILL NOT LIVE TO SEE ME DESTROY HIM."

Raseri drew in a deep breath, and Camille knew she would not survive the fire to come. Futilely, in a two-handed grip she thrust out the stave, as if it would ward the flames, and she shut her eyes and turned her head aside, death even then on its way.

A great blast of fire spewed forth, but it touched not Camille. She opened one eye to see the last of it gushing into the sky.

And then Raseri looked down at her and at the staff in her hands. "Lady Sorcière sent you here?"

Of a sudden, Scruff scrambled out from the pocket and to Camille's shoulder.

"Yes, my lord Dragon," said Camille, her voice tight and quavering with residual tension and dread, as well as with disbelief that she was yet alive, Camille herself feeling as if she would collapse at any moment, and she abruptly sat down on the stone. She put her head between her knees and said, her voice a bit muffled, "Indeed I was sent by the Lady of the Mere. —Oh, not specifically here, yet she did start me on my way. 'Twas Chemine, the Lady of the River who sent me to you, for only—"

"Chemine?" The Firedrake's glittering, golden serpent eyes flew wide in surprise. "That cannot be. She would not do such, for I slew her mate on her wedding night, or so it is I recall."

"Nevertheless, she is the one who sent me, with her son Rondalo as my guide, for you are the First of the Firsts, and perhaps only you can aid."

Raseri peered down into the valley, and his forked tongue flicked out, and he hissed, "Are you certain this is not some trick? I see Rondalo now riding in haste this way."

"Oh, no," cried Camille, leaping to her feet, "he will break his sword-oath."

"Scruff," called Camille, holding open the vest pocket; the wee sparrow hopped in. Then swiftly she cast off her rucksack and bedroll and waterskin and then removed her cloak. She stood on the lip of the ledge and whirled the garment by its collar 'round and 'round o'erhead.

Finally Raseri said, "He's stopped."

Camille continued to whirl the cloak.

"He's turned back."

Arm weary, Camille lowered her cloak and saw in the distance, among the great boulders strewn along the valley floor, Rondalo riding away.

As Camille donned her cloak once more and Scruff scrambled back to his usual perch, Raseri said, "Well, now, if one of my sworn enemies has sent you to me for aid, and the other sworn enemy acted as your guide, then there is a tale here for the telling, and I would hear it all."

Darkness had fallen, and Scruff was now asleep in the high vest pocket, and by the growing argent light of the waning gibbous moon half-risen, her tale now come to an end, Camille looked up at Raseri.

The Dragon sighed. "No, Camille, I know not where lies a place east of the sun and west of the moon." Even as Camille started to weep, Raseri added, "Yet do not despair, for although I am indeed the First of the Firsts, there might be in Faery some who are even older than I."

"Older? How can that be?"

" 'Tis said they have been in the world since the very beginning of time."

"Where can I find these eld ones?"

"I am not at all certain, but there is a river you may follow, and they might be found nigh. Yet it is perilous in the extreme to go along those banks and worse still to fall into its flow."

Camille glanced at sleeping Scruff. "Peril from what? Monsters? Serpents from the seas in those waters?"

"Worse," replied Raseri. "It is the River of Time, that which the Fey avoid; none whatsoever go nigh, for it is said that should one travel along the River of Time, then mortal he will become."

"A river of time?"

"Aye, for all time flows in a stream out from Faery, to spread over the earthly demesne." Raseri looked down at Camille, then gestured outward. "Where else would time issue forth but from out of this mystical place?"

"But I thought time touches not Faery."

"In the main, 'tis true, for in Faery, time is confined to the river, perilous in the extreme; but in the mortal lands it spreads out over the whole of the world and becomes diffuse, attenuated, and is somewhat less dangerous. In Faery, all Fey avoid the river, going 'round rather than across, for we want not to suffer time's ravages should we travel along its banks or fall into its flow. But in the world of mortals, the Fey on occasion do swim within time, for there it is weakened. Still, should we spend overlong in the world of men, we might turn mortal ourselves. Have you not heard the tales of Fey falling for the love of a mortal man or woman, and becoming mortal themselves? That's because they overextend their stay in the earthly realm. To retain their immortality, Elves and other such oft vanish from the mortal lands and return to Faery, else mortal they would become. And though the River of Time does run through Faery, none I know travel thereon."

Camille sat silent for a moment, then she fished in her rucksack. "I must signal Rondalo that all is yet well."

She unscrewed the brass sealing cap from the wick and lit the small brass and glass lantern; then she paced out to the rim of the ledge and stood awhile, slowly swinging the light back and forth. Finally, she stepped back to Raseri's side and blew out the lantern and capped the wick once more. As she set the lamp aside to cool ere returning it to her rucksack she said, "Though it would seem quite perilous for Fey to go nigh, the River of Time will not affect me more than it ordinarily would, for I am mortal already. Even so, you say those who might aid can thereat be found?"

"Aye. 'Tis rumored that three sisters live along its banks and, if true, they are the eldest of the eld. Too, it is also said that all things are revealed in due time, and mayhap along the banks of Time's River you will discover just where lies a place east of the sun and west of the moon."

Camille glanced at her stave and said, "Raseri, I would go."

"Then, lady, because of all you have said, I will take you to the place whence the river springs, and mayhap you'll find that which you seek. Yet beware, for, if all things are revealed in due measure, what you may discover woven in the tapestry of time could in the end be salvation or doom for you or your Alain or both. His fate as well as yours may already be sealed."

"What you say might be true," replied Camille, "nevertheless, I would go."

"So be it then," said Raseri. "Take rest now, and we shall take flight at first light."

"Take flight?"

"Aye, You did not expect to walk, did you? Nay, I shall bear you thither, you and your wee sparrow."

"But I—"

"But me no buts, my lady, for it is a long way, and you have not the time."

At the dawning, even though Scruff complained that he was hungry, as she had done every day, Camille treated the sparrow's wing with a tiny dab of salve. She looked up to see Raseri watching. "He was wounded by a thorn and cannot fly," said Camille, by way of explanation.

"Mayhap where we are bound," rumbled Raseri, "your tiny bird will improve, for 'tis said time heals all wounds."

"Oh, do you think? I do so hope, for I would see him take to wing."

As Camille fetched some millet seed for Scruff and sprinkled it on the stone, Raseri turned his head and flicked out his forked tongue, tasting the frigid morning air. And he said, "Rondalo yet waits afar."

Camille glanced down the vale, yet it was too dark for her to make out aught. She drew out a biscuit from her rucksack and took a bite, and in a moment said, "Tell me, Raseri, how came you to do battle with Rondalo's père Audane?"

Even though he was a Dragon, Raseri managed a shrug. "All I know is that on Audane's wedding night, he and I fought fiercely. As to why, I cannot say. Whether or no he wounded me, that, too, is not in my ken, and how I finally slew him, I know not. Only that I did. My first true memory is of being here in this fastness. I was alone in Faery for some while, but then, nine or ten moons later, I was aware that Chemine had come to Faery bearing Audane's sword and giving birth to Rondalo. Beyond that, I know little."

Camille shook her head in puzzlement. "Tell me then, are all Firsts as are you: knowing nought of what went before you each came unto Faery?"

"So it seems," said Raseri, peering toward the oncoming light.

Camille fell silent and took another bite. Around the mouthful, she said, "Have you heard of the Keltoi?"

"Indeed. Most in Faery know of the legend. Wandering bards all; those whose tales caught the ear of the gods, and they in turn made Faery manifest."

Camille swallowed and took a drink of water. "Well then, Raseri, answer me this:

"What if it is true that, as they wandered across the face of the world, the Keltoi did tell their tales, and the gods did listen, and they so enjoyed what they heard they made Faery manifest so that they could be entertained by the stories that followed? Mayhap long past, 'round a campfire a gifted Keltoi began a tale, the first one the gods listened to, and it went something like this:

"Once upon a time there was a terrible Drake named Raseri, a Drake who breathed flame. And in a hard-fought duel with an Elf named Audane, Raseri slew the Elf. Yet it was Audane's wedding night, and he had lain with his bride ere the battle, and some ten moons after the terrible death, Audane's grieving widow, a Water Fairy named Chemine, birthed a son. And Chemine gave over unto the wee lad Audane's silvery sword, the one with the arcane runes hammered down the length of its blade, and she said, 'One day, my Rondalo, you will battle with vile Raseri, foul murderer of your sire.' "

Camille fell silent, and Raseri cocked his head and said, "Mayhap 'tis true that such did happen. Even so, where does that lead?"

"Oh, don't you see, Raseri, ere that tale mayhap there *was* no before, no existence whatsoever for Faery, no existence even for you. Mayhap that's when Faery began. Mayhap that's when you were born full-grown. Mayhap there was no Audane, yet even if there was, if the legend of the Keltoi and the gods is true, then it is no fault of yours he was slain. Instead 'tis completely the fault of the Keltoi who told that story, the first the gods had heard, and this blood vengeance, this sword-oath Rondalo swore, should instead have been sworn 'gainst the tale teller, or the gods who made it true, for in truth they are the ones in combination who did murder Audane."

Raseri grunted, but otherwise did not reply, and Camille ate the remainder of her biscuit in silence, her thoughts tumbling one o'er the other.

Finally Raseri said, "If you have the truth of it, Camille, then much needs setting aright."

"Wh-what?" said Camille, shaken from her musings.

"I said, have you the truth of it, much needs setting aright. Even so, there is this to consider: although the Keltoi, or gods, or in combination, are responsible for much grief and rage, they gave me, they gave all of us, life as well. Without them we would not be. Hence, if the legend is true, we owe them our very existence. Those tales, though fraught with peril and desperation and fury and sorrow such as they are, without them we would not be."

Camille nodded, somewhat abstractedly, and Raseri tilted his head to one side and said, "You seem preoccupied, Camille. What were your thoughts that I so interrupted?"

Camille glanced at Scruff and then at the Drake, then out to where Rondalo might be, and she shrugged and said, "I was just wondering whose silver tongue or golden pen is telling the tale we find ourselves in."

Raseri's booming laughter echoed among the peaks, but when he looked down at Camille, she wasn't laughing at all.

"The sun rises, Camille," said the Drake.

Camille looked to see that the sun was just then edging up through a col between peaks. Camille stood and stepped to the lip of the precipice and once again whirled her cloak 'round and 'round above her head. Then she donned it and took up her bedroll and waterskin and rucksack and slung them onto her shoulder, and as she started to slip the stave into the rucksack loops—

What's this?

A hairline crack ran a small way from the bottom of the staff upward toward the withered lower end of the carved stem of the garland.

Did I somehow do this?

"Camille," said Raseri, nodding toward the rising sun.

Quickly Camille shoved the stave into the loops, then took up the sparrow. She glanced at Raseri's great, leathery wings, now partly unfolded, and said, "I'd better put you in the pocket, Scruff, else you might be blown away."

Scruff *chp*ed a time or two, but then settled in, and Camille asked, "Where shall I, um . . ."

"You can straddle the base of my neck," said Raseri, bending low and crooking a foreleg on the side where Camille stood.

Using the leg as a stepping block, Camille clambered up and took seat. A double row of great barbels ran the length of Raseri's neck. "May I use these for handholds?" asked Camille, grasping the pair before her. They were somewhat soft and a bit flexible, like the barbels 'round the mouths of some kinds of fish.

"Use what?" replied Raseri, craning his neck about. "Oh, those. Indeed."

"I would ask two things more, my lord Dragon," said Camille.

"And they are . . . ?"

"Fly over Rondalo so that he might see I am all right."

"I shall do so. And the other . . . ?"

"Ignore any of my screams you might hear."

With booming laughter, Raseri stepped to the lip of the sheer precipice and leapt out into space.

Camille sucked icy air in through clenched teeth as down the Drake plummeted, wind whistling past and blowing back her hood, her hair to stream out golden behind, the rocks below rushing up to meet them. She closed her eyes and gritted her teeth, for she knew they surely must crash, yet she stubbornly refused to scream. But then—*Whoosh!*—Raseri's vast, leathery wings began beating, and he arced through the nadir of his dive and began to climb into the sky. Camille opened her eyes, as up and up he spiralled, and she gasped in wonder, for the view from the height was magnificent. Why, it was almost as if she could see the whole of Faery, though surely not. And she glanced down at Scruff, who was chirping in joy, craning his neck out from her pocket so that he could see. Then Raseri turned and flew back over his firemountain, and Camille saw that it was hollow, and thin tendrils of smoke streamed out from fumerols below.

Down the vale arrowed Raseri, toward Rondalo's campsite, and, as they flew over, the horses shied and would have bolted, but for the tethers holding fast. Raseri circled and Camille waved, and Rondalo waved in return, a look of astonishment on his face. And then Raseri wheeled and thundered away, the rising sun at his back.

And down below, Rondalo sighed, and watched them wing into the distance—his implacable foe bearing off the woman he had come to cherish. When at last they were gone from sight, Rondalo stepped to the horses and stroked muzzles and soothed the animals with soft and gentle words. Finally he broke camp and saddled the mounts and laded the packhorse and then slowly rode away, his path taking him in the opposite direction from that in which the Drake had flown.

High across the world of Faery did the Dragon Raseri soar, mountains and rivers and steads and cities, villages and forests and lakes, and barren wastes of ice or sand or rock all passing 'neath his wings. And Camille was enthralled, for never had she imagined what flying would be like, and here she was, high in the sky, chill wind streaming through her hair, clouds like foreign castles and great châteaus rising all 'round. Scruff in her pocket chirped his approval, and Camille then knew what a loss the tiny sparrow had suffered, unable to fly as he was. Momentarily, Camille's wind-driven tears became tears of sympathy, but then she was distracted by a great herd of shaggy animals thundering across the grassy plain below.

The sun slid up the sky and across and down, yet Raseri's wings never seemed to slow, never seemed to tire. Through looming walls of twilight they flew, Faery borders, eight or nine altogether . . . Camille uncertain as to which.

But finally, as the sinking sun touched the distant horizon, the Drake began to circle down. "Yon is the river," he called out to her, but, though she looked, Camille could see nought of a stream.

"Where?" she cried. "I can make out no river."

"See the high, grassy ridge jutting above the forest below? Just down the long slope you will find the origin, else you will see nought whatsoever."

Camille's gaze first found the hillock far under, and then downslope she saw a glimmering, and of a sudden Camille could see a silvery ribbon originating at the glimmer and threading through the forest. How she had missed it, she could not say, yet there it was. She looked away and then back, and lo! the river had vanished entirely. Yet when she looked at the slope again, and then down to the glimmer, of a sudden the stream reappeared. Once more she looked away and again the river vanished, completely absent to her searching sight until she returned to the origin.

As if sensing Camille's trial, Raseri called out, "It seems one cannot see the full flow of time lest one starts at the beginning."

Camille let her gaze follow the course of the silvery stream, and in the far distance she could see a great glint of water—perhaps a vast lake, or even an ocean or sea—into which Time's River did flow.

Down spiralled Raseri and down, to finally come alight upon the knoll.

"This is as close as I will go," said the Drake, and he bent his neck low.

Again Camille used Raseri's foreleg as a stepping block as she dismounted. She stretched and twisted to get the kinks out.

As she did so, "It begins there, the River of Time," said the Dragon, pointing with his head downslope.

Camille could see in the distance, a cascade plunging over a linn, yet it seemed the water itself had no origin, either that or it sprang directly from a misty cloud hovering above, the vapor itself glimmering as if of a gleaming within.

Camille looked at the sky and judged the lees of the day, the sun some halfway set. "I should reach the linn ere darkness falls. If not, I have my lantern to guide me. Would you walk down with me?"

"Would that I were braver, yet I'll not gamble 'gainst time. Even so, Camille, you have little to fear in these environs, for all Fey shun this place. Still, stay on your guard, for who knows what troubles time can bring? I would say this as well: you have given me much to ponder, and I thank you for that. Mayhap someday I will be able to repay you for that which you did bring."

What did I bring? Camille wondered. Yet she said, "Oh, Raseri, by bearing me here you have more than paid whatever debt you might imagine you owe, though for the life of me I cannot think why you would believe such."

"Perhaps one day we will both know," said Raseri. "But now I must fly, for yon is a peril I cannot face—the ravages of time."

"Then go, O Lord Dragon, and be well," said Camille, and she curtseyed there on the ridge.

Raseri dipped his head and then said, "Ward your eyes." As Camille put a hand to her brow, with a great leap and thunderous flapping, Raseri took to wing, pebbles and dust and weeds and grass swirling about in a great cloud, Camille battered by the wind of his launch.

Up he circled and up, and then with a great skriegh, he arrowed away, his dark ruddy scales glittering crimson in the light of the setting sun. And it was then that Camille remembered a time in the Winterwood as she rode upon the back of the Bear, a great fell beast flying high above and sounding the very same skriegh. *Was that Raseri even then?* She watched the Drake fly away, the splendid creature he was, and when she could see him no longer, down the slope and toward the linn she did go.

She reached the waterfall as twilight ebbed toward night, and she set camp on the slope just above the cascade, and placed sleeping Scruff on a low branch of a sapling at hand. As she settled in for the night, she looked with curious eyes at the cataract; even this close, in the light of the stars, it seemed as if the water came out from nowhere at the very edge of the linn, though the silvery mist above may have obscured its source.

As Camille prepared to go to sleep, of a sudden she remembered the stave; she lit her small lantern and examined the hairline crack. *I don't remember it reaching this far, and I surely did nought to cause it to lengthen, for it has been affixed to my rucksack all day, but for the gentle trip down from the ridge above.*

Sighing, Camille started to lay the staff aside, but then, though she knew what she would find, she counted the blossoms remaining, starting with the one awither and progressing to the one atop. *One hundred yet linger, though the bottom flower is nigh perished. Two hundred sixty-six days agone, a scant one hundred left. A year and a day and the whole of a moon beyond, that's all she said I would have. And I have squandered— No, Camille, not squandered. Used. I have used two hundred sixty-six days in all to reach this place. Even so, am I any closer whatsoever to finding my beloved Alain?*

Camille blew out the lantern and capped the wick to keep the oil within the reservoir no matter the lamp's orientation, then placed it near at hand.

Silently, the stars wheeled in the sky as Camille was lulled asleep by the *shsshing* fall, for here at the linn and perhaps nowhere else could the passage of time be heard.

28

Future

In the nascent light of the very next dawn, Camille was awakened by the sound of weeping, and she sat up to see a silver-haired maiden sitting at an apparently empty loom in the hovering mist at the precipice of the falls. "Woe betide the world," the demoiselle wailed. "Oh, woe betide the world."

And Camille saw squatting under the loom a shaggy little man, or creature, covered in long, unruly hair—*Much like the being I saw in Les Îles, but this one is much uglier and certainly hairier.* And he gibbered and ran his hands along the cloth beam, then scuttled to the linn and made motions of throwing, as if somehow dragging unseen fabric from the bar to hurl it over the edge of the falls.

At the maiden's side a golden spinning wheel stood silent on the flat stone of the dry streambed along which water should have coursed to supply the cascade, yet nought flowed at all, though the cataract itself sprang from nowhere to thunder down into the river below.

Casting aside her blanket, Camille sprang to her feet and cried out, "Ma'amselle, Ma'amselle, what is amiss?"

The maiden turned, anguish in her gaze, and—*Oh, my!*—her eyes were like unto silver. "I have lost the end of my thread, and if I do not find it quickly, what is to be will not transpire, and time itself will be broken."

What? How can that be?

With tears brimming, the maiden mutely appealed for help, and even though Camille could see nought whatsoever on either the loom or the spinning wheel, she rushed down to aid. As she reached the demoiselle's side, Camille said, "Where did you last have it? —The thread, I mean."

"On the tapestry," cried the maiden, gesturing at the loom.

Camille frowned—"What tapestry?"—but reached out and gasped in startlement, for her touch told her that indeed there was fabric on the loom, yet it could not be seen.

In the dim light of the new morn, carefully, slowly, Camille ran her fingers lightly over the nonvisible cloth, searching by feel for the end of a misplaced thread, her unaiding gaze lost in the moment, alighting on runes carved in the breastbeam, runes which spelled out the name Skuld.

"I cannot find it here," said Camille.

"Oh, but it must be there," wailed the maiden. "I had it not a moment ago."

"There is another place to search," said Camille, and she scrambled 'neath the rig and ran her fingers along the underside of the fabric, and the ugly little man gibbered at her, his breath foul, his eyes glaring as he motioned for her to move aside so that he could continue with his arcane rite.

Yet Camille did not yield as she felt all along the bottom, and, in spite of the hairy man's angry jabber, she thought she could hear the sound of one or mayhap two other looms weaving nearby—the clack of shuttle and the slap and thud of treadle and batten—and though Camille glanced this way and that, she saw them not.

Of a sudden—"I have it!" cried Camille, grasping the dangling, unseen thread 'tween forefinger and thumb.

"Clever girl," said the maiden, smiling, a bit sly it seemed. "Do not let go of it, please." She took up a very-fine-toothed, golden carding comb hanging from the distaff of the golden wheel. "I need to start spinning a new thread from the Mists of Time."

Camille's eyes widened in amaze as the demoiselle reached up with the comb and teased a wisp out from the shimmering vapor. Somehow she managed to grasp the tenuous strand itself, and she fed the hazy filament through the eye in the golden spindle tip and over a hook on the flyer arm, and then down and 'round the spool. Then she gave the wheel a sharp whirl, and lo! it continued to spin, though no one pressed the treadle. And gleaming vapor was pulled down from the mist and twisted into a glassy thread that vanished even as it was spun. Long moments it turned, yet of a sudden the spinning wheel stopped, and the maiden plucked the bobbin loose and mounted it to the shuttle. Even as she did so, another bobbin abruptly appeared on the spinning wheel, no hand setting it there, and again the wheel began to whirl, as if that new spool were right then being wound with invisible thread. The maiden paid it no heed, as she fetched the end of the new-spun, unseen thread from the bobbin on the shuttle in hand, and she took from Camille's fingers the end of the invisible thread of the cloth on the loom.

As Camille scrambled out from under the rig to sit on the dry stone just back from the linn and watch, the maiden tied the new thread to the old—or so did it seem she was doing from the movement of her fingers—and she placed the shuttle in the loom shuttle race and then sat down; and the moment she did, the loom of itself began furiously weaving.

The hairy creature under the loom gnashed his teeth, and cursed in a tongue Camille did not know, and vanished.

"Who was that, and what was he doing?" asked Camille.

"That was Uncertainty, enemy of the future, an agent of Chaos who would have all things return to the formless, disorderly state whence both Faery and the mortal world came."

"Why was he—?"

"Hush, child," said the demoiselle, her argent eyes staring into the silvery vapor, her gaze intent. "Let me weave that which I see in the Mists of Time; when I catch up, we will talk. Break your fast while you wait."

Suddenly, before Camille appeared utensils and a fine porcelain plate laden with food, but food not quite like any she had ever seen, familiar and yet not, as if it had come from a different time. Yet though the meal was cold, the aroma was appealing, and so she ate: the bread the whitest and lightest she could imagine, the meat well spiced and tender, the strange red and orange fruit tangy and tart, the greens crisp, and the deep, deep brown confection so sweet, so marvelous, it brought tears to her eyes.

Even as Camille ate, she watched the wheel and loom in amazement, as many new-wound bobbins flew from the spinning wheel to the warp beam, to somehow keep the warp threads replenished, while other bobbins mounted themselves on shuttles to wait their turn at the weft.

Just as Camille finished her breakfast—the utensils and plate to vanish—the silver-haired maiden smiled, for the loom had slowed to a moderate pace, the spinning wheel turning in synchronization, twisting time's thread out from the hovering mist, full-wound bobbins and shuttles replacing empty ones.

"Ma'amselle, I am Camille."

"And I am Skuld," replied the maiden, not taking her gaze from the mist.

"A strange name, that," said Camille.

"Perhaps no stranger than Camille," replied Skuld, smiling. "Mine is a very ancient name."

"Is your loom ancient as well? I ask, because I saw the word Skuld carved thereon."

The maiden smiled again. "The loom and I are both quite antiquated, primeval in fact."

Camille looked at the demoiselle. "You do not appear antiquated. In fact, were I to guess, I would say you are no older than I am, mayhap even younger."

"Oh, la, child, believe me, I am eld beyond counting."

"If true," said Camille, "then perhaps you are one of three I have come to see: one of three sisters that Raseri said might be found along the shores of Time's River."

"Raseri the Drake?"

"Aye, he brought me here."

"Ah, then it did come to pass, just as I wove."

"Just as you wove?"

Skuld gestured at the loom and said, "In the tapestry of time."

"Ma'amselle," said Camille, "a tapestry it may be, yet I cannot see that which you weave.

"I know, child, for the future is hidden from most mortal eyes . . . from most immortals, too."

Camille nodded. "Indeed, Lady Skuld. Still, that's not why I am here. I need your—"

"I know why you have come, Camille. Did I not say that I wove it into the tapestry?"

"Yes, but—"

"Humor me, Camille, for it is not oft I have visitors. I will in good measure deal with your question. But ere then, I ask, what do you know of time?"

Camille took a deep breath, then exhaled and said, "All I know of time is that it flows from the past through the present to the future."

Skuld laughed. "Ah, but that is just backwards."

"Backwards?"

Skuld pointed at the silvery vapor. "These are the Mists of Time; here is where all things begin, a future flowing toward the present, to wash over all mortal things and stream into the past. Here, child, here at the start of the River of Time is the future; it is the beginning of all things, whereas the past is the end of all, for there, at the end of time's flow, all things come to rest, buried in antiquity."

Camille frowned and said, "Perhaps it is all relative, depending on whether one looks at time as a flow streaming o'er the mortal world, or if one looks at it as a mortal moving forward through a flow of time."

Skuld laughed again and said, "You are quite clever, my child," the maiden at the loom calling Camille "child" even though Skuld herself appeared to be no older. "My sisters will delight in you."

"Ah, then," said Camille, her heart a bit lighter. "Raseri was right, assuming your sisters live on this river too."

"They do," said Skuld. "Have you any sisters?"

Camille nodded. "Five . . . and a brother as well."

"And what do folk say of them?"

"Until of recent, very little. But now that they have wealth and a mansion, they are courted. —My sisters, that is. My brother Giles is yet too young to be sought out by prospective brides. Regardless, I believe that folk say my sisters are quite fetching . . . certainly Lord Jaufre does, the old roué. —But tell me, Lady Skuld, what do folk say of you and your sisters?"

Skuld smiled. "Many things: some curse us; some bless us; some say nought, while others make up fanciful tales. Some men have it all wrong about the three of us. They say that one of us spins the thread of a man's life, and that one of us measures the thread, while the third one cuts the thread. But that is obviously wrong, for my sisters and I seldom interfere in the affairs of others—oh, at times we do intervene when someone fails to live up to the terms of a wager, but in the main we stay aloof. Too, occasionally when times are dire do we take a hand, but even then we follow a set of rules. Ah, but the men who say we spin and measure and cut the thread of a man's life do have it wrong, for time and fate are continuous, flowing from the future through the present and into the past, washing over all on the way to the Sea of Oblivion."

Camille frowned and slowly shook her head. "I yet find it difficult to comprehend the flow of time as you tell it to be."

"Why so?"

"Well, is it not true that what a man has done affects what he will do? Do not the events of the past shape those of the future? And does that not mean that the events of the past occur *before* those of the future? Is not the past merely prologue for that which is to come?"

Continuing to watch the mist, Skuld said, "As you yourself pointed out, Camille, it all depends on whether one perceives the past and present and future from the standpoint of one who is moving through the wash of time, whereas my sisters and I perceive it from the point of view of the flow itself as it washes over those standing still. Hence, I weave, as do my sisters, shaping the great tapestry of time. Together we depict that which might come to be, that which is happening in the moment, and that which has gone. As for my part, the patterns I set thereon are not quite fixed, for they are mutable by those depicted. Hence, the tapestry is a living thing, and I alter what I portray even as I weave. My middle sister alters it again by what occurs, and my third sister binds it forever. Hence, in a sense, you are right: for those who stand in the flow of time, the past *is* prologue, even though it is gone beyond recall, though from my view the past is yet to be."

As Camille pondered that enigma, the shuttle slammed side to side, bearing the weft of time back and forth through the warp, the treadle setting the pace, the batten pounding the threads home, the unseen cloth growing. Finally Camille said, "I am quite amazed that you—or perhaps your splendid loom— can weave an invisible tapestry."

Without looking away from the mist, Skuld said, "Invisible to you, perhaps, but not to me." Then Skuld pursed her lips. "If you wish, I can make visible to your eyes the events and other such it contains—great wars to come, men flying in machines through the air, and the like—but heed: should I give you such knowledge of the future, you may bring even greater disaster to all. Even so, I will show you if you so desire."

Hearking back to her discussion with Alain concerning predestination versus free will, and about knowing the future, Camille said, "No, Ma'amselle, I'd rather not see. Still, I would like to know if I will succeed."

Skuld raised an eyebrow. "If I say yes, will you try less hard? If I say no, will you abandon your search?"

Camille shook her head. "No, for you yourself said that what you weave is mutable, hence, even though I might welcome the knowledge, still I or others might make it change. And so, whether the answer is yea or nay, I would go on, either to preserve the yes, or to alter the no."

"You are wiser than your years, Camille," said Skuld.

"Oh, I think not, Lady Skuld, for if I were, I would not now be searching for a place east of the sun and west of the moon. And that is why I came, to ask where such a place does lie, for at that place is my Alain, or so I have been told."

Skuld said, "You need ask my middle sister, for, from your point of view, she is much older than I, while I think of her as being much younger, given how differently you and I perceive the flow of time to be."

"But haven't you already woven into your tapestry the place I seek?"

"Mayhap, Camille. Even so, you still must ask my sister."

"Where can I find this sister?"

Yet weaving, Skuld said, "My sisters and I are bound by a rule: no answers of significance or gifts of worth can we give to anyone without first a service of value being rendered to us—which, in my case, you have certainly done—but even then we must ask a riddle and have it correctly answered. Hence, resolve me this: from that which is yet to come, unto the singular now, what am I?"

Camille glanced down through the growing dawnlight at the River of Time and said, "You are the Future."

"Indeed," said Skuld, "and a gift from and for the future you shall have." She tilted her head toward the turning spinning wheel. "Take my finest golden carding comb and keep good care of it; hold on to it to the very end, for then it might do you some good."

"But, Lady Skuld," protested Camille, "Should the thread snap again, time itself will be broken have you not the comb to tease out a new thread from the mist above."

Skuld shook her head. "I have another, my child, though not fashioned of gold; hence, you must take this one, else Faery itself might fall, for there is one who will pollute the River of Time even more than the one I now place on my tapestry."

Camille looked at the loom where the invisible depiction grew. "You now weave someone evil?"

"Aye, a monstrous man yet to be; one who will reach out his arms to take in the masses and clutch them unto his breast; one who will do a little three-step jig dance of victory; one who will start a dreadful holocaust. Regardless, Camille, you must take the carding comb, else one will come and destroy Faery itself by polluting beyond all recovery the very River of Time."

Camille sighed, yet did was she as bade and took up the golden carding comb. "Again I ask, Lady Skuld, your middle sister, where can I find her?"

With a flick of her eyes, Skuld glanced at the horizon, bright with the oncoming sun. And with her right hand she gestured downstream and intoned:

> "As grain is to stones that roll and grind,
> Moments are crunched in the weft of time,
> Seek the like and my sister you'll find."

Again Skuld glanced at the bright horizon, and she said, "And this I will tell you as well: leave not the banks of time's flow, else surely you will lose the stream."

And in that very moment the limb of the sun edged over the rim of the world, and so vanished Skuld and loom and spinning wheel all, and day came on the land.

And Camille heard Scruff instantly chirping, for he would have millet seed.

29

Present

Camille sighed, for Skuld had vanished with the coming of the sun. She turned toward Scruff. "All right, my wee companion, you'll have your millet." She trudged upslope to the camp and rummaged in her knapsack, then scattered a bit of seed on the ground before the sparrow, Scruff having awkwardly fluttered down from the low branch on which he had spent the night. As he pecked at the grain, Camille set about breaking camp. She paused a moment to examine the stave and groaned in dismay, for not only had the crack lengthened, but another split had started as well.

I have not overly used the staff. What is happening here?

Swiftly she counted the blossoms.

Ninety-nine remain.

As she slipped the stave through the loops of the rucksack, she glanced once more at the blossoms and again at the cracks.

I wonder . . . The first crack started when there were one hundred blossoms left. The second at ninety-nine. Will another crack appear at ninety-eight? Is Lady Sorcière telling me that time grows short?

Camille raised her face to the sky and cried out, "I know, Lady Sorcière! I know!"

Scruff looked up from the millet seeds and cocked his head. Then he began pecking away again.

While waiting for the sparrow to finish, Camille stepped to where she could clearly see the cascade.

Like a spring bubbling up from the ground, where the true source cannot be seen, so too does the fall of time issue from an unknown source, perhaps out of nowhere, right at the brim.

Scruff gave a chirp, as if to say, All done, and Camille stepped to her waterskin and poured the wee bird a drink in a cup she had acquired just for him. "It won't do, I think, to drink from time's flow, Scruff. Raseri seemed to believe it would be a terrible thing to fall into the stream, and so I think we'll completely forgo those silvery waters, except to use them as a guide to Skuld's middle sister."

When Scruff had had his fill, and had taken his morning bath, Camille put his cup away and slung her goods and lifted Scruff to her shoulder. Then she looked at the river.

"Which side, Scruff? Which side should we follow? It would not do to walk down the incorrect bank and find ourselves on the wrong side of time. I mean, Raseri also seemed to think no one should swim in the River of Time, hence, if we found ourselves on the opposite shore from Skuld's sisters, well, then, since we must not swim across, we'd have to come back here and walk 'round the end. Still, the question remains: which side should we take?"

Camille frowned in concentration, remembering. "Ah, Lady Skuld pointed with her right hand, and so we'll walk along the right-hand side rather than down the sinister."

Camille crossed the stone streambed above the falls, then made her way down from the linn until she reached the bank below, and then she began to stride forward, following the silvery flow.

Yet as she paced, the sun seemed to rise rather swiftly into the sky, and in less than a quarter candlemark by Camille's reckoning it had come to the zenith. Camille stopped and, shielding her eyes, frowned up toward the golden orb.

All seemed normal, but she waited.

The sun slowly crept across the sky.

"Hmm . . ." said Camille. "Let us see, Scruff."

She started downstream again.

The sun sped forward.

Again Camille stopped, and once more did the sun eke ahead.

"Oh, Scruff, methinks days will be quite odd, here along time's flow, but there's nought to do but press on."

Downstream she paced, and within what she judged to be another quarter candlemark, the sun set and dusk drew across the land.

Scruff chirped in confusion, but nevertheless went to sleep.

Within another quarter candlemark, a waning gibbous moon arose. And another quarter after that, dawn came into the sky.

Scruff awoke, yet he was not hungry, and neither was Camille.

On Camille walked through a second swift day and night, perhaps a candlemark in all, and as day came once again, she paused, and the sun returned to a normal pace. Camille unslung her waterskin for a drink, but as she recorked it and looped it over her shoulder, she took in a sharp breath and pulled the stave from her rucksack. Two more cracks had appeared, and the blossoms numbered but ninety-seven.

Tears welled in Camille's eyes. "Oh, Scruff, each candlemark we follow time's stream a blossom will wither and vanish. I must go away from here and— But wait. Lady Skuld said, 'Leave not the banks of time's flow, else surely you will lose the stream.' It must be just the same as when we flew high above, and I looked away, and the river vanished. Oh, Scruff, if we leave these banks, we will lose the very flow. Yet along these shores is where the middle sister lives, and if we do not find her, then I think we'll not find Alain."

Dejectedly Camille slumped to the ground. "Ah, me, but what a dilemma. Even if we stay still, a blossom will wither each day. But if we continue, blossoms will vanish each candlemar—" Of a sudden her eyes lighted. "What if after we find the middle sister we go back the way we came? Will the blossoms retur—?" Camille looked hindward. Only forest met her eye. Of time's flow there was no sign.

Her heart leapt into her throat, and swiftly she looked forward again and sighed in relief, for the river yet streamed from this point onward.

"Only in Faery," she muttered, and she got to her feet. "We have no choice, Scruff, but to go forward, for the middle sister I must find. Let us hope she is but a few strides ahead."

Onward she stepped, the sun racing across the sky and setting, only to rise and set again and again, the waning moon rising later and turning crescent and then new and then waxing, blossoms withering and vanishing, splits riving the stave, as Camille and Scruff went on.

Altogether, nearly thirty candlemarks of trekking along the banks of Time's River had elapsed, days and nights flying by— and some eight more candlemarks had been spent resting, where the passage of time returned to its normal ways; at this very moment, sixty-nine blossoms remained on the stave. But now that

Camille continued along the River of Time, the morning sun was on swift rise.

Rounding a bend in the river, Camille saw a mill, its great waterwheel—if it could be called such—turning in time's flow. She went on, the sun rising with each step, and by midmorn, she reached the building. Old it appeared, quite ancient, yet it seemed sturdy enough, and Camille could hear millstones grinding inside. She stepped past a bench sitting outside the open door and peered in. It seemed no one was there, yet the great bhurstones turned.

And then she remembered Skuld's words:

> *"As grain is to stones that roll and grind,*
> *Moments are crunched in the weft of time,*
> *Seek the like and my sister you'll find."*

"Oh, Scruff. Perhaps this is where we will find Skuld's sister."

Camille stepped inside. Great gears on axles groaned o'erhead, driven by the wheel, and they in turn drove the great bhurstones, though there was no grain to grind. All through the mill went Camille, past a wide opening looking out on the world, past another breach in the wall which opened out onto Time's River where the lower part of the great waterwheel turned. On she went, looking this way and that; strangely, midmost, a skylight was affixed in the ceiling above, and a slanting beam of sunlight shone down, slowly creeping across the floor.

But Camille found no one in the mill, and no sign of loom or spinning wheel.

"Well, Scruff, we'll wait here, for I am certain that's what Lady Skuld's words did mean."

Camille stepped to the door and out to the bench, where she sat in the sunlight and waited.

Slowly the day grew onward, the golden orb gradually arcing toward the zenith.

Still Camille waited, and Scruff settled down on her shoulder, the wee sparrow content to simply bide.

And time edged past.

And just as the leading limb of the sun entered the zenith, Camille heard weeping from within.

"Allo!" called Camille, stepping inside. "Who is—?"

"Oh, please help me, please help me, I have lost the end of

my thread, and if I do not quickly find it, woe betide the world, for that which is now will then not be."

Past turning gears went Camille, to come upon a motherly woman, middle-aged she seemed, with pale yellow hair, and she was crawling on the floor before a loom, feeling about for her lost thread.

Once again a shaggy little man seemed to be ripping fabric away from the cloth beam and bearing it to the opening at the waterwheel and casting it into the flow.

As she had done with Skuld, Camille rushed forward to aid, even though here, too, the thread was invisible to her eyes. Camille dropped to her hands and knees beside the woman, Scruff scrambling to retain a perch. And as the wee sparrow chattered angrily at the hairy little man, Camille asked the woman, "Is it not lost in the tapestry?"

"Nay, the thread upon the weaving is well marked, but the feeding thread broke and fell."

Feeling the way before her, Camille crawled toward the loom, and above Scruff's irate chatter and the grinding of the axles and gears and stones, Camille thought she could hear the sound of one or two other looms, but they were nowhere to be seen.

Of a sudden—"I know!" cried Camille, and she sprang to her feet and stepped to the loom, and by feel she found where the thread left the golden shuttle, and she followed it to its end. "Here it is," said Camille, and she handed it to the woman, who looked with golden eyes at Camille and smiled slyly and said, "Clever girl."

In but an instant the woman had tied the thread on, and sat down at the loom, and it began frantically weaving, the spinning wheel at her side turning in synchronization, apparently spinning invisible thread out from the sunlight streaming in through a skylight above.

In that moment, the hairy little man growled and vanished.

"It is good to see Uncertainty gone," said Camille.

" 'Twas not Uncertainty, but his brother Turmoil, enemy of the present, and, just as is his brother, Turmoil, too, is an agent of Chaos."

Camille looked at the loom, and to her surprise she could see a single, visible thread running across, various shimmering colors along its length, colors which changed with each clack of shuttle and slap of batten.

Camille also noted that carven in runes on the breastbeam was the name Verdandi.

"You, I take it, are Lady Verdandi?"

"Aye, and you are Lady Camille," replied the woman, staring out the broad opening, as if viewing events beyond. "Now, hush, child, and let me weave. When I catch up, we can talk. In the meanwhile, break your noonfast."

On the floor appeared utensils and a wooden trencher laden with steaming food: well-done beef slices and a stewed turnip along with a cup of rugged red wine and a great slab of coarse bread. Thereon as well was a small amount of oat grains. Smiling, Camille sat down and placed Scruff beside her and scattered the grain before him. And then she dug into the hot food, savoring every bite, for it had been many days since her last warm meal—rabbit over a campfire, eaten with Rondalo some thirty-four days ago, or mayhap but five days past, depending on how one counted the candlemarks along the River of Time. Unlike the meal provided by Skuld, this was food Camille was used to, for it was food of her time.

Even as Camille finished the last of the provender—the utensils and trencher to vanish—the frantic pace of weaving slowed.

"What do you weave, Lady Verdandi?"

"I fix on the tapestry that which is now: folks working in fields, folks shearing sheep, and other such. Would you like to see?"

Camille shook her head, and watched as Scruff pecked at something in the cracks of the floor, a beetle most likely. And she said, "I think that such sights are perhaps not meant for mortals, the viewing of events all the world over at the very moment they occur."

Verdandi laughed, but she did not take her eyes from the opening. "My sister Skuld says that one day to come, folks will be able to see distant events even as they happen. How that can be, I know not, yet Skuld is seldom in error. I know, for I amend the tapestry of time for those things she did foresee but were changed by extraordinary effort."

"Oh," said Camille, "but I do hope I do not have to do so to find my Alain."

"Child, you are already making such an effort, and I do hope you succeed, else the world will be the worse off."

At this pronouncement Camille's heart hammered wildly, for if the fate of the world were added to her quest for Alain, it would seem too much for a simple farm girl to bear.

To still her racing heart, Camille concentrated on the clack and slap and thud of the loom, its rhythm somehow soothing, the loom where, but for a single weft thread, an invisible tapestry grew. Finally, Camille said, "Would that I could see my love at this moment, even if he is the Bear. Do you weave such?"

"Mayhap, child. Mayhap."

"Then let me ask what I came to ask: where lies a place east of the sun and west of the moon? Lady Skuld said you would know."

"I believe, Camille, she sent you to me to ask, but she did not say I would know."

"Well, Lady Verdandi, *do* you know where such a place is?"

Her golden gaze yet focused on the opening, Verdandi said, "You will have to ask my sister."

Camille groaned. "The third sister?"

"Aye."

"Downstream, I assume."

"Indeed."

Again, Camille groaned. "And here I was hoping to leave this flow. Just where downstream?"

"Let me ask you this," said Verdandi, "what is the color of time?"

Camille sighed in exasperation, yet, just as she had humored Lady Skuld, so would she humor Verdandi. She took two breaths and exhaled slowly, then said, "Well, the Mists of Time whence the future comes were silvery, though the future itself seems to be an invisible color, at least to most of mankind, for most of us see it not. I suspect, though, that to you three who weave the tapestry of time, the color of the future must be quite plain to all your eyes."

Verdandi smiled. "And what of the past? Has it a color?"

Camille turned up a hand. "If it does have a color, then to mankind it is perhaps the hue of shadows and moonlight, or mayhap the color of death, for it is buried beyond recall."

Verdandi laughed and kept weaving and asked, "What of the present, then?"

Camille looked at the golden sunlight twisting down onto the spindle and being spun into invisible thread by the golden spinning wheel. Then she glanced at the thread on the tapestry aweave. Finally she said, "In spite of the golden sunlight and the many hues I can see on that single bit of weft, I would think that the color of the present must be the same as the color of a flash, since both exist for but this moment."

Again Verdandi laughed and then said, "Urd will enjoy your company."

"Urd?"

"My sister, and as you have rightly surmised, she lives downstream. To you she will seem much older than I, though to me she seems much younger."

Camille nodded and said, "And where might I find this sister? —Other than just downstream?"

"Answer me this riddle," said Verdandi. "Caught on the cusp of ago and to be and trapped forever in the eternal now, what am I?"

Camille glanced out at the waterwheel turning in the River of Time. "You are the Present."

"And a present you shall have," said Verdandi, tilting her head toward the loom. "My finest golden shuttle; take good care of it, and do not yield it to anyone except perhaps near the end, for then it may do you some good."

"But, my lady, what if you need it?"

"I have others, my child, though not fashioned of gold; hence, you must take this one, else Faery itself might fall."

Sighing, Camille stepped to the loom and when the thread came to an end, the shuttle flew into her hand, while another did take its place.

Camille turned back to Verdandi. "Again I ask, my lady, your sister Urd, where can I find her?"

With a flick of her eyes, Verdandi glanced at the skylight, where the sun passed above. And with her right hand she gestured downstream and intoned:

> "Ebon is the Oblivion Sea,
> A gape of darkness where all things flee,
> There binding time my sister will be."

Again Verdandi glanced at the skylight above, and she said, "And this I will tell you as well: when you leave the banks of time's flow, then you will lose the stream."

And in that very moment the trailing limb of the sun exited from the zenith, and so vanished Verdandi and loom and spinning wheel all, leaving Camille and Scruff alone in the ancient mill.

And the river flowed and the wheel turned and the great bhurstones ground on.

30
Past

Some three and a quarter swift candlemark days after leaving the mill and continuing on downstream, at a candlemark dusk, Camille stopped and made camp, the second such stop she had made along the River of Time, and again she and Scruff rested through an ordinary night. When dawn came, she and Scruff broke fast, and then onward they pressed, swift days passing with every candlemark, blossoms fading, vanishing, splits fissuring the stave. Camille paused now and again to eat or drink and to feed her hungry and quite confused sparrow, for to the wee bird it seemed no sooner had day come than night and sleep quickly followed. Another fifteen and a half candlemarks passed, and Camille and Scruff spent another night acamp, stars slowly wheeling through the vault above, following a bright waxing moon some two days past half-full.

When morning came, once again Camille and Scruff took up the trek, and some ten candlemark days later, at a turn ahead, high stone bluffs loomed on either side of the river, a gorge through which the flow ran. Toward this ravine Camille went, the swift day growing with every step. As she drew nigh, the sun passed through the zenith, and Camille could see a dark opening in the nearmost wall.

"Scruff, I believe yon is the place whither we are bound, for no doubt 'tis 'a gape of darkness,' and Verdandi did say:

" 'Ebon is the Oblivion Sea,
A gape of darkness where all things flee,
There binding time my sister will be.' "

Toward this gape Camille went, and she came to where the shore turned to flat stone, as if all the soil had been scrubbed down to the primal bedrock itself. Along the stone she travelled, the swift sun trailing down the sky, its candlemark pace matching her strides. Finally, as the rapid day came to late afternoon, Camille threaded through a scatter of boulders to reach the breach in the sheer stone wall. She looked inward; a cavern receded into blackness beyond, and there was no sign of a weaver or a loom or a spinning wheel.

"Well, Scruff, just as we waited at the mill for Verdandi to appear, so shall we wait here for Urd. If I am wrong, then on the morrow we will go onward and hope to find another gape."

And so they waited at the mouth of the cave, Camille and Scruff, as the sun gradually edged down the sky. A candlemark passed and then another, and finally the sun dipped into the horizon.

And still they waited. . . .

Time eked forward. . . .

Scruff scrambled into the high vest pocket, preparing to bed down for the oncoming night.

And the moment the last of the sun disappeared—

"Oh, help me, help me. I have lost my bobbin, and woe betide the world if I find it not, for history itself will be unraveled, and all will become undone," wailed a white-haired crone, crawling around on the bedrock beside a golden spinning wheel near a silent loom.

And the loom itself held a great tapestry, completely visible to Camille, but instead of the fabric being wound about the cloth beam, the tapestry trailed from the loom and across the smooth stone and disappeared into the darkness of the cavern.

And there beside Camille at the mouth of the cave, a cursing, hairy little man struggled to pull great lengths of the tapestry out from the gape and toward the River of Time, for he would cast it in.

"Where did you last have it?" cried Camille as she sprang forward to aid the crone.

"In my hand, here at the spinning wheel," keened the ancient woman. "But I dropped it and it rolled away, and now I cannot find it."

Camille searched the bedrock about the golden wheel, yet she saw no spool. Even as she searched, she frowned in concentration. "Wait a moment," she called. "The stone here is not level, but slopes down toward—"

Quickly, Camille scrambled to the loom and below, where once again, though she could not see them, she heard the sound of one or two other looms aweave. Yet her purpose was not to locate other looms, but instead to—"I have it!" cried Camille, snatching up a bobbin partially wound with black thread, and she scrambled out from under and handed it to the crone.

"Clever girl," cackled the old woman, smiling a toothless smile and casting Camille a sly glance; the ancient's eyes were entirely black. The crone mounted the spool to the spinning wheel. Then from the spindle, she grasped between thumb and forefinger what seemed to be a tendril of shadow, a tendril which came from the blackness of the cavern itself. The ancient fed the tendril through the hook, then somehow tied it to the black thread on the spool. She gave the wheel a sharp spin, and then sat down at the loom, and it began frantically weaving as the woman stared with her jet-black eyes into the cavern's ebon gape.

At that moment the hairy little man cursed and vanished.

"Another agent of Chaos, I presume, and brother of Uncertainty and Turmoil," said Camille.

"Aye," replied the crone. " 'Twas Obscurity: enemy of the past."

Camille glanced at the breastbeam. Carved thereon, as she expected, were runes spelling out the name Urd.

"Lady Urd, 'tis you I've come to find, sent by your sisters."

"I know, child, yet let me weave. We will talk when I have caught up. In the meanwhile, break your duskfast."

Of a sudden, before Camille appeared a clay bowl, and she took it up and frowned at the contents: it was filled with what at first she took to be a soup, yet it was pulpy and green, and seemed to be much like slime one would find on a pond. Even as Camille's mouth turned down at the thought of consuming such, Urd said, "Eat up, child, for it is one of the oldest meals in the world."

Camille sighed and resigned herself to at least try. No utensils were provided, and so she used her first two fingers, dipping in and bearing the wet, scumlike coating to her mouth. She managed to choke down the first lick, its taste somewhat like that of the stalks she had chewed on when crossing the grasslands. She dipped in her fingers again and dragged more slime to her mouth.

As she ate, Camille realized she could see the pattern upon the tapestry, yet parts of it were quite blurred, as of dyes that were not fixed, as of colors that ran. In some places, though, the depiction was quite clear, while at others the fabric seemed entirely blank. Yet even as she scrutinized the tapestry, the patterns at a given spot seemed to shift about, to change slightly, or to change altogether, or to vanish entirely.

By studying the tapestry and distracting her mind, Camille managed to eat all of the slime and to do so without gagging overmuch. And just as she finished, the pace of the weaving slowed.

Camille set the clay vessel down to the stone, and, as with the wooden trencher and fine porcelain provided by sisters past, so did this bowl vanish, too.

"It gums quite good, eh?" said Urd, smiling her toothless smile. "Tastes good, too."

Camille sighed. "Mayhap a better term to describe it would be, um, 'nourishing.' "

The crone cackled. "Quite right, Camille. Quite right."

Camille frowned at the fabric. "Why do you weave such a tapestry? One where the colors run and patterns change and great blank spots exist."

Without taking her gaze from the ebon gape, Urd said, "Oh, child, the pattern set thereon is quite well-defined, precise and clear to all who can truly see; without error, I bind all that has gone before as it did in fact occur. 'Tis simply because you have mortal eyes that the past seems quite unclear. Even to most immortals much of it seems unclear as well, but to mortal eyes the pattern is yet worse."

"Why so?"

"Much of mankind tries to ignore the weaving, often trying to change what the pattern shows, rewriting history to suit their own needs, though the events they would alter are quite plain to eyes which behold the truth."

"Mankind rewrites history?"

"Aye, child, at least the victors do, though in the end it is the survivors who will have the final say, can they winnow out the truth, or if not, make up that which is either fanciful or as they would have it be. Even so, most of what they tell will shift from era to era."

"And because I am of mankind, you say I cannot see the truth?"

"Nay, child, that I did not say. Some see the truth for what it is when it comes upon them. Still, there is much you do not know, for you have not the lore. But even if you had much wisdom, some things yet would be obscure to you, for they are beyond your understanding as well as beyond the knowledge you have. But despair not, for I think you will never twist the truth simply for your own ends, though you may not see it when others do so."

"Be that as it may, Lady Urd, I did not come to discuss the truth or relevance of history, but instead I came to ask if you know where I might find a place east of the sun and west of the moon."

"You are welcome to look at the tapestry to see if it is there," replied Urd, gesturing at the long train leading into the dark cavern.

In the growing dusk, Camille lit her small lantern, and then slowly walked alongside the tapestry, searching for . . . she knew not what. Still the pattern seemed begotten with runny dye in places, some places obscure, some murky, and some places blank, other places shifting even as Camille looked on, yet in still other places the scenes were quite clear: folks in loincloths hunting with spears, other folk digging in fields and dressed in sandals and with cloth bound 'round their waists and buttocks and up through their legs, others on rafts poling along rivers, still others making passionate love, and here Camille did flush. She saw all manner of endeavors, the depictions so lifelike that one might think of them as actually being real living people, though many were very old, and some seemed to be on the verge of death, while others were in caskets; and there were graves and ruins and great monoliths and other curious things of antiquity, things that might once have been but might no longer be. Strangely, every time Camille looked at the tapestry, it seemed to have altered, as if the figures and scenes themselves were moving, changing, shifting about.

Into the cave by lanternlight Camille followed the tapestry, the cloth wending away into the dim recesses within, where it finally disappeared under ever-increasing layers of dust, though the cavern itself went on and on.

Camille sighed and turned about, for she had not spied aught in the pattern which would aid.

Returning to Urd, Camille said, "I found nothing of that which I seek, and so again I ask, know you where such a place might be."

"Answer me this riddle, child: running on the rim of now to oblivion, what am I?"

Camille looked through the growing dusk at the River of Time and then replied, "You are the Past."

Without glancing away from the ebon gape, the old woman crowed with pleasure and said, "And it's past time I should give you a gift." She nodded toward the spinning wheel. "Take my best bobbin, the one of gold, and keep good care of it. Do not yield it to anyone except perhaps near the end, for then it might do you some good."

"But what if another calamity occu—?"

"Take it, child, for other spools I have, though none as fine or of gold."

Sighing, Camille took up the golden bobbin, a bobbin in a queue of spools, as if awaiting its turn at the spinning wheel. And then she said, "Please, Lady Urd, do you know where is a place east of the sun and west of the moon?"

With a flick of her eyes, Urd glanced at the horizon, dusk nearly gone. "I know of someone who might, for he has travelled far and wide."

Hope sprang into Camille's heart. "Where can I find this traveller?"

Again Urd glanced at the horizon, and then she intoned:

> "There are winds that do not blow,
> But flow across the sea;
> A master of one might know
> Where such a place doth be."

Once more Urd glanced at the fading dusk and said, "And this I will tell you for nought, for I have seen it in my weaving:

> "Nearly dual,
> It is the key;
> That which two fear
> Shall set four free."

Just then, the fullness of night fell, and Urd and loom and spinning wheel and tapestry vanished all.

Camille cried out, "Wait! The riddles, what do they—?" But in the ravine only her echoes responded to her cry, and she realized she would get no answer at all . . . and neither of the two riddles meant a thing to her.

Camille made camp there at the cave—placing Scruff on a

boulder high—and ere she went to sleep, she counted the blossoms on the split and cracked and splintered stave: forty remained.

As tears brimmed in her eyes, she pondered her encounters with the three sisters and wondered if she had chosen the right course, for it had cost her dearly to travel along this way, especially upon these shores, where many blossoms had vanished, and all she had to show for it were two conundrums for which she had no answer, as well as a carding comb, a shuttle, and a golden spool, and these in response to her three straightforward answers to three very simple riddles.

But wait! Lady Skuld said: "My sisters and I are bound by a rule: no answers of significance or gifts of worth can we give to anyone without first a service of value being rendered to us— which, in my case, you have certainly done—but even then we must ask a riddle and have it correctly answered."

Now the service I performed was the finding of lost—Oh, my! Ladies Skuld and Verdandi could easily have found their own missing threads, for although they were invisible to me, they were certainly not invisible to them. And as for Lady Urd, a lost bobbin would mean little, for she had many more. Why would they do so? —Test me with trivial tasks, that is. Perhaps it was to aid me on my way. But what aid have I been given? Two riddles I know not how to answer. Three quite commonplace gifts, but for the value of gold they bear. Yet those are the gifts they gave me, gifts supposedly of worth. Yet even though gold is precious, perhaps their value is— Camille's eyes widened in speculation. *Mayhap they are magical in some manner!*

Camille fetched out the carding comb and loom shuttle and spinning-wheel spool, golden all. By lanternlight she examined them carefully, yet they seemed no more than what they were— comb, shuttle, and bobbin. She sighed. *Even if they are magic, I am no mage to use them.*

Camille put the gifts away and blew out her lantern and lay down to sleep.

She slept not well at all beneath the waning moon, for her dreams were filled with strange, hairy beings posing riddles unanswerable.

The next dawning, Camille was awakened by Scruff's insistent chirping, and she groaned up and fed the sparrow and took a biscuit for herself. To her dismay, she found her water was all gone, and she gestured at the river and said to Scruff, "But we'll not drink from that flow, my friend."

After breaking fast, on downstream she went, a swift day rising behind. Yet just before a leftward then rightward jog in the gorge the bank itself disappeared, and she had little choice but to follow a narrow path up the sheer rise, for to do otherwise would lead to wading in Time's River, and she certainly would not do that. And as she climbed, she heard an unusual sound, somewhat like that of very distant but nearly continuous, rolling thunder, yet at the same time, not. Wondering at what it might be, on upward she went, to come into a breeze, a facing wind that grew stronger with every step. And salt was in the air.

At the top of the rise, with her golden hair streaming in the wind and her cloak billowing out behind, she found herself on a headland, looking out upon a deep blue indigo sea.

"Oh, my, Scruff," breathed Camille, "an ocean."

Camille was taken by the wonder of the sea, the first she had ever seen, and her gaze was irresistibly drawn to the horizon afar, the waters reaching on beyond. And she stood a good long while, taking in the salt air and staring out at the endless and vasty deep. Finally, she said, "Oh, Scruff, is this where time spreads out over the mortal world, and if so, then does the deep blue ocean we now see from above become the sky if seen from below?"

Scruff did not answer, and long, rushing waves rolled across the water to thunder and thunder against the base of the cliff, spray flying up to be caught on the wind.

Of a sudden Camille gasped. "Or is this instead the Sea of Oblivion, where all of time does flow?"

Camille slumped down to the sward on the headland high, and she said, "Regardless, I have come to the end of Time's River, and time is running out, for there are but thirty-nine blossoms yet on the stave. Thirty-nine days and a whole moon beyond, that's all the time that remains."

Camille looked to the left and drew in a sharp breath, for the shoreline below lay unbroken for as far as the eye could see. Then she looked back the way she had come; the River of Time was gone.

And down in the sea, waves rolled in and in, unheeding of the girl above.

31

Winds

Camille sat awhile on the headland above the thundering sea, Scruff clinging to her shoulder and facing into the stiff breeze. Long moments passed as the sun edged further up the sky. Finally, she roused herself and glanced at the growing day. "Well, Scruff, Lady Verdandi did say that when I left the banks of time's flow, I would lose the stream, and of that I am glad, for time out of joint is not to my taste."

"*Chp!*" chirped Scruff, as if he totally agreed.

Camille stood. "Though I cannot answer the riddles posed by Lady Urd, still we must press on . . . but which way, my friend? Which way? Left? Right? Inland?"

Camille scanned the shoreline as far as she could see in either direction, but she espied no sign of habitation whatsoever. Of a sudden, Scruff *chp!-chp!-chp!*ed, and, rising over the horizon, sails appeared, swiftly growing taller, and then a hull came into view. And driven by the wind abaft, over the sea it rode.

"A ship, Scruff. A ship. Oh, how glorious."

Camille watched awhile as it hove across the water.

"It seems to be heading somewhere off to our right, Scruff. Perchance 'tis an omen telling us which way to go, for perhaps . . ."

Camille pulled the stave from the rucksack loops, taking care to not snag a splinter on the cloth. "Lady Sorcière, were it any stave but yours, I would wrap it tightly with leather or cloth, or bind it with straps, all to deal with the splits and cracks and splinters. Yet I deem you meant it to be thus, and so wrap it I shall not. Instead I shall again walk with it, for mayhap, contrarily, it cracks from disuse."

And, stave in hand, off Camille set, following the rightward shoreline, as the ship asea plunged across the rolling brine, the wind driving her swiftly. And rising across the horizon after, came a seething, dark wall of clouds.

"A storm is coming, Scruff," said Camille, her cloak flying in the wind. Onward she strode across flowing grass on cliffs above the sea, hoping to find shelter ere the blow came.

On she walked and on, a candlemark and then two, the land rising and falling, the storm drawing nigh, and just as she topped a long upward slope, with a hard-driven blast the tempest did blow ashore at last. And through thickening gray sheets of rain hurled by a pummelling wind, Camille saw spread out before her a broad harbor sheltered by seaward hills, ships riding at anchor within, and a seaport town arcing 'round.

The hard rain pelting down, the wind moaning among the buildings, Camille saw ahead a signboard swinging wildly in the squall, a leaping fish depicted thereon, the words Le Marlin Bleu circling 'round. It marked the very first inn she had come across after entering the town. In the rain and wind she ran for the door and lifted the latch, and a hard gust snatched the handle from her grip and slammed the panel wide.

"Shut the door, boy," shouted a man above the howl of the storm, scrambling for papers swirling about behind the counter as the panel slapped to and fro. "I said shut the door, else the storm itself'll blow us all away."

Camille lunged to catch hold of the panel madly swinging. Then she struggled against the wind to shut the wild thing, pushing it to with her shoulder. Finally, she got it closed and latched, and relative quietness descended, the moaning wind shut out. Thoroughly drenched and dripping, she cast back her hood and turned toward the man at the counter, who yet chased after paper. Shedding her cloak, she looked at Scruff in the high vest pocket, his feathers soaked. Bedraggled, he looked up at her and grumped a short, sharp "*chp!*" Camille laughed and said, "You look like a wet dog, my friend."

"Who you callin' a wet dog, boy?" came the voice from low, the man down on hands and knees and reaching under a desk for a loose receipt.

"Oh, sieur, I meant not you," said Camille, stepping forward. "I was speaking to my companion."

"I didn't see you come in with any—" Voucher in hand, the

man rose to his feet. "Oh, pardon, ma'amselle, I thought you were, um—"

"My companion is here in my pocket, good sieur, and we would like a room, and a hot meal, too, and warm bath, and a good long drink of water."

"*Chp!*"

"Oh, and some grain for my friend. Oats, rye, barley, if you please. He is a bit tired of millet."

The man cocked a skeptical eyebrow at Camille and the sparrow, and Camille fished about in her rucksack and then plunked a gold coin down to the counter.

The man's eyes lit up and he quickly said, "Right away, ma'amselle." He turned and called out, "Aicelina, à moi cet instant!"

There came a soft knock on the door, barely heard above the moan of the wind and the drumming of rain on the shingled roof.

"Entré!"

Dressed in a borrowed robe, Camille looked up from her just-finished meal of haddock and red cabbage and green beans and black bread. A dark-haired young maiden, certainly no older than Camille, and perhaps a year or two less, stood at the doorway looking in.

"Mademoiselle, your bath is ready."

"Merci, Aicelina." Camille took a last sip of tea, then stood. "Keep guard, Scruff," she said to the dozing, wee bird, perched on the back of the chair before the red coals on the hearth, wind groaning down the chimney.

"Mademoiselle, shall I add another brick of peat to the fire?"

Camille glanced at the hearth and then at Scruff. "Non, Aicelina. I believe the room is now warm enough. Besides, he is quite comfortable as it is. —Now where is the bathing room?"

"This way, mademoiselle."

Camille, barefooted, followed Alicelina down the hall—doors on the right, windows on the left—and gusts and rain rattled pane and sash. And Camille said, "Aicelina, I have been pondering a riddle given me. Know you of winds that do not blow, but flow across the sea? The reason I ask is that I have been advised to seek a master of such."

Aicelina opened the door at the end of the hall. She turned to Camille and said, "Non, mademoiselle, I know of no such thing." And as wind whistled 'round a corner outside, the maiden's brown eyes widened and she glanced through the windows at the storm without. "Mayhap 'tis a mage, for 'tis said some are masters of the wind. —Oh, but wait, that would be a wind that blows, rather than one that does not." Aicelina frowned and fell into momentary thought, but then realizing where she was, she moved aside. "Your bath, mademoiselle."

Camille stepped into the chamber; a tub of steaming water sat waiting. Aicelina followed and said, "Fresh towels on the bar, mademoiselle, and soap in the dish, three scents in all: mint, lilac, rose. And a fresh sponge is on the board. Is there aught else I can do?"

"Merci, Aicelina, it is enough."

Aicelina started to leave, but then turned back and said, "About your riddle, mademoiselle . . ."

"Yes?"

"This is a port town, a seaport town."

Camille nodded and said, "The very first I've ever seen, Aicelina. I'm a farm girl and, but for a handful of drawings in a book in Fra Galanni's library, I know little of ships and boats. Yet when I topped the long hill above the town and saw all the ships at anchor, oh what a thrilling sight it was. —But what has this to do with my riddle?"

"Well, mademoiselle, your riddle speaks of masters, and there are masters of ships, and the ships themselves—"

"Of course!" exclaimed Camille, grabbing the startled girl and embracing her. "And the ships themselves flow across the sea. Oh, merci, merci, Aicelina."

Yet after the girl had gone, and Camille had slipped into the soothing water, as she luxuriated in the warmth she frowned. *But how can ships be winds that do not blow?*

"Well, now, young lady, for a tot of rum, I'll answer your question."

It was the next morning, and Camille stood on a dock along the harbor. The storm had blown itself out sometime during the night, and the skies were blue above. Even so, great waves yet crashed against the breakwater at the harbor mouth afar, remnants of the blow.

"And how much would that be? —The cost, I mean."

The eld man looked her up and down, as if gauging her

wealth, his eyes widening at the sight of the sparrow on her shoulder. Then he said, "A bronze."

Nearby, a lounging youth snorted. "A tot is but a copper, ma'amselle." The oldster shot him a glare.

Nevertheless, Camille handed the man a bronze. "Now, sieur, my answer."

With surprised eyes, the old man looked at the coin in his hand, then glanced down the dock at the Bald Pelican, a ramshackle tavern sitting ashore just beyond the planking. Then he looked at Camille and said, "Your answer is tied up at pier thirty-two; she's being laded for a long run." He bobbed his head, then turned about and trotted away as fast as his legs would bear him, for *ten* tots of rum awaited, and perhaps out of generosity for a good-paying customer such as he was about to be, the barkeep would set up the eleventh for nought.

Camille looked at the youth. "Which way?"

The lad pointed.

Three-masted she was, and broad, with a wide and flat low prow and a high deck aft, her length some thirty-five paces in all, and her hull was painted red. On her bow were two glaring yellow-orange eyes, and in slashing black lines, a strange symbol was inscribed behind and below each eye. She was tied up at pier thirty-two, and a bustle of dockworkers labored at loading bales and kegs and crates onto the cargo nets of the large vessel, seamen aboard cranking the windlasses and raising the goods and swinging the booms about, to lower the nets down through the hatches and into the bays below.

The crew adeck were men like none Camille had ever seen: the cast of their skin a yellow-tan, their eyes tilted like those of Elves, yet their ears were not tipped. All had hair jet-black, curled in a loop behind and tied by a small bow. And they spoke in a strange tongue, the words short and sharp and at times harsh-sounding.

Most were dressed in red pantaloons, their arms and chests bare, yet among the crew were warriors, or so Camille thought them to be, for each was armed with two gently curved swords held to their waists by broad golden sashes wrapped 'round vibrant red robes.

"Quite a sight, eh, Mademoiselle Sparrow?"

Camille turned to see beside her a brown-haired, brown-eyed, brown-bearded man of middling years. He glanced at Scruff and smiled, then added, "The ship, I mean."

"Indeed, sieur, for never have I seen such. But that is no wonder, for, in truth, never had I seen any ships at all before yester.
—Do you know its name?"

"Her, ma'amselle."

Camille turned up a hand, an unspoken question in her eyes.

"All ships are female, ma'amselle; and yes, I know her name, and I'll trade you her name for yours."

Camille dropped her gaze from his and turned to look at the ship. "I am Camille, sieur."

"I am Jordain, harbormaster here, and she is the *Higashi No Kaze.*"

"The *Higashi No . . . ?*"

The harbormaster smiled. "The *Higashi No Kaze.* I am told by her master it means *East Wind.*"

Camille's heart leapt with hope. *There are winds that do not blow, but flow across the sea.*

"Sieur, I must see this master."

Jordain pointed. "He's there on the poop."

Even as Camille's gaze followed the harbormaster's out-stretched arm to see a formidable figure standing on the high deck astern, she said, "No, M'sieur Jordain, I mean I must speak with this master. It is urgent I do so."

He, too, was dressed in a red robe, though elaborate yellow-gold dragons were depicted thereon. About his waist was a broad red-and-yellow sash. His feet were stockinged in white, and strange black sandals he wore. Like his crew, his eyes were tilted, his complexion a yellow-tan. He, too, had his black hair tied in a curl behind by a small black bow. In his right hand he held horizontally an open red fan. Before him, on the straw mat where he knelt, his two gently curved swords lay in jet-black scabbards, one sword longer than the other.

On his knees on a separate straw mat to the left of the man and a bit behind, the interpreter, one of the crew, said, "Lord Hirota says, there can be no such place, Jordain san." The interpreter had not once looked at Camille.

On the floor of the captain's cabin, Jordain and Camille also knelt on woven straw mats—"tatami," Jordain had called them—Camille to Jordain's right and slightly behind.

Again Hirota spoke, his words chopped short as if each were cut off by an axe, and Camille wondered if Lord Hirota's scowl was perpetual.

When Hirota fell silent, the interpreter said, "Lord Hirota says, though there are many strange things in Faery, a place east of the sun and west of the moon is not one of those, for *Tsuki Musume*, um, Daughter Moon, is quite disobedient, for she sometimes runs ahead of, um, Father Sun, and sometimes lags after, sometimes hides her face and sometimes shows it brazenly."

Camille, her heart falling, said, "Then he knows of no such place?"

The interpreter yet looked only at Jordain, and when the harbormaster nodded, the interpreter spoke rapidly to Hirota. Hirota turned his head and gazed at Camille, the look in his eyes quite insolent, and, without saying a word, he snapped the red fan shut.

"No," said the interpreter, looking at Jordain.

Camille sighed.

Hirota then said swift words, his haughty eyes never leaving Camille, and the intepreter said to Jordain, "Lord Hirota says, he has never seen hair of gold before, and he wishes to know if you have any more such as she."

Jordain looked at Camille, a faint smile tugging at the corners of his mouth, though there was interest in his eyes as well. "Are there?"

Camille blushed, but said, "If I had a fan, I would snap it shut."

Jordain turned and said to the interpreter, "Tell Lord Hirota she has closed her fan."

After the interpreter spoke, Hirota growled and looked away from Camille.

"At least he didn't ask about your sparrow," said Jordain, "though I have no such reticence."

Camille smiled. "Scruff is my travelling companion."

Jordain waited for more, yet Camille added nought.

They walked on down the docks, passing ship after ship, some lading cargo, others off-loading.

"Your port seems quite busy."

"Aye, for 'tis the season for trading. We have fine wool and wine and cognac and brandy and other such to export, while the ships bring goods from afar."

"And that's why the *East Wind* is in port?"

Jordain nodded.

"Then tell me, are there any other ships herein named after the winds?"

"Certainly none currently in port as great as the *Higashi No Kaze*, though there are three others who might sail in one day soon."

"What about ships that are not as great, yet named after the winds?"

"Why is it you want to know?"

Camille sighed and said, "I search for my true love Alain. He is gone to a place east of the sun and west of the moon, or so did Lady Sorcière say. And I was given a riddle to solve, a riddle which will lead to him, or so it is I hope."

Jordain sighed. "Your true love, eh?"

"Indeed. I love him more than life itself." Camille's voice dropped. "It is my fault he is missing."

"There is a tale here to tell," said Jordain, "and I would hear it. Yet the riddle first."

Camille glanced up at Jordain then said:

> *"There are winds that do not blow,*
> *But flow across the sea;*
> *A master of one might know*
> *Where such a place doth be."*

"Ah," said Jordain. "Now I see why you seek ships named after the winds. Let us go to the harbor office, and we shall see what ships are harbored that answer to such."

Registered in port there were currently nine ships with names, some of which needed to be translated, that evoked the winds—*Breeze, Windsong, Squall, Little Cyclone, Sea Breath, Gale, Storm Runner, Villion's Bluster, Wind Walker*—and a tenth craft named *Puffer*, though Jordain thought this last but a small boat named after a fish.

Over the next two days, Camille and Scruff visited every one of these craft, yet none of the masters knew where the place she sought did lie.

"I thought not," said Jordain. "Most were coastal runners, and not ships that sail across the five oceans and the seven seas."

"That many?" asked Camille. "—Oceans and seas, I mean."

"Those are the ones in Faery I know of," replied Jordain, "though 'tis said there are more—some claim nine oceans in all, and as many as eleven seas."

Camille stood silent for a while, looking over the harbor, and then she said, "When first we met, you spoke of three other great ships named after the winds, ships that might come."

Jordain nodded. "Aye, they are the *Hawa Kibli*, and *Aniar Gaoth*, and the *Nordavind*. Fear not, Camille, if any come across la Grande Mer—the Great Sea—and into port, I will send a runner to fetch you. Where are you staying?"

"At the Le Marlin Bleu, but any runner you send must at times find me elsewhere—at mapmakers, for example. Yet I will tell the clerk at the Blue Marlin where I am bound, and the runner can ask him. Oh, and in the evenings, the runner will find me at La Lanterne Rouge, where I will be singing."

Jordain's eyes widened in surprise. "The Red Lantern? But, Camille, it is quite an unruly place, and though there are women who work there, I think they are not your sort."

Camille said, "I will only be singing, Jordain, not, um, not, well, you know. Besides, I have been told that every ship's captain and crew sooner or later comes to the 'Lantern, and as I did in Les Îles, I shall ask each audience if anyone knows whither lies the place I seek."

"Bu-but—" Jordain began to protest, yet Camille stopped him with a thrust-out palm.

"As I said, Jordain, I will simply be singing."

Jordain sighed. "When do you begin?"

"This very eve."

Jordain shook his head and turned away, peering out over the water. Then he pointed. "There goes the *Higashi No Kaze*."

As she watched the red ship tack toward the harbor entrance, Camille frowned and said, "Her sails are not like the other ships I've seen leaving port."

"Aye, they are not," said Jordain. "But for that matter, the whole ship is different, her bottom is quite flat with but a small keel, and the rudder is long and angles out, somewhat like a lengthy oar. Her sails are called lugsails and have four corners down the outside border; they're made of coarse cotton and braced flat by long wooden strips running from the haul to the edge. And she's equipped with oars for the crew to use when the wind does die. No, not like other ships is she, yet quite seaworthy in all, they say, though I myself wouldn't want to be aboard her in a heavy storm."

They watched as the great ship made her way to the mouth of the harbor and then on out to sea, where she turned to the larboard and soon vanished behind the upsloping hills to the headland, her strange sails the last to disappear.

Camille sighed. The *East Wind* was gone, along with her yellow-tan crew.

There came a soft tap on the door, and when Camille opened it, a huge man filled the frame, his hat in hand. "Miss Camille?"

"Yes?"

"Ma'am, I'm t' go with y' t' th' Red Lantern."

"Sieur?"

"I'll be waitin' down below."

He turned to go, but Camille called out, "Wait!"

The big man turned back, brushing the shock of red hair out of his pale blue eyes.

"Who are you, and why are you going to the Red Lantern with me?"

"I'm t' see that no one does y' wrong, Miss Camille."

"Does me wrong?"

"Aye. 'At's what th' harbormaster sent me t' do."

"Jordain." Camille's word was a statement, not a question.

" 'At's right. Mister Jordain."

"And if I need no protection . . . ?"

"Oh, you will, miss," averred the big man. Then his mouth formed an *O*, as if he just remembered something. "And, miss, my name is John, though most know me as Big Jack."

"Well, Jacques, I—"

"No, no, miss. Not Jacques. Jack. And it's Big Jack at that."

"Well, um, Big Jack, tell Jordain that I thank him for his offer, and I thank you as well, but—"

Jack held up an admonishing index finger. "No, no, miss. He said you'd like as not try t' say no, but he gave me instructions, he did, and I'll not take a no."

Camille sighed and said, "Well, Jack, er, Big Jack, I suppose it can't harm if you tag along."

After the mêlée at the Red Lantern was over, and after the three men who had tried to carry Camille up the stairs had been smashed unconscious by single blows of one of Big Jack's massive fists, Camille no longer objected to him being about. In fact, after but two nights, his very presence meant that when

Camille took the stage a quiet would descend, for Big Jack would stand up in the center of the throng and glare all 'round; and a hush would fall over the boisterous crowd, each person there wondering if he was the one Big Jack was getting ready to maim. And then Camille would begin to sing, and Big Jack would smile and sit down, to a great sigh of relief. And her singing brought laughter and tears to the eyes of captains and crew alike, and even the ladies of the Red Lantern would pause to listen, some weeping softly. And now and again, as she had done in Les Îles, Camille would sing to a wee sparrow.

As before, at the conclusion of every performance, she would ask if anyone there knew of a place east of the sun and west of the moon, and though sailors and masters looked at one another, none could tell her where such a place might be. . . .

. . . And thus did eighteen days pass, eighteen blossoms withering to vanish since Camille had been in Leport. Twenty-one blossoms remained on Lady Sorcière's staff, new splinters and cracks yet riving the stave with the coming of each new day.

"Mademoiselle! Mademoiselle!" cried the lad. "The harbormaster sent me to fetch you. He says to tell you the *South Wind* has come."

Over Scruff's chirping objections, Camille snatched him up from his breakfast of grain, and she grabbed up the staff and followed the lad out from the common room.

Down to the docks she hastened, following the trotting lad, and he led her to one of the piers, where was berthed a ship fully as large as the *Higashi No Kaze* had been.

Yet this ship had a pointed prow, and her lines were long and low, though a high deck arose at the stern, and a smaller one at the bow. She was three-masted, and brown was her color, her furled sails brown as well. Her name was written on her prow in serpentine letters, letters which Camille could not read. Her crew was dressed in long, flowing robes, their faces dark brown, some nearly black beneath their colorful turbans. At their waists they bore sharply curved swords as well as curved and keen-pointed knives.

Jordain stood on the dock with a small, dark man dressed in pale brown robes, sandals on his feet. He had black hair and a black beard, as well as a flowing black moustache below his quite aquiline nose. His black eyes lit up as Camille approached.

Jordain said, "Lady Camille, this is Captain Anwar, master of the *Hawa Kibli*. Raiyis Anwar, I present Lady Camille."

"*Chp!*"

"And her sparrow, Scruff."

Anwar laughed, and, with a great flourish of his right hand, he deeply bowed. Camille curtseyed in return.

Then Anwar smiled, white teeth showing. "Lady Camille, Harbormaster Jordain tells me you seek a place?"

"Yes, Master Raiyis, I do."

Again Anwar smiled. "My lady, 'raiyis' is the word for 'captain' in my native tongue. Please, call me Anwar."

"And you, sieur, please call me Camille."

Anwar made a small gesture with his hand, somewhat like the flourish of his bow. "Now, about this place you seek."

"All I know of it, Captain Anwar, er, Anwar, is that it lies east of the sun and west of the moon."

Anwar shook his head. "I know not where such a place is. In fact, unless it moves, unless it cycles on a crystal sphere of its own, somehow gliding between those spheres upon which the sun and the moon do ride, I do not know how such a place can even be."

Tears brimmed in Camille's eyes, and Anwar took her free hand in his and said, "I am sorry, my dear. Yet do not yield all hope, for strange is the realm of Faery, and your place might be real after all."

Then Anwar turned to Jordain. "Is the *Aniar Gaoth* or the *Nordavind* in port? Or the *Higashi No Kaze*?"

Jordain shook his head then added, "The *Higashi No Kaze* sailed away some days past, and Lord Hirota did not know where the place she seeks might lie."

Anwar nodded. "Then perhaps it is written that the Elves will know . . . or the iron-bearing Dwarves."

"Elves? Dwarves?" asked Camille.

Anwar nodded. "Jordain told me of the riddle you have: 'There are winds that do not blow, but flow across the sea.' Camille, many are the vessels in Faery named after the winds, but only four of these are great ships of the sea. If any would know where this place you seek might be, it would be the captains of such. Yet, alas, the master of the *East Wind* did not, and I, master of the *South Wind*, know not either. But there are two ships left: the *Aniar Gaoth*—the *West Wind*—is a vessel with an Elven crew; her master may know, for he has travelled wide, as has the Dwarven master of the *Nordavind*—the *North Wind*."

Camille gestured at the harbor. "But Captain Anwar, those two you name, they are not here."

"Nevertheless, Camille, it is the trading season, and they will come soon or late."

"Then let us hope they come soon," said Camille, "for if they come late, it will not matter."

Another fortnight did pass, fourteen more blossoms gone, when came the word that the *Aniar Gaoth* had docked. Again Camille rushed to the pier, following the lad that Jordain had sent, Big Jack now striding after, for he had decided Camille needed protecting in the day as well as the nights at the Red Lantern. And so, down to the docks they did go to where the Elvenship lay.

She was long and low and slender and sleek, her bow knife-sharp, her stern club-blunt, her hull a deep blue. No fo'c's'le nor stern castle did she bear, but instead low decks fore and aft. And her three masts were tall and raked back, with yardarms wide and many. She would carry an enormous amount of sail, all of it now full-reefed, though Camille could see they were pale blue and with a sheen like that of silk. She was half-again longer than either the *Hawa Kibli* or the *Higashi No Kaze* had been.

As to her crew, Elves were they all—alabaster skin tinged with gold, tilted eyes in narrow, high-cheekboned faces, tipped ears, and lithe grace. They were armed with glittering swords, and horn-limb bows and deadly arrows, and long-handled, gleaming spears. Silks they wore, and satins, and they spoke in a lilting tongue.

Jordain was waiting. "Welcome to the *West Wind*," he said. Then he escorted her up the gangway, Big Jack following in their wake. Elves paused in their activities to watch this golden-haired maiden with a sparrow on her shoulder pass by, many smiling, some essaying courtly bows.

Jordain led her aft, then down a short ladder to a passageway below—Big Jack bending down to keep from bumping his head—and into a captain's lounge. At a chart table centermost, a flaxen-haired Elf pored over scattered maps, and he looked up as they entered.

"Cabhlaigh Andolin, I present Lady Camille; my lady, Captain Andolin." Jordain glanced at the sparrow and added, "And ere he objects, on her shoulder is her companion Scruff."

Andolin made a courtly bow, murmuring, "My lady," and Camille curtseyed and replied, "Captain."

Andolin looked at Scruff and smiled, then turned to Big Jack, who thrust out a hand and said, "My name's John, but all call me Big Jack." Andolin's clasp was swallowed in Big Jack's grip, and the Elf seemed glad to get back his hand whole.

Andolin then turned to Camille. "My lady, Harbormaster Jordain has told me of your riddle and of the place you seek." He gestured at the scatter of charts on the table. "Yet I find nought to satisfy your quest, for I think no place can exist that lies east of the sun and west of the moon, not even in Faery."

Camille burst into tears.

The blossoms withered one by one, until all were gone but one. And there was but one great ship left whose captain might know. Camille no longer had the heart to sing, though she felt she must. Yet night after night none in her audience could tell her where was the place she sought. And every day she had haunted the docks, watching the harbor entrance, watching for her last hope. Yet the *Nordavind* did not come and did not come, as the blossoms withered away until there was left but one.

And now in the gloom Camille sat on the dock, her songs at the Red Lantern done, and she waited, her hopes all crashed down, but still she sat waiting, waiting for a ship, waiting for the *Nordavind*, waiting for the *North Wind* to come.

Camille's spirits were as black as the night, for it was the dark of the moon. Yet the docks themselves were lit by lanterns scattered here and there and by the stars shining down from above. Off to one side and lurking in the shadows stood a large man: Big Jack yet on guard.

"Oh, Scruff," said Camille to the sparrow asleep in her pocket, "do you remember what the old woman said back in the very last village on our way to Raseri's lair? When we asked if any knew where lay a place east of the sun and west of the moon, she said, 'Only the North Wind would know.' I do pray that she is right. And I pray to Mithras that the *North Wind* will come. Yet I have little hope, for the last blossom even now—"

"Make ready to tow!" came a distant call.

Camille stood to see whence came the cry.

At a dock afar she could see the Elvenship alight with lanterns, and a bustle of activity aboard.

She walked down to see what was afoot.

Captain Andolin stood on the stern, issuing orders, Elves haling on halyards and climbing ratlines. Towing ropes had been affixed to bow and stern, and rowing gigs awater and manned stood ready to haul the ship away from the slip.

When Andolin fell silent, Camille called, "Are you and the *West Wind* leaving, Captain?"

He looked down at her. "Aye, my lady, we are." He glanced over his shoulder out toward the night sea. Then he turned back and asked, "Can you not feel it?"

"Feel what, Captain?"

"The ever-worsening twist in the aethyr, the growing warp and bend." He pressed a hand to his forehead as if in distress.

"No, Captain, I cannot. I don't even know what you mean when you say 'aethyr,' and I certainly do not feel any twisting or warping or bending. —Are you in pain?"

"I would not name it pain, my lady, though it is much like an ache."

"What is amiss, Captain, and is there aught I can do to aid?"

"Only distance will help, Lady Camille, and we are making ready to put such distance 'tween us and Leport as swiftly as we can." Andolin then called down to two Human dockworkers, "Cast off fore! Cast off aft!" Hawsers were uncoiled from 'round mooring posts and thrown into the water. Even as Elves drew the hawsers in, Andolin called out, "Rowers, row!"

Slowly the great Elvenship *Aniar Gaoth* drew away from the dock, the men in the towing gigs rowing to pull her away.

"But, Captain, I still do not know what is the matter," called Camille.

Andolin looked down at her and grimly said, "Iron is coming."

Then to her he said no more, instead turning and calling out to his Elven crew, the captain totally consumed in swiftly getting his ship under way.

Camille watched a bit longer, then she sighed and walked back toward her place of vigil, a large shadow following.

Iron is coming.

Nigh mid of night, even as the *Aniar Gaoth*, silhouetted against the stars as she was, slid beyond the harbor mouth to vanish from view, Camille heard the dip and pull of many oars, and a guttural voice calling out: *"Roers, gjøre i stand!"*

In the starlight and the light from the lanterns adock, Camille could make out a long, low craft gliding across the water, many oars stroking, and it appeared the ship was heading for a nearby slip. Camille stood and watched, and oars dipped and dipped, and the voice called out, *"Mindre! . . . Mindre! . . ."*

The craft slowed, and slid toward the slip.

"Åres på!" came the cry, and all the oars were shipped aboard. Then the long boat slid into the slip and broad-shouldered, short men leapt out to— Nay! Not men. But Dwarves instead, like those she had seen in Les Îles.

And in the lanternlight on the dock, Camille could make out runes on the bow of the ship, runes she could read, and they named the ship *Nordavind.*

The *North Wind* had come at last!

And even as the Dwarven crew moored the vessel to the dock, the very last blossom disappeared from Camille's split and splintered stave.

32

Commission

Even as Camille approached, she recognized the craft for what it was: a raider ship . . . or so Fra Galanni had said in response to Camille's inquiry about a picture in one of his books. "A terrible raider ship from the North, bearing tall, flaxen-haired, blue-eyed men, and you would think them sent from Mithras Himself, they with their proud ways. Yet they are not from Mithras, girl, but instead from one they call Woden, and a grim god is He. For His followers come in their longboats, their Dragonships, girl, with their axes and their shields and murderous ways to pillage and rape and despoil. You'd best never see one, Camille, yet if you do, run away as fast as you can." Or so Fra Galanni had said.

Yet now Camille was hastening toward the craft, rather than running away, for this was the *Nordavind*—the *North Wind*—and she would speak with the captain of the Dragonship.

As to the ship itself, it was long and low and open-hulled, and Dwarven war shields were arranged along her sides. Her hull was klinker-built—long overlapping oaken strakes running fore to aft—and even though she had ribs and crossbeams thwartwise for bracing, still her hull had a serpentine flexibility that caused the craft to cleave sharply through the water, yielding a nimbleness beyond that which her narrow keelboard alone would bestow. And she was swift, for her length was a full fifty paces, yet her width was but barely five. She could mount as many as four masts, each with a square-rigged sail angled by a beitass pole to make the most of the wind. She also carried thirty-five pairs of narrow-bladed, spruce oars, trimmed to length so that all could strike the water simultaneously in short, choppy strokes, the oars now resting amidships on three pairs of trestles. A steerboard rudder was mounted at the starboard rear to guide her on her journeys.

As the Dwarves unladed the craft, Camille stopped one bearing a keg on one of his broad shoulders and said, "Your captain, sieur. I would have a word with your captain." Yet even as she spoke she noted that not only was this Dwarf wearing an iron or steel chain mail shirt, so were they all.

Iron is coming, said Andolin, and this must be what he meant.

The dark-eyed, dark-haired, dark-bearded Dwarf, a half a head shorter than Camille, said, "Captain Kolor is the one you want, lass." He turned and called out, *"Kolor, en pike til se du!"*

"En pike?" The response came from a Dwarf standing at the far end of the ship.

The keg bearer pointed at Camille and called back, *"Pike, ja!"*

Kolor gestured for Camille to come to him, and she said to the keg bearer, "Merci, sieur," then began wending her way through the bustle of iron-clad Dwarves as they unladed their cargo.

And as she walked toward Kolor, Camille noted that the Dwarves' axes and war hammers and maces and dirks and crossbows and quarrels and shields were all of iron and steel.

Ah, and did not Captain Anwar speak of the iron-bearing Dwarves? And Alain's brother Borel said, "A few who sail the seas carry weapons of iron, of steel. It protects them from some of the monsters of the deep. They seldom bring it onshore, however, and then but in direst need." No doubt, these are some of those mariners Borel had been speaking of.

Finally, Camille reached the captain, a Dwarf who could have stood no more than four-foot-one. He had honey-blond hair and a honey-blond beard and his eyes were pale blue.

He cocked an eyebrow as she stopped before him.

"Captain Kolor, I am on an urgent mission, and I need your help."

"And you, my lady, are . . . ?"

"My name is Camille, and of late consort to Prince Alain of the Summerwood. Yet he is missing, and I believe you know of the place where he could be."

"Lady Camille, if I know of it, you need but ask. Has it a name?"

"Sieur, I only know it lies east of the sun and west of the moon."

Kolor frowned and said, "My lady, I do not think such a place can even be."

Camille drew in a sharp breath. "Captain, are you saying—?"

"What I am saying, Lady Camille, is that I know of no such place in either Faery or the mortal world."

Of a sudden Camille's knees gave way, and she collapsed to the dock, her stave clattering down at her side, and she buried her face in her hands and sobbed. Kolor stepped forward to aid her, but from nowhere it seemed, Big Jack was kneeling beside her, and he glared up at the Dwarf and gritted, "What did you say to her?"

In spite of the difference in their relative sizes, a steely look came into Kolor's eyes, and he said, "I but told her I did not know where lies the place she seeks."

Big Jack ground his teeth, and for a moment it seemed he was caught on a cusp, trying to decide whether to comfort Camille or to lay this Dwarf by. Unflinching, Kolor stood ready for either. But finally Big Jack softly said, "Lady Camille?"

"Oh, Jack," she sobbed, "I was hoping Urd was right."

"Urd!" cried Kolor, reeling back. "Did you say Urd?"

Yet weeping, Camille looked up at the Dwarf. "Lady Urd, yes. She told me of the winds that are not winds. She and her sisters Verdandi and Skuld aided me."

"Maiden, Mother, and Crone, girl, didn't you know who they were? The Fates, that's who. The Fates! Am I to be cursed by the Fates themselves?"

They sat in the Bald Pelican, the night nearly faded away, the tavern empty of all but Camille and sleeping Scruff and Kolor and Big Jack, as well as a drowsy barkeep and a drunken old man lying under one of the tables, mayhap the same old man to whom Camille had given a bronze days past. Camille was just coming to the end of her tale, Big Jack's eyes wide in wonderment, for this was the first of it he had heard.

". . . and then Lady Urd said,

> " 'There are winds that do not blow,
> But flow across the sea;
> A master of one might know
> Where such a place doth be.'

"And so, by happenstance, I came unto Leport and found the four winds—*East-*, *South-*, *West-*, and last of all, your ship, Captain, the *North Wind*—but none of the masters of any of the four seem to know where lies the place I seek, in spite of Lady Urd's words."

Kolor slowly shook his head. " 'Twas not by 'happenstance' you came to Leport, Camille, for the Fates—Maiden, Mother, and Crone—all had a hand in your coming. And heed, though the Fates control Destiny, 'tis said they must not interfere, must remain aloof, and can only give gifts for services rendered. Still, at times, at dire times, they do take a hand, and I can only conclude that times are dire, for they did take a hand with you. Yet we do not know what portends, but for their words that one might come who will pollute the River of Time beyond redemption. Yet even though dire times are in the offing, even then the Sisters cannot give gifts unless a riddle is answered properly. 'Tis then and only then they can bestow such gifts upon the one they would aid. Then the one given the gift can ask a question, and even then it may or may not be answered, and if answered, the reply comes in the form of a riddle. In your case, Camille, all such did happen: three favors, three riddles, three answers, three gifts, three questions, three replies couched in riddles."

"But Captain, the three gifts they gave—comb, shuttle, and spool—but for the gold they contain, are quite ordinary." Camille looked at Kolor and then Big Jack and asked, "What good can they possibly do?"

Kolor shrugged, and Big Jack turned up his hands.

Camille stared into her mug of tea grown cold and said, "Regardless of the gifts and riddles, my quest seems come to an end, for none knows of the place I seek."

Long silence fell over the trio, but then Kolor said, " 'Tis true I know of no place which lies east of the sun and west of the moon, but there *is* a place which might have something to do with your tale: 'tis an island nearly beyond the rim of the world itself, and it is an evil place, peopled by Trolls and Redcap Goblins and their Human thralls, or so the escaped slave we picked up at sea told us ere he died."

"Escaped slave?" asked Jack.

Kolor nodded. "On one of our voyages we came across a Human adrift on a log, and when we plucked him from the sea, we found his leg to be gone from the knee down, torn off by the same creature that had destroyed his raft. He had managed to bind the stump, but, in spite of the salt of the sea, it had gone bad in the long, hot days ere we got to him, and he was out of his mind. Yet among his babblings he said he had been the pilot of the *Swan*, but the ship met ill fortune, and he and his crew had been castaway upon a place he named Troll Isle. There they had been seized by Goblins, Redcaps that is, and made into thralls, joining the other Human slaves castaway there before.

"We treated him as best we could, but he was too far gone, the stump of his leg poisoning all the rest of him. Yet he had moments of lucidity, or so it seemed, and he talked about the isle:

"Mountainous it is, he said, some forty miles across or so, covered with forest for the most part, but for the slave-tended fields. A formidable citadel sits above a ramshackle town, and one might think the fortress worthy of conquering, for within might lie great treasure, but the escapee said not—only Troll gold was therein.

"He was one of the field slaves, and over a long, long period, he managed to slip away enough times to make a raft and provision it with food and water.

"Then one night he went to the cove where he kept it hidden, and pushed off and away. By the time we found him, he had sailed for several moons, driven by the winds when they blew, drifting on the currents when not, living off the sea and rain when his own supplies gave out.

"I asked him where was this isle, and he marked it on one of my charts, and if it is truly where he said, then he had made a remarkable journey from there to where we took him up from the sea.

"He died babbling, muttering nonsense, and screaming of Goblins and Trolls, and there was nought whatsoever we could do but wait and then give him back to the sea.

"As to the island itself, I only know it as a place on a chart; my crew and I have never been there, for if we are to believe the dying man's description, it is warded by a mighty fortress peopled by well-armed Goblins and Trolls, and, because of that, and because of what the escapee said, I deem there is no cargo of worth or booty of value to be had, and the only gold therein is Troll gold, a low-grade fusion of iron and brimstone, its glittering promise totally false, for it is of little worth.

"Yet since much of your misery and that of your Prince Alain seems to be entwined with the acts of Redcaps and Trolls—"

"Olot," gritted Big Jack, making a fist.

Kolor grunted and continued, "—then maybe this island is the place you truly seek, though, Faery or no, I think it will not lie east of the sun and west of the moon."

Camille turned up her hands. "Captain, think you that we can give credence to a man dying of delirium?"

"That I cannot say, Lady Camille. Yet, if his tale is true, if he was indeed a pilot, then there may be an island of Trolls and Goblins and Human thralls at the place he marked on my chart, and Trolls and Redcaps seem to be at the bottom of all."

Camille sighed and shook her head. She pondered for long moments, no one saying aught, but finally she looked out the window and said, "To do nought whatsoever will in itself accomplish nought. Your isle seems to be the only choice I have left. —List, if you will bear me there, I will pay you with the golden gifts: comb, shuttle, and spool."

Kolor blenched, and he thrust his hands out in refusal, saying, "No, no, Camille. I would not take what the Fates have given you."

"Oh, would that I yet had the jewels I did sew into my garments, but they were stolen, and so I have little to—"

"Lady Camille, since the Fates themselves sent you to me, it means that my ship and crew and I have been commissioned by the Dread Sisters Themselves to be at your behest. Aye, we will bear you to that wicked place, if it is truly there, for the Fates so decree, but we will do so reluctantly, for I would not willingly put you in such peril extreme."

Big Jack, who had said little, glanced at Camille's stave. "When, Cap'n Kolor? When will you take us there? What I mean t' say is: time grows short."

Kolor looked at the big man. "You mean to go as well?"

Big Jack glanced at Camille and nodded. "I was told t' protect her, and protect her I will."

"Oh, Jack," said Camille, "you don't have to go. It's likely to be—"

"Quite dangerous," said Big Jack. "All th' more reason for me t' go." Then he turned to Kolor. "As I said, time is short. When do we go?"

Kolor took up the split and cracked stave—the blossoms gone, the carved vine withered—and examined it closely. Then he started, his eyes flying wide, and turned the stick into the lanternlight to see it more clearly. " 'Twas the dark of the moon when we docked, yet look." He laid the staff down on the table and pointed to the dark disk just below the grip at the top. A hairline-thin pale crescent marked the disk along the right-hand perimeter.

"And a whole moon beyond," breathed Big Jack. "And a whole moon beyond. . . ."

Captain Kolor sucked air in between clenched teeth and he looked at Camille and said, "Oh, my lady, I am sorry; I neglected the import of Lady Sorcière's words."

Camille felt her heart plunging. "Sieur?"

Kolor sighed and shook his head and tapped the stave. "A whole moon beyond is not enough time, for the isle is far, and the winds are against us; we simply cannot reach it in a moon."

33
Asea

Tears welled in Camille's eyes. "Cannot reach . . . ?"
   Kolor shook his head. "Not in a moon." He looked into
his mug of ale, peering at the foam.

Big Jack reached out his enormous hand and enveloped
Camille's, and he said, "Captain—"

But Kolor thrust out a palm to stop Big Jack's words; the
Dwarf's brow furrowed in concentration as he peered into his
mug as if trying to capture an elusive thought. And then his eyes
widened in remembrance, and he grimaced and murmured,
"Unless . . ."

Camille and Big Jack waited, but Kolor said no more.

"Unless what, Captain?" said Camille.

Kolor took a deep breath and dipped a finger into the froth
and raised it up and stared at the pale lather. Then he licked his
finger clean and looked over at her. "Unless we sail across the
Sea of Mist."

Camille frowned. "The Sea of Mist?"

Kolor let out a lengthy sigh. " 'Tis said it is a short lay of
water, Camille, though I've never been there. Too, they say
therein a terrible monster dwells—a breaker of ships, a killer of
all who attempt to cross. No vessel has ever won through, but if
we could sail those waters and out, then mayhap we could reach
the island in just under a moon."

"If no ship has ever won through," said Big Jack, "then how
do you know it's but a short stretch across?"

Kolor glanced at Scruff sleeping in Camille's pocket. " 'Tis
said a message bird was loosed at dawn to fly from side to side,

and from the time it took, the lay was judged. Even so, ships are not birds, and those waters are deadly."

"What kind of monster is it?" asked Camille.

Kolor turned up his hands. "I know not, lady, for none has ever survived to say."

"Then how do you know it is a 'breaker of ships'?"

"Wreckage drifts out, Camille. And before you ask, reefs and shoals could account for such wrack, but there are no signs of grounding on the remnants."

"Monster, reefs, shoals, or no, if it'll get us to the isle in a moon, then that's what we should do," declared Big Jack, "sail the Misty Sea."

Camille held up a cautioning hand. "Oh, Jack, I don't know whether—"

"Camille," said Kolor, "a commission was I given by the Fates, and I would not go against Them."

Camille looked at the Dwarf. "Is there no other way?"

Kolor glanced at Big Jack and said, "Not any that will get us there in a moon."

Big Jack looked to Camille for affirmation, and she sighed and then silently nodded.

"Done and done!" Big Jack declared.

"May the Three Sisters truly be with us," said Kolor.

"When do we leave?" asked Big Jack.

Kolor looked out through the window at the rising dawnlight. "It will take the full of this day to reprovision, but we can set sail as soon as that is done."

"What about the tide?" asked Big Jack.

"No need to wait for the outflow, not with the *Nordavind*," said Kolor, standing. "Now I must recall my crew and tell them of the task the Fates have cast our way."

As Camille rose to her feet, Kolor added, "Rest this day, lady, and bid your farewells."

Big Jack said to Kolor, "I will fetch th' lady when all is ready."

Kolor nodded, then turned toward the door, Camille and Big Jack following. And as they stepped from the Bald Pelican, with a new day on the air, Scruff awakened and scrambled to Camille's shoulder and demanded to be fed.

As she broke fast with Scruff and Big Jack in the common room of the Blue Marlin, Camille said, "Jack, will you tell

Madam Maquereau at the Red Lantern that we will be leaving on a voyage, and that I will not be singing there again?"

"Uh-huh," said Big Jack, shovelling eggs into his mouth.

"Also, if you can find Jordain, tell him as well what it is we do."

"Mmm-hmm," said Big Jack, bobbing his head. Then, speaking around the mouthful of eggs, he added, "Though with th' *Nordavind* in port replenishing her stores, I suppose Harbor-master Jordain already knows."

They finished the meal in silence, Scruff pecking away at the barley seeds. Then, after Big Jack was gone, Camille settled her bill with the desk clerk, paying for that day as well, and she asked that Aicelina prepare a bath for her, the last she would have for many days to come.

When Aicelina knocked on Camille's door, Camille gave the girl a silver for herself, saying, "You have served me well, Aicelina. Scruff, too, bringing his grain as you have." Then Camille gave her another silver and said, "We are going on a long journey, a moon there and back, and I will need more grain for him, and since we will be going by water, the grain will need protection from spray."

"Oui, mademoiselle," said Aicelina. "I shall have them put it in a double sack, the outer one tarred. And what grain would you have?"

"A mix of oats, barley, rye, wheat, and millet."

"And how much?"

Camille shrugged, then said, "Enough to last the full journey, and a bit more, should something go awry. Three moons in all should do it."

"I shall purchase ten pounds," said Aicelina, then looked at the silver in hand. "Oh, mademoiselle, it will not take a silver or even a bronze for such a small amount."

"Keep whatever is left over, Aicelina."

Aicelina's eyes widened and she bobbed a curtsey. "Thank you, mademoiselle. I shall fetch it now." The girl started to turn away, but then turned back. "Oh, and your bath is ready." Then she was gone.

Night had fallen when came a tap on the door. Camille opened the panel, and in the lanternlight stood Big Jack, an enormous bronze battle-axe over his shoulder. "Th' *North Wind* is ready, Lady Camille. Captain Kolor says t' come."

Camille fastened her cloak 'round her shoulders and took up her bedroll and waterskin and rucksack, the stave affixed in the loops. Then she fetched sleeping Scruff from his perch on the back of a chair, and, blowing out the lantern, said, "Let's go."

At the dock Jordain stood waiting. "Camille, I know you feel you must do this thing, yet to sail the Sea of Mist is tantamount to throwing yourself from a cliff."

"We have no choice," said Camille.

"Besides," said Big Jack, hefting his battle-axe, its keen edge glinting in the light of the dockside lanterns, "it's not like we're going in unprepared; I've got Lady Bronze here, and th' Dwarves . . . well . . . you know Dwarves."

"Fear not, Harbormaster," said Kolor, just then stepping forward, "the Fates are on our side, or so I do believe."

Jordain shook his head. "Nevertheless—"

"Harbormaster," said Kolor, "there is no other way."

Jordain sighed and said, "Then I can but wish all of you well, especially you, my lady." And he took Camille's hands in his and kissed them, then released her and stepped back.

Moments later: "Åres rede!" called Kolor, and Dwarves took up spruce oars from the trestles.

Then Kolor called to the docksmen, "Cast off fore! Cast off aft!" and the mooring hawsers were uncinched and dropped into the water.

As Dwarves hauled in the lines, "Skubbe av!" Kolor called.

And fore and aft, oars were used to shove away from the dock. "Roers, åres til vann!"

Dwarves fitted the oars through holes in the upper starboard and larboard strakes and slid them out into the water. Kolor said, "Brekki," and a brown-haired Dwarf stepped forward and began rhythmically chanting "Strøk! . . . Strøk! . . . Strøk! . . ." And as the Nordavind backed away from the pier, Camille in the prow raised a hand in au revoir to Jordain, and the harbormaster sighed and waved in return.

Soon Kolor commanded Brekki to turn the craft, and the oarchief called for the rowers on the starboard to back water, while those on the larboard stroked ahead. And when she was turned about, the oars were shipped aboard and square sails were raised on all four masts and the beitass poles angled to catch the wind. Swiftly the craft surged forward and toward the harbor mouth. Past lanternlit ships moored at anchor glided the Nordavind, sailor's songs and sea chanteys drifting o'er the water from some. Camille looked back at the town of Leport, brightly lit in the night, her eye finding the Red Lantern, and she wondered if anyone therein did sing. Onward sailed the ship, most of the eighty Dwarves looking aft as well, for their shore leave had been quite brief—but from mid of night to dawn. Yet they knew the Fates could not be denied, and so they groaned and watched Leport recede—they, too, singling out the Red Lantern—until they sailed past the harbor mouth and out into open water, the *North Wind* asea at last, its ultimate goal a point in the ocean marked on a chart by a dying, delirious man, a place where might or might not lie an island of Goblins and Trolls.

Camille sighed and turned to face forward, looking across the starlit deeps, wondering what peril or joy or grief lay in the waters ahead.

"There," said Kolor, pointing. To the fore and standing across their course reared a great wall of twilight, a border of Faery there in the sea.

For nearly a fortnight in all they had sailed across the deeps, the pale arc on the dark disk on Lady Sorcière's staff growing every day, keeping pace with the moon, turning from crescent to half and beyond, and now it was nearly full, a thin bow of darkness yet remaining along the left perimeter. And in that fortnight the *Nordavind* had sailed through stormy and fair weather alike, in seas smooth and choppy and raging, the wind brisk and agale and nonexistent, and there Dwarves did row. Camille had fared quite well, no matter the seas or the weather or wind, but Big Jack had, as he said, spewed his guts more than once. And in these days Camille had discovered that the amenities aboard a Dragonship were nonexistent, for she had not even the meager privacy that a burlap curtain in her père's crowded cottage had given. She had learned to relieve herself over the side just as did everyone else, and to take care of her courses as best she could, though for the most part, Big Jack and the Dwarves looked the other way. Scruff, however, seemed disgruntled out upon the sea, for it held no beetles or grubs to scratch up, no trees to perch in, and no flopping dust whatsoever. And still every day Camille had treated his injured wing with the salve, working the joint tenderly, Scruff's small peeps quite unsettling to her as she did so.

But now in the dawntime, with the moon having set a candlemark past, they had come to a looming wall of twilight there in the middle of the deeps. Faces had turned grim, and weapons were placed at hand, for beyond the shadowy marge lay the Sea of Mist.

"Guide her true, Belkor," said Kolor to the redheaded Dwarf at the steerboard tiller.

"*Bestandig, Skipskaptein,*" replied Belkor, his jaw set at a jut.

And driven by a brisk wind, toward that dim ambit they did run.

Big Jack took up Lady Bronze and stood ready, the great battle-axe agleam in the first rays of the sun rising off the port beam.

And just as the golden orb broke free of the rim of the sea, through the Faery border the *Nordavind* slid to come into a cold, clammy mist, a damp, grey fog shrouding all. And the sea-blue sails fell slack, for therein was no wind.

"*Åres rede, tie,*" whispered Kolor, the order passed on down the line.

Quietly, Dwarves took up oars from the trestles.

"*Roers, åres til vann, tie.*"

As quietly as they could, the Dwarves fitted the oars through the strake holes and slipped them into the water; 'round the shafts where they fitted through the openings, they muffled the oars with cloth wrap. Then, facing aft, they sat, their sea chests acting as seats.

Now Kolor signed to his oar-chief Brekki, who stood just ahead of the tiller, where all the rowers could see him. Brekki put his finger to his lips, and, with measured strokes of his hand down through the air, the Dwarves began to row to his mute cadence, the dip and plash of blades nearly silent.

When Camille looked questioningly at Kolor, he whispered, " 'Tis a tactic we use in perilous waters. At times, though, when edging up on a foe, the rowers stand and face forward as they stroke, axes and shields at hand. But for long pulls, much of the stroke comes from the legs, and so we sit."

On they went through the grey fog, the mist swirling in coils with their passage, a chill dampness seeping through all. Scruff ruffled his feathers, fluffing them outward to stay warm. Camille held open her high vest pocket, inviting him to take shelter within, but he did not accept.

On went the *Nordavind*, oars quietly dipping in concert, ripples of the craft's passage spreading wide to vanish in the gloom.

And though they could not directly see the sun, a vaguely

brighter glow in the chill, cloaking mist showed where it was. A candlemark passed, and the nebulous shine angled upward as the hidden sun crept into the unseen sky above.

Of a sudden, Scruff chirped and grabbed a golden tress and leapt into the pocket.

"Captain," hissed Camille, urgency in her whisper. "Peril is nigh."

"Peril?"

Camille pointed at the sparrow, frantically tugging on her hair.

Kolor stepped forward and whispered to Brekki, and Brekki silently signalled the rowers, *Åres oppe!*

Oars were raised from the water, and the *Nordavind* glided and slowed.

Big Jack held Lady Bronze at the ready.

Camille gripped her split and splintered stave.

All eyes stared into the grey fog, but its chill grasp thwarted vision beyond three or four boat lengths in all.

Moments later, from the larboard, a swell washed through the water, the *Nordavind* bobbing up and down with the passage of something huge and unseen.

In silence they waited, Camille hardly daring to breathe.

Finally, the undulations quelled, and Scruff regained his perch upon Camille's shoulder.

"We can go on," whispered Camille, pointing to the sparrow.

Kolor looked at the wee bird in wonder, and then hissed to Brekki to proceed.

Once again oars quietly dipped in synchronization, and the *Nordavind* glided on.

And still the dim glow of the sun edged up through the shrouding mist.

A candlemark passed, and then another, fog aswirl in their slow wake.

Time edged forward.

Another candlemark slid by, and then once again Scruff snatched a tress and dove into the pocket, and again Camille hissed a warning to Kolor. Oars were raised, and all fell silent, but for *plip*s of water dripping from the blades. Left and right did eyes stare through the grey shroud, and once more to the larboard did a surge in the water come, this time close enough to see the point of the heave as something enormous just under the surface passed by. Yet what leviathan thing or creature caused the bulge, none could say, for only the surge did they see.

Once more they waited in silence, until finally Scruff took to Camille's shoulder again. And once more did they quietly row.

And still the glow of the sun crept across the fog, yet it did not burn away the cloaking mist, as if the shroud itself defied all. Even so, the sun, or rather its diffuse glimmer, provided a guidepost to steer by, else they could have been rowing in circles, for all Camille knew.

Becloaked in mist, across the chill, glassy sea they went, Brekki mutely marking the beat, oars dipping in concert, the *Nordavind* gliding in near silence, though ripples of passage spread wide.

The glow of the sun passed through the zenith and started a slow slide down the sky, and still the ship went on, none knowing how far they had come nor how far was yet to go.

And somewhere in the deeps, an unknown thing did glide.

"Captain, ahead," sissed Big Jack. "I think I see . . ."

The day had fallen toward midafternoon, the glow now angled in the shroud off the starboard beam, and all hands wondered if they would ever come to the end of this dismal murk, with its chill dampness reaching unto the very bones. Yet the fog seemed to have thinned a bit, and Camille and Kolor strained to see what Big Jack—

"There!" sissed Camille.

A distance ahead and dimly seen through the clammy mist a wall of twilight reared up into the sky.

" 'Tis the border," grunted Kolor, grinning. "We've come to the far side."

Forward they glided, Brekki meting out the slow and silent beat.

Yet as they neared, Scruff again grabbed a golden tress and dove into the pocket.

Åres oppe! Brekki silently signalled.

Slowly the ship glided to a stop.

plip! . . . *plip!* . . . *plip!* . . . dripped the lifted blades.

No heave in the water came.

No leviathan moved past.

plip . . .

They waited . . .

. . . eighty-three souls afloat on the glassy surface of a windless, becloaked sea.

A full candlemark slipped away, the diffuse glow of the unseen sun eking downward through the mist.

And still Scruff remained in the pocket.

"*Skipskaptein* Kolor," whispered Brekki, then he glanced at Camille and switched to the new speech, "if we do not move soon, we'll be caught on this sea in the night."

Kolor nodded, but did not reply.

And still they waited . . . silent on a waveless sea. . . .

The glow sank. . . .

Kolor glanced at Camille and turned up a hand.

Camille glanced down at Scruff. The wee bird yet trembled in the high vest pocket, tugging now and again on her hair. She looked back at Kolor and shook her head.

Finally, Kolor took a deep breath and whispered to Brekki, "Ahead a stroke at a time, long pauses in between. If something lies in wait, mayhap we can slip by."

Brekki signalled, and oars dipped and pulled a single stroke.

Ripples eased across the water. . . .

The ship glided forward then slowly came to a stop.

Another single stroke . . .

More ripples . . .

Another glide and stop . . .

Another str—

From below the Dragonship itself, monstrous suckered tentacles came looping up out of the water to lash through the fog and grasp at the sides of the ship. Recoiling Dwarves cried out and snatched up axes at hand, to hack and chop at the boneless limbs, but their blades did not cut. A huge, slimy arm wrapped about Belkor at the tiller and he was wrenched overboard, his screams lost as he was lashed under the chill sea. A tentacle whipped 'round one of the sternward Dwarves, and Kolor snatched his axe from his belt and leapt forward to hack at the slimy thing, to little effect, the tough hide resisting his furious blows, and the shrieking Dwarf was yanked into the water and down. Another ropy arm came coiling at shrilling Camille, but Big Jack, shouting a wordless howl, with a great overhand stroke slammed Lady Bronze down onto the grisly member, shearing through, black blood flying wide. As the shorn-off tentacle lashed and writhed, the gushing stump was whipped back into the water, and the creature below went mad. The water foamed in its fury, and a great stench filled the air. And then another tentacle came hurtling out of the water to whip around

Big Jack and savagely contract in a crushing embrace. Without conscious thought, screaming, Camille leapt forward and slammed Lady Sorcière's staff down on the ropy arm, and lo! a splinter stabbed in, and the tentacle fell limp to the deck, to be slowly dragged back overboard. Released, Big Jack staggered and fell, Lady Bronze clanging to the deck, even as another tentacle whipped forth. Shrieking, once more Camille struck with the staff, and that arm too fell slack. And again she struck and again, and two more tentacles fell away. And shrilling, Camille raced down the ship, striking left and right, left and right, left and—

Of a sudden the monster was gone, leaving stunned Dwarves behind.

Camille stumbled forward another step or two, then fell to her knees, weeping hysterically.

"Quick," shouted Kolor, even as he leapt to the steerboard. "To the strokes! Let us leave this bedamned sea behind."

Dwarves leapt to obey the command—some oars broken, some gone, some yet in the strakes—and in moments the craft was under way, Kolor calling the cadence, for Brekki was among the missing.

Wincing a bit from bruised ribs, Big Jack lifted Camille up in his massive arms and carried her to the bow. And he sat with her in his lap and stroked her hair as she clung to him and sobbed uncontrollably.

And even as Scruff scrambled free of the vest pocket, they came to the twilight border and through and into the slanting sunlight beyond. And a strong wind blew off the starboard stern, filling the four square sails, and across the waters fled the *Nordavind*, leaving the Sea of Mist behind.

Steadily the *Nordavind* hove across the deeps, days passing one by one, the disk on Lady Sorcière's staff waning from full, to gibbous, to half, and then crescent, time rapidly running out. And when there were but four days left ere the whole of the moon would be gone, in late afternoon, a broad, mountainous island came into view. Camille stood in the bow of the Dragonship, her heart thudding in her breast. Delirium or no, the dying man had been right, for not only was an island where he said it would be, but Camille could see a great citadel sitting on a high hill, the mighty fortress looking down upon a small, seashore town. As to the rest, much was covered with trees, though a great spread of cultivated fields surrounded the citadel itself. It had to be Troll Island.

"This ain't right," said Big Jack behind her. "You going alone onto th' isle just ain't right."

Camille shook her head. "We've argued this out for a whole week, Jack, and my mind is firm: Lady Sorcière said I must go alone, and alone I will go."

At Camille's side, Kolor said, "It's no use, Big Jack. Besides, she's right. If Lady Sorcière said to go alone, then you, me, my crew, we'll just have to let be."

"Still, it just ain't—"

"Jack, I am the only one who can easily pass for a Human slave, not the Dwarves, and certainly not—"

"But I'm Human," protested Big Jack.

"Oh, Jack, you'd stick out like a sore thumb, big as you are, towering over everyone else. No, you'll need to stay. Besides, I'd rather not have combat if there is a way to set my love free without blood being shed."

"My lady," growled Kolor, "I caution you: Trolls and Goblins or no, this may not be the place where your Alain doth be." Kolor gestured at the lowering sun. "There sinks the sun, and the horns of the moon punctured the sea nearly three candlemarks past. Hence, this is not a place lying east of the sun and west of the moon. As I've said before, Faery or no, such a place cannot be."

Tears brimming, Camille glanced at her stave then took a deep breath and said, "Nevertheless, I am going."

"And you should take me with you," said Big Jack.

Angrily, Camille brushed her tears aside and snapped, "No!"

Big Jack's face crumpled, and Camille reached out a hand, but then let it fall to her side. "Jack, hear me: I will go alone and discover for myself whether or no this is the place where Alain is kept prisoner. Then and only then might I need you and the Dwarves to aid, but only if there is no other way." Camille glanced at the Dwarven crew—sixty-seven in all counting Kolor, thirteen lost to the monster of the sea. "I have seen all the death I can stand, and I would have no more."

"Wishes or no, my lady," gritted Kolor, "if it becomes necessary, then death there will be."

Camille glumly nodded, yet added, "But only if unavoidable." She turned and looked at Big Jack and then Kolor, and was satisfied by a reluctant nod from each.

"All right, then," said Kolor, "as we have discussed, just after darkness, we will set you ashore a bit away from the town. Then to avoid accidental discovery, we'll shove off and stand out to sea. With our masts unstepped and our blue sails draped over the wales, from a distance we'll look just like the waters; only someone seeking such should be able to sight us. There we'll await your signal: lantern or fire. Have you the oil?"

Camille nodded and pointed to her rucksack. "The three flasks you gave."

"But list, Camille," said Kolor, now glancing at Big Jack. "Should we not hear from you in a timely manner, we'll not stay hidden long."

Big Jack clenched a fist and nodded.

Camille sighed and said, "Agreed."

Kolor then glanced at Scruff on her shoulder and said, "Keep an eye on that wee bird, for he is a wonder to have. Nought else I know of can tell when hidden peril is nigh."

"Indeed, Captain, a better sentry I could not have." *Except at night*, she silently added, *wee little sleepy bird.*

Twilight fell upon the ocean, and the *Nordavind* glided silently toward the isle. Soon they lowered sail, and rowed the last sea-league or so, to finally slip into a cove. Big Jack jumped over the side and waited.

Attired in a threadbare dress—the only thing of hers that she yet owned that had come from her père's poor cottage—and with Scruff asleep in the high pocket above her left breast she had sewn thereon, Camille shouldered her rucksack and bedroll and waterskin and took up her stave and turned to Kolor and said, "Lady Sorcière said unlooked-for help would come along the way, and it most certainly has, but none more so than you, Captain." She kissed Kolor on the cheek, then waved au revoir to the Dwarves at the oars, then turned to waiting Big Jack. With tears in his eyes he reached up and lifted her across the top wale and sloshed to the beach and set her to dry land. Camille gently placed a hand to his wet cheek and, with a bravado she did not feel, she said, "Fear not, Jack. I'll be all right. After all, what could possibly go wrong?" And she gripped his collar and pulled him down and kissed him where tears ran.

Then she turned and started up a low dune and inland.

When Camille reached the crest she looked hindward. The Dragonship was backing water, pulling away, and in spite of Lady Sorcière's admonition, she almost cried out, "Wait! I would have you come along!" But she did not, for well did she know, but for one of the gifts—Scruff—she must go alone.

And so she went over the dune and down, then turned leftward and headed for the ramshackle town, where 'twas said Human slaves did dwell.

Her face smeared with dirt, her golden hair tied in a worn scarf, a small bundle of branch-wood on her shoulder as would a slave bear, Camille entered the streets of the town only to find them vacant. By starlight alone she made her way along the cobblestones. Of a sudden a voice hissed, "Here now, do you want to get yourself killed, out after curfew as you are?" Startled nearly out of her wits, Camille jerked about to see a dark figure in a doorway. Frantically, the figure motioned, "Quick, in here you stupid girl, before the patrol comes."

Now Camille could hear a tramp of feet nearing, and before she could react, the figure—a man, she thought—jumped out and clutched her by the arm and jerked her toward the opening, her bundle of sticks flying from her shoulder to clatter to the cobbles. "Har!" came a cry, and the sound of running, even as the man, wrenching her about, darted back and snatched up the bound branch-wood. He then yanked her 'round opposite and dragged her through the doorway and shut it behind, darkness plunging down, alleviated only by a faint ruddy glow of a few coals on the hearth. As Camille and her rescuer stood holding their breath in the dimness, the clatter of arms and armor and the slap of running feet hammered past.

Soon all fell quiet . . .

. . . *But for the pounding of my heart.*

After a moment, by the dull glow of the dying coals Camille saw the dark shape of the man move across the room, and she heard the scratch of a match, and in the wavering light he lit a tallow candle and turned and held it high, the better to see just who this fool was who had been out after curfew.

And Camille leapt forward and embraced him, crying, "Lanval! Oh, Lanval! It's you!"

34
Citadel

"*Chp!-chp!-chp!-chp! . . .*"

"Oh, Scruff," exclaimed Camille, pushing away from Lanval and looking into the high pocket. "I'm so sorry."

In the candlelight, Scruff looked up at Camille and cocked his head and chattered away, scolding her for mashing him between her and some man.

With wide eyes, Lanval, shabbily dressed, looked on this dirt-smeared girl, a girl bearing a rucksack and waterskin and bedroll, a girl with an angry little bird in a pocket on her thin-worn dress. "Mademoiselle, do I know you?"

"Lanval, it's me, Camille."

The steward of Summerwood Manor gasped, now seeing that the person under the dirt, this demoiselle, was indeed Lady Camille. He set the candle to the table, the tallow sending up a thin strand of smoke to add to the soot on the ceiling above. Then he took her by the hands and said, "Oh, my lady, what are you doing here in this terrible place?"

"Is my love Alain on this isle?"

"Aye, mademoiselle, the prince is here, a prisoner in the citadel."

Camille's knees nearly gave way, her relief so great in finding at last the place where her love was bound.

"My lady," said Lanval, reaching out to brace her, and he aided her to a chair at a table.

Camille took several deep breaths then said, "I have come to set him free."

As Lanval stepped to the fireplace and pulled two bricks

away, he said, "I am afraid that cannot be done. Not only does a fortress hold him, but so do the Troll curses."

"One by Olot and the other by his daughter?"

"Aye. Yet how know you this?"

"From something the Troll said in the Winterwood."

"Ah, I remember: you did meet Olot there," said Lanval, reaching in the hole behind the bricks. "—Here it is." He removed a small canister. "Until that encounter, 'twas but one curse, and that by the daughter."

"One or two, it matters not," said Camille bitterly, "if only I had known the content of the curses, then mayhap none of this would have happened. Oh, Lanval, it is all my fault disaster whelmed the manor."

"Nay, Lady Camille, not your fault, but that of the Troll-cast magic." Lanval popped the lid from the canister. "We'll have a spot of tea, and you can say how you came."

"But how did you get here, Lanval? Was it the wind?"

Lanval added a bit of branch-wood from Camille's bundle of sticks to the dying coals in the hearth, and hung a kettle on a fire iron and swung it over the blaze. Then he turned to Camille and said, "Aye, it was the wind; we whirled across the sky in that terrible howl, the Prince and the entire household of Summerwood Manor—all, that is, but you—to plunge down on this appalling isle to join the slaves already here as thralls to the Goblins and Trolls."

Tears welled in Camille's eyes and ran down her cheeks, and she said, "Oh, Lanval, I was stupid and foolish, and thus the calamity fell. A year and a day and nearly a whole moon agone, I contrived by candlelight to see Alain's unmasked face; that's when the curse struck and that awful wind did come."

Lanval sat down at the table across from Camille and said, "Nay, my lady, again I say, 'twas the fault of the Trolls, the cham and the chamumi and the ancient dread magic that somehow did come into their hands."

"Cham? Chamumi?"

"Troll words," replied Lanval. "Cham means king; chamum, queen; and chamumi, princess. Regardless, Chamumi Dre'ela, the Troll princess, set a curse upon the prince long past: Alain spurned her advances, and so she cursed him—broke a terrible amulet of clay she wore about her neck, one of Orbane's devices, we think."

Camille said, "One of the Seals of Orbane, or so Lord Kelmot thought."

"Lord Kelmot?"

Camille nodded. "He aided me after the terrible wind took you all away. I told him of the clay amulet Olot wore, and Kelmot spoke of the seals."

Lanval said, "Seals of Orbane: Olot had one, and Dre'ela another. Regardless, when Dre'ela broke hers, Alain was cursed to take the form of a bear in the day, though he could be either man or bear at night, whichever he chose. Further, Dre'ela's bane was such that he could never marry anyone but her. To this she added that if Prince Alain ever fell in love, and if his true love ever did discover that he was both man and bear, then he would have to marry Dre'ela in a year and a day and a whole moon beyond."

"Marry a Troll princess?"

"Aye. The wedding is three days from now."

Camille's face fell, and she glanced at the split and splintered stave. "Then *that* is the reason for the time I was given."

An eyebrow raised, Lanval looked at her, but she explained not. Instead she said, "Oh, Lanval, we must do something ere then."

The kettle above the fire began steaming. Lanval got up to attend it, and Camille glanced at Scruff, the sparrow again asleep in her dress pocket. While Lanval prepared the tea and once more hid the canister, Camille carefully set Scruff to a shelf above the table, where he ruffled a bit and then settled as she sat back down.

While they waited for the tea to steep, Camille said, "The second curse then, it was the cause of the wind." Her words were a statement, not a question.

"Aye, the cham, the Troll king, Olot, set a terrible curse on Prince Alain there in the Winterwood that night he and his Goblins assailed you and the Bear."

Camille nodded and sighed.

As Lanval poured two cups of tea, he said, "When you and the Bear first arrived at Summerwood Manor, the Prince told us that if you ever saw his face, then he and the entire household staff would be transported to this isle, and we would all become Olot's slaves. Hence, the seamstresses immediately set to making the masks he would wear, and that's how you first saw Prince Alain—his features hidden. Yet masks or no, the prince said that Olot had further added that none could tell you the reason for concealment else the curse would come due regardless."

"Yes," said Camille as she watched tea leaves swirl and settle in her cup, "the secrecy: all could know but me."

"Aye, my lady—not only of Olot's curse regarding seeing Prince Alain's face, but also of Dre'ela's curse were you to learn Alain and the Bear were one and the same. We simply could not tell you, though all else but you could know."

"Can we not break these curses?"

"Many mages tried, my lady—you saw numbers of them there at Summerwood Manor—yet none succeeded. Orbane's cursed clay amulets are simply too strong."

"There must be a way. There must."

Lanval shook his head. "I'm afraid only the Fates could defeat such great and powerf—"

Camille's eyes widened. "The Fates!" she blurted.

Lanval looked at her curiously.

"Lanval, we might just have a chance, though at the moment I know not how." An elusive thought skittered along the edge of Camille's mind, yet it was gone ere she could capture it.

"My lady?"

"Lanval, I have a tale to tell you, a story to unfold." Camille blew on her tea and took a sip and then began:

"After I committed my stupid mistake and the terrible wind came and hurled you all away, Lord Kelmot aided me in finding the Lady of the Mere. She was there that dawntime, sitting in the hollow of the oak, and both Alain and Kelmot had told me that she does not appear unless something dire is in the offing. Even so . . ."

When Camille's tale came to an end, the golden carding comb and shuttle and spool lay on the table along with Lady Sorcière's staff. One at a time Lanval picked up the gifts and examined them and then set them back. Then he sighed and looked at Camille. "Fates or no, I know not how these might be used to break the curse. Have you any thoughts?"

Camille turned up a hand. "None." Again Camille felt that there was something she should know lying on the edge of her mind, yet once more the wisp of a thought vanished.

Lanval frowned. "Would that the prince could advise us, for he is quite well-read and perhaps would know how to use these to the good."

"Is there any way I can see Alain?"

Lanval shook his head. "He has been kept prisoner in a suite of windowless, Goblin-guarded rooms in the citadel. None are permitted to see him but Olot, Dre'ela, and Te'efoon."

"Te'efoon?"

"She is the chamum, the queen."

Camille frowned. "No one else is permitted therein but Trolls?"

Lanval nodded. "Just those three."

"What about those who clean the chambers, change the bedding, and—"

"My lady, it is clear you have never seen how Trolls and Goblins live. There is no cleaning of rooms, changing of bedding, or the like. However, you do remind me that there are those who take drinking water and food to the prince's quarters, but they only enter when Alain is the Bear, and even then, the Bear is not present, but in a separate chamber in those same quarters, and so—Bear or prince—none ever sees him but the Trolls. They isolate him, for they have some vile plan they would not have upset, and the prince is at the center of all."

Camille looked at the three Fate-given gifts. "If I could be one of those who serve the prince, mayhap I can use the opportunity to bribe the guards."

Lanval's eyes widened. "Better yet, mayhap you can bribe the chamumi."

"Dre'ela?"

"Aye. She oversees those who bring the food and water, and I know she is quite fond of true gold; when we first came, every gold thing we had, be it ring or brooch or coin or aught else, she stripped and kept as her own, fashioning necklaces and bracelets and bangles from it all."

"Oh, Lanval, if she does love gold that much, then perhaps I do have a chance." Camille gestured at the gifts. "Surely these are true gold."

"Aye, they are," said Lanval. "Rare on this isle, for here only glittering Troll gold is found."

"Kolor spoke of it," said Camille. "—Troll gold, I mean. Quite worthless, he said."

"Indeed it is," said Lanval. "But list, Lady Camille: in your recounting did you not say the Fates warned you to keep these gifts. If so, then giving them to Dre'ela would be a mistake."

Camille shook her head. "Non, non. What the Sisters said was to hold on to them until near the end, for then they might do me some good." Camille glanced at the dwindling arc of light yet remaining on the dark disk of Lady Sorcière's stave. "Three days is all we have, Lanval, and so we *are* near the end; now is the time for their use."

Lanval frowned and said, "Lady Camille, I beg of you, try to remember the exact words of the Sisters, for if you relinquish the gifts when you should not, then even the Fates will fail."

Lanval's admonition struck Camille pale, and she somberly nodded and said, "I will, Lanval. I will."

The next dawning, Redcap Goblins came pounding on the doors. Camille and Lanval were rousted out and, along with two-score of others, were marched through the cool morn up toward the citadel, while the bulk of slaves—poorly dressed, as were all—were herded to work in the fields. Camille thought she caught a glimpse of Blanche, but she could not be certain. Even so, she did not cry out, for Lanval had told her the Goblins would lay about with whips should anyone speak. Camille had wondered how she could get Scruff to remain silent, and she had tried to leave him behind, yet he would have none of it, insisting instead on going with her. And so he was hidden in her high breast pocket, and he remained silent and still—peril was at hand, and he uttered not a peep. In another pocket, Camille carried what she thought might be the least of the gifts of the Fates: Urd's golden spool; though whether it was truly the least, she could not say. Yet it was the smallest of the three, and as such it best fit the plan she had in mind. Camille had carefully considered Lanval's warning concerning the Sisters' words of gift giving, and the other two gifts were hidden next to Lanval's meager hoard of tea in the hole behind the bricks.

As they approached the citadel, Camille's eyes widened in wonderment, for it was truly a formidable fortress, its great stone walls rearing up to castellated heights, towers in the corners fitted with arrow slits. Surrounding all stood a deep, dry moat embedded with sharpened spikes and stakes. A massive drawbridge spanned the moat, and a huge, bronze-clad gate stood open. Just inside the gate, in the mouth of the entryway was a portcullis raised high—fangs ready to drop on intruders, heavy bars to prevent entry as well. Above the gate a great, runic symbol—an *O*—was carven in the stone, and Camille could not but wonder who had it so sculpted—*Olot, most likely*, she thought. Across the bridge and into a passageway that jinked right and left they went, murder holes above, ready to rain death down upon any who won past the moat and gate and portcullis. At the exit of the corridor piercing the walls another portcullis and gate stood. Across an open, paved courtyard they were herded and through two massive, recessed doors, which led into the castle proper.

They came into a great hall, and the stench was nearly unbearable. Camille clapped a hand to her nose and mouth.

"Take swift and shallow breaths," whispered Lanval, "and breathe through your mouth only. Soon you will become accustomed to it."

How she would ever become accustomed to such a reek, Camille could not imagine, but she did as Lanval advised and took quick, barely drawn breaths. As the Goblins prodded them on inward, Camille looked 'round the great hall. By the early-morning daylight seeping in through high windows, she could see the chamber was filthy, with food rotting and shards of bones scattered across the floor. Flies buzzed among the litter of garbage, and a squirm of maggots wormed within the corpse of a small animal Camille could not identify. Spiderwebs filled nooks and crannies, and in one corner what seemed to be a mounded pile of excrement lay. Tables and benches marked this as a dining hall, with dirt and grease layering much of the furniture, and snoring Goblins lay about, some on the tables, others under.

A Goblin called out, "Rat catchers, to your traps!" and a score of slaves separated out, each with a guard, and they vanished through doorways and up stairs and down.

Camille watched them go, wondering what was afoot, yet she was shoved in the small of her back to stumble across the floor, one of the Goblin escort snarling, "No lollygagging, turd, or I'll take the whip to you."

Lanval turned to protest, but Camille shook her head *Non*, and so he said nought.

Past a low, one-step dais at one end of the room they were herded; three massive chairs of state set thereon. Through an archway they were goaded and into a huge kitchen beyond, and there they set to work, preparing a great breakfast for their captors.

"Would that I had some poison," mumbled a worker, and Camille saw that it was Cecile, one of the seamstresses with whom she had had such cheerful times in the sewing circle of Summerwood Manor. Even so, Camille said nought, having been warned by Lanval that should the Goblins even inadvertently find out who she was, then Olot would be the next to know. And so Camille pitched in as did everyone else, the whip the price of dawdling.

Soon great pots of porridge were bubbling, and a hundred or so carcasses of rats were gutted and skinned and set asizzling upon spits. Too, great pots of tea were brewed, and now Camille knew where Lanval had gotten his tin of leaves, though how he had managed to do so under the very noses of the ward, Camille could not say.

Finally, guards snarled orders, and the hot gruel and cooked rats and brewed tea were hauled into the great room to be served to the now-clamoring Goblins, Redcaps all.

That group was replaced by another, and that one by another still. But soon all Redcaps on the isle had broken their fasts, and finally meager portions of gruel were prepared for the slaves, and half of the kitchen crew was drafted to take the porridge unto the thralls in the fields.

But Lanval had Camille remain behind, for now they prepared food for Olot and Te'efoon and Dre'ela. An enormous number of rats were set to broil, and a great pot of oil of a sort—somewhat like that of olives—was heated, along with a cauldron of vinegar.

A gong sounded, and Lanval murmured to Camille, "We will serve them when they get seated. You are to stay behind, else if Olot sees you, in spite of the dirt smeared on your face and your golden locks bound in a scarf, still he might recognize who you are."

Even so, Camille stood in the shadows at the archway to watch as the Trolls came down a lengthy stairway along one wall and into the dining hall.

Olot led, and he was yet the same: a hideous, massive, nine-foot-tall Ogre with yellow eyes and green-scummed tusks, and he was still dressed in what looked to be the same greasy animal hides he had worn when Camille first saw him.

Next came a female Troll, "Te'efoon," whispered Lanval. A head shorter than Olot, she stood perhaps eight feet tall. If tusks and talons could be called dainty, then hers were a bit more dainty than Olot's, though her tusks were still scummed and her talons long. Te'efoon was dressed in what looked to be mottled green velvet, though the green could have come from mold. Sprigs of hair sprang from her dangly ears and one of her wide nostrils as well as from a large mole on her chin, though not a sign whatsoever grew on her knobby head. She was spectacularly ugly

Yet even more ugly was the third Troll, Dre'ela, some seven-foot-six or so. She had her father's tusks and her mother's hair and even longer talons than either. But worst of all was the cut of her burlap dress, for she had little modesty, and now and again as she descended the stairs—

Camille flinched away from looking at such a hairy and obscenely bright red—

"Stay here," again hissed Lanval, and then he and the others took sizzling hot rats and the oil and vinegar out to the low dais to serve the cham, chamum, and chamumi.

Yet crunching on a mouthful of rat bones, Dre'ela strode into the kitchen and smirked 'round her tusks at the women standing there. And she stood and stroked a necklace made of rings and brooches and bangles of gold strung on a hemp cord. Looped about each wrist as well were bracelets made of cord-hung golden rings and such. When none of the women reacted, Dre'ela growled and croaked, "It is time to feed my groom." Then she simpered and said once again, "My groom."

With a bucket of water, Camille stepped forward and into Dre'ela's miasma, much like the reek of her Troll sire: that of a rotting animal burst open after lying dead afield for a full sevenday in the glare of the hot summer sun, though in Dre'ela's case, there was a heavy overlay of musk.

Camille could feel wee Scruff's body trembling where he hid in her high pocket, yet in spite of knowing how frightened he was, she was careful to keep a vacant-eyed, slack-jawed, dull-witted look on her face. Even so, she, too, was afraid: afraid that Dre'ela would realize this slave was someone new, and then she would be exposed. Yet the chamumi's yellow gaze passed over Camille with no interest whatsoever. After all, she was merely a slave.

And as Lanval took up a great bowl of porridge, and Cecile bore several cooked rats, Dre'ela turned on her heel and led them all outward and across the chamber and up the long staircase.

And as they came to a hallway above, Camille softly canted a singsong chant:

"True gold is quite fine,
So softly gleams mine,
    Some think it surely best.
Troll gold is better,
Bright it does glitter,
    Outshining all the rest."

As they neared a Goblin-warded door, again Camille softly chanted her singsong cant, and Dre'ela whirled about and snarled, "What is that you are caterwauling, you piece of Human filth?"

Only then did Camille remember Chemine's warning: "Let not this girl sing to Goblins and Trolls."

Keeping the dull-witted look on her face, Camille then simply spoke the cant:

"True gold is quite fine,
So softly gleams mine,
    Some think it surely best.
Troll gold is better,
Bright it does glitter,
    Outshining all the rest."

A calculating look came into Dre'ela's yellow eyes, and she gazed at Camille's hands and wrists and neck, and upon seeing no gold there, the chamumi said, "Have you gold? True gold? I'll give you bright Troll gold for such."

"Oh, oh, would you, ma'amselle?" said Camille, digging in her pocket for the spool, a gaping smile on her face. "I-I love bright shiny Troll gold." Yet then she paused. "Bu-but, I-I'd also like to see your groom. Not as the Bear. No, not as the Bear. Not the Bear." Camille frowned, as if trying to dredge up a concept beyond what her slack-jawed look implied. And then she vacantly smiled and said, "Not Bear, but when he is Human. I-I hear from the others who once worked where he lived that he is pretty, too." Again Camille furrowed her brow, as if slow thoughts moved through her mind. Then she grinned again and said, "Maybe even as pretty as Troll gold, but not as shiny. Not as shiny."

"See my groom? I should think not, for only I can—"

In that moment Camille took the golden spool out from her pocket and held it up for the chamumi to see. Dre'ela's eyes widened, and she reached out and snatched the spool from Camille. "A wedding present," said Dre'ela.

"C-can I-I see the groom tonight?" asked Camille, smiling a gape-jawed smile.

"Certainly not," snapped Dre'ela. "None are to see him until after the ceremony, when I become the Princess of Summerwood."

"I-I will bring you another golden wedding present tomorrow if you let me see him tonight."

Dre'ela's eyes flew wide. "You have more true gold?"

"I-I know where to find some."

Dre'ela's eyes narrowed and she looked at Lanval. "Does this dull-wit have more gold?"

Lanval, holding the great bowl of porridge, shrugged and said, "Chamumi Dre'ela, I know not. Yet what harm would come of letting my daughter Naïf see the prince?"

Dre'ela glanced at the golden spool and then at Camille and said, "Very well, Naïf, you may come to see my groom tonight, but you must bring more gold on the morrow."

Lanval cleared his throat and, when Dre'ela looked at him, he said, "What of the curfew, Chamumi Dre'ela? If my simple daughter is to be out after dark, she will need a permit."

Dre'ela turned to Camille. "I will send an escort to your hovel this night. Set a lit candle in your window."

As Camille bobbed her head in understanding, she hid both glee and disappointment behind her half-wit countenance: glee for she would see Alain at last; disappointment for she would not be free to come and go on her own.

Dre'ela turned and signed to the guard. The door was opened, and, following the chamumi, Camille and Lanval and Cecile entered one chamber of a suite, where they set down the water and porridge and cooked rats and then took up the previous day's bucket and pot and left. Camille had been hoping to see the Bear, yet, as Lanval had said, he was not in the rooms they entered. *Mayhap he will detect my scent, if Dre'ela's stench doesn't cover all.*

That night, when Redcaps pounded on the door, Lanval looked at Camille and held up a cautionary hand; he glanced at the bricks behind which were hidden his cache of tea and the shuttle and carding comb, and now even sleeping Scruff, then he answered the summons. Goblins bulled inward, shoving the steward aside. And they began pulling the bedding apart and overturning tables and chairs and opening drawers and such. They searched through Camille's rucksack, tossing clothing and vellum and pen and ink aside and all else they found of no worth to them, though, after sniffing to see what it was, they kept the flasks of oil; they found the pocket sewn within, yet nought of value was there, for Camille had left all coinage hidden nigh the sandy cove where the *Nordavind* had landed. Thoroughly they searched all—room, bed, furniture, drawers—even stirring through the ashes within the fireplace. Lastly they pawed Camille and Lanval, searching for whatever might be hidden upon them, yet they found nought. At last they snarled at Camille and escorted her out, leaving Lanval to clean up the mess left behind.

As the steward closed the door, he smiled to himself and glanced at the untouched bricks, for well had he anticipated what Dre'ela's Redcaps would do. Then he stepped across the room to retrieve Scruff from the hollow behind the bricks, fully expecting to be scolded by the little bird.

As the chamumi poured a score of Troll-gold nuggets into Camille's waiting hands, Dre'ela said, "Remember, stupid girl, you must bring me a gift of true gold on the morrow, and I will give you even more of this much brighter gold."

Camille grinned foolishly and crowed:

> *"True gold is quite fine,*
> *So softly gleams mine,*
> > *Some think it surely best.*
> *Troll gold is better,*
> *Bright it does glitter,*
> > *Outshining all the rest."*

Camille laughed and shoved the nuggets into her pocket and then gaped up at Dre'ela and said, "I-I would like to see the groom now."

Dre'ela signed to the Redcap guards, and the door was opened.

With her heart hammering in her breast, Camille followed the chamumi into the entry chamber, where Dre'ela paused before a mirror to admire her new bangle of true gold, the spool now on its own hemp cord about her neck. Finally, she turned and led Camille past the day's porridge pot and water bucket and into a room beyond, and there in a great, canopied bed lay Prince Alain asleep.

Camille nearly burst into tears, but whether they were to have been tears of joy at seeing his beautiful face or of distress that he was unaware, she did not know. Yet she could not let Dre'ela suspect that aught was afoot other than a simpleton desiring to see the groom. And so she held her emotions to herself, and reached into her pocket and drew out a nugget and managed to gape a grin and say, "Oh, he is quite pretty, almost as pretty as shiny gold. Can I-I stay awhile and try to see which is prettier?"

No answer came and Camille turned and saw that Dre'ela was back before the mirror and turning the bobbin this way and that, watching the candlelight gleam on the spool.

Swiftly Camille stepped to the bed and she put her hand to Alain's lips and then shook him by the shoulder. "Alain, Alain, it's me," she whispered. "Alain, wake up."

But the prince lay slack, unresponsive, almost as if he'd been—

"What are you doing, oaf?" snarled Dre'ela, striding into the chamber.

Camille started, and then turned with a lackwitted grin and held up the Troll-gold nugget and said, "I-I was trying to see which is prettier, shiny gold or the groom."

Dre'ela glanced at her own golden bangles and then at Alain, as if she, too, were trying to decide which was prettier. Then she grabbed Camille's wrist in a painful grip and jerked her from the room, saying, "You've seen him, and that's all you bargained for. I'm sending you back."

In spite of Dre'ela's clawlike clutch, "C-can I not stay in the castle?" asked Camille, hoping the chamumi's answer would be yes, for surely Alain would waken, and if she could somehow divert the guards—

"No, you fool of a Human," snarled Dre'ela. "You know treacherous slaves are not permitted in the castle at night."

Camille hid her disappointment behind her lackwit face and said, "Th—then tomorrow night I-I will give you more true gold, and you will give me shiny gold, and I-I will see the groom again, eh?"

Dre'ela's yellow eyes gleamed with the thought of more gold from this fool, and she said, "Oh, yes, Naïf. . . . Indeed."

* * *

"I think he was drugged, Lanval," said Camille, bitterness in her voice.

Lanval blew out a sigh of exasperation. "Drugged? I wouldn't put it past her."

Camille's shoulders slumped in despair. "What will we do, Lanval, what will we do? I mean, there are only two days left, and I can't talk to him if he's drugged. And Dre'ela is there in the chambers as well. I need to be alone with him to see if he can tell us how the Fates or their gifts might be used to break the remaining curse."

"I know not, my lady, yet there is this I *do* know: we must not let hopelessness or gloom o'erwhelm us, else we are fordone ere we begin."

Camille took a deep breath and let it out. "You are right, Lanval. It is time to think and not lose heart."

With effort, Camille set aside her emotions, and she fell into long thought. Finally she said, "Have you any cord, Lanval?" At the steward's puzzled nod, Camille grinned and said, "I believe if I give Dre'ela a piece of cord along with the golden shuttle, she will step out from the chamber and back to the mirror to fix a new necklace. That will occupy her a short while. Yet it still leaves me with Alain being drugged."

Lanval turned up his hands, but then Camille exclaimed, "A note!" She rushed to her rucksack, tossing aside the things Lanval had so carefully repacked. "I can leave a note in his food, mayhap in his porridge. Then, no matter how Dre'ela is drugging him, he can be on the alert for such and avoid it."

A frown crossed Lanval's face. "You must be careful in what you say, for should the guards or Dre'ela or Olot or Te'efoon discover your note, it must not let them know aught."

"Can they even read, Lanval?"

"I don't know, my lady, but we must assume that they can."

Camille nodded and sat awhile, then finally penned:

Every bird is wary in what it drinks and eats,
especially a tiny brown sparrow sitting in a tree,
scruffy little soul just like . . . ~C~

Camille then frowned and said, "Ah, but I know how the Bear eats, and he is likely to gobble this note down should I place it in his food. We must find another way."

She locked at Lanval, but he shrugged.

And then Camille said, "I know! I'll scent it with something I am certain does not exist in that castle."

"What is that, my lady?'

"Soap!" said Camille, and she rummaged through her rucksack and drew out the last of the Summerwood Manor soap she yet had, now nought but a chip. As she rubbed it across the vellum, she said, "We'll slip it under the porridge bowl, where the Bear will surely scent it." She paused and looked at Lanval. "Oh, my, but there is this: will Alain know of the note if the Bear does find it?"

"I believe so, Ma'amselle, for once he said that when he is a man he remembers all the Bear has done, though when he is the Bear at times he has trouble holding on to his Humanity. Or so the prince did say."

"Good " declared Camille, folding the vellum over and over, then dripping candle wax along the edges to seal the ink against liquid; "Just in case," said Camille.

Then she rubbed more soap over the outside. "Surely the Bear will scent this."

"But what if he does not?" asked Lanval. "What will you do if on morrow night you find the prince asleep?"

"If this fails, then when I return tomorrow night I will slip out and hide nigh the cove till day comes on the land, and then set a signal fire to call Kolor and the Dwarves and Big Jack. I had hoped to avoid combat, but we may have no other choice."

Lanval shook his head and sighed.

"What?" asked Camille.

"My lady, I think it will take a miracle for any to invade that stronghold."

A bolt of fear shot through Camille's chest, but she said, "Then let us pray it does not come to that."

As Camille followed Dre'ela up the stairs, she heard a peculiar chanting. Ere coming to the top, Dre'ela paused and pushed out a hand to hold Camille back, and they waited. When the chanting ceased, the chamumi went on, Camille following. At the landing, Camille saw down the corridor and just disappearing 'round a corner a blot of darkness streaming tatters and tendrils, like a ragged shadow moving away, and it seemed to Camille she heard muttering in the tattered shadow's wake. It reminded Camille of something or someone, and just as they reached the Goblin-guarded door, she remembered the ragged silhouette that had flown across the face of the moon the night the Goblins had come to Summerwood Manor, the night Lord Kelmot and the Lynx Riders had slain them all. Too, it was the night the Goblins had slaughtered two of the black swans, and the rest had flown away. Yet what might that streaming black thing have been, or the one that had vanished 'round the corner, Camille could not say.

Dre'ela motioned the guards to open the door, and then she turned to Camille and held out a hand. "I'll have my wedding gift now."

Camille reached into her pocket and pulled out the cord and the shuttle. "Chamumi Dre'ela, have you my shiny?"

Dre'ela's eyes widened with greed at the sight of the golden shuttle, and she hurriedly gave Camille another score of Troll-gold nuggets and snatched the shuttle and cord from Camille and rushed in to stand before the mirror. Camille slipped past her and into Alain's bedchamber. The prince lay on the bed, one hand tightly clutched and held to his chest.

Rushing to his side, "Alain, Alain, my love," whispered Camille, " 'tis—" But there was no response, though the prince did breathe. Camille shook him, yet he lay slack. Then Camille opened his fist, and therein was the note Lanval had hidden under the porridge bowl that very morn. *He found it and read it and knew I was here, and he was waiting for me. But then, somehow, he could not avoid being drugged . . . or, wait! Bespelled!* That *was what the chanting was about. Someone bespelled my love with sleep. Oh, what am I going to—?*

"See my pretty?" croaked Dre'ela.

Camille tucked the note into her pocket and then, hoping that Dre'ela would not see the tears running down her face, she turned and gape-mouth grinned and held up a nugget and said, "Shiny."

Dre'ela stood in the doorway, her golden-shuttle necklace gleaming in the candlelight next to the golden spool.

"It wasn't a drug," said Camille weeping, "but a spell instead. He had the note. He had the note. Yet it will do us no good."

"There, there," murmured Lanval, as he held her and stroked her hair. "It will be all right. It will be all right."

Camille pushed herself away. "How can you say that, Lanval? Tomorrow is the very last day, the very last day of all." She snatched up the stave and shoved it toward Lanval. "See!" A hairline-thin crescent was all that was left on the dark disk.

"My lady, you said yourself, you will signal the Dwarves."

"But, Lanval, it was you who said it would take a miracle for any to invade that stronghold."

Silence fell between them, but finally Lanval said, "I see no other choice. You must slip out to the cove and set the signal fire. And even though I would rather be at your side, I must stay behind to be in the citadel then, so that I can try to open the gates and let them in."

Camille's eyes lighted with a bit of hope. "If you can get the gates open, then there *is* a way to invade after all."

Lanval took up matches and candles and handed them to Camille. "They took the oil, yet use these to start a fire with dry branches, and when it is well burning then cast green ones on. That should raise a plume for the Dwarves to see."

Camille nodded and packed her rucksack. She took up the cane and slid it through the loops, then fetched sleeping Scruff and put him in the high breast pocket. "Ready," she said at last.

"When the next patrol passes," said Lanval. He blew out the candle and went to the window and raised the blind and peered into the darkness beyond. Long he looked, and then he gasped.

"What is it?" asked Camille, making her way through the darkness to his side.

"Across the street," he whispered. "On the roof."

Camille stared through the darkness, and finally in the starlight she made out the silhouettes of three or four Goblins atop the low building opposite.

Lanval said, "No doubt they are Dre'ela's guards, waiting to follow you wherever you might go to fetch items of true gold."

"Can we not provide a diversion, something to draw them away?" whispered Camille.

Lanval hissed, "I could do so, but then who would open the gates?"

Camille sighed. "Let us wait, for mayhap they will go away after a while, or even fall asleep."

Long did they wait, yet the Goblins remained alert. Finally Camille said, "Mayhap we can set this house afire and in the confusion I can slip away. —Oh, but no. Wait. If we set the house afire, then the Dwarves will think it the signal, and come entirely too soon."

Plan after plan they examined, rejecting them all. The only

one which seemed to have a chance of succeeding was to place against one wall all the wood they could gather, including the furniture, and setting a candle among tinder such that when it burned down far enough it would start a fire . . . sometime after they were in the citadel proper, they hoped.

And so it was they closed the blind again and broke apart the table and chairs and bed and the drawers in the one chest of drawers, and added the firewood, too.

Dawn came, and Goblins went through the town pounding on doors, rousting everyone out. Lanval lit the candle that stood among wood shavings just ere his own door was hammered upon, and he and Camille stepped outward, she with her rucksack and stave and Scruff in the high pocket, and the last of the golden gifts in the pocket at her waist. As they started away amid the kitchen crew, Camille looked back. Redcaps dropped down from the low roof of the building opposite Lanval's, and—

Oh, no! They're going in to search Lanval's place once more.

Moments later, one of the Goblins charged back out holding the candle aloft, and he yelled, "You'll pay for this, you Human dung, once the cham finds out."

Tears flooded Camille's eyes, yet she brushed them angrily away. *No time for tears, Camille, but for finding a way out of this mess.* And she thought furiously, yet nothing of worth came to mind.

It was only as they crossed the drawbridge that she noted that *all* the slaves were being herded into the castle.

And lo! she found herself walking alongside Blanche, and at Blanche's side strode Renaud.

"Blanche," she hissed, " 'tis me, Camille."

Blanche gasped, surprise in eyes so dark they were black, and by this feature alone did Camille then know that this was truly her Blanche. "Camille?"

Camille nodded.

Blanche jabbed Renaud and whispered, and Renaud turned his own grey eyes to Camille in surprise.

As they tramped through the jinking passageway through the citadel wall, Camille whispered, "You do not work in the fields?"

Blanche shook her head and reached out and clutched Camille's hand and said, "None shall work in the fields this day, the day of the chamumi's wedding."

Camille sucked in air through clenched teeth, and Blanche squeezed Camille's hand in sympathy, but ere she could say aught else, they passed into the castle proper and Camille and Lanval and the kitchen crew were separated out and set to cooking, while the remainder of the slaves—all but the rat catchers—were put to work cleaning the great hall, for here would the wedding be held and the cham, chamum, and chamumi would have the chamber look quite splendid on this, Dre'ela's wedding day.

Breakfast came and went and food was taken to the Bear, and still Camille had no plan. The great hall was swept and shoveled and, time after time, slaves carried litter out through the gates to cast it into the depths of the dry moat.

Midmorning came, and then late morning, and finally, as the last of the trash was borne outward, the great gong sounded, and Redcaps came running, and all the slaves were gathered into the great hall, for Chamumi Dre'ela would have many guests at her nuptials, even if some were nought but Human slaves. And so, with the Goblins wielding scimitars and tulwars and spears and standing ward, all the slaves were gathered in and all the Goblins as well, and the great doors were shut behind, for the chamumi would have no one sneaking out during the upcoming ceremony. Again the gong sounded, and, amid huzzahs from the Goblins, the cham, chamum, and chamumi, *and the Bear* came down the long stairway, the Bear a pale yellow-brown.

The wedding was at hand.

And Camille could not think of aught to do.

While Goblins yet shouted, the three Trolls took to their thrones, and they left the Bear at the foot of the low dais, perhaps as a sign of his servitude.

Once again the gong sounded.

Silence fell.

Olot stood and held out his hands as if in benediction, and he smiled, his scum-coated tusks gleaming as of fresh, green slime.

And then he bellowed for all to hear, "In but moments my fine and lovely daughter"—a great shout of leering approval broke out, and Dre'ela stood and awkwardly curtseyed, golden spool and shuttle on hemp twine about her neck dangling and swinging, along with stolen rings and brooches and other such, all made into bangles for neck and wrist. She sat back down, not at all modestly, and some Goblins crowded forward the better to see. Nodding his approval, Olot continued: "Soon my fine and lovely daughter will be married to the Prince of the Summerwood." Now Olot gestured at the Bear, and once again Goblins howled in delight. Olot raised his hands, and when quiet fell, he said, "A prince who is cursed to be a Bear by day, though he may choose to be a Man or a Bear by night, a curse my daughter herself laid upon him for spurning her advances, and now he must wed her, for his Human lover found out he was the Bear. And by my own curse, he and his household were brought to this isle to serve us, for his Human face was seen by his Human lover, who betrayed him despite being warned. And so by the geas set upon him by my clever daughter, he must marry her, and she is greatly aroused by the prospect of mating with a Bear." Now all the goblins hooted with excitement, and Dre'ela smiled her own tusky smile.

Olot held up his hands, and quietness fell. "Why should we do this? Why mate my daughter to a filthy Human? Or even a Bear? Heed! I have been planning this ever since our former master was thrown into the Great Darkness. Once we were free of him, I said to myself, *no more* would we bow to *any* master. Instead, we and our kind will become the masters ourselves. And as masters it is our due to live in the lap of luxury. And we will do so in Summerwood Manor and rule the Summerwood, for, with this marriage, Dre'ela will be the rightful and true princess of all therein."

At this pronouncement, Chamum Te'efoon hooted with glee and clapped her hands, and all the Redcaps whooped in elation.

Olot let the shouting nearly run its course. Finally he raised his hands and called out, "Now let us get on with the ceremony, and it's a formality, I know"—he grinned a tusky grin—"but does anyone wish to challenge this wedding?"

And even as Redcaps smirked at one another, from the back of the chamber a small voice said, "I do."

35
Challenge

Olot's yellow Troll eyes flew wide in disbelief. "What?" he roared, glaring out over the assembly, looking for the miscreant.

"I do so challenge!" Camille cried out. "I challenge, for the prince is consort to me!" Shaking off Lanval's restraining hand and gripping her staff, Camille pushed forward through the throng. As she emerged from the crowd to step toward the low dais, she cast off her head scarf, and her golden hair cascaded down. And many slaves—those from Summerwood Manor—now gasped in recognition.

"You!" cried Chamumi Dre'ela, rage in her eyes.

"You!" cried Olot, lust in his.

The Bear raised his nose in the air and snuffled, then rushed to Camille's side, and she threw her arms about his neck.

Even as she hugged the Bear, Te'efoon roared, "And just who are you to make such a claim?"

Camille stood and called out, "I am the Princess of the Summerwood, consort of Prince Alain."

"You claim to be his wife?" shouted Te'efoon. "Were banns posted, a king notified, perhaps the king of Faery?"

Camille stood defiantly, yet she said, "No. No banns. No notification of a king. Yet we are joined by the bonds of love and also by common law."

"Ha!" shouted Olot. "Since I am the first cham, the first king, to know of this, I deny that a marriage between you and he ever took place."

But Camille was not to be deterred, for she had finally captured the elusive thought that had skittered 'round the edge of her mind—a thought concerning the Fates and wagers and living up to the terms of a contest. She looked into the faces of all three Trolls on the dais—cham, chamum, and chamumi—and said, "Nevertheless, I do challenge."

A great hubbub filled the hall, among slaves and Goblins alike, for this chit of a girl challenged a Troll.

A great smile swept over the faces of the Trolls, tusks gleaming greenly, and Cham Olot raised a taloned fist and said, "Then I name the terms: combat to the death."

Rage in his eye, the Bear reared up on his hind legs and roared, his black claws ready to strike.

Goblins shrieked, and Dre'ela cried out in fear. Chamum Te'efoon leapt up to flee, her throne crashing over backwards. Olot quailed, thrusting his hands out before him, to ward off any coming blows.

And, lo! Scruff struggled up out of Camille's pocket and took to wing! The tiny sparrow *flew*! Camille gasped in astonishment as up and 'round he circled, and then shot through a high window slit and away. Yet Camille had no further time to wonder, for even then the Bear took a step toward Olot.

"Remember my curse, Bear: if you kill me, then you die," shouted Olot.

Camille reached out a hand, trying to stay the Bear, and she cried, "Oh, Bear, oh, Alain, I would not have you die. Better that it be me."

But the Bear was not to be deterred, and took another step forward.

Olot threw up both hands. "All right, all right, not combat to the death. She can name the challenge, but I shall name the terms."

At that, the Bear looked back at Camille, and she nodded.

The Bear dropped to all fours.

"One of the terms," said Olot, looking at Camille, "is that whatever you choose, the means for such must be in this chamber."

Again the Bear looked at Camille, and again she nodded, all the time her mind racing: *What can I possibly challenge him with? A singing contest? No! Remember Chemine's warning: "Let not this girl sing to Goblins and Trolls." Besides, Trolls and Goblins no doubt think that croaking or roaring is splendid singing, and I can do neither, hence I would lose were one of Olot's stipulations be that goblins would judge.*

What about échecs? I am a fair hand at that game. We could use the squares of the stone floor as the squares of the board, and slaves and Goblins as the pieces. Ah, but the Goblins are the only ones with weaponry, and they would slay a slave every time Olot captured a piece, and surely he wouldn't let the slaves bear weapons on their part. No, not échecs.

"Come, come, girl," growled Olot. "Name the challenge."

Camille looked at the Bear and then at the slaves, then turned to Olot and said, "Riddles. A game of riddles."

The Bear settled back on his haunches, even as a murmur whispered through the slaves.

"You have named the challenge," said Olot, "and these shall be the terms: again I say the riddle must concern something within this great throne chamber." Olot laughed, his gaze sweeping about, for well did he know the room, free of debris though it now was.

A murmur of dissatisfaction rumbled through the slaves, for these terms meant that many a riddle could not be posed.

But Camille looked about the chamber and agreed.

"You ask; I answer," said the cham.

Again Camille nodded, then she said:

> *"To and fro does it go,*
> *A long thread trailing after,*
> *Leaving weaving in its train,*
> *The tapestry of the crafter."*

Olot looked stunned, glancing back at Chamum Te'efoon and Chamumi Dre'ela. And Dre'ela held up the shuttle dangling about her neck and said to Camille, "This, you stupid girl: a weaver's shuttle."

Camille frowned and said to Dre'ela, "It was your father's to answer, but this once I will accept interference." Camille then turned to the cham. "Is that your answer, too?"

"It is," said Olot, both cham and chamum beaming proudly at their very ugly offspring, Dre'ela simpering at Olot and Te'efoon in return.

"Perhaps you shouldn't have listened to your daughter, sire, for you lose," said Camille.

"*What?*" Roared Olot and Dre'ela and Te'efoon together. "What else can it be?" shouted Olot.

Camille pointed to the base of the overturned throne and said,

"To and fro does it go,
A long thread trailing after,
Leaving weaving in its train,
The tapestry of the crafter."

And there under the throne a spider was repairing the last of its web, weaving back and forth between the legs of the upset chair of state. "The answer is a spider," said Camille. "Now I'll take my Bear and leave."

Some of the slaves laughed at the cleverness of this chit of a girl, many of those from the household of Summerwood Manor clapping. But at growls from the Goblins and the brandishing of swords and spears the mirth was swiftly quenched.

"Three!" roared Olot. "You must pose three altogether, and should you lose even one, then you lose all. Those are the terms."

At this the Bear growled, and so did some of the slaves, but Camille nodded her agreement, saying, "Three it shall be, my lord, yet this time and the next you and you alone must answer."

The Troll cham glanced at his daughter and wife, and then at the golden-haired girl he would most dearly like to bed. Finally he nodded his agreement.

Camille again glanced about the chamber, and then she said:

" 'Round and 'round 'tis spun,
On which the thread is wrapped;
'Round and 'round 'tis spun,
Until it is fully lapped."

Chamumi Dre'ela pulled the golden spool on its cord from 'round her neck, and she began tossing it up and catching it, even as she stepped in front of her sire and glared at him and jerked her head toward the bobbin.

Olot looked at her and growled, "You were wrong the last time, daughter." He gazed about the chamber, and then laughed and said:

" 'Round and 'round 'tis spun,
On which the thread is wrapped;
'Round and 'round 'tis spun,
Until it is fully lapped."

And then it was the cham who pointed at the upset throne, where the spider turned a captured fly 'round and 'round as it wrapped it in webbing. "The answer is a fly," crowed Olot. "The fly is spun up in webbing for the spider to hang in his larder."

As slaves groaned, for surely Camille had lost, Camille said, "This time you should have heeded your daughter, sire, for she had the answer all along: it is a spool, a spinning-wheel spool."

"See!" shrieked Chamumi Dre'ela in fury.

"Spool?" roared Olot.

"Indeed, my lord," replied Camille.

The slaves now hooted aloud at clever Camille's second out-witting of the cham of Goblins and Trolls.

"This is trickery," roared Olot. "No more riddles with double answers, answers which you can pick and choose the one I do not guess." The cham flexed his great thews and said, "For the third and last challenge, I want a physical contest, not one of twisted words. And recall, should you lose this one, then you lose all."

Camille was stunned, for although she was keen of mind, what could she physically challenge the Troll with? And it had to be something within the chamber.

'Round she looked, and 'round, but nothing came to mind. Finally, in despair, with tears in her eyes Camille looked at her beloved Bear, her beloved Alain. And there, matted in the Bear's fur was a great blob of candle wax, the wax she had spilled on Alain that terrible night when all had been snatched away, the wax a sign of her betrayal of him. But then she realized that the very thing which had doomed him might also be his salvation.

She turned to the Troll cham and announced, "The third and last challenge, sire, is to clean the Bear of candle wax, but no single hair of the Bear's fur may be harmed, else you lose."

Shoving Olot aside, plucking and pulling on the Bear's fur, scraping with her talons, Dre'ela tried her best and failed, the wax stubbornly clinging to fur. And the Bear did growl all during the trial, yet he stood quite still.

Chamum Te'efoon snarled, "Out of the way," and she shoved the chamumi aside. And with sweat beading on her knobby, bald head, she, too, plucked and clawed at the growling Bear, her talons a bit more dainty, if dainty could be said of Troll talons. Yet, she had no better success than did her daughter.

Olot hurled the chamum aside, and he clawed at the wax, to little effect, and the Bear added a show of teeth to his growl.

Then Olot whirled on Camille and snarled, "This is an impossible task. None can do so. I declare the contest null and void."

"But if I clean it," said Camille, "then you lose, agreed?"

Sneering, Olot nodded his concurrence.

Camille reached into her pocket and pulled out the third and last gift: the golden carding comb, the comb Skuld told her to hold on to till the end, for then it might do her some good.

"Not fair," snarled Dre'ela.

Te'efoon nodded and called out to Olot. "Our daughter is right, for this pretender has a comb."

But Camille replied, "The only rules were, whatever the contest, it had to concern something in this chamber, and this comb was certainly in the chamber."

A rumble of agreement muttered among the slaves.

Camille knelt before the silent Bear and combed the fine, fine teeth through his fur, and in but moments, all the wax was gone, and not a hair on the Bear had been damaged.

"Now I will take my Bear and leave," said Camille.

"Never!" cried Olot. He turned to the Goblin guard and bellowed, "Kill her!"

"For the Lady Camille," shouted Lanval, turning to the nearest Goblin and smashing a fist in its face.

"For the Lady Camille," shouted Blanche, kicking a Goblin in the gonads even as Renaud crashed a bench over another's head.

And the hall erupted in sound and fury, some slaves grabbing up whatever came to hand and attacking the foe, while others fought with nought but fists, feet, and teeth. The Bear roared and reared up, and with mighty blows smashed aside Goblins left and right, keeping them back from Camille, though she shrieked and flailed away with her staff whenever one did come nigh.

Even so, the Redcap Goblins had bladed weapons—spears and tulwars and scimitars—and nearly all of the slaves did not, though a few here and there had managed to wrest a blade away from a downed Goblin. And so the tide turned, for bronze sheared through hands and arms and legs, necks and guts, and slaves fell, pierced or hacked or slashed, and red blood streamed in rivulets across the floor.

But then—*Boom! Doom!*—the great doors to the castle came crashing inward, and, led by a tiny sparrow, the Dwarves, with their axes and war hammers and maces swinging, rushed into the fray, Big Jack and Lady Bronze among them and slaying Goblins with every strike.

Redcaps fought with fury, yet the iron of the Dwarves shattered goblin bronze, and Redcaps shrieked and tried to flee, only to be cut down from behind. Te'efoon and Dre'ela fled screaming up the stairs, but, just as they reached the high landing above, Scruff flew into the face of Te'efoon, and she reeled back and lost her balance, and she reached out to grab on to anything to save her from the long fall, her talons snatching Dre'ela's necklaces of stolen gold, and shrieking, together they tumbled over the edge to plummet headfirst to the stone floor below, skulls cracking open like rotten melons, necks snapping like twigs.

Chirping, Scruff flew back down to Camille and alighted on her shoulder, yet she paid little heed; all the battles had ended but one, and Camille cried out in distress, for with battering fists, Olot hammered back the Bear, staggering the massive bruin. Yet this enraged the Bear, and, mad with unbridled fury and striking mighty blows, he savaged the Troll cham, smashing him to the floor. But Olot threw up a hand and squealed, "Remember my curse: if you kill me, then you yourself are slain."

"Oh, Bear," cried Camille, "I would not have you die."

And in that moment the Bear hesitated, but Big Jack shouted, "Well, Troll, I am not so cursed!" And with a single blow of Lady Bronze, Olot's head went flying.

And with the last bane gone, the Bear vanished, and there stood Alain.

And so it was at that very instant, at the instant Camille's Alain had been set free, it was high noon above, with the new moon lagging on one side of the zenith and the sun just passing beyond, and in that moment the island could truly be said to lie east of the sun and west of the moon there at that time and place.

Yet even as Camille rushed into Alain's arms, she looked about at the dead and the dying—slain Goblins and slaughtered slaves and three very dead Trolls—and at the grief-stricken survivors, those with loved ones dead, and at the wounded crying out for aid. And Camille burst into tears and clutched at Alain and buried her face in his shoulder, for even more death had come, and it was all because of her, or so it was she did think.

Both Kolor and Lanval called for the untouched survivors to

begin binding the wounds of the injured. And as most of the Dragonship crew and many of the household of Summerwood Manor set to the task, both the captain and the steward turned toward Alain and Camille. But then Kolor started and gasped in disbelief, and he breathed, "Maiden, Mother, and Crone, but am I seeing true?" And he pointed at the dais, where an ebon-cloaked, hooded figure appeared . . .

. . . and then another . . .

. . . and then one more . . .

. . . and all the Dwarves did kneel.

36
Pledge

Dark as ravens, the three figures stood unmoving, the hoods and hems of their black cloaks outlined respectively in silver, gold, and jet. Two held staves; one did not. All in the hall before them fell silent, but for the groans of the wounded and the sobbing of Camille. Then the silver-trimmed figure stepped to the edge of the dais and said, "Weep not, Camille, for you did well."

Camille looked up into Alain's face and then disengaged from his embrace and turned toward the dais. "Lady Sorcière," she gasped, and wiped at her tears ineffectually.

The figure cast back her hood, revealing silver eyes and silver hair, and Camille curtseyed low and said, "Forgive me, Lady Skuld, I took you for someone else."

Even as Skuld smiled enigmatically, the other two figures cast back their hoods, revealing golden-eyed, yellow-haired, matronly Verdandi, and black-eyed, white-haired, toothless, ancient Urd. And all the Dwarves dropped their gazes, for surely it would be unwise to stare into the face of Destiny, be it beginning, middle, or end.

And though the three Fates now stood before the assembly, Camille thought she could faintly hear the sound of three looms weaving.

Amazement in his eyes, for there stood Wyrd and Lot and Doom, Alain bowed, and all former slaves who were able bowed and curtseyed as well, Big Jack lowering Lady Bronze and bowing, too.

"Pish, tush," said Verdandi, waving a negligent hand. "This is no time for formalities. Instead, care for the wounded."

As Dwarves and Humans resumed the task of tending the injured, Skuld looked at Camille and said, "Although what Fate gives, most assuredly Fate can take away, we three would be most appreciative if you would return the gifts to the givers."

"Oh, indeed," said Camille, and she took the carding comb from her pocket. "Here is one"—she stepped forward and gave over the golden comb to Skuld—"but I'll have to get the other two, for the shuttle and bobbin are on—"

—Yet of a sudden the shuttle was now in Verdandi's hand and the bobbin in Urd's. Camille was relieved, for now she wouldn't have to touch Dre'ela's corpse. And then the golden gifts vanished, as if returned whence they had come.

Camille looked back at Alain, and he yet held wonder in his eyes, for not only were the three Fates standing before him, but it appeared his love had had dealings with them. She held out her hand and he stepped to her and took it, and together they faced the three Sisters.

With her stave in hand, Verdandi lifted the gold-trimmed hem of her cloak and stepped down from the dais and looked up at Big Jack and said, "Would you walk with me?" Big Jack bobbed his head and offered his arm, and together they moved among the those who were injured, Lady Verdandi saying a word here and touching a cheek there, and all seemed the better for it.

"Here, you, up off your knees," snapped Urd, gesturing at Kolor. "A hand if you please."

Kolor leapt to his feet and aided Urd to step down from the dais, the crone then leaning on him as she shuffled among the slain, prodding Goblins and Trolls with her walking staff, as if to make certain they were truly dead.

But Skuld remained on the dais, and she looked at Camille and said, "It would please me much if you would give me the other gift as well, for truly it is mine."

Camille frowned. "But my lady, what other gift—?" Camille furiously thought: *The only other gifts I was given are—*

In her left hand, Camille yet held on to the stave, and she gave it over to Lady Skuld. And lo! the moment Skuld took the staff, the splits and cracks and splinters vanished, and the vine blossomed again.

"Then you are the Lady of the Mere," said Camille in wonder, "and Lady Sorcière, too."

Skuld nodded. "As I said, there at the beginning of the River of Time, my sisters and I are bound by rules, and no matter that

I am Skuld or the Lady of the Mere or Lady Sorcière, I must follow those rules. Did you not pledge service to me there on the edge of the mere, and answer riddles ere I responded to your need, telling you where to find your love as well as giving you the staff and the sparrow?"

At mention of the wee bird, sudden tears came to Camille's eyes, and she reached for Scruff on her shoulder to return that gift as well. But Skuld thrust out a hand of negation and said, "No, you will yet need the sparrow for the great peril which is yet to come."

Even as Camille's heart leapt to her throat, Alain put a protective arm about her. Then he gestured at the dead Goblins and Trolls. "But Olot and his minions are slain, my lady. Of what peril do you speak?"

"Camille yet owes me a service, Prince Alain, and it will be more perilous than that which she did for you."

A look of hardness came into Alain's grey eyes, as if he would challenge Lady Wyrd Herself, or face dangers dire, but at that moment Camille quietly asked, "What would you have me do?'

"No, my love," said Alain, "not you alone, but we two together." He turned to Lady Skuld. "What would you have us do?"

Camille bowed her head, dreading the answer, but Skuld smiled and said, "Fear not, Camille, for I would not ask either you or Alain to betray your consciences. As to the service itself, it is impending, for the one who would pollute Time's River beyond all repair is yet to come, and there is one before him who stands athwart your path, an acolyte who even now prepares the way for his return.

"But that event wends down the River of Time and will not wash over the worlds for yet long whiles."

In that moment Verdandi as well as Urd returned to the dais, Big Jack handing Verdandi up, Kolor handing Urd. And the three then stood side by side, and the sound of weaving looms again came faint on the air.

Skuld looked with silver eyes at Camille and said, "Remember this, Camille: even though what I have seen is now woven in the tapestry of time, great efforts by the determined can alter those events. Heed, you and Alain and any who walk at your side have time to prepare and mayhap even change that which I have foreseen, for it is only when Verdandi weaves and Urd binds that the pattern of the tapestry is fixed."

"I remember," said Camille.

Skuld turned to her sisters and asked, "Is there aught you would add?"

Verdandi looked at Camille and Alain and said, "For now, return to Summerwood Manor, and enjoy the immediate days."

Urd cackled and winked at the two, then pointed a shaking finger at Camille, and said, "Remember all I have told you, child, *all* . . . and act."

The clack of shuttle and slap of treadle and thud of batten swelled, and of a sudden the Sisters vanished, the sound of weaving no more.

"Maiden, Mother, and Crone," breathed Kolor. "Maiden, Mother, and Crone."

37

Restoration

Camille, aiding Renaud to splint Blanche's broken arm, found herself next to Kolor, who was helping Big Jack bind a wound across a woman's back. "How did you get here so quickly," she asked, "from your station asea?"

"We were not there," replied Kolor.

Camille glanced at Kolor and frowned. "Not there?"

"Did I not say when you went ashore that should we not hear from you in a timely manner, we would not stay hidden long?" As Camille nodded, Kolor said, "Well, when we had not seen any signal for two full days and nights, we slipped into the cove just ere this dawn, and then—"

"And then we argued about what to do," growled Big Jack. "I was all for—"

Kolor snorted. "He was all for an immediate raid, but the Goblins were locked up in this great fortress, and if the prince were prisoner within, well . . . —This is a formidable redoubt and—"

Big Jack's jaw jutted out. "And if we'd gone over th' wall in th' dark like I wanted to—"

"But the dawn was already upon us, Jack."

"All because of your dithering," shot back Big Jack.

Kolor sighed and said to Camille, "But then you and the others were marched from the town to the citadel, mayhap to be locked up as well. I thought Big Jack was going to attack the fortress all by himself, yet we managed to talk him out of it, for we believed surely you would think of something to do, Camille, or so it was we hoped."

Big Jack nodded, but made no comment as Kolor continued: "Long we waited, and long we watched as load after load of rubbish, it seems, were hauled out of the castle and thrown from the bridge into the moat. As the sun neared the zenith with the yet-to-be new moon still in its grasp, we heard the distant sound of a gong, and all the walls were abandoned, and lo! the bridge was left down with the gate wide ajar. Now we debated whether or no we had been seen and whether 'twas a Redcap ruse to draw us into a passage with murder holes above."

Fashioning a sling, Renaud grunted and shook his head. "We were all in, and they thought no one else was about, and so, what was there left for them to ward against? Nothing, they believed."

Kolor nodded in agreement and said, "As we discovered when we heard another distant gong, and shortly thereafter, Camille, your wee bird came flying straight for us, and we knew you were in trouble, and that no signal would come, though mayhap you'd sent the sparrow."

Camille shook her head. "Scruff did it all on his own." She looked at the bird, delight in her eyes. "And he flew, oh, how he flew. It was marvelous."

"Indeed," said Kolor, "and we were quite surprised, him with his wing and all. —Regardless, Big Jack took off running, little Scruff leading the way, and we were right behind. And a bit of trouble we found you in, too."

"There, Blanche," said Renaud. "All done."

Her forearm now splinted and in the sling, Blanche turned to Kolor. "Thank you, Captain, you and your crew. Thanks to you as well, Jack. Without your aid, we would have all been slain." She looked at Renaud, tears in her eyes, and whispered, "All." She pulled Renaud to her and kissed him.

Her own eyes tearing, Camille looked for Alain. He was kneeling and speaking to Jules, the lad with his head bandaged and but a stump for a hand. But then Renaud said, "Come, my lady. More need our aid."

Camille turned and followed the blacksmith, and they stopped at the side of a bleeding man, moaning and rocking and holding close the corpse of a woman slain.

At last all of the wounds had been bound, broken bones splinted, and the injured were moved to suitable quarters in the seaside town and made comfortable.

Then those who had escaped unscathed began the task of removing the dead from the citadel, to be buried or set upon pyres or slipped into the sea, as was the custom of their folk, wherever they were from. Forty-six Humans had died, twenty-one of these from Summerwood Manor. No Dwarves had been slain in the battle, though three had been slightly wounded. All eighty-two Goblins and the three Trolls had been slaughtered, and these were dragged to a bluff and hurled into the sea.

And even as this was being done, a Dwarven horn sounded, and hurtling through the sky came a Dragon on the wing. Dwarves scrambled to arm themselves, though what they might do against a terrible, fire-breathing Dragon, none could say. But Camille called out, "Kolor, Kolor, stand down your crew. 'Tis Raseri come to the isle." But Kolor was not in the courtyard, was instead casting Goblins into the sea, and the Dwarves left on guard took up axes and maces and shields.

Raseri circled 'round the towers, then settled down atop the wall castellations, his rudden scales with black running through gleaming dully in the afternoon sun.

And lo! upon Raseri's back rode an Elf, all alabaster and gold. And Camille called out in amaze, "Rondalo, Rondalo, do my eyes deceive, is it truly you?"

Rondalo, a sword girted at his waist, leapt to the banquette and strode along the wall and down one of the ramps.

Camille grabbed Alain's hand and crossed the courtyard, tugging the prince after.

Even as Rondalo approached, he pressed a hand to his forehead, a look of distress in his eyes.

"What is it, Rondalo?" asked Camille as she came to a stop before him.

Rondalo looked about, then he said, "Iron."

On the wall above, "Iron!" boomed Raseri, then he bellowed at the sky: "IRON!"

At this great shout, Dwarves flinched back, and Big Jack came running out through the doors of the castle, Lady Bronze in his grasp. Then he looked up to see Raseri, and though Jack blenched, onward he came to stand ward at Camille's side.

Yet pressing his hand to his temple, Rondalo said, "My lady, we came to help, but we saw as we circled above, these iron-bearing Dwarves had already dealt with the Goblins and Trolls."

Raseri flexed his great claws and said, "Too bad we arrived too late to join in the battle."

"But how did you—? No, wait. Lord Rondalo, may I present Prince Alain of the Summerwood. Prince Alain, Lord Rondalo. Without his help I would not have found you."

Both Rondalo and Alain bowed to one another, a look of resignation in Rondalo's gaze, a look of reservation in Alain's.

"And on the wall above is Raseri, also without whom I would have failed."

Alain grinned and said, "We met once, apast. Even so, Lord Raseri, I thank you for your aid." Alain bowed, and Raseri dipped his head.

"Lord Rondalo, Lord Raseri, this is Big Jack, who aided me as well."

Big Jack bowed to Rondalo and Raseri, and then he said to Rondalo, "You came with th' Dragon?"

As Rondalo nodded, Camille said, "But you and he are mortal enemies; I do not understand."

Rondalo smiled and said, "It is Raseri's to tell."

The Dragon lowered his long neck down and said, "I thought many long days about what you said, Camille, especially the Keltoi tale you told of me and my battle with Audane on his wedding night, and then the coming of Chemine.

"I followed the trace of Rondalo's taste until I came upon the bard in a village where the cattle were quite stampeded, perhaps because I snacked on a couple. Then—after some back and forthing, and shoutings, and brandishings of blade, and blowing of fire—I spoke to Rondalo about what you had said, and together we agreed that perhaps you were right. We declared a truce and I flew Rondalo to Les Îles, where we put the premise before Chemine. And since neither Chemine nor I can remember aught of a battle between Rondalo's sire and me, nor of anything ere we found ourselves in Faery, we both thought you might have had the right of it. Chemine in turn consulted seers and such, but they were of no aid. Finally, we three decided you indeed had the right of it: it was a Keltoi tale the gods made manifest. Chemine's hatred of me then abated greatly, as did that of Rondalo, and so we declared the truce would last for a year and a day and a whole moon beyond, a time we picked because of you."

Camille looked at Rondalo. "But what of your sworn oath of vengeance?"

Rondalo turned up a hand. "You showed me the way around it. If I never visit Raseri's lair, I need to fight no Dragon. But even if I do go to his lair, I think the only combat we may do is a game or two of échecs."

Raseri raised his head up and looked about and then hissed, "More iron bearers come running."

"Kolor and the burial detail, I shouldn't wonder," said Big Jack.

"Oh, Jack, would you tell him, tell them, to stay away. The iron affects Rondalo . . . Raseri, too, it seems. It twists the aethyr, warping it, bending it, or so I was told."

As Big Jack rushed off, Rondalo looked at Camille in surprise. "You know of iron's effect on the aethyr?"

"Not really. It was what Captain Andolin said, when he and the *West Wind* left Leport because the *North Wind* with its crew of iron-bearing Dwarves was even then coming into the harbor. Caused an ache, he said."

"And a disorientation," said Rondalo, grimacing. "Still, even had we known of the iron, we would yet have come."

"Well, I'm certainly glad you did," said Camille, "for both of you are my friends, and my heart rejoices to see my two friends have set an old enmity aside and have become comrades. Even so, how did you find us here?"

Raseri said, "Flying well above the River of Time, I followed the faint trace of your taste to Leport; there I landed upon the headland, and Rondalo went down to speak with the inhabitants, for I believe they all hid under their beds at the sight of me."

Rondalo smiled and said, "Harbormaster Jordain told me that you were striving to reach Troll Island beyond the Sea of Mist. I went back up to the headland, where Raseri waited, and the only island either of us knew that lay beyond those baleful waters was this one, Orbane's stronghold of old."

Alain's eyes flew wide in startlement. "Orbane? This was Orbane's isle?"

As Raseri and Rondalo both nodded, Camille said, "Olot said his former master had been cast into the Great Darkness; *that* was Orbane. And the carved *O* above the gate . . . I thought it was for Olot, but instead it must signify Orbane."

She turned to Alain. "Oh, love, don't you see, that explains how the Trolls came across the Seals of Orbane, the seals which they used to curse you. Olot must have found the seals after Orbane was gone."

Rondalo said, "Yet it still does not explain how the Trolls came to know the way of their working, for the Trolls have no magic of their own. I think they must have had help from a mage, someone skilled in the art."

Camille took Alain's hand. "Perhaps the same someone who cast sleep upon you, my love, or so I do think happened the night you held my note, and most likely the night before."

Alain's grey eyes turned grim. "If it is true that a mage aided the Trolls, we need search the citadel for him."

Camille frowned. "Search we should, yet I think no mage is here, for surely he would have attended the wedding were it so."

"Mayhap you are right," said Alain, "yet if there is no mage here now, he may one day return, and we must be ready." He paused a moment and then added, "I'll ask Big Jack and Kolor and his crew to help me search the castle, and if we find no mage, then we'll stand ward against his return."

Camille nodded and said, "When we search we must be alert for someone streaming tatters and tendrils of shadow, for that is what I saw when the Goblins came to Summerwood Manor, and again when I believe you were bespelled by sleep.

"Yet, heed, a mage is not all we need to seek, for Lord Kelmot told me there were seven Seals of Orbane. Two were used to curse you, Alain—one by Dre'ela and one by Olot, all to gain control of the Summerwood—but what of the other five? Surely *those* we need to find."

Alain said, "Agreed. And if any are found, they must be destroyed."

Raseri growled. "I wouldn't be so quick to destroy them, Prince Alain, for they do have some good uses."

"How can anything that curses be good?" asked Camille.

Raseri turned his yellow eyes upon her and said, "Two were needed to trap Orbane in the Castle of Shadows; I know, for I was there."

Camille's eyes flew wide at this bit of news, but Alain said, "Then that leaves three."

"I would help you search," said Rondalo, "but the iron—"

Camille laid a hand on the Elf's arm. "I would not have you nor Raseri be anguished any longer. Alain and Big Jack and the iron-bearing Dwarves and I can deal with that which is yet to be done, and I would ask you to go away from here and to a distant place of comfort."

Raseri gazed at Camille and Alain and said, "But I would fly you both back to the Summerwood."

"We will sail back with Captain Kolor on the *North Wind*," said Camille.

"Then I would suggest, my lady," said Rondalo, "that you sail around the Sea of Mist rather than across it. They say there's a monster within."

"There is," said Camille, grimly. "It took thirteen of Kolor's best down into the sea."

"One day you will have to tell me that tale," said Rondalo. "It sounds like one the bards should sing."

"I would hear it as well," said Raseri. "But not here amid the twist of iron." Then he looked at the Elf and shifted a wing. "Rondalo?"

Rondalo reached out and took Camille's hand and kissed it. Then he bowed to Alain and said, "You are fortunate indeed."

Alain nodded, then gripped Rondalo's hand, and said, "Come to Summerwood Manor, my friend, for, as a bard, you must hear her sing."

Rondalo quirked a smile and winked at Camille and said, "He's not yet heard your tale, eh?"

Camille laughed and said, "Not yet, Rondalo, but soon."

Alain looked at Camille and then Rondalo, once again reservation in his gaze.

Then Rondalo strode up the ramp and mounted Raseri, and the Dragon said, "I, too, will come to Summerwood Manor, when it is time." Then Raseri looked at the stone castle and a small lick of fire curled from his mouth. "It's been long since I did battle with one of magekind, yet I will return now and again to see if a mage is about."

Rondalo grinned and his hand went to the pommel of his sword. "I will accompany you, fell Drake."

"Done and done," said Raseri. Then he looked down at Camille and Alain and said, "Shield your eyes."

Camille and Alain each put a hand to forehead, and with thunderous flapping of his leathery wings, Raseri took to the air, dust and sand and small pebbles swirling and pelting about in the courtyard below.

Raseri circled once and again, then came swooping in low o'er the wall, and he called out, "Had I known that this was the place east of the sun and west of the moon, you could have been here much sooner."

Booming with laughter, up he flew and up, spiralling into the sky, and then he arrowed away and was soon lost to sight.

When the Dragon was gone, Big Jack and Kolor and the Dwarven burial crew came in through the gate. And Kolor looked at Camille and Alain, and asked, "What did he have to say?"

Alain took a deep breath and then exhaled. And he replied, "He told us this was Orbane's stronghold, and three of the cursed seals are missing, and there may be a mage about."

That night, Camille and Alain took to one of the abandoned houses in the small seaport town, and they lay down together for the first time in a year and a day and a whole moon beyond . . . yet even as they kissed, even as a wee bit of fire kindled in the heart of each, both Camille and Alain fell asleep of weariness.

The next dawning, though, after grain and a cup of water had been set out for Scruff, Alain took Camille gently in his arms and kissed her long and deeply, she returning his ardor. And they explored one another most thoroughly, Alain quickening, Camille softening, fire running through their loins. He slipped inside her, and she rose to meet him, and in the sharing did they complement and fulfill one another and become complete themselves.

Scruff paid no heed to the gasps and moans of either, nor of Camille's calling out of "Oh, Alain. Oh, Mithras, sweet Mithras."

A moon altogether they searched the citadel—Orbane's former stronghold—with the Dwarves tapping on walls and floors and lintels and mantels and stairwells and corners and bookcases and desks and other such, looking for hidden panels, secret doors, disguised caches and catches and levers, without any success. Yet in some chambers in the towers they discovered scrolls and tomes and alembics and astrolabes, and containers of minerals and powders, and boxes of dried plants and flasks and vials of liquids, and crystals and stone tiles marked with runes, and jars of various animal parts, many suspiciously like those of Humans and perhaps of other beings, and five decks of arcane cards somewhat like those Lisane had used, though these held symbols and depictions that to Camille seemed somehow obscene. In a room far below, past the dungeons deep, they found more scrolls and tomes, pamphlets as well, along with mortars and pestles and mineral salts and burners and the like. Too, there was evidence—water and a sleeping pallet and food partially eaten, food gone stale but not moldy—that this room had of recent been used, yet by whom, none could say.

But of shadow-streaming mages and clay amulets—the Seals of Orbane—they found nought whatsoever.

In that same moon the citadel itself was cleansed of all traces of Goblins and Trolls, the former slaves discovering a large and unused supply of soap with which to wash down the floors and walls and tables and counters and all other surfaces the Trolls and Goblins had defiled. Much of the bedding had to be burned, as it was clearly beyond redemption, though stores of cloth were discovered, and the Summerwood seamstresses set about making new sheets and coverings.

In that moon as well, the former slaves declared Alain and Camille to be the new prince and princess of L'Île de Camille, for that is what they now called it.

Finally, Alain decided that they had searched all they could, and he gathered together the populace, and he asked them what they would.

"My lord," said one of the former slaves, "I and mine would stay, for in spite of ill memories the isle itself is quite pleasant, with rain aplenty and good soil and fair weather for the most. With its bountiful sea and plentiful crops, we could find no better were we to return whence we came."

Calls of agreement sounded throughout.

Alain looked at Lanval. "My lord," said the steward, "I have spoken with the staff of Summerwood Manor, and we would return with you. Captain Kolor says there is room on the *Nordavind* for the forty-eight of us who survived, fifty counting you and Lady Camille."

Camille glanced at Kolor, and he grinned and said, "We'll be a bit crowded, but she'll take that many back to the distant shores."

Alain nodded and then said, "Is there aught any would add?"

A woman stepped forward and curtseyed. "My lord, who will govern us? Who will have the final say if you and Lady Camille are not here? You are our prince and princess, and we would have you stay."

Now a clamor of agreement rose up among those remaining.

Kolor looked at Alain. " 'Tis a worthy addition to your holdings, Prince Alain, for long have mariners needed a seaport in these remote waters. I ween it would be bustling with trade in a trice, were it to become known to explorers and captains far and wide."

Alain looked at Camille, and she said, "Appoint a steward until we can send someone in our stead."

Now another clamor arose, and finally the woman turned

and raised her hands and quiet fell. Then she said to Alain, "We don't want someone in your stead, my lord and lady, though a steward we will abide. Have you no kindred to send to watch over us as we wait your permanent return . . . or even an occasional visit to this far-flung outpost of yours?"

"My kindred are all watching over principalities of their own," said Alain. Then he smiled and glanced at Camille and said, "Yet there is a youth who is kindred of Camille who would make a splendid prince regent once he is trained."

Camille's eyes widened in surprise, and she turned to Alain and said, "Giles?"

"The climate seems right," said Alain, smiling, "with its warm days and cool nights. And from what you say of him, he has the temperament and humor to be kind and gentle. Too, if he is as clever as you, well then, who could ask better?"

Camille smiled and nodded, but then frowned. "But who will train him, who be steward here until Giles is ready, assuming he even takes up your offer?"

Now it was Alain who frowned. "Even after Giles is trained, he will need a right-hand man." The prince looked over at Jules, the lad's own right hand gone. "Or perhaps a left-hand man." Alain stepped to the boy. "Jules, would you train as steward of this isle, to serve Prince Regent Giles?"

Jules grinned and dipped his head. "Indeed, my lord prince."

Alain smiled and then turned and faced Lanval, and said, "There is one whom I would trust to train—"

Lanval thrust out a hand of negation. "My prince, there is a better choice." Lanval turned to Andre the gardener and said, "Will you, old friend, come out of retirement and train both of the lads? After all, it was you who trained me and then took to your flowers. Besides, they need a good gardener here, for the fields have improved considerably since you took a hand."

Andre shook his head, then said, "Very well, Lanval. Very well, my prince. But I would return to Summerwood Manor once the lads have reached their years and are well prepared."

Camille stepped forward and kissed Andre on the cheek. "I will miss you, my friend," she said. "Train them well and quickly, for I look forward to your return. There is much that needs tending in the gardens of Summerwood Manor."

Camille then stepped to Jules and embraced the boy and whispered, "I could think of no better companion for my brother Giles."

"Done," said Alain, then he looked about. "Is there aught any would add?"

Big Jack cleared his throat, and when Alain nodded his way, Jack said, "Someone who knows arms and armor needs t' stay and teach these folk how t' defend themselves, not only from sea brigands, but also from th' mage, should he return. Now there's plenty of tulwars and scimitars and spears left, and so I'm thinkin' that I'll stay behind, at least until these folks are ready."

Alain grinned and said, "Well and good, Jack, and so shall it be. You will make a splendid armsmaster."

Big Jack nodded and then added, "But I do have one request, Prince Alain." Then Jack looked at Kolor. "I would ask that the *North Wind* come back in a year and a day and a moon beyond and take me on as crew, for in spite of my spewing my guts now and again, with what other mates can one take on Goblins and Trolls t' lay them by th' heels."

Kolor raised an axe and said, "I would welcome you and Lady Bronze, and so shall it be done."

And thus it was decided: Jack would stay as warchief for a year and a day and a moon, and Andre would remain as steward, with Jules as his understudy, and, if agreeable to the lad, Giles would be sent and be trained as Prince Regent of L'Île de Camille.

Another fortnight passed ere all was ready, and with tears in her eyes, Camille bade au revoir to Jules and Andre and Big Jack, and when she kissed the big man on the cheek, she whispered, "Thank you, Jack, for doing to Olot what my Alain could not, for with one blow of Lady Bronze you set him free."

Big Jack shuffled his feet, his own eyes brimming, and he managed to choke out, "My lady, should you ever have a want, all you need do is ask."

Then the *Nordavind* set sail, with sixty-seven Dwarves aboard, along with forty-nine souls of the Summerwood, counting Alain and Camille and Scruff.

They did not sail through the Sea of Mist, but went around instead.

All in all it took seventy-two days to reach a port on the far distant shores, Kolor dropping anchor at the town of Atterrage in the Bay of Abri, for it was much closer to the Summerwood than other ports in Faery.

They spent a week in Atterrage, resting and arranging for

transportation. Alain also arranged with Kolor to return to this port on his way to get Big Jack, some ten moons from then, and take on Giles as a passenger and deliver him to the L'Île de Camille, or to give passage to whomever Alain chose as regent-in-training should Giles not wish the task.

Finally came the day of departure, with the *Nordavind* going one way, and the household of Summerwood Manor going another. With tears in her eyes, Camille bade au revoir to Kolor and crew, and just as Big Jack had vowed, so too did Kolor pledge that should Camille ever need him and his crew again, they were at her beck. She kissed the Dwarven captain on the cheek, and then stepped back to Alain.

And Camille and Alain stood adock in the dawn and watched as the *North Wind* once again blew out over the waters. And when they could no longer see the ship, they sighed and turned about and left the sea behind.

Two fortnights after, as dusk drew down on the land, a train of ten red coaches came curving up the oaken lane and unto Summerwood Manor, and to Camille's wondering eyes, the place stood warmly lit by lanterns of welcoming. As Camille and Alain alighted from the lead coach, tiny Lord Kelmot strode forth to greet them, a lynx padding at his side. Scruff, asleep in Camille's pocket, took no note of the cat.

As the other red coaches disgorged their passengers, "Welcome home, my lord and lady," said Kelmot, with a wee, sweeping bow. "I was told you were on your way."

Alain bowed and Camille curtseyed in return, and Camille said, "But how, who—?"

" 'Twas a message from Lady Sorcière," said Kelmot, "delivered by Jotun the Giant, though he was very small when I spoke with him, yet quite a bit larger when he left. Regardless, my lord and lady, welcome home." Kelmot stepped aside and gestured Camille and Alain within.

Alain offered Camille his arm, and together they entered the manse, Lanval and the staff following after. And they found the place well lighted and clean and set to rights, the damage of the wind all gone.

Camille looked down at Kelmot, an unspoken question in her eyes. He grinned and said, "I called upon a few friends of mine to help—Brownies, I believe you would name them, though to me they are the Nis and the Pech."

"Where are they?" asked Camille. "I would like to thank them for—"

Of a sudden, Alain put a finger to Camille's lips. "My love, one should never thank a Brownie, else he will leave in high dudgeon."

Camille frowned, but then smiled and curtseyed to Lord Kelmot and said, "Well, if that is the case, my wee friend, my thanks do then go to you."

Kelmot smiled and bowed in return, then leapt astraddle his lynx. He grinned his catlike grin, catlike teeth and catlike eyes agleam, and he said, "I am glad you are safely home, my lord and lady, and now I must be off to mine." And the lynx bounded out through the open door and vanished into the dusk.

Alain closed the door after, and turned to Camille and said, "Well, my love, I wonder what there is to do, now that our guest is gone."

Camille looked at Alain in all innocence and said, "Indeed, what is there to do?" Then she grinned and said, "I'll race you." And she darted for the stairs.

38

Mazes

They sat in the game room, playing échecs. It was Alain's move. As he studied the board, Camille studied him, for though she had lived with Alain for a moon and a fortnight on L'Île de Camille, and another seventy-two days with him on the *North Wind,* and then even more days in Atterrage and on the journey to Summerwood Manor, she yet marvelled at the fact that she could see his beautiful face and see him in the daytime, to stroll the grounds of the manse or to take meals in the gazebo or to wander the hedge maze or to do whatever they would, all with the sun above.

Finally Alain exhaled, and turned his king on its side. "You take this one, my love, yet I'll take the next."

"Ha!" said Camille, grinning as she set the board again, with its spearmen and warriors and heirophants and such.

A discreet knock came at the door, and Lanval entered. Alain looked up. "Yes?"

"My prince, 'tis a trivial thing, but someone has stolen the small lockbox."

Camille laughed. " 'Twas I, Lanval. I am the miscreant. I had forgotten all about it. You'll find it buried in Andre's compost pile by the stables. I hid it after I took some coins to see me through my quest, though little good it did, me being robbed in Les Îles. Dig in the center, and there it will be. —And, oh, by the bye, you'll find it damaged; I had to break in with a hammer and chisel . . . Renaud's."

Alain laughed. "Quite the burglar are you, my dear? Tools and all?"

Camille fluttered her eyes at Alain and said, "Why, whatever do you mean, sieur? Would I even know how to handle such devices? I am sure I would be all thumbs."

They both broke out laughing.

Lanval smiled and shook his head and left them to their games.

Alain sobered and said, "Burying the box in compost, that was clever, my dear. But even more clever was presenting to Olot those double-answer posers, and challenging him to remove the wax, and solving the riddles of the Fates Themselves."

Without comment, Camille smiled at Alain, then gestured at the board. She would play white this time.

He nodded, and she unconventionally opened the game by stepping forward the spearman who stood just to the right of the white queen's heirophant.

As Alain pondered his response, Camille's eyes wandered to the échecs board on the central table, the one reserved for Alain's sire and dam should they ever be found. Then she stared up at the portrait of Lady Saissa, she with her black hair and black eyes. Then she turned and looked at Lord Valeray's portrait, grey eyes and dark hair, though not as black as the lady's. And as she looked, a thought eased at the edge of her mind, something that Alain had said, yet she could not quite recall what it—

"Your move, Ma'amselle Burglar."

Camille grinned, and studied the board. Alain had sprung his black king's warrior across—

"I have it!" she shrieked, Alain starting back. Camille leapt up from the table and darted to peer at Lady Saissa's portrait, then whirled and dashed across to Lord Valeray's. "Alain, I might know where your parents are."

"What?" Alain, scrambled to his feet. "Where?"

"Oh, love, I might be wrong, but you said that I had solved the riddles of the Fates Themselves, but there is one I had not, for I knew not then what it meant. I still might not know what it means, but I do hope I am right."

"Which riddle is that, Camille?"

"Urd's last."

" 'Tis done," said Alain. "The ribbon is laid."

"Good," said Camille, "for they know not the path, and we can but hope the ribbon will guide them, for neither of us nor anyone else must lead; 'tis my belief they need do this voluntarily, else it might have no effect."

Alain nodded.

Camille hugged him. "And be prepared for disappointment, for I am not certain I am right. But if I am, then something wonderful will happen."

At Alain's second nod, Camille said, "You go on in; I'll be at the gazebo. And remember, when I ring the bell—"

"I remember," said Alain, his voice tight with tension.

With Scruff on her shoulder, Camille turned and headed for the gazebo, while Alain entered the hedge maze.

A quarter candlemark later, just as the sun reached the zenith, Blanche stepped from the manor and started for the gazebo, a tray of food in her hands. And at nearly the same time, Renaud rounded the corner of the manse and headed for the gazebo as well.

When they arrived, as Blanche laid out the lunch on the table—bread and cheese and petit fours and tea, and a small bit of millet seed for Scruff, who hopped down and began pecking away—Camille craned her neck about as if looking for someone and said, "Renaud, the prince would like to know how goes the crafting of shoes for the horses to come, now that the Bear is gone. But I don't see Alain at the moment. Hmm . . . " Her eyes lighted on a small bell on the table. In spite of her tension, she laughed gaily and said, "I know, why don't I just ring for him?"

"Oh, Camille," said Blanche, "the prince isn't someone you just—"

But Camille took up the bell and jingled it quite hard, the tinkle ringing across the sward.

As Camille set the bell back to the table—

"Help! Help!" came a cry.

Scruff lifted up his head.

"Oh, help me!" came another cry.

Scruff took to wing, flying for the maze, even as Camille cried out, "Alain, Alain!"

" 'Tis the prince," gasped Blanche, but Renaud was already running toward the hedge.

Camille scrambled to her feet and followed Blanche, the handmaiden running swiftly after Renaud.

Now others ran toward the maze, one of these Lanval, though he and they were yet a distance away.

Renaud was first to the entry, where he hesitated, for he did fear this place: "I think if I ever went in there, I would lose my-self forever," once he did say to Camille.

Then Blanche reached the entry, and she hesitated too, for she shared Renaud's fear.

But then Alain called out again, "Oh, help me! Help me!"

Gritting his teeth, Renaud, with Blanche right behind, darted inward, both casting their fears aside. Without realizing it, Renaud followed a long ribbon lying on the ground and twisting into the labyrinth.

Camille stopped at the entrance, and even as Scruff flew back over the hedges and landed on her shoulder, chirping an irritated "chp!" Lanval arrived. "Keep the others out, Lanval," Camille said, then she darted within.

Twisting and turning, Renaud and Blanche ran through the high hedgerows, the ribbon guiding their feet. Winding and weaving, jinking left and right, at last they came to the very center of the maze, and there they found Alain waiting, standing beside the statues of his parents.

And even as they gaped at the completely unhurt prince, and then looked full at the effigies, a great burning came over the smith and handmaiden; Alain cried out and leaped forward to aid, but the furious flames cast no heat, and the two within were not harmed. And so he stepped back, as Camille, now at the center as well, chanted Urd's final allusion:

> "Nearly dual,
> It is the key;
> That which two fear
> Shall set four free."

And Blanche and Renaud disappeared in the flames as the glamour burned away, and when the fire dwindled and vanished, where they had been now stood Lady Saissa and Lord Valeray, each of them somewhat dazed.

In the faraway town of Lis, there where Camille had first boarded the red coach, in the stable across the street from the Golden Trough, two people who but for the hue of their eyes were twins of Camille's Blanche and Renaud, two people who had had no memory of who they had been, two people who, some eighteen years past, had titled themselves Clarisse and Georges, those two people suddenly knew their identities: they were the true Blanche and Renaud. How they had lost their memories, how they had been whisked from Summerwood Manor to the town of Lis those eighteen years agone, they had not the vaguest idea, though each of them knew that magic was somehow involved.

But in the maze at Summerwood Manor: "Mother! Father!" cried Alain with tears in his eyes, and he embraced them both.

Great was the rejoicing there in the labyrinth, and great the joy as well when the King and Queen of the Forests of the Seasons emerged arm and arm with Alain and Camille.

Lanval bowed low and glanced at Camille and then said, "My lord Valeray, my lady Saissa, your quarters are ready and raiment has been laid out, for we were expecting you."

Valeray raised an eyebrow. "Expecting us?"

Lanval canted his head toward Camille and said, "The Lady Camille told us you would come . . . or rather that you might."

"It was someone we trusted," said Lord Valeray, "one of magekind who had been here before and has come since, and who cast the curse that transformed us, and in evil glee made us fear the very thing which would set us free."

"The sight of our likenesses in the heart of the maze," said Lady Saissa.

"Was this done using a clay amulet?" asked Camille.

At Valeray's nod, Alain growled, "A Seal of Orbane." Then he looked at sire and dam and asked, "And who was this trusted mage who came and did this to you?"

Rage filled Lady Saissa's eyes, and she said, "It was—"

"Hradian!" exclaimed Camille. "The witch Hradian."

Saissa looked at Camille in surprise. "Yes, but how did you know?"

Camille turned up a hand. "When you said it was someone you trusted, then did I remember how Hradian was dressed: the crone accoutered in black, with black lace frills and trim and danglers. She looked as if she were streaming tatters and tendrils of shadow, just as was the silhouette that flew across the moon, just as was the glimpse of the figure I saw there in Orbane's citadel. And when she came to Summerwood Manor, ostensibly to remove a curse, she was sly-eyed and leering. Oh, how she must have gloated, knowing that she was at the root of all."

Saissa and Valeray both nodded, for even though they had been restored, they yet remembered all that had occurred when they were Blanche and Renaud. But Alain frowned and said, "At the root of all?"

Camille turned to Alain. "Oh, don't you see, my love, this is the mage who must have traded her services to Olot in exchange for some of the seals he had found there in Orbane's stronghold; she told him and Dre'ela how the seals did work; she transported Olot and his Goblins to the Winterwood the night they attacked the Bear; and when Borel and his Wolves came, she whisked Olot away to safety; she transported as well the Goblins to Summerwood Manor to fetch me after you were gone. She is the one who bespelled you with sleep, there in the citadel. All of this I do believe. Too, she must be the one the Fates said stood athwart our—" Camille's eyes widened in remembrance. "Oh, my . . . I just recalled: Lisane—the Lady of the Bower—when she read the cards for me she said I was greatly opposed by two beings unrevealed: by the Magician, and by the Priestess who appeared to be but an acolyte of the Mage. She also said the Mage was somewhat off center of her reading, which meant he was not directly engaged in my immediate quest for you; even so, she believed he was somehow responsible, though the acolyte seemed more involved, but from behind the scenes. The mage must be Orbane, and the priestess, the acolyte, that must be Hradian."

Alain gritted his teeth and said, "If Orbane is behind all, he is the one the Fates Themselves fear, for if he is set free from the Castle of Shadows, he will indeed pollute the River of Time beyond all redemption."

Saissa and Valeray both looked from Alain to Camille in puzzlement, and Valeray said, "You must tell us the full of your tale, Camille, for as Blanche and Renaud we know only parts thereof. When we know all, we need to gather Borel and Liaze and Celeste and decide what to do. For if Orbane is involved, then all of Faery and the mortal world as well are in dire danger."

That night as they lay in bed, Alain said, "Back when my parents first vanished, the reason the trackers failed to find a trace of their leaving the manse is because my sire and dam never left at all. And the glamour made everyone who knew Blanche and Renaud believe that he had grey eyes and she had black. Yet as you know by what you saw as you waited for the red coach, the true Blanche and Renaud have eyes of dark blue and brown. 'Tis only now, after the curse is gone, we do remember it so."

Camille took Alain's hand and said, "Even as I boarded the red coach, I told them I would resolve just who they were, perhaps long-lost kindred or such. Yet now we know the truth, and with the curse lifted, they should know as well, for they were cursed, too, or so Urd's riddle would seem to say. We need send someone to the village of Lis to bring them here, that is if they wish to come back to Summerwood Manor, where they would be welcome, and we do need a smith. —Oh, and this I remember as well: when I boarded the coach, I was told by a repugnant little man that the eyes are windows to the soul, and it seems he was right after all."

Alain laughed and drew Camille close and kissed her and said, "Ah, Camille, who else but you would think to look within a person to find another hiding inside."

A fortnight later, Giles arrived, riding with the courier who had gone to fetch him, the lad nearly thirteen now. Camille rushed out to welcome him, and though he was glad to see Camille, he seemed quite somber. He momentarily brightened when a sparrow came flying to alight on Camille's shoulder, but then he fell glum again.

"What is it, Giles, what has happened?"

"Oh, Camille, Maman is dead."

"What?"

Giles sighed. "When no gold came from the prince that third year . . . well, you know that some of the young men courting our sisters did pitch coins down the garden well and make various romantic wishes—wishing for a kiss or to touch a breast or something even more daring, and I believe Joie and Gai complied, to what extent I don't know. Regardless, while fishing up the wide, fine-mesh net she had hidden down in the water of the well to catch the coins ere they reached bottom, Maman fell in and got tangled in the net and drowned."

Tears welled in Camille's eyes. "Oh, poor Maman." Yet Camille's sorrow was mingled with relief: sorrow, for Maman was dead; relief, for Maman was dead. Even so, it was her mère who had drowned, and silent tears ran down Camille's face. She embraced Giles and held him a bit, but then disengaged and wiped her eyes. Then sighing, she took Giles by the hand.

"Come, we will have a meal in the gazebo, and you can tell me all else."

As they strolled across the sward, Giles looked about. "Where is your Prince Alain?"

"At the moment I believe he is with his sire and dam inspecting the new horses, yet he will come soon. And we have something to ask you, something which I believe you'll find quite remarkable."

They walked on in silence, a silence finally broken by Giles as they reached the steps of the gazebo: "Your mansion is more grand than ever ours was."

Camille nodded distractedly, then said, "Tell me, Giles, how is Papa holding up, now that Maman is gone?"

"Papa ran away with a femme du cirque; he took the place of a clown who had died of a bladder infection after being struck in the face by one."

"What?" said Camille, shocked. "Papa ran away with a—"

"With a femme du cirque," said Giles. "And he seems blissful, living on the road as he does and being a clown and cuddling with his circus girl."

They mounted the steps and sat down, and Celine brought them lunch, the girl handmaiden to Camille, taking the place of she-who-was-Blanche but who now was Queen Saissa.

As Scruff hopped to the table to peck away at a portion of barley, "What of our sisters?" said Camille.

"All are married."

"All? Married? Even Lisette?"

"Oh, yes. —Er, well, she was. You see, after our mansion burned down—"

"The mansion burned down?"

Giles nodded as he bit into a peach.

"Perhaps, Little Frère, you ought to tell me all."

Giles sighed and said, "After the gold did not come from the prince, and Maman was discovered drowned—clutching a coin, a glare on her face—we found enough gold and silver and bronze in the net to keep us going for awhile. Then Joie and Gai got married in a double ceremony and— "

"Married to whom?"

Giles looked at Camille as if wondering just why that was important, but he said, "Javert and Philippe. Anyway—"

Camille held out a hand. "Which one married which?"

Giles sighed heavily and said, "Joie married Javert and Gai

married Philippe." Giles paused, as if waiting for another of these unimportant questions, but Camille gestured for him to go on.

"When Colette got married"—Giles glanced at Camille—"to Luc, Lord Jaufre invited us all to his estate near Rulon, and that's when Papa ran away with the circus. I hardly recognized him in those bloomers and that high, pointed hat, his face all white but for his big red nose and those shoes and—"

"Enough," said Camille. "Go on with the rest."

"Well, Papa left Lisette in charge, for she was the last but for me, and she said the money was running out. And so she married Lord Jaufre and—"

"She married that fat old roué?"

Giles nodded. "For his money, I think, for she did say she would send funds to me, and she moved to his estate and left me in charge of ours.

"For a while, things seemed all right, but, increasingly, Pons wouldn't—"

"Pons, the majordomo?"

Giles nodded. "Pons wouldn't follow my orders, and so I told him to pack his bags and be out by the morrow. I never did like him and his ways.

"In any event, that night the mansion caught fire, and all was lost. You see, living out where we did, there weren't enough of us to quench it.

"Pons was missing, along with what little money I had left. Some think he died in the fire, but I don't believe it is true. Regardless, now that the mansion was gone, I then went to live with Lisette and Lord Jaufre, him being the closest and all."

Camille sighed and said, "And that's where our courier found you?"

Giles shook his head and said, "No, he found me at Felise's."

Camille frowned. "Felise? What happened to Lisette?"

"She ran away with the apothecary."

Camille's eyes flew wide. "What? But what about Lord Jaufre?"

"He wasn't a nice man, Camille."

"Not nice? What do you mean?"

"Well, every night when he and Lisette went to bed, he would take those dogs with him."

"Dogs?"

"Hounds," said Giles. "Big ones."

Camille turned up a hand. "And . . . ?"

"Night after night I could hear Lisette crying, and Lord Jaufre laughing, and the dogs panting."

"Oh, my," said Camille, shuddering, imagining the worst, then shying away from that thought. "Then *that's* why she ran away."

"Non," said Giles. "She ran away with the apothecary after Lord Jaufre died of acute indigestion, or so the apothecary who was also the coroner ruled. We buried Jaufre the next day, along with his six dogs, who, strangely, died that very same night as well."

Camille drew in a sharp breath, but otherwise remained silent, her imagination running wild in another direction.

"Lisette became a very wealthy widow," said Giles, "and that's when she ran away, and I moved to Felise and Allard's."

Camille shook her head. "What's the apothecary's name?— The one Lisette lives with."

"I don't know," said Giles. "Besides, she doesn't live with him."

"Doesn't live with—"

"Non, Camille. Within a week or two, news came that the apothecary had vanished, run away said Lisette. But she is all right, quite happy, I think, for Felise told me Lisette is often seen gadding about with a young man on each arm."

Camille fell back into her chair and gazed wide-eyed at Giles. "And here I thought *I* had had an adventure, but it seems to me that you—"

"Camille!" came a cry, and she turned to see Prince Alain riding toward her on a handsome bay.

Overwhelmed with the wonder of it all, nevertheless Giles accepted the regency of L'Île de Camille; he would spend some time under the tutelage of Lanval, learning to read and write and to keep the books, as well as beginning to understand all that being a prince regent entailed. He would continue this way until it came time to leave for the port of Atterrage, there to meet with Captain Kolor and take the *North Wind* to the isle. Once on the isle, it would be Andre who would take up Giles's education, and Giles would train alongside his steward-to-be Jules. In the interim at the manor, Giles attended all matters concerning Alain's principality of Summerwood, for he needed to be tutored in affairs of state as well as those of estate . . . one event of which came just nine days after Giles's arrival.

"Oh, Giles, come quick," said Camille. " 'Tis a rade, a rade, a magnificent rade, for Alain's sisters and brother have come."

"Raid?" blurted Giles. "Do I need a weapon? I don't know how to use one. Perhaps I could wield a club or throw rocks."

Camille laughed. "No, no, Little Frère. Not an r-a-i-d, but an r-a-d-e. Now quickly, dress in your finest, for Celeste and Liaze and Borel are here, and Borel has brought his Wolves."

As Giles hurriedly dressed, Camille ran to her own closet and called for Celine. With the handmaiden's aid, she slipped into an elegant indigo gown, a sprinkle of white pearls across the bodice and tiny white insets in the sleeves. Celine shod Camille in indigo slippers and gave her a white fan for her wrist, and the handmaiden wove indigo ribbons throughout Camille's golden hair.

Then down the staircase Camille dashed, Scruff flying after, Giles coming behind, and they stood in the portico door and *ooh*ed and *ahh*ed as they watched the cavalcade come, with Borel's Wolves loping into view first. Then came a splendid procession of high-prancing horses, with decorative tack and high-cantle saddles and riders accoutered in silks and satins. Up the white-stone way they came to curve 'round before the manor in great panoply and then to stop. As attendants stepped forward and took the reins of the horses, Camille grabbed Giles by the hand and hurried to stand on the granite-and-malachite, oak-tree inlay in the great welcoming hall, Scruff now on her shoulder.

Alain came to stand beside them, as did Lord Valeray and Lady Saissa.

And then Lanval at the entry called out, "The Ladies Celeste and Liaze and the Lord Borel."

But as Celeste and Liaze and Borel saw their sire and dam whole and hale before them, and saw Alain standing in daylight uncursed, all formality dissolved into laughter and tears and hugging and questions flying and answers lost and Scruff's agitated chirping.

". . . and with the resolution of that final riddle, thus were your parents restored."

Silence fell 'round the great dining table as Camille's recounting came to the end, and each one there pondered what they had been told, some for the second time. Finally Borel said, "What would you have done Alain, without this girl?"

"Married a Troll, I expect," said Giles.

Borel looked at the lad in surprise, but then burst into guffaws of laughter, all others joining in.

Yet when it died down, Valeray said, "Thanks to 'this girl,' as you called her, Borel, he was spared that hideous fate, as were we all. Nevertheless the question remains, now what are we to do? Stop Hradian, I would say, ere she finds a way to release Orbane."

Murmurs of agreement circled the dining table, and Celeste said, "Borel, when you last located the witch, it was in the Winterwood, correct?"

Borel nodded. "Aye. There in the cursed part."

Saissa sighed. "I was so sad when I first heard that a part of your most lovely demesne had fallen under bane."

Borel nodded and glanced at Camille and said, "Probably cursed by Hradian herself to keep curious eyes away."

"And on the most direct route unto the mortal world," said Liaze. Then she added, "Not that anyone ever goes there but our dear brother Alain, and whatever for, I wonder?" Then she grinned at Camille.

"Are you two married yet?" asked Celeste.

"The banns are posted," said Alain—he glanced at his father—"and a king notified."

Borel looked from sire to brother, and said, "What say somewhile after the wedding, we three get a warband together and run down the witch?"

"Done!" said Alain

"Done!" said Valeray.

"Done!" said Camille.

All at the table looked at her in startlement, all but Alain that is. Lord Valeray frowned and said, "One moment there, my daughter-to-be, we will be opposing magic, and that's no place for a girl."

"Father," said Alain, a bit sharply, "ne'er were there a braver girl with a truer heart nor a more clever wit, and without her, you and mother and I would all be captives of Olot and his Redcaps on Troll Island, and I would still be cursed as a Bear and be married to Dre'ela, and you would yet know yourselves to be Blanche and Renaud and be slaves to Goblins and Trolls. And as for opposing magic, she has done so, though perhaps not directly. Too, she faced down a Dragon, and battled a monster in the sea, and which of us can say we've done the same? Nay, sire, no matter the peril, she is welcome to come, along with her little Scruff too, for did not the Fates so say? Surely, sire, you would not challenge the Ladies Wyrd, Lot, and Doom."

Lord Valeray took a deep breath and let it out, then shook his head and said, "I would not be so foolish. Welcome to the warband, daughter-to-be. We set out after the wedding."

Epilogue:
Afterthoughts

Thus ends this part of the tale which began long ago upon a
winter's night.

—Oh, and although I am not certain, there is this to ponder:
just as Elves and other such Fey can become mortal by living
overlong in mortal lands, who's to say the reverse is not true?
Mayhap by living in Faery overlong, Camille herself could become one of the Fey. If so, then she and Alain, if they manage to
survive the peril ahead, might have a chance of living quite hap-
pily ever after in those places therein that now and again lie east
of the sun and west of the moon or so I have been told.

*I was just wondering whose silver tongue or golden pen
is telling the tale we find ourselves in.*

Afterword

Perhaps the original fairy tale, "East of the Sun and West of the Moon," did come from the Norse, and I do hope that those folk in the Scandinavian countries forgive me for seasoning the story with a French flavor. But in a nod to the Norse, I *did* bring Dwarves into the tale, and they *did* sail the sea in a Dragonship, both clearly Nordic in origin. Even so, if my version of this tale is true, perhaps in the mortal world the Norse tale did come from those very same Dwarves—Kolor and crew—carrying it back to the fjords and steadings and telling it to those they found there.

Lastly, there is this: every place but the poles on this planet lies east of the sun and west of the moon at various times of the month (when both sun and moon are in the sky and the moon is anywhere from new to full). But in Faery . . . who knows? For strange and wonderful are the ways therein.

—Dennis L. McKiernan
Tucson, Arizona, 2001

About the Author

Born April 4, 1932, I have spent a great deal of my life looking through twilights and dawns seeking—what? ah yes, I remember—seeking signs of wonder, searching for pixies and fairies and other such, looking in tree hollows and under snow-laden bushes and behind waterfalls and across wooded, moonlit dells. I did not outgrow that curiosity, that search for the edge of Faery when I outgrew childhood—not when I was in the U.S. Air Force during the Korean War, nor in college, nor in graduate school, nor in the thirty-one years I spent in Research and Development at Bell Telephone Laboratories as an engineer and manager on ballistic missile defense systems and then telephone systems and in think-tank activities. In fact I am still at it, still searching for glimmers and glimpses of wonder in the twilights and the dawns. I am abetted in this curious behavior by Martha Lee, my helpmate, lover, and, as of this writing, my wife of forty-three years.